125

8-3

GO5850

D1029818

# FLYING WILDCATS

# FLYING WILDCATS

EDITED BY

## LEO MARGULIES

THE HAMPTON PUBLISHING COMPANY

NEW YORK

COPYRIGHT, 1943,
THE HAMPTON PUBLISHING COMPANY
NEW YORK, N. Y.

PRINTED IN THE UNITED STATES OF AMERICA

# CONTENTS

# MALTA MASQUERADE

*By*

## ROBERT SIDNEY BOWEN

## I

THE sun was a fading ball of flame balanced on the western rim of the Mediterranean. The shadows of night were rushing up with all the speed and ominousness of an approaching hurricane as the U. S. Aircraft Carrier *Bennington* slowly traced a huge circle in the sunset-tinted waters. To port and to starboard her destroyer escort trailed her like so many faithful watch dogs.

Aboard the *Bennington* there was not a single smile. From Admiral Porter down to the lowest rating, every officer and seaman went about his job grim-faced, or stood raking the darkening heavens through binoculars.

One of those topside was Lieutenant "Stud" Stacey. He was six-two, who had a pair of shoulders to go with his height. And he had earned the right to wear the Navy Cross under his wings that day in December when the treacherous sons of the Rising Sun slammed down on Pearl Harbor.

Four of those rats had not pulled out of their dive that day, and Stud Stacey was the reason.

With one arm hooked around a port crash net stanchion, Stud searched the heavens until his eyes smarted. He slowly lowered the glasses.

"It can't be navigation," he muttered. "Old Saunders is a homing pigeon if there ever was one."

"The best," said Lieutenant Jay Bell who stood at his side. "So they must have bumped into trouble."

"And they had orders to fly with radios dead," Stud said. "Nobody's supposed to know we are here in the Mediterranean."

"No, nobody!" Jay agreed. "Except maybe half the Italian and Nazi Secret Service. Wonder how long the Old Man's going to stick here?"

"Until dark," Stud said. "And that'll be in a few minutes. Six planes, and not a sign of one of them. Maybe, though, they'll catch us after dark, and come aboard under flares."

"Not a chance," Jay said, and shook his head. "I checked with the flight officer. They had fuel until seven-fifteen. It's seven-thirty now."

At that moment, as though Admiral Porter suddenly realized that further waiting was a waste of time and a danger to the *Bennington,* the huge aircraft carrier suddenly went cutting due westward at increased speed. Stud Stacey took one final look at the shadow-blurred heavens, and slipped the binoculars into their case.

"Jay," he said, "all of those boys were pals of mine. I've got to find out, for sure. We can't just steam off and leave them to fall into the drink!"

"They're in the drink already," Jay said quietly.

"Look," Stud said grimly, "we've got a twin-engined Grumman utility amphibian aboard. And she's got tanks for fourteen hours. If we took off just before dawn we could cover the whole area of their flight, and catch up with the *Bennington* by noon, easy. We might find some of the boys still floating."

"*We*, huh?" Jay murmured.

"They were your pals, too, weren't they?" Stud shot at him. "Also, you're a good navigator. You don't want to come along?"

"Sure, I do," Jay said. "But there's the little matter of Admiral Porter, and some of his fourstripers. Maybe they won't like the idea."

"That's what we'll find out, now," Stud Stacey said and turned. "Come on."

Stud's hands felt wet and clammy, and a cold lump tried to clog up his throat. He had seen buddies of his die in the air, and there had been a few other occasions when a plane or two had roared off the flight deck, never to be seen again. But this time, six planes had gone away. Six Curtiss SOC scouting jobs with a pilot and observer-gunner in each ship. They had apparently headed in the general direction of the British-fortified island of Malta.

At a definite time the *Bennington* had reached the rendezvous point where the aircraft were to be met, but the patrol planes had not put in an appearance. No word from them had been received.

And now that the zero point for fuel had come and gone the *Bennington* was steaming away.

Presently Stud and Jay were going through the routine of gaining an interview with the ship's commander. There was still a lot of flaming red on the western lip of the Mediterranean when they were ushered into the admiral's quarters. With the Old Man were Captain Drake, Flight Operations Officer, and Commander Jenkins, senior Section Leader.

The admiral returned their salute, and gave them a hard, quizzical stare.

"Yes, Lieutenants?" he said. "Your request said 'urgent.' What's it all about?"

"The missing patrol, sir," Stud Stacey said. "We have a Grumman amphibian aboard. Lieutenant Bell and I would like to make a search patrol and rendezvous with the *Bennington* around noon."

"What makes you think you can find those patrol planes?" the admiral asked in a heavy tone.

"Lieutenant Bell and I simply want permission to try," Stud said. "We might find some of them floating in the water and could pick them up with the Grumman amphibian. I . . . Well sir, every man in that patrol was a good friend of mine."

"Sit down, both of you," the admiral answered. "We were about to ask for a volunteer searching team. Sit down, and I'll give you as much of the picture, as I know."

Stud Stacey and Jay Bell waited, and Admiral Porter was silent for a moment. He stared at the huge detailed chart fastened under the glass top of his desk, then suddenly jerked his head up, as though he had decided what to say.

"As you know," he began, "this Attack Force of which

the *Bennington* is a member, is supposed to be a surprise in these waters. We are here to help the British Fleet units cut the Nazi supply lines from Sicily to Tunisia and Libya. Our real job, though, is to help in keeping Malta a workable base. The Nazis want to knock out Malta for keeps, and are throwing every unit of their *Luftwaffe* they can spare into that job. For that matter, perhaps more units than they really can spare.

"But they are going to go all-out for Malta, and the devil with the cost. They've got to have it or their North Africa aspirations are sunk. So that's our immediate job—to help cut the Axis supply lines in general, but to keep Malta's head above water in particular."

The admiral looked at his chart again.

"The Axis raid bases in Sicily," he went on presently, "are at Siracusa, Marsala, Palermo, and Messina. British raids have done some damage at those bases, but not much. The British have been forced to remain at Malta, go up when Nazi raiders arrive, and knock the spots off them.

"That's where we are to enter the picture. Plans have been worked out to give the Nazis the works at both ends. While the British are giving them trouble over Malta, planes from this Attack Force will raid their bases in Sicily, and also catch the Nazi survivors on the way back. If it works out the way we hope Nazi air losses will be three times what they can stand, and—we also hope—they'll give up ideas about Malta."

The *Bennington's* commander scowled darkly into space. There was a glitter in his dark eyes and his lips were pressed tightly together in a thin grim line.

"That patrol this afternoon went out for scouting only!" he suddenly said. "It's leader had strict orders to avoid *all* contact with enemy aircraft. He was not even to get close to Sicily. The job was to scout for enemy surface ships in nearby waters. We wouldn't be pulling much of a surprise if Axis surface craft spotted our planes far out to sea. Before we start throwing punches, it is necessary for us to learn the exact location of *all* Axis surface units. Then we can know how best to maneuver to avoid them. Above all, we want to keep our presence a secret as long as we possibly can."

The admiral made a helpless gesture with one hand.

"What happened to that patrol, I haven't the faintest idea," he said. "Lieutenant Commander Saunders had orders to keep radios dead. However, in a real emergency he had permission to make contact with us. In code. We picked up absolutely no signals at all."

"Would you call meeting enemy planes, and being forced to engage them, an emergency, sir?" Jay Bell asked.

"I would, and so would Saunders," the admiral replied instantly. "I have considered the possibility that they were surprised and perhaps shot down. Such a possibility doesn't make sense however. Dog-fights don't last long, but there would be plenty of time for Saunders to get some word back to us. There is just one thing that might have happened. They lost their way, and sat down in the water rather than reveal their location, and ours, to enemy ears."

"Not a chance of that, sir!" Stud spoke up quickly. "Old —I mean, Lieutenant Commander Saunders could find a rowboat without charts or instruments. He'd never miss a rendezvous through faulty navigation."

"You're probably right," the admiral said with a faint smile. "Navigators don't come any better. Now, your attention. Here's their flight chart for the patrol."

Both lieutenants gave their absolute attention to the chart and memorized every word the admiral spoke.

Eventually the senior officer leaned back and looked at them.

"I think I should remind you that you're taking on a very dangerous mission," he said quietly. "If you bump into enemy planes you won't stand a chance in that amphibian, even though she carries machine-guns. You, also, will fly with a dead radio. However, for you an air fight *cannot* be considered an emergency. An emergency for you will *only* be something that directly bears on the immediate safety of the *Bennington*. You will be strictly on your own. Is that clear?"

"Perfectly, sir," Stud and Jay replied in the same breath.

"Very well, then," Admiral Porter said, with a nod. "I'm turning you over to Captain Drake for final instructions. Incidentally though, you will not be connected with the *Bennington* in any way, once you take off. Remove all *Bennington* insignia from your uniforms. Carry no papers, or other identification. And the *Bennington's* markings are to be removed from your plane. Leave only the usual Navy markings. The Axis probably suspects that U. S. Navy units are here in the Mediterranean, but we're not going to let them find out *which* units. Well, that's all. Good luck, Lieutenants. And God-speed there and back."

## II

A hundred times during the last five minutes Stud Stacey had opened his mouth to start a song, or to make a bit of conversation. Each time, though, something seemed to stick in his throat and not let anything out.

The Grumman had been in the air almost five hours now. During every minute of that time he, and Jay Bell in the amphibian's co-seat, had kept their eyes glued on the rolling Mediterranean. Except that when the dawn sun brightened the sky they had taken a few glances at the surrounding heavens.

But below or above, they had seen nothing to make a pulse quiver.

"So help me!" Stud finally burst out. "Even a look at a Musso destroyer would help. How we making it, Jay?"

"Right on course," Jay replied wearily. "We'll make landfall at the southern tip of Sicily in another five minutes. I'd like to go in close and high for a quick look."

"At what?" Stud asked.

"Don't know," Jay said. "Been getting hunches. Got a feeling something's going to pop. That sea and sky! Enough to make you figure anything!"

Stud shot a quick side glance at his flying mate. He saw the taut, strained face, the tiny wrinkles at the corners of the eyes, and the way the lips were compressed. It was not hot in the amphibian's pilot compartment, yet Jay's forehead was dotted by tiny glistening beads of sweat.

Stud raised one hand to his own forehead and felt sweat

there. His own facial expression was probably much the same as Jay's.

"The way I feel I don't care a hoot what your hunch turns out to be," he finally growled. "Nix on holding this course after we make landfall, though. If we get too close to shore we might get spotted—and this job doesn't silhouette like any Axis crate. If they should come tearing up . . . What's the matter?"

Jay had suddenly lunged forward and was peering narrow-eyed down off the port bow. Stud leaned forward himself and took a look. He saw only the sun-bathed blue swells of the Mediterranean.

Jay shot out a stiff finger and pointed.

"There!" he said in a tight voice. "Sight your eye along my finger. Something in the water, like the tail of a plane. Wait till a swell moves it and it catches the sun. There! See it?"

Stud suddenly caught the faint flash of color down in the water about a mile ahead, and a quarter of a mile or so to port. It wasn't exactly a flash of color. Rather it was a sort of half silverish and half golden glow that outlined itself against the blue of the water. But Stud knew that it was the tail of a half-submerged plane. One of the missing scouting aircraft from the *Bennington!*

He couldn't say anything. The tail of that half-submerged plane, swaying slowly to and fro, was like a silent farewell from men he had known and loved. Just the tail of a half-submerged plane and nothing else. No floating parachutes, and no floating wreckage of other planes. The cockpits were under water, so if the pilot and observer were aboard they were dead there. And if they weren't in the cockpits they were dead some place else.

"I'm going down and land, Jay!" Stacey suddenly got out harshly. "I've got to find out why, if I can."

"Go on down," Jay muttered. "Just don't pile us up, that's all."

Stud throttled the twin Wasps and sent the Grumman amphibian circling downward. He landed as close to the floating plane as he dared, and then with Jay in the hull nose to fend off he water-taxied slowly toward the doomed craft.

When Jay made fast with his fendhook, he killed the engines and came forward. They leaned far over the hull nose and peered down into the clear blue water. Then Stud slowly let the air out of his lungs.

"Both pits empty," he heard his voice say. "They aren't aboard."

"It's Dick Saunders' ship," Jay said. "See that forward cockpit hatch? See that thing caught on it and swaying around? That's Dick's scarf. That wild blue and red one he always wore. Must have got it yanked off as he bailed out."

Stud let his eyes wander toward the tail section that was above water. It was peppered with bullet-holes. It looked as though it had been used for a target by a dozen planes.

"Shot down!" he muttered. "The whole ship's riddled like a sieve. So they did have an air scrap! But why didn't they get something out over the radio? You can't get *six* ships all in a flash!"

"Maybe you can," Jay got out. "But where are the other five? They—"

Jay cut it off short and he and Stud stared skyward as they heard the drone of aircraft engines. The sun blinded them, but when they did see it they were too surprised and relieved to move. It was a Supermarine "Walrus" reconnaissance of the Royal Air Force, Fleet Air Arm. And it was coming down straight at them, with throttled engines.

"Did those boys just now spot us," Stud muttered, "or have they been tagging us all along?"

"Don't know," Jay said. "And I also don't know what *they'd* be doing way out here in that flying chicken crate. They'd stand less chance against Axis planes than we would. But I sure hope they've got something to tell us."

For a brief second Stud was startled. He glanced back toward his cockpit, then returned his gaze to the British amphibian sliding down. It landed with a lot of splashing some hundred yards or so to starboard. Then its pilot taxied slowly around and approached the U. S. Navy plane head-on.

It came to a stop a dozen feet away. A figure popped up out of the hull nose like a rabbit coming up out of its hole. In his hands he held a short-barreled, wicked-looking sub-machine-gun! And with it pointed at the two U. S. Navy flyers he barked a command in a guttural accent.

"Don't move, or you will be dead men!"

As a million crazy thoughts exploded in Stud Stacey's head, he glared pop-eyed at the figure in flying garb in the British reconnaissance amphibian. He was unmistakably German, but for the first few moments Stud was utterly unable to make that truth stick in his brain, though he knew that the German use of such British planes was a fairly recent variation of an old trick. It was the same with Jay Bell.

"Hey, what's the big idea?" Stud finally blurted.

The German in the British amphibian smiled broadly and made a gesture with the submachine-gun. Another man appeared at his side. "You Americans should have remained at home until you learned how to play at war with real soldiers," this man said. "Place your hands above your heads, please. We are boarding you."

A film of red rage clouded Stud Stacey's eyes. He had a mad desire to lash out and make a grab for the German's gun. The hulls of the amphibians were touching noses and the barrel of that submachine-gun was no more than a couple of feet away.

However, before Stud could act on his crazy urge the second German quickly stepped aboard the American plane and went quickly to the hull door in front of the pilot's compartment. Stud turned impulsively but a jab in the arm from the machine-gun stopped him cold. He turned back and glared into the smiling face.

"So it's true, huh?"

"True?" the German echoed, with a puzzled look.

"That you Huns have been cleaned out of most of your own planes!" Stud Stacey cracked.

The German's taunting smile disappeared for a moment, but quickly came back.

"We will talk of that at another time," he said in a flat voice. "You will now crawl back aft to where my comrade is waiting for you. Be foolish if you wish. It does not matter to me. Move, please."

The two U. S. Navy pilots eyed him for a brief moment, then obeyed. They did so for two sound reasons. One, because their deaths would not explain this cock-eyed mystery to them, and the other, because the German with the sub-machine-gun acted as if he hoped they would not obey.

They ducked down into the hull and crawled back to the pilots' compartment and through it to the cabin amidships. There the other German awaited them, with a Luger in his hand. He frisked them for guns, found none, and shoved them down into seats. He took a seat across from them where he could drill either one at the drop of a hat.

The German with the machine-gun came back to the pilot's seat. He had left his machine-gun behind, but his holstered Luger was where he could grab it in nothing flat.

Through the compartment door opening Stud could just see the British amphibian. Still another German had appeared in the hull nose and he pushed the two craft apart. Then the British amphibian taxied away and took the air.

The pilot at the controls of the U. S. Navy plane got his engine started, jitterbugged with them for a couple of minutes, then took off himself. As the hull left the water Stud turned and looked at Jay. His flying pal was a picture of dumbfounded amazement and blazing anger. He caught Stud's look and groaned through clenched teeth.

"What a big help we turned out to be," Stud muttered. "I—"

He suddenly caught the faint smile on the face of the German who held the Luger on them. The smile meant that the man understood English, and was thoroughly enjoying himself.

"Well," he said, "we can tell our grandchildren that we at least served with the British Fleet Air Arm, Jay."

Jay caught Stud's quick half wink. He played up.

"Yes," he said. "And what a bright idea you had! Requesting that we be transferred for service with the British Fleet Air Arm. Rot! I wish I'd told you to go alone, and stayed home."

Stud glanced out the cabin window. The United States Navy amphibian was high in the air by now, and, from the position of the sun Stud could tell they were flying due west. And six other planes had suddenly appeared in the sky! All British, too. Six British Fairey "Fulmars" of the Fleet Air Arm.

Wild hope began to build up in Stud but it died a sudden death as he glanced at their German guard. The man had also sighted the approaching planes, and didn't seem worried in the least. In fact, as he saw Stud look at him he smiled and nodded.

Stud scowled and returned his gaze to the Fulmars. They came sweeping in close and took up escort positions. Stud Stacey could see part of the British Supermarine Walrus that was leading the aerial parade. He could also see the thin dark line on the horizon far ahead.

"Sicily!" he said to himself.

### III

Some fifteen minutes later the thin dark line on the horizon had become a good big hunk of land. Italian-owned and Nazi-ruled Sicily.

Stud had never seen the place in his life. But it was Sicily all right, because when Stud looked toward the north he could see volcanic Mount Etna towering up into the blue heavens.

A moment or two later the German at the controls nosed the Grumman downward. Another few minutes and the amphibian was landing on the surface of an airfield that seemed to hold all the German and Italian planes in the world. There were hundreds of them, ranging from Messerschmitt 109s to giant troop-carrying transports.

Stud Stacey guessed that it was the gigantic air base at Siracusa, and as he gazed at the mighty array of war aircraft a dull throbbing ache surged through him. What a target! What a perfect target for the British, if they would only stop pecking around in Libya and concentrate all of their big stuff on this air base! It was the kind of target that couldn't be missed from any altitude.

No wonder Malta was being plastered night and day. There were enough planes here to keep up that pace with no plane going out more than once every fourth day.

"What a target!" Stud muttered. "Why don't they smack it, but soon and plenty?"

"Don't forget, pal," Jay said. "Great plans for Nineteen Forty-four. It's been in all the papers. Well, here comes the reception committee. Maybe we'll get a hint or two now."

The "reception committee" consisted of six high-ranking officers of the German *Luftwaffe*. In their shiny boots, baggy pants, and dangling medals, they presented the usual ludicrous pictures of what the well-dressed Hun officer should wear.

But there was the heart and the brain of a baby killer in

every one of those uniforms, and so Stud and Jay were in no humorous mood as the committee came to a halt and waited for them to be ushered out of the amphibian. Six pairs of piglike eyes started giving them the up and down. Then the senior officer came a step or two forward and poked a stiff finger at Stud.

"Your name, section number, and ship?" he boomed in English.

"Al Smith," Stud shot back at him. "Section Twenty. Macy's Basement."

The senior Nazi grunted and shot a keen look at the Grumman. When his eyes swiveled back to Stud there was a sneer on his lips.

"So there is an American aircraft carrier in Mediterranean waters?" he said.

"One?" Jay echoed before Stud Stacey could speak. "There are six, and two more on the way. Anything else you want to know?"

The German ignored him and looked at the Nazi who had piloted the Grumman. He addressed him as Colonel von Scholtz, and asked what had happened.

"*Leutnant* Stivers and I were on high patrol over the area where we met those six American-made planes yesterday, *Herr Kommandant,*" von Scholtz told him. "Fortunately we were between them and the sun. They did not see us. We saw them land to inspect one of the destroyed planes that had not yet sunk. We landed and took them prisoners.

"Meuller flew our plane back. I believe, *Herr Kommandant,* that they are from the carrier base of those planes we destroyed yesterday. There are no markings on the aircraft, just as there were none on those planes yesterday. Nothing but the U. S. Navy insignia. But that is enough."

They had spoken in German, and Stud's three years of German in college was strained to the limit. He managed to get it, though he maintained a blank expression as though he were quite ignorant of what was being said. But he was pleased by the look of anger and worry that skipped across the *Kommandant's* face. Then the Hun addressed as *Leutnant* Stivers spoke up.

"They talked with each other," he told the senior Nazi. "They were broken-hearted at being captured, but were glad they could tell their grandchildren that they had served a week with the British Fleet Air Arm. It is possible that they and a few of their planes have been loaned to the swine British."

The *Kommandant* glared at his prisoners.

"I must find out for certain!" he suddenly snarled. "Take them away, and search them to the skin. There are ways for us to find out the truth!"

The *Kommandant* turned on his heel and strode away, followed by his entourage. Stud took that opportunity to impress von Scholtz with his ignorance of the German language.

"What's biting him?" he asked. "What was he raving about?"

"Nothing," the German said. "He spoke about a matter that does not concern you. You will come with me, please."

The German pilot and a couple of bullet-headed, bullnecked field guards escorted Stud and Jay across the air base and into a stone building. What Stud saw on the short walk both excited and depressed him.

There seemed to be more planes than he had seen from the air. At least more troop transport planes. And gathered about each transport were swarms of German paratroops. They were going through the exercises of piling into the planes, jumping to the ground, and racing toward mounds of machine-guns, hand grenades, ammunition, and such. It was a picture of Nazi thoroughness. Practice, practice, and more practice.

For what? Some months ago it had been Crete. Shortly it was meant to be Malta. Grimly Stud realized that these Germans were preparing for an air invasion of the British island stronghold in the central Mediterranean.

This stone building which Stud Stacey and Jay Bell entered was to all intents a jail. There were barred windows and steel doors. The American prisoners were stripped to the skin, and each given a dirty pair of work pants, and their own shoes. Then they were led to a darkened room, and the door was slammed savagely behind them.

"Well," Jay said as they both tried to adjust their eyes to the gloom, "the recruiting officer promised me I'd see the world, and he wasn't wrong."

"Yes," Stud agreed. "Only—"

He stopped short, seeing movement in one of the bunks. A man stood up and limped over toward them. By the shaft of pale light that filtered through the single window the Americans saw that he wore the uniform of a flight lieutenant of the Royal Air Force. But he looked more Russian with his beard of two months' growth at least. He peered at them and smiled.

"Yanks," he said. "I'm Flight Lieutenant Witherington. I say, you are Yanks, aren't you, though you have no uniforms."

The voice was as English as London Bridge, but caution shot through Stud as he shook the proffered hand.

"That's right," he said, and introduced Jay Bell and himself. "The Huns seemed to have a yen for our uniforms. They gave us these pants, instead."

"Oh, you'll get your uniforms back," Witherington said with a laugh. "Did the same thing to me when I was captured. Hope to find secret messages in the lining, and all that sort of rot. But, I say! What are you two Yanks doing here? Don't mean to pry into your private business, you know, but are there Yanks in this part of the world?"

"With the R.A.F.," Stud replied cautiously, looking around him as he spoke. "What happened to you?"

"Oh, you're airmen?" the Englishman said. "Allah be praised. We speak the same language. If you'll pardon me I'll sit down. This leg of mine isn't up to snuff today. So Yanks are with the R.A.F. at last, eh? Splendid!"

As the Englishman eased himself into a chair, Jay and Stud also sat down. They looked at the man questioningly.

"Oh, yes," he said. "Didn't answer your question, did I? Sorry. What happened to me? A victim of the latest dirty Nazi trick, you might say. Out on patrol with two of my chaps. Ran across another British patrol. Four of the beggars. Then it happened so suddenly I didn't know what had happened until it was all over."

"What?" Jay Bell probed.

"They were British planes," the Englishman said harshly. "But Jerry blighters were flying them. Caught me and my two chaps for fair. My two chaps died, but somehow I got thrown clear, and remained conscious just long enough to yank my rip-cord. I woke up in this beastly hole. One of the guards told me I came down on land. Mashed up my leg a bit, but it's on the mend, now. Near as I can figure it was a little over a month ago. They were pleased to inform me that my pals had gone down in flames. Didn't bail out."

"Tough!" Stud Stacey murmured sympathetically, and tried to study the man in the bad light. "How-come the Nazis have British planes, though? Where'd they get them?"

"Lots of places, unfortunately," the Englishman replied. "We left a few in Greece. Crete, too, and of course, France. Also, a few of our chaps have been forced down here and there. The Libyan campaign, you know. Those that were damaged they patched up, and there you are."

"But with all the crates they've got, why would they want British planes?" Jay asked.

The Englishman leaned forward and peered at them intently.

"I say!" he murmured. "Just where did you say you were stationed? What R.A.F. unit?"

"Fleet Air Arm," Stud said quickly. "I'm afraid you'll have to let it go at that."

"I was hoping," the Englishman said sadly, "that you were from the American Fleet Air Arm, or whatever they call it. We've heard rumors at Malta that some units of the

American Navy were coming over to lend us a hand. An aircraft carrier, or two. But it's quite all right if you chaps wish to keep mum. Chap shouldn't even trust his brother these days. But, I say! If you were shot down, what about the markings on your planes?"

"No markings," Stud said. "So you were at Malta, eh?"

"Quite," the Englishman said and laughed. "But that's no secret to the Nazis. There were markings on my plane. But you asked about the Nazis wanting British planes. Rather obvious, I'd say. Malta, of course. A chance to fool our ack-ack gunners and do a strict bit of reconnoitering. Jerry wants Malta. Did you notice all the transports and paratroops they've got out there? Malta is due for it bad most any day now, I'm afraid."

"And what are Malta's chances?" Stud asked.

"Decidedly poor, unless we get a lot of help."

There was a moment of silence, then Stud asked the rather obvious question.

"Why hasn't the R.A.F. bombed the tar out of this place? Holy smoke! A good strafe of all they've got here would turn the place into a ten-alarm inferno! It's a perfect target!"

"Agreed." The Englishman nodded slowly. "If I were R.A.F. Middle East O.C. I'd order the raids, and the devil with anything else until we were through with this job. But I am only a squadron flight lieutenant. Of course, though, there are problems. There are not enough bombers at Malta. Much too small and risky for operation of the big fellows. A bit too far away for raids from Cirenaica and Egypt.

"Also, they need every bomber they have there to prevent Rommel from getting a sudden and disastrous jump on us.

The real reason, though, is this place itself. They'd get the alert well in advance and put a hundred of their fighters in the air for every bomber we could send over. But, good Lord! I wish some kind of an attempt could be made before it's too late! Malta is doomed if we just sit back and wait. Or if American forces don't get over here quick and give us a hand."

The urge to tell the Englishman the truth zoomed up in Stud, but he beat it down. He was certain the man was all that he pretended to be, but feeling certain didn't make something an absolute fact. There were other reasons, too, for him to keep his mouth shut. The main one was that Nazis probably were listening in on this little chit-chat session. He and Jay had had that pot-bellied *Luftwaffe* big shot more than a little buffaloed. For the sake of all concerned, particularly the *Bennington* far out to sea, it was best to keep things that way.

At that moment the door was banged open and a couple of armed guards appeared. By grunts, and gestures with their Lugers, they indicated that Stud and Jay were to accompany them.

"See you again, Witherington," Stud said as he got to his feet. "Good luck, and keep punching."

"Quite," the man said and smiled. "And watch the blighters for tricks, chaps. They're cagey beggars."


IV

The base *Kommandant's* office could serve as a model for the administration office of any modern airport. As the guards pushed Stud and Jay inside they could imagine passengers asking questions about transport take-off and arrival times.

A second look, however, revealed that the place was definitely a *Luftwaffe* establishment. There were pin-pointed maps on all the walls. There were flight charts. There were three or four short-wave radio sets. Everything needed for the operation of military aircraft on a gigantic scale.

The *Kommandant* and *Leutnant* von Scholtz were the only two officers in the huge room. There were a few junior grades at the radio sets, but the polished boot flunkies of the *Kommandant* were missing.

The senior Nazi ordered the two guards to withdraw. Then he beamed at Stud Stacey and Jay Bell, waved them to chairs and offered them cigarettes.

"We know all about you, Lieutenants," he said in flawless English, "so you can relax. There is no need to be on your guard. And, oh, yes. Your uniforms will be returned presently."

Stud and Jay accepted cigarettes because they wanted a smoke, even if it was the brand of mildewy hay the Nazis call tobacco. They lighted up and smoked in silence while the *Kommandant* watched them. Presently he frowned slightly and leaned forward.

"You are not interested in what happened to your aircraft carrier?" he suddenly asked.

Stud kept his expression blank.

"What carrier?" he asked. "The British have several out here."

The *Kommandant* laughed softly, but there was no mirth in it.

"I mean your American carrier!" he said.

"American carriers in the Mediterranean?" Jay Bell echoed. "Hot dog! Now there *will* be some action in these parts!"

"I'm speaking of the American carrier you took off from early this morning," the German said coldly. "To search for six of her planes that did not return from a patrol yesterday afternoon. I might add that those six planes will never return."

"That's what you think!" Stud replied.

"That's what I know!" the German snarled. "All six planes were shot down. There were no survivors."

"And by your dirty rats flying captured British planes!" Stud shouted, as his blood started to boil. "It would have been the other way around if they'd been flying under their own colors."

"War is war," the *Kommandant* continued. "The only thing that concerns us is winning it. And we shall win it! Yes, we took care of your comrades in the manner that English prisoner described to you. They will never return to your carrier."

A cold wave rippled up and down Stud's back, and he thanked his stars he had kept a strict check on his tongue while Jay Bell and he had talked with Witherington, the R.A.F. flight lieutenant. So the Nazis *had* been listening in on that conversation. And now this pot-bellied Nazi thought he was leading them into a nice little trap. Stud grinned, thin-lipped.

"My pal and I were searching for those planes, yes," he said. "But we didn't take off from any· American carrier. And neither did they. And if you think bunking us in with an Englishman, fake or otherwise, will get you anything, then just guess again."

"If there was an American carrier in these waters you wouldn't be sitting at that desk," Jay Bell said. "You'd be down in a raid shelter. Maybe you will be there pretty soon, at that."

The base *Kommandant* listened with a half-smile. He sighed heavily and gestured with his hands, palms up.

"Very well, then, if that's the way it must be," he said. "You give me no choice. You possess information that I desire, and I intend to obtain it. For the last time! Are you from an American aircraft carrier?"

"What's an aircraft carrier?" Stud asked blandly.

"All we fly is gliders," Jay said.

The *Kommandant* reached into a desk drawer, pulled out a handful of stuff and dumped it on the desk.

"Look at those things!" he barked.

There was a solid gold identification bracelet with Witherington's name and rank engraved on it. There was a handkerchief marked with the initial "W." There was a small snapshot of the R.A.F. pilot and a good-looking girl. There was also a much creased pocket-size Union Jack. There were also other items that proved that Witherington was English and a member of the R.A.F.

"So what?" Stud said and looked up.

The German smiled, the kind of a smile that made little fingers of ice clutch at Stud's heart.

"I just want you to be sure the swine is English," the Nazi said. "The dog has been our guest five weeks now. At first he was a fool, as you two are. I believe he will stop being a fool now. And that you will, also!"

The *Kommandant* turned to Colonel von Scholtz, and spoke in German.

"Have the English swine removed to the blockhouse," he ordered. "Have him made ready for a little questioning. You, Colonel, will do the questioning. I will be along with these two prisoners presently."

Colonel von Scholtz saluted and stamped out of the place, leering at Stud and Jay. As the door closed the *Kommandant* ignored the two Yanks and gave his attention to some papers on the desk.

Stud pondered the chances of Jay and himself breaking out of the place and making a wild dash for one of the many planes out on the huge field. He stopped pondering, however, when he suddenly saw how closely a couple of the flunkies at the rear of the huge office were watching him. And they had Lugers in their hands.

Stud's thoughts were bitter, heart-crushing. The mystery of Dick Saunders and his patrol pals was a mystery no longer. No wonder no signals had been picked up by the *Bennington's* radio. Dick Saunders, like Witherington, had come across a flight of British planes. Like Witherington, Dick had probably thought nothing of their joining forces.

And then it had been too late. Each Nazi had picked his man, got in close, then fired with all guns. A blank-range, cold-meat blasting of the American pilot and observer. The bullet-holes in Dick's half-submerged plane was proof of how close those masquerading killers had been. Dick, and his boys probably had died before any one of them could so much as put his lips to the flap-mike, much less speak into it. Apparently none had been as lucky as Witherington and been hurled clear of his plane before death struck him down. They all probably were at the bottom of the Mediterranean now.

And today Jay Bell and he had been caught. Caught cold by a Nazi trick that was as simple as it was deadly. Their lives had been spared, however, for a good reason. The Nazi butchers of Siracusa were planning a gigantic blow against the British stronghold of Malta. But fear was holding the Nazis back.

Surprise and strength were their two best weapons. But suppose surprise and strength were suddenly sprung on them? That's what obviously worried the pot-bellied Nazi sitting there at his desk. He was not sure of Malta's strength. He was not sure, either, whether American Navy units had arrived. Shooting down U. S. Navy-marked planes yesterday had given him much cause for suspicion. Capturing Stud and Jay today had obviously added to that greatly.

Until he knew for certain just what he would be up against he didn't dare strike his sledge-hammer blow at Malta. And in some manner the wounded Witherington seemed to have a big place in his plans.

The *Kommandant* suddenly grunted and pushed up from his desk. He nodded at his two prisoners, then toward the door.

"Everything must be ready and waiting by now," he said. "You will walk in front of me out the door."

When the two Yanks stepped through the door two German guards dropped into step at their sides. The parade marched across the field.

Again Stud took in all the "sights" in the time allowed. And again his heart seemed to turn into a chunk of ice, though his blood boiled. What a mess a flock of American or British bombers could make of this whole place, if given half a chance! The entire base was like a gigantic powder-keg with wings.

The long lines of bombers carried enough bombs to flatten any fair-sized city, to say nothing of the ammo dumps, and fuel dumps located about the outer fringes of the base. True, raiding bombers might never return from this spot, but Stud felt that any sacrifice would be repaid ten times over in destruction to such a vital Nazi base.

"If I get away," Stud mumbled, "I'm going to yell for a raid on this place, even if I have to yell all the way back to the White House!"

"If I get away?" A bitter laugh rose up in his throat. Sure! That should be easy! All he and Jay would have to do would be to knock about fifty thousand Nazis kicking, grab a ship and take it off between the solid showers of steel that would come up at them, and then maybe have to shake off four or five hundred planes that would most certainly give chase. Easy. In a story book!

The parade marched into a squat, one-story building that contained only one room. The windows were high and let in just enough light to see by. The walls were stone blocks, and the floor was of cement.

There was no furniture in the room. Just four posts sunk

into the cement at the rear end. Dark stains, and bullet marks on the rear wall told what those posts were used for. Even the air smelled of torture and death.

Stud walked into the room, then stopped dead. His brain swirled with sudden anger as he saw the Englishman.

Witherington was stripped to the waist, and his wrists were lashed to one of the posts, above his head. His eyes were closed, and his lips were pressed together in a thin line as though to seal up groans and moans. But his jaw was set defiantly, and he was trying to hold his head high.

Beside him stood von Scholtz, without his tunic. In his hands he held a short, thick bull-whip. And two flaming red welts across Witherington's back were horrible evidence that von Scholtz had been getting in a little practice.

Stud whirled on the *Kommandant,* only to be grabbed and pinned helpless by the two guards.

"You barbarian devil!" he shouted hoarsely. "You rotten, no good rat! A whipping post!"

The German seemed not to mind. He fixed his glittering piggish eyes on Stud and smiled.

"An English practice, according to history," he said with a sneer. "And used extensively in your United States, too. And, of course, very effective. Colonel von Scholtz! Get the prisoner's attention! I wish to speak to him!"

Von Scholtz' arm swept down and the bull-whip made a sickening crack as it bit into the skin of Witherington's back and drew blood. The Englishman shuddered, but not a sound came from between his clamped lips. The *Kommandant* walked forward.

"The time has come for you to talk, swine!" he snarled.

"You will tell me all you know of the Valletta defenses in Malta. Of course you won't reply at once. But you will eventually."

The *Kommandant* suddenly turned and stabbed a fat finger toward Stud and Jay.

"And when *you* are ready to spare him further agony, speak up!" he shouted. "Tell me about the American aircraft carrier, or see him die there at that post! And you two in a similar manner, later!"

"The devil with the dirty beggar, Yanks!" Witherington cried out. "Don't tell him a bloody thing!"

*Crack!*

The whip in von Schultz' hands bit deep, and a gun seemed to go off in Stud's brain. All became roaring red, and he hurled himself blindly toward von Scholtz.

"You beast!" he screamed wildly. "Let that man alone or I'll kill you with my bare hands!"


V


Stud Stacey's outstretched hands were but a foot from the throat of von Scholtz when he was suddenly pulled up short and slammed down onto the floor. The two guards who had grabbed him fell on top of him, and through a whirling blur he saw the metal barrel of a Luger slicing down at his head.

He jerked his head to the side and lashed up with his free fist. He experienced the wild momentary satisfaction of feeling his fist crash against solid bone. Then the ceiling sort of dropped down on him.

For a long time he didn't have a clear idea of just what was taking place. He seemed to be floating in a world of utter darkness. Yet, at intervals the darkness would be banished by a sheet of red or orange or yellow that flared up in his brain. And on each of these occasions there would be a thunderous roar in his ears, and stabbing pains throughout his body.

Finally the roar and the lights faded away, and only the pains remained. He came to, to find himself sitting on the cement floor in a pool of water. And right at that moment a fair portion of the Mediterranean hit him in the face. He let out a shout of anger and glared up at the guard who held an empty bucket.

"Take it easy, Stud," he heard Jay say. "He's got his gang with him."

Stud looked at his pal who stood with a guard's Luger about an inch from the back of his neck. Slowly Stud got to his feet. The guard dropped the bucket and closed in with his Luger.

"You should give your watch dogs a couple of medals," Stud said to the *Kommandant*. "They certainly saved your dirty hide that time."

"And *I* saved yours!" the Nazi answered. "I could have given the order to kill you, but I spared you for the time being. I want you to be *impressed*. Colonel von Scholtz! Continue!"

Von Scholtz slapped the bull-whip against Witherington's bleeding back.

"Well, swine?" he shouted. "You will answer our question, yes?"

The Englishman was half-slumped against the whipping-post as though dead. Von Scholtz gave him another vicious lash with the whip, and Witherington's whole body quivered.

"Speak, you swine!" von Scholtz screamed.

But not so much as a groan slipped past Witherington's tightly clamped lips. As von Scholtz lifted the whip again Stud let out a yell.

"Hold it!" he cried. "That man has something you can never lick! More nerve than your whole blasted German army! Let him alone. It's my turn, now!"

The *Kommandant* shot him an angry look.

"Your turn?"

"Right!" Stud snapped and walked away from the guard's Luger, as though it was not there. "Tie me up, and see if you can get any better results."

"Thanks, old man," came the muffled voice of Witherington, "but I don't mind it. The dirty beggars must have their sport, you know."

Stud looked at the *Kommandant* and grinned, tight-lipped.

"I guess you'll have to kill the three of us," he said evenly.

"We wouldn't tell you the time of day," Jay Bell told them.

The *Kommandant* might never have seen other than cringing victims in his torture and execution chamber. At any rate he stood stock-still and stared at Stud in angry bafflement. His face became beet-red and wild wrath flared up in his eyes.

He half-turned as though to scream an order at von

Scholtz but checked himself. A cunning look took the place of the anger in his eyes. He seemed well pleased with some sudden and secret decision. He had opened his mouth to speak when the ungodly wail of the raid siren blotted out all other sound. The *Kommandant* stiffened, but regained control of himself in a flash.

"Perhaps you are right," he said to Stud. "Perhaps all three of you dogs would die before you would speak. I will consider this matter, and see you again, later."

The *Kommandant* barked an order at von Scholtz, and the two guards, then all four raced away, leaving the prisoners alone. Stud ran to Witherington and started fumbling with the ropes that bound the Englishman's wrist. With Jay's help he freed the British flier and lowered him gently to the floor.

The man smiled his thanks, then closed his eyes tight and clenched his fists to keep from fainting. Stud and Jay could only stare helplessly at the man's bleeding back for there was nothing with which to cover the whip welts.

Witherington opened his eyes, took a deep breath, and a little color came back into his face.

"I only hope I catch up with that von Scholtz beggar some day," he said, with a crooked smile. "Just hear those planes! False alarm, of course. We'd never bomb here in daylight. But it shows the blighters have got the wind up, no end!"

Stud listened to the roar of German planes going off the base and stared in frank admiration at Witherington.

"You've certainly got what it takes," he said. "Frankly, I was scared stiff the rat would call my bluff. Don't know whether I could have taken a beating, or not."

"It's not a pleasant business," the R.A.F. pilot said. "I'd like to know, though, why he suddenly changed his mind. He's a tricky devil. And it wasn't because you convinced him that we wouldn't speak. Not the Nazi nature. They have absolute faith in the power of torture. No, the blighter has got something else up his sleeve. I. . . . I say!"

The Englishman's face suddenly went deathly white.

"Think I'll lie down a bit," he mumbled. "Sorry to be like this. But watch the blighter, you Yanks. Full—of tricks. Try—to get you to—"

Stud and Jay caught the man as he fainted and gently turned him over, to lie face-down on the floor. Jay ran over to the bucket the guard had left and found there was still an inch of water left in it. He came back and sprinkled the water on Witherington's back. Stud was angrier by the second.

"Jay," he muttered, "you and I are elected to get him away from here!"

"But how?" Jay asked.

"I don't know!" Stud said. "But we've got to find a way. Witherington, there, rates *out*. And we could do with some of the same thing ourselves."

With a quick nod Stud started a tour of the blockhouse. The windows were too high for him to see out, and there was nothing in the place to stand on. There were two doors, one at the front and one at the side.

He tried the front door. It was locked and bolted. He glanced at the side door, shrugged and walked over to it just to make sure. He mechanically took hold of the knob, twisted—the side door was not locked!

He opened it an inch and found himself staring at the broad back of a guard and at the air base beyond. He caught a flash glimpse of Nazi Messerschmitt One-tens coming in to land, then he quickly shut the door and stood there trembling in wild excitement.

"Great Pete, Stud!" came Jay's whisper at his side. "The darned thing isn't locked!"

For a long minute the two Navy pilots stood staring at each other. Jay finally found his tongue.

"The dopes slipped a cog this time!" he whispered fiercely. "All we have to do is nail that fat slob out there, and we'll have our pick of the planes. Did you see them? Messerschmitt One-tens, practically within spitting distance. With all this air activity going on we could slip off, and they wouldn't know the difference!"

Stud's heart was pounding wildly against his ribs, and the blood was surging through his veins. If they *could* get off in a One-ten, and were given half a chance, they could reach the *Bennington* in a couple of hours, easy. Yet, as those wild thoughts raced through his brain he felt uneasily that there was some obvious and important factor that he was missing completely. Some thought was in his brain, but he couldn't pin it down.

"Yes," he finally said. "We get the guard, then you and I carry Witherington to that first One-ten. We park him in the radioman's seat, then we get going. But—"

"But what?" Jay demanded. Stud shook his head.

"There's just something—I mean. . . . Oh! There's part of the picture we're missing, Jay. Don't know how to put it in words exactly."

"Maybe you'll think of them when we're back on the *Bennington*," Jay said. "We've got to get going because it'll be dark soon. And we'd have enough trouble hunting the *Bennington* in daylight. Get Witherington up on your shoulder, Stud. I'll go out and take care of that Nazi baby. Boy! Am I going to love clouting him! Come on! Let's go!"

Stud scowled darkly at the closed door, then heaved a sigh, and shrugged.

"Okay," he muttered. "Give me a hand getting Witherington up on my shoulders. Sure you can handle that Nazi alone?"

"Any six of them! Jay. Don't wait to watch it. Keep going to the nearest plane and pile him aboard. I'll be right on your heels."

They picked up the unconscious British pilot and carried him to the side door. As they straightened him up so that Stud could take him across one shoulder Witherington groaned, opened his eyes in a blank stare, and mumbled a few words.

"Watch beggars—full of tricks—all kinds—clever tricks."

At the mumbled words a great white light seemed to flare up in Stud's brain. He stiffened, and looked wildly at Jay who looked back at him in alarm.

"What's the matter, Stud?" he asked sharply. "That going over they gave you? Look, I'll carry Witherington, and you—"

"Shut up!" Stud whispered. "It just came to me. What Witherington just mumbled. This is the answer to that Nazi big slob's crazy actions. The old spider inviting the fly into his parlor."

"You gone screwy?" Jay demanded. "What are you raving about?"

"The *Bennington,* you chump!" said Stud. "Don't you get it? This door was left unlocked on purpose! That Nazi *wants* us to make a break. He's probably waiting some place to see us pile out of here and into one of those planes. Maybe he didn't figure we'd take Witherington along, but I don't think he'll mind much. Jay! We could crawl over to one of those planes, and nobody would stop us!"

"For Pete's sake, Stud!" Jay said hoarsely. "I don't get it!"

"They want us to bust out of here and take off because they figure we'll head straight for the *Bennington!*" Stud said with forced patience. "They've got ships in the air now, waiting for us. That Nazi is no dope, Jay. He knows there's a Yank carrier or two somewhere in these waters. He doesn't dare make a move until he finds out where they are and sends his dive bombers to keep him occupied. Don't you see? He knows he'll get nothing out of us. So he's trying this gag. He's willing to pass us up, if we can only lead him to the *Bennington!*"

"We'll take off and high-tail for Malta. He'll figure the *Bennington* is at Malta," Jay answered.

Stud shook his head.

"No soap," he said. "I still say that dope is no dove, see? He'll have plenty of planes between here and Malta to cut us off if we head that way. The way he worked on Witherington proves plenty things he doesn't know about Malta, but it's a cinch he knows that there aren't any Yank naval units there."

"So what do we do?" Jay growled. "Give it up and have a good cry?"

"Shut up and let me think!" Stud replied. "I. . . . Hold everything! I've got it! We'll go the lunkhead one better. You cart Witherington off in one plane and I'll grab a second plane. You head west and up as fast as you can. I saw some clouds when I had that quick look just now. Head for them, lose yourself, then work your way south-ward and around toward Malta. Maybe you'll pick up a British Navy boat on patrol. Land in the water and have them take you aboard. But make it to Malta, if you can. You're a good enough navigator even with German instruments."

"Thanks!" Jay said, giving him a hard look. "And you? Why two planes?"

"I'll ride herd on you, of course. And—well, if we smack into trouble, two ships will be better than one. Now, quiet. Here, I'll hoist Witherington up on your shoulder. And I'll do the slugging act on that guard outside. Come on, Jay. Button your lip. This is the way we'll play it!"

## VI

Jay gave Stud a long suspicious look, then leaned forward and caught Witherington around the legs so that the English-man slumped head-down across his shoulders. A lump rose up in Stud's throat, and he came close to reaching out and grabbing Jay's hand. He refrained, however, because such a gesture would reveal his own thoughts. And Jay was just stubborn enough to refuse to go through with *that* kind of a play.

So Stud simply slid past Jay and closed his hand over the knob of the door. His heart was striving furiously to pound out through his ribs, but his decision was made, and that was that.

Yeah, he would ride herd on Jay and Witherington, but not the way he suggested. This was going to be the great big beautiful and final blackout for him. But he would give these cursed Nazis here at the Siracusa base so much to worry about that they wouldn't have time to pay any attention to Jay and Witherington. He'd—

Gingerly he eased the door open an inch. There was still all kinds of activity going on about the field, but when he saw there were no Germans near the line of Messerschmitt One-tens, and that the guard had even backed a step or two closer to the door, he knew that his figuring had been correct.

The Nazi big slob had planned it to be this way. He figured he was going to pull a fast one. But not if Stud Stacey could prevent it!

Easing the door open wider, Stud paused just long enough to glance back over his shoulder at Jay and wink, then he went out the opening like a shot from a gun. He slugged the German guard behind the ear probably before the Nazi even heard anything, then was streaking headdown toward the line of Messerschmitt One-tens.

He had a crazy impression that every eye on the field was looking at him. He also had the impression that machine-guns would start snarling in the next split-second, and that his legs would be kicked out from under him, and he would sprawl flat in his own splashed blood.

Nothing happened, though. If there were shouts and cries he didn't hear them because of the pounding roar in his ears. And if any bullets did come his way he didn't hear them either. And then he was right alongside the nearest One-ten. He skidded to a halt and whirled around as Jay came charging up.

Grabbing Witherington, he hastily motioned Jay up into the pit. Then he hoisted Witherington up, and waited until Jay had the unconscious Englishman jammed down in the rear pit. Then Stud ducked under the belly of the One-ten and leaped toward the next in line.

It was then that he saw the third ship, a One-ten refitted as a light bomber. There were eggs in the wing racks, and it seemed as though the One-ten was begging Stud to take it. He was ducking under the belly of the second Messerschmitt in line when he heard Jay's engine's roar out their song of power and felt some of the vicious prop-wash slapping against him. Then he was under the second Messerschmitt and making a flying dive for the pit of the plane fitted with bombs.

As the seat of his pants hit the leather cushion he heard the savage snarl of machine-gun fire. But he did not waste even a precious split second to jerk up his head and take a look. If all his figuring had been cockeyed, it was too late to turn back now. Anyway, he had a personal job to do no matter what happened to Jay and Witherington. He had a few monkey wrenches to toss into the Nazis' well-laid plans for Malta. Yeah! a few monkey wrenches fitted to the racks under this Messerschmitt's wings!

As the thoughts raced through Stud's brain he had juiced the Benz-Daimler engines into life, and kicked off the wheel brakes. As the One-ten lunged forward as though coiled steel springs had suddenly been released, he jerked up his head and took a look.

Not fifty yards in front of his on-rushing plane a Nazi Heinkel One-thirteen was settling down to earth! He jumped on right rudder, closed his eyes, and prayed. He felt his left wingtip brush something, then his plane was bouncing forward lightly on the wheels.

And there was the snarl and crackle of machine-gun fire all over the place; whether it was directed at him, he didn't know. Whether his ship was being hit, he didn't care. He had the One-ten off, now, and it was going to take more bullets than the Nazis had to stop him.

When he was no more than a hundred feet up he leveled off, banked to the left, and stuck the nose down a hair. Out the corner of his eye he caught a flash glimpse of Jay's Messerschmitt climbing upward toward the west like a rocket with something mighty important on its mind. He choked out a sob of joy and gave all of his attention to the job at hand.

He was slicing down through the air straight for the line of giant troop transport planes. The paratroops gathered about them suddenly became as a nest of ants stepped on. They went washing off in all directions. And with a wild bellow Stud jabbed the trigger trip of his guns and air cannon.

Nazi paratroops seemed suddenly to fill the air in front of him. But he wasn't particularly interested in them. His objective was the ammo and fuel dumps just behind them. Ammo and fuel waiting to be put aboard the transports.

He reached those dumps like so much speeding light, yanked the lever that sent a brace of his "eggs" hurtling downward, then hauled the Messerschmitt's nose straight up toward the sky. For what seemed like ages utter silence closed in about him. He knew that his engines were screaming with power, but he couldn't hear them.

His lips were working furiously, but he seemed unable to hear the shouts that spilled out from between them. It was as though he were zooming straight up through a perfect vacuum. Nothing but silence, and more silence.

Then something let go. The earth seemed to split apart below his zooming plane. The very heavens seemed to split apart above it. All the wild savage forces in the world grabbed hold of his One-ten and sent it spinning and flip-flopping off through the air like a dried leaf in a tornado.

In a dull, abstract sort of way he knew that he had not got enough altitude before his brace of bombs exploded and touched off all that steel-cased destruction down there. He wondered if the One-ten's wings had been ripped off. He wondered if he were just sitting in the fuselage alone, and sailing through the air like a rocket. Every square inch of his skin was drawn as tight as a drumhead, and a great crushing weight was trying to push the sides of his head together.

And then suddenly he was clear of the crushing invisible forces. It was as though he had been under water with air locked in his burning lungs, and had suddenly popped up to get his head above the surface.

For a few seconds there were only dancing red dots before his eyes. Then something brushed them away, and he realized that he was not zooming toward heaven any more. The One-ten was tearing earthward and spinning like a top. Before his brain could command his muscles to function, instinct took charge, and he mechanically eased back the throttles and pulled the One-ten out of the spin.

It was then he saw the sea of red and swirling black clouds of smoke that marked the western border of the air base. There were no signs of the troop transport planes now. Nothing but fire, and black smoke. But the boiling sea of flame was lapping out in all directions. Lapping out toward other lines of Nazi aircraft. The Nazi planes were not all in line, though. Many had pilots in them, and they looked like so many cockeyed beetles as they scooted this way and that in a desperate effort to get up into the air. Nobody seemed to pay much attention to the other fellow, with the result that they were locking wings and piling up in all directions.

As Stud laughed harshly and sent the One-ten rocketing down toward fuel stores on the south side of the base, and not far from the base administration buildings, a mighty thunderous clap seemed to drive his ear-drums straight into the middle of his head. And at the same time he saw scores and scores of tiny bullet-holes appear in the One-ten's wings and fuselage nose.

His greenhouse shattered to bits and seemed to melt away. A white-hot spear of flame cut across his left shoulder. Another one dug its way across his right hip. Just a touch of white fire, and no further pain. He suddenly felt numb all over, but he could still move his hands and feet.

"Try it, rats!" he shouted. "Just try and do it before I dump the rest of them!"

Hunching well forward over the controls, and trying to steel his half-numbed body against the next hail of death from above that would surely cut off his life, he sent the One-ten pile-driving earthward and straight at the fuel dumps. In the last split second allowed he flattened out, let all of his eggs go, and let the Messerschmitt rocket straight forward.

Blurred objects flew past underneath his wings. He thought he saw guns spitting fire at him. Something came hurtling down on fire so close to his right wingtip that he was sure he could feel the heat. He jerked his head around and made out the silhouette of a Heinkel One-thirteen just before the craft struck ground and disappeared in a cloud of blood-red smoke.

"Heinkel down in flames?" he mumbled dazedly. "What gives, anyway? Did I nail one of the rats, and didn't realize it? Oh well. It's getting dark. What goes on here! I can't see. I. . . . Yes, I can. That's water down there. I must be over the water. And Nazi planes all around. Jay! Did you make it, Jay? Boy! You should have seen the mess I made. It was beautiful, Jay. All reds and yellows, and. . . . What am I doing? Jay isn't here. He can't hear me. Maybe I'm going crazy. Maybe this is the way it feels. Sure, I'm going crazy, and passing out. I. . . . But they're not shooting Stud

Stacey down. Nix! I'm landing. I'm going to sit down in that nice cool water—down. . . !"

"But how long, sir, will it be before he's up and around, and in good health?"

"Two weeks, I fancy. Three at the most. Got a body of iron, this Yank has. But why are you so anxious to have him all fit again? Can't wait to get your flying mate back on the job, what?"

Words were coming to Stud Stacey from a long way off. Coming to him from down a long black tunnel. Two people talking. Something familiar about one of the voices. But it was so dark. Who was he? Where was he? And why was it so dark? It. . . .

He remembered now. He had been killed. He hadn't made that water landing. He had crashed in, and now he was dead. But why was it so confoundedly dark? And why couldn't he see the—

But suddenly he could see. Not exactly see, because the darkness had simply changed to a soft white glow. But hold it! It wasn't all white. There were shadows. No, objects.

He found himself staring up into the grinning face of Jay Bell. There was a lot of bandage wound about Jay's head, and his arm was in a sling. But he was grinning, and he certainly didn't look dead. And he started to talk as another man in medical white hovered near him.

"Three weeks, you've got, Stud, the doc says. Three weeks to get as good as new again. And then, pal, I'm going to pop you right on the button. Pull a fast one, would you?

Try to be the big hero? Knew you had something like that in mind, so Witherington and I stuck around."

"Huh?" Stud heard his lips mutter. "What do you mean, you stuck around? I saw you heading west, like I ordered."

"Like I ordered, he says!" Jay Bell said. "Sure, we headed west, but when you dumped those first eggs we came back. Witherington came to and he was fit to be tied when he got wise to the picture. I didn't feel so happy, myself. So we beat it back.

"Only had the chance to shoot one Heinkel off your neck, though. You'd turned everything so haywire they weren't paying much attention to us. What a mess you made of that joint! Don't know whether you'll be court-martialed or not, but Admiral Porter was here yesterday, and I got the hunch he was kind of sore. He'll probably tie a medal around your neck for a weight, and toss you into the drink. Not a bad idea, when I think of what you tried to pull on your old flying pal."

"Now talk sense, Jay. What happened, and where am I? And how did we get here, and where's Witherington?"

"Give me a chance!" Jay hurried. "This is a base hospital at Malta. Witherington's in the next room, and getting along swell. He and I came here by air. A British destroyer brought you. After you'd dumped the last of your eggs you went hightailing south over the water about two hundred feet up. Witherington and I hightailed after you. A couple of Nazis made a few passes, but their hearts weren't in it. They were all flocking back to the volcano you'd made of that place.

"Anyway, something went haywire with your ship. You

made a hop, skip, and a jump landing. I guess Providence let Witherington and me see a British destroyer right then. We were about twenty miles off the northern tip of Malta. The destroyer heaved a few at Witherington and me before they caught on that we were trying to lead them to you. They were cagey for a while but finally made for your floating wreck and picked you up. And here you are. I told them the story and they contacted the *Bennington*."

"And Admiral Porter seemed sore?" Stud asked, with a frown.

"Well, call it disappointed," Jay said with a laugh. "Seems he had a raid on that base all figured out, and set to go. But you upped and grabbed all the fun for yourself."

"There's other bases up there," Stud mumbled sleepily. "And he can have my share of fun with them. I've had enough to hold me for a while. So, shove off, Mister. I've got a date with sleep. Thanks for everything—though. Many—thanks."

"Rot," Jay snorted, but he was grinning as the silence of sleep came to Stud Stacey again.

# MEDALS FOR JOSEPHINE

*By*

OSCAR J. FRIEND

JUNGLE, mountain, hillside clearing, and more jungle. Josephine roared along sweetly at her cruising speed of 227 m.p.h. In the bomb bay amidship one of the transparent belly panels had been removed, and in the aperture a high-speed intricate camera was clicking away, taking innumerable pictures of the Burmese terrain below under the expert hand of Sandy Stone.

Sandy was an ex-cowboy from Texas, an A-1 bombardier, an expert aerial photographer—and an incorrigible individualist. Josephine was a Lockheed Hudson medium bomber. To the brass hats she was a unit and a number in an American air squadron cooperating with the R.A.F. in the Burma campaign. But to her crew she was—Josephine, a gallant old girl of the air who had been through many hazardous flying hours with her four boy friends.

A voice sounded in Sand's headset. The pilot, Lieutenant Bill Duffy, from Maine. A better skipper never flew a ship.

"Sandy, d'you really think those nasty little squirts are using poison gas in the area?"

"I don't know, Bill, but I wouldn't put anything past the dirty little zeros. We'll know when we get back to base and have these negatives developed."

Down below, Sandy could barely make out activity on the part of the invading brown troops. In between sections of jungle and upland country there were occasional lines of trucks, temporary ammunition dumps, spots where there were accumulations of what could be gas shells and bombs, concealed gunnery—things which would come out in better relief on photographs which would be studied painstakingly.

For Josephine was not on a bombing mission. Her bomb bay had been unloaded and camera equipment had been installed in her capacious belly for photo reconnaissance duty. Unattended and alone, unarmed, save for "Hot Dog" Weimer, the forward gunner and "Sugar Babe" Munroe, rear gunner from Missouri, Josephine was prowling the Burmese skies.

Hot Dog Weimer, former tailor from Brooklyn, was peering ahead. He saw nothing suspicious through his plexiglas greenhouse. Only the dimly seen activity of the ground forces far below.

It was the lanky Missourian who gave the alarm.

"Better get high behind, Bill," he called through the intercom as he rose to his feet in his rear power turret and scanned the horizon behind them. "We done flushed us a covey of Mitsubishis. They're coming up on our tail. How come you didn't see 'em, Sandy?"

"Musta took off of that brown field we passed a ways back," said Sandy. "I thought that looked like a camouflaged airfield."

"How many?" asked Duffy crisply as he fed more soup to his pair of Cyclone engines.

"I count ten," reported Sugar Babe Munroe. "And I think they're Nakajimas instead of Mitsubishis. Come on, you yellow rats, and get a taste of Josephine's stinger!"

"We can't ditch them," said Bill Duffy grimly. "They've got at least a twenty-mile edge on us. Don't let 'em get under us, Sugar Babe. We're vulnerable there. Hang on tight, gang, I'm going to drop some altitude in a dive."

"What?" cried Sandy into his mike. "And get full of ack-ack? Don't mind me, but think of all this film I've shot."

"I am thinking of it," said Duffy. "We've got to get it back to base. You heard the colonel's orders—and you know how the old boy gets when he isn't obeyed. We got to try to run for it. If those Nakajimas are A.N.Ones, they'll blast us out of the sky."

"Not Josephine," contradicted Sandy. "She's brought us through worse than ten Japs. Remember that time north of Corregidor—"

"But not in one lump," said Duffy curtly, tersely. "Shut up, Sandy. Your job is to take pictures. My job is to get Josephine back to base all in one piece."

"Aw, Skipper," growled Sandy. "Turn and give Hot Dog one shot at 'em."

"He'll get it," said Sugar Babe, firing a warming burst from his turret gun. "They're between us and home."

"Hot dog!" exclaimed the forward gunner. "Swing us around, Bill, and I'll stitch them Japs to the sky."

Josephine tilted her nose downward under the pilot's

steady hands and roared into a power dive for gaining speed. Gradually she veered on right rudder to arc around in a beautiful swing toward the west. The flight of Naka-jimas came into view for both pilot and forward gunner. Down in the bomb bay Sandy was cursing and mumbling helplessly to himself.

All he could see was jungle below him. All he could hear was the roaring of the Cyclones. He was definitely out of this fight save in the possible rôle of a clay pigeon. His three buddies were having all the fun, and it irked him.

Then both rear and forward guns went into action as Hot Dog and Sugar Babe got enemy planes in their ring-sights. All creation seemed to break loose for a minute, and an omi-nous staccato rattled along one wing and crawled up the fuselage toward the bomb bay until a dexterous maneuver of Bill Duffy's caused Josephine to veer out of danger.

Sandy glared at the neat row of holes which had stopped appearing just a couple of feet away from his position and his precious camera. Then he saw a flash of red, and bits of a Nakajima suddenly littered the sky to one side and began raining groundward as one honorable Japanese boy went to meet his ancestors.

"Right on the nose!" cried Sugar Babe. "That's one horse-fly that won't nip Josephine on the flank."

"Hot dog!" shouted Gunner Weimer through the inter-com. "Look what's coming, Bill. A squadron of P-Forties out of the south, or I never learned my silhouette manuel."

"Looks like Major Frost's squadron returning from a mis-sion," clipped out Bill Duffy. "Now watch these Nakas air out."

"Green cows!" groaned Sandy Stone. "I can't even see my own rescue. Why'd I ever study to be a bombardier in the first place?"

He heard Duffy communicating with Major Frost and then felt the big ship swerve and dip to clear out of the mêlée. The flight of P-40s droned by to engage the Jap fighters like a swarm of angry hornets.

"Okay, Sandy?" checked Lieutenant Duffy as he straightened out on his course.

"Yeah, Skipper," growled the Texan.

"Come in, Sugar Babe," went on the pilot.

"Snug as a bug in a rug," answered the Missourian.

"How about you, Hot Dog? You look all right from here."

"Never worked up a sweat, Skipper," reported Weimer. "Didn't even have a chance to get my guns hot."

"You birds oughta been down here with me," groused Sandy. "My shoes are full of sweat and my collar's still smoking."

Lieutenant Duffy set Josephine down lightly on the field at Bundraang. This was the area under the control of Colonel Bigby, wing commander of the American Air Force cooperating with the British Army and R.A.F. in Burma. British and Indian jungle fighters were in the second week of assault on three temple-studded hilltop positions from which the Japanese were defending Rathedaung, the strategic village on the Mayi River some twenty-five miles north of Akyab.

The action was on a small scale because of the inability of either side to bring in large forces for jungle fighting or

more armament because of the terrain. Supply lines, mostly
by sampan, were slow and uncertain. Only expert cooperation by the air arms made progress at all possible.

"Home again, gang," said the pilot. "All right, Sandy,
hop over to the photography shack with those films while I
report to Colonel Bigby."

Colonel Bigby was not a martinet or a dyspeptic, but he
was under considerable anxiety and strain over the present
campaign—not to mention the heat and the annoying insects and the difficulties of reconciling Allied commands.
He listened to Lieutenant Duffy's report and then snorted.

"Very well, Lieutenant," he said crisply. "But you should
not have attempted to engage those enemy fighters. Your
mission was photo reconnaissance only. Get those pictures
here as quickly as possible. A big movement is in the making. Confound Major Frost. Why didn't he escort you in?"

An hour later the squadron of P-40s came roaring in.
Major Frost hastened to report to the colonel. His report
tallied essentially with that of Bill Duffy.

"We chased the Nakajimas, sir, well back over the Jap
lines, shooting down two of them. Then they flew into a
low-hanging cloudbank, and we sought altitude to catch the
Nips on the other side. But they never came out of that
cloud, sir. We lost them somehow, Colonel Bigby."

"I see," snapped Colonel Bigby. "They disappeared—disintegrated—went up in smoke."

Major Frost reddened behind his ears. He glanced at
Lieutenant Duffy. Then: "I didn't say that, sir. But I don't
understand how my whole flight could lose them so completely."

"Did it occur to you, Major Frost, that you might have lost your whole flight, chasing into enemy territory after a few Nakajima fighters? That might have been a trap—and you were returning from a special and important mission."

"Yes, sir, I know, sir," answered the major. "But I found Lieutenant Duffy under attack, and—"

"You should have driven off the enemy and escorted Lieutenant Duffy's plane back to base instead of chasing off to leave him wide-open to another possible attack. Of all the men at this base you are the one man who should realize the importance of your mission and that of Lieutenant Duffy."

"Yes, sir," agreed the major, saluting and biting his lips.

Lieutenant Duffy looked from one to the other of his superior officers without making the slightest sound. He felt like crawling away, but he couldn't escape. The colonel went on irascibly.

"So those Jap planes simply disappeared in a cloudbank, eh? Major, your squadron just let a group of little yellow men outfly them, and you jeopardized your mission by pursuing enemy planes so far afield."

"Colonel Bigby," burst out Bill Duffy, "if you please, sir, it was my fault. I communicated with Major Frost by radio and asked for his assist—"

"That will do, Lieutenant," the colonel cut him off shortly. "You have already made your report. Major Frost was perfectly right in coming to your aid, but he exceeded himself when he chased those Jap planes behind their own lines. One more violation of this sort or disobedience of exact orders by any man in this wing and I'll ground him and have him transferred. Is that clear, gentlemen?"

"Why not have him court-martialed?" Bill Duffy added silently to himself as he saluted in unison with Major Frost.

Sandy Stone broke up the seance at this moment by breaking in with a handful of damp pictures. He saluted quickly and held out the prints.

"The rest of those shots of that area photographed today, Colonel," he said.

"Good," said the colonel a bit more mildly. "Take them into the other room where Captain Grayson is making the map. Come along, Frost. You, too, Duffy."

In the next room Captain Grayson was busily pinning photographic sections of a huge relief map to the top of a big table. He took the damp pictures from Sandy Stone, riffled through them quickly and with an expert eye, made some measurements, did some trimming with a pair of shears, and began fitting the new pictures into his map.

The other men looked on in silent interest. The map was a creditable relief map of the surrounding area, reaching from some ten miles north of Rathedaung almost to Mandalay. Major Frost's eyes widened slightly as he noted where the newest pictures were being fitted into the map. Bill Duffy and Sandy Stone merely ogled. They knew what they had been photographing, but they hadn't the slightest idea what it was all about.

"Gather closer, gentlemen," ordered Colonel Bigby briskly. "Have a look at this map. Maybe you will begin to understand the importance of what I am about to tell you. Here,"—he pointed with a blunt finger—"is Maymyo, about thirty-five miles northeast of Mandalay. It is at present a strong Japanese supply base. The railroad yards, shops, mainline trackage and rolling stock are all in Jap service.

"While the British and Indian troops are concentrating up here at Rathedaung, our job is to make a heavy bombing raid on Maymyo and cripple supply and communication lines. Major Frost, your squadron has been doing reconnaissance and photography work southward as far as Mandalay, while Lieutenant Duffy has been photographing the terrain between here and Maymyo. The point is, gentlemen, we cannot locate any strong Jap airfield or bases—nothing to explain or account for the amount of ships the enemy gets into the air. Our purpose is to bomb Maymyo at daybreak tomorrow morning, but we don't want to be surprised by a lot of Mitsubishis and Nakajimas coming up from anywhere this side of Mandalay. That, in short, is what you gentlemen have been doing for the past two weeks—hunting for airfields which can accommodate big flights of enemy planes.

"Since you have failed to discover anything of this nature, we can only deduct and presume that any heavy aerial umbrella the Japs can bring to bear must come from Mandalay or points south. As soon as Captain Grayson studies this map and these newest pictures, if he finds nothing to contradict this assumption, I will give you official orders for a raid at daybreak on Maymyo. Blast these gnats and jungle junebugs!" And the colonel slapped viciously at the tiny swarm of winged pests reconnoitering his nose.

"A raid on Maymyo?" repeated Bill Duffy. "Colonel, have I permission to put—Josephine—er—my bomber back into fighting condition to take part in this raid?"

The colonel's sharp gray eyes bored into Duffy's blue ones. "You not only have permission, Lieutenant, you have my explicit orders to do so. You have finished your photography mission, and I want every possible ship to take part in this all-out raid on the Jap supply center."

"But wait a minute, Colonel Bigby," objected Sandy Stone. "I'm not satisfied with our photography. There's a section we flew over today that I want to get more pictures on. I think that's the spot where those Nakajimas got on our tail—about fifteen miles north of Maymyo. I think—"

"I fancy your skipper and Major Frost have heard enough of that area," Colonel Bigby cut the sergeant bombardier off curtly. "You have pictures of that area, Captain Grayson?"

"Yes, sir," answered the cartographer. "Lieutenant Duffy's flight today brought them in. Here they are."

"That's what I'm talking about," burst out Sandy. "There's a big brown field, half-field and half-jungle, that I want to photograph more thoroughly. I think those Nakas may have come up from—"

"That will do, Sergeant Stone," said the colonel shortly. "You will dismantle your camera equipment and get ready for a bombing raid. And, Lieutenant Duffy, you had better notify your crew as to my instructions about obeying orders explicitly. Major Frost will be in command of the flight. Grayson, where the devil is that oil of citronella—or something to keep these blasted bugs at bay?"

"Yes, sir," said Duffy, saluting stiffly.

"That will be all, Sergeant Stone," said Major Frost, eyeing the angry Texan significantly.

Duffy indicated that his bombardier was to follow him out, and withdrew.

"What gives with the major?" Sandy demanded as the pair trudged toward the makeshift hangar where Josephine was getting a quick overhauling.

Bill Duffy searched himself for a cigarette and briefly explained.

"That didn't give Colonel Bigby a reason for dressing everybody down," protested Sandy. "Anyway, Major Frost only did what anybody else would have done. And, Bill, it's about that very area that—"

"Forget it," advised Duffy. "You heard our orders. We're flying a bombing raid to Maymyo. And we're broken men if we don't follow orders. Major Frost will see to that. Now, get busy and fix Josephine up for carrying bombs."

Grudgingly Sandy Stone obeyed. But, as he worked, he kept shaking his head and mumbling to himself. Major Frost's story about Jap planes disappearing in a cloudbank didn't sound as much like nonsense as it did an unexplained mystery which had a logical solution somewhere—somehow.

After mess Sandy made his way to Headquarters shack where he found Captain Grayson sweating over the big map.

"Mind if I come in, Captain, and have a last look at the pictures?" the bombardier asked.

"Not at all, Stone," said Grayson.

For nearly an hour Bombardier Stone poured over the big relief map with a magnifying glass. He paid particular attention to the area over which he had been flying this afternoon. The spot which fascinated him the most was a point about two-thirds of the distance from Bundraang to May-myo, the place where the Nakajimas had appeared so mysteriously and then had disappeared just as suddenly when Major Frost's squadron had driven them off from the attack on the fleeing Josephine.

"There was a low-lying cloudbank over eastward, as I remember," muttered Sandy to himself. "It could have masked this area from Major Frost's squadron."

He continued to examine the map, regretting that his photograph of the spot in question had not been made at a closer elevation, that he didn't have a number of other shots of the same spot for comparison. Nevertheless, his keen eyes studied and weighed things until gradually a difference in depth and perspective began to show.

And, suddenly, he had it. The actual truth leaped out at him all at once—like an optical illusion wherein where one stares for a long time at a drawing of something concave which, in the blink of an eye, magically becomes something convex.

It was the angle of the shadows of the trees that gave the secret away. Different photographs in various parts of the big map, taken at different times of the day, naturally showed shadows at various angles and in various stages of foreshortening. But the spot that was half-field and half-jungle threw shadows that didn't jibe with the shadows of other photographs made this same afternoon.

Bill had been flying Josephine southward. That put the afternoon sun on their right hand, throwing ground shadows to the left. The suspected area had foreshortened shadows which indicated that the sun should have been almost directly overhead. The jungle stuff was nothing but a painted canvas—camouflage! The real trees and objects that actually stood out here and there threw their correct shadows to the left. But one tiny section was false. That could only mean the screened entrance to an underground hangar. Hundreds of planes might be safely stored there, coming out through the masked entrance and using the field for taking off and landing.

Sandy dropped the magnifying glass and rushed it to Major Frost's quarters. But the major didn't even give him a chance to talk. Doubtless his neck was still smoking from contact with the colonel.

"I don't want to hear any more about that area, Sergeant," he said curtly.

"But it is about ten miles behind the Jap lines," protested Sandy. "It's fully fifteen miles this side of Maymyo, and if we have all our ships concentrating on Maymyo—"

"Which we will," said Major Frost crisply. "You heard the colonel's orders, and I will not tolerate the slightest breach of flying discipline. Any more out of you, and I'll ask Lieutenant Duffy to ground you and use another bombardier."

"Leave me out of one of Josephine's flights?" gaped Sandy incredulously. "No sir. I—very good, sir. Good-night."

He saluted and quickly withdrew. They weren't going to deal him out of a night flight and a bombing raid. No, sir— not if he had to sew up his lips. But the colonel was stubborn and the major was crazy. Why, if all of the American bombers with their rather inadequate protection of fighters were concentrating on bombing Maymyo, and a heavy flight of Jap fighters came from nowhere in their rear and took them by surprise—well many would come through, but the slaughter would be terrific.

Sandy set his lips in a grim line. He knew what he had to do. And he knew that if he was wrong—and there wasn't the least possible chance for verification—he was headed for a court-martial and disgrace.

Two hours before daylight flight after flight took off from the field at Bundraang, circled for altitude, fell into battle formation, and headed south to wreak Allied vengeance on the Jap base at Maymyo. Josephine, fortunately, was in the left flight of a bomber squadron. High above, Major Frost led his squadron of protective P-40s, combat eagles which would blast down any Jap fighters that come up and come down to do battle with the raiding bombers.

But no thought had been given to a possible attack from the rear. And Sandy Stone crouched in the bomb bay of Josephine and grimly scanned the starlit terrain below through a pair of night glasses. He knew what he had to do. He hadn't dared talk before. And he groaned slightly as he speculated on whether or not Bill Duffy would listen to him, would heed him now.

"Skipper," he spoke hoarsely into the inter-com. "Bill?"

"What's the matter, Sandy?" came back Duffy's crisp voice. "You sound peculiar."

"Are Sugar Babe and Hot Dog cut in?" asked Sandy.

"Of course," said Bill cheerfully. "Don't we all four fly this old girl as one?"

"Well, listen, gang," said Sandy rapidly. "I couldn't make

the brass hats listen to me. I studied that relief map last night—those pictures we shot yesterday. I discovered the secret of those Nakajimas that jumped up on our tail. Frost was right about them disappearing. Here's how it is."

Rapidly he told the whole story.

"Good glory!" groaned Bill. "Why didn't you tell me before?"

"You heard the colonel's orders. I wasn't going to let them ground me."

"Maybe you're wrong," said Hot Dog. "You didn't get a chance to recheck."

"That's possible," admitted Sandy, "but I'll bet every cow in Texas that I ain't. Anyway, it's take a chance that I'm right and save the entire flight, or gamble wrong and get the four of us and Josephine in dutch."

"How?" demanded Sugar Babe. "What can we do now?"

Sandy drew a deep breath. Then:

"We can leave this flight mission and bomb the devil out of that camouflaged underground entrance! We can bottle all those Jap planes up down there like rats. We'll protect the flight at any rate."

"And suppose there are no Jap planes in an underground base there?" asked Bill Duffy calmly.

"Curtains for us and Josephine," admitted Sandy succinctly.

Another pause. Then:

"I can't make such a decision," said Duffy. "It wouldn't be fair to the rest of you fellows."

"Say, who commands this plane when we are coming on target?" drawled Sugar Babe.

"The bombardier, of course," answered Duffy.

"We haven't got a special navigator," went on Sugar Babe significantly. "If Sandy says we're coming on target and instructs you how to fly, you have to obey, the way I see it. I'm voting to ride it out with Sandy."

"Make it two of us," declared Hot Dog Weimer. "I want to put a tuck in the seat of their pants."

"Okay," said Duffy coolly. "You guys asked for it. Take over, Sandy."

A sob of thankfulness choked the Texan. He *had* to be right now.

"Coming on target," he said huskily. "Bear six points left, Skipper."

Five minutes later Josephine was skimming smoothly over the suspected area. Following Sandy's terse directions, Duffy put the ship into a dive. Like an exultant eagle Josephine roared down out of the dawn.

Sandy, the bomb bay open and ready, tripped his releases, and a stream of finned torpedoes and bombs rained down to blast the camouflaged area to bits. As the bomber pulled up and zoomed out of the dive there was a brief period in which all the world seemed to stand breathless, chilled, frozen—and afraid.

And then a harsh rose, a crater of fiendish red and yellow blossomed on the ground below them, a satanic flower which was instantly masked by billowing clouds of white and black smoke.

"You were right, Sandy! You were right!" shrieked Hot Dog Weimer. "They must have had detectors down there.

Look, Skipper, half a dozen fighter planes already got out of the rat-hole and they're taking off on our tail."

"Turn Josephine around, Bill," yelled Sugar Babe Munroe. "Let's go back and polish off them gnats for the colonel."

"Hot dog!" exulted the forward gunner. "Look out, you Japs. Here comes Brooklyn."

"Here comes the United States," corrected Bill as he maneuvered Josephine in the fastest reverse the gallant ship had ever looped.

And then the roaring of angry hornets droned in the sky, and Flight A of Major Frost's P-40s came diving out of the southern heavens.

After that it was pandemonium, a madhouse, for a time. The Jap planes taking off had no more chance than a handful of buzzards in a blizzard. Only one P-40 was knocked down, the pilot bailing out.

Then the radio communications began to crackle.

"You idiots get back into the Maymyo flight formation!" roared the angry voice of Major Frost. "What do you mean by this insubordination?"

"We're out of bombing ammunition, Skipper," called Sandy.

Duffy relayed this information.

"Then head back to Bundraang," ordered the major. "I'm grounding you until I get back to report to the colonel." And then he added: "My apologies for not listening to Sergeant Stone last night. After you're court-martialed, I'll cite all four of you for medals."

The flight of P-40s went roaring away. Duffy ruddered

his ship around to head for base, and the four of them lifted their voices in a barber-shop quartet:

"Come, Josephine, you're a flying machine, going up, or coming down. . . ."

# SEALED ORDERS

*By*

## NORMAN A. DANIELS

FRANK CORRIGAN, in the Lockheed P-38, roared at three hundred and fifty miles an hour over the Java Sea. At sixteen thousand feet, he could see the island of Java sprawled out to the south. Frank's job was to keep a weather eye out for Jap raiders based on Celebes, unhealthily close by. There had been raids on Java—serious ones, because the Japs could reach their objective in short flying time.

He liked it way up here. He was master of the sky. Upon him rested the responsibility of not allowing Java to be blitzed by an extremely strong force. Other pilots were roaring over the seas, too. And back on Java, strong formations were ready to take to the air at the first radio warning from the patrols.

Frank Corrigan stood on one wing for the sheer deviltry of it. The Lockheed was a brand-new, beautiful baby. There were too few of them in the South Seas. Handing one over to Lieutenant Frank Corrigan had been the same as telling him point-blank that he was a trustworthy pilot.

Then Frank Corrigan's eyes narrowed a bit. Miles away, he saw a number of tiny specks in the sky. Instantly, the nose of his plane shot upward as he strove for a good ceiling. At twenty thousand he darted into a cloud and waited. The radio was at his lips, and all he had to do was snap the switch. But until he was certain that his eyes had not been just hopefully seeing things, he had to wait.

He soared out of the cloud shortly after. Then he had a good glimpse of the force that was heading toward Java. At least thirty Jap planes! Frank snapped the radio switch and gave vent to a whoop of delight.

"Enemy formation coming in! Thirty or more. Here we go again!"

He darted down suddenly. The Jap armada was well ahead of him now and totally unaware of his presence. They were traveling at nearly top speed, intent on surprising the United Nations forces on Java and bombing as many grounded planes as possible.

Frank revved her up to three hundred and ninety m.p.h., near the top speed of this interceptor-fighter. Both motors purred smoothly as if they were also eager to get into the scrap. Not once did Frank Corrigan think of the odds against him. The fact that thirty Japs were below him meant nothing more than additional prey. He had done his job of warning the base. Now he had to split up that formation if possible, hold them in check until the other boys could get upstairs and take part in the argument.

The Japs were flying at about eight thousand feet, apparently secure in the belief that their arrival would be a distinct surprise and shock. Frank dived at them, finger brushing lightly over the surface of his firing button.

The pilot of the last Jap plane never knew what happened. Shells from Frank's cannon smashed through the cowling. That pilot died long before his ship did.

Frank kept on diving. They knew of his presence, now, but that was all right with him. His course took him under one Jap plane which he smeared with a tracer. Then he came up to swoop at a third. This one took a burst of machine-gun bullets and let go with a thick stream of black smoke.

Frank did a fast rocket loop, came up under the belly of another and peppered him out of the fight. The formation was breaking up fast now. The Japs were trying to get away from this flashing, crazy Yank. Frank felt some slugs smash into the tail portions of his ship, but she only quivered a bit and kept going.

He spotted the Jap squadron leader, brazenly circling back to take on this lone Yank. Frank Corrigan whooped again, rolled slightly to the starboard side and escaped the first of the Jap's tracer bullets. Then his cannon started to spit. Both planes were roaring straight at one another with a speed that was almost incredible.

One moment Frank saw the Jap there. The next he saw only a smudge of smoke. Later, a few pieces of lighter débris floated down.

There were two of them pouncing on him now. Frank looped again, passed through the concentrated fire of the pair and got above them. They scurried in opposite directions. Frank went after one of them. At four hundred m.p.h. he rapidly overtook the Jap, stayed about a hundred feet above him and held his fire. The two planes got so close that Frank could see the yellow face of the pilot looking over his shoulder. That pilot was worried plenty.

Frank knew the others would be upon him in a moment and he also saw that a score of the planes had resumed their formation and were streaking toward Java. He watched the cowling of the Jap plane come slowly into the cross-sights of his cannon, then he threw a dozen shells at the craft.

The cowling was ripped apart. The Jap plane fluttered like a moth with singed wings. It turned over on its back for a moment or two, then started a long, slanting glide to earth. There was no living hand at the controls.

Frank came back fast. Jap fighter planes were trying to overtake him, but that Lockheed could show her heels to anything the Japs owned. He breezed after the score of bombers. They were the ships whose destructions .really meant something.

Frank realized they were almost over Java now. The running fight had been toward land all the way. He darted down, straight into the middle of the pack. If he could hold them, harry them for five minutes longer, the interceptors would be in the sky to finish the job.

His guns lambasted one bomber, the aim shifted and another took a terrific amount of punishment. The rest hastily split up, formation being highly dangerous now. But during his maneuvers, Frank realized the fighter escort of Japs would have come into position. He twisted his head and gave a grunt of surprise. They were right over him. Two had already started to dive.

He squirmed to get out of their way, but a terrific explosion almost burst his eardrums. Things were blacked out for a few moments, then he realized that he was losing altitude at a dangerous rate. The cowling had been shattered. One engine was straining furiously. Jap fighter planes circled closer for the kill.

There was an interruption of those tactics a moment later though. Franks rashness had paid dividends. Yank interceptors were roaring toward the battle. The Jap bombers wheeled away without having let go with a single egg. There was no time for them to do any bombing now. Their main worry was how to get away.

At full throttle, Frank climbed as high as he dared. There were still a pair of Japs trying to come in for the kill, but they were also wary of this crazy Yank. They had seen enough of their own ships go down to know he was not a clay pigeon.

Just to keep them worried even more, Frank threw some steel their way. At twelve thousand he knew he had reached his ceiling with that sputtering engine. The plane was doomed. He knew that, but a moment later he got concrete evidence of it.

One of the Japs came rushing in, guns spitting. The Lockheed buckled and gave up the ghost. Frank saw part of one wing fly off and he didn't wait any longer. By using all his strength he managed to get the shattered cowling back, climbed out and dived into space. One hand clutched the ring, but he didn't pull it. The Jap was diving at him, waiting for the chute to check his descent to a mere drift and then those machine-guns would take care of him.

Frank Corrigan kept turning over and over. Now and then he had a glimpse of the Jap and saw with satisfaction that he was getting smaller and smaller. Then he pulled the ring. The silk blossomed out, jerked his fall short and two seconds later he was on the ground.

He ran into the chute, trampled the air out of it and cut himself loose. The Jap roared down. But a Yank interceptor was on his tail. The dirt, only about fifty feet to the left of where Frank stood, seemed to be studded with thousands of geysers. He flung himself flat.

The Jap lost his head. With the Yank pounding away at his tail, he didn't come out of his dive until too late. A wing scraped the ground. A bolt of flame encompassed the Jap ship and with a great ripping of metal, she broke into pieces.

Frank wiped sweat off his face, got his bearings and trudged wearily toward Operations base. It was early evening when he stumbled into the commander's shack and saluted.

Colonel Drake looked him over. Drake was a tough man to work for. He usually considered only the faults of his men, rarely their successes.

"Corrigan," he accused, "you wrecked a new Lockheed today. Not that it wasn't worth it, but those ships are difficult to obtain way out here. You should have broken off the engagement as soon as the interceptors were in the air. I tried to tell you that by radio, but you either had the instrument shut off or you paid no attention."

"It was shut off, sir. I wanted to concentrate on my job.

It was too late to break off, sir. The Nips were coming at
me from all directions."

"All right," Drake said. "Stand at ease, man. You look
so blasted uncomfortable. Sit down, if you wish. Have a
cigarette . . . Corrigan, I've a request here from our Naval
forces for a good man. I understand you are familiar with
Navy planes."

"Yes, sir. Flew them for more than two years."

"Good. That means you automatically get this assignment.
Being a lone fighter as you've proved more than once, you
ought to like this job and it might take some of the gross
recklessness out of you. At midnight, a Navy car will call
for you. Further orders will come from your new commander. After making a report to Intelligence, you'd better
get some rest."

Frank snuffed out the cigarette. Was Colonel Drake punishing him because he had plunged head-first into that un-
equal fight so that Java would be saved from a bombing?
That was the devil of a reward. He saluted, made no comment and walked out.

He kept stewing over the situation instead of sleeping.
What kind of an assignment did the Navy have for him?
With what ship? So far as he knew, all craft were in action
far from Java. At least he hadn't spotted even a torpedo boat.
The Dutch had a few ships laying about for protection, but
even their fleet was at sea. . . .

Midnight found Frank climbing into a car. An ensign
greeted him with a grin, but answered no questions, pro-
claiming that he only followed orders and didn't know why

the devil the Navy had to call on the Army for even one man's help.

They stopped at the end of a dock where a motor launch was waiting. The ensign helped Frank into the swift little craft and it tore straight into the darkness of the Java Sea. Half an hour later, the ensign signaled with a blinker light. It was answered, but although he strained his eyes, Frank Corrigan couldn't see any ship.

Then he gave a gasp. It was a submarine! The biggest undersea craft he had ever laid eyes on. There were two guns aft, two forward. Big fellows. A square, roomlike structure was amidships. Frank had never seen a sub that looked just like this one.

He climbed onto the bridge and shook hands with Lieutenant Commander Paul Kent. Kent was young, eager-eyed, but didn't look resplendent in his greasy uniform.

"Glad to have you aboard us, Lieutenant," he said to Frank earnestly. "Don't ask me why you were selected, or what you are to do. I don't know. There are sealed orders in my safe. Can't open them for a day or two."

Frank gasped. "A day or two? Say, how long am I supposed to stay cooped up aboard this death-trap? Listen—I'm a pilot. I'm used to space—millions of miles of space. I'm used to speed and fast action."

"Maybe you'll get it," Paul Kent grinned. "Well, come below."

Frank followed the sub's commander into the narrow confines of the craft. Paul drew a sharp breath, squeezed himself through a narrow door and into one of the smallest rooms Frank had ever entered. One man crowded the place. Two absolutely jammed it.

Paul sat down on the edge of a bunk, which he pulled down from the wall. There was nowhere else to sit so Frank sat down beside him. He was aware that motors were humming smoothly and there was considerable activity in the control room.

"What the heck!" he said. "I lost a new plane and the colonel lands on me hard. But is this any kind of punishment for an aviator? Cooped up aboard a submarine? They might as well have thrown me into a dungeon. What am I supposed to do—grow wings on the sub and fly her?"

Paul laughed. "Growing the wings isn't necessary. We've got 'em. There's no point in grousing. Right now we're a hundred feet under the surface and moving into action."

Frank Corrigan looked unhappy. "I don't like being shut up like this. Why didn't you get a Navy flyer if you need an aviator? I can't see what good one is on a sub."

"There were no Naval flyers handy," Paul Kent said. "I know that your colonel was asked to supply the craziest pilot in his group. A guy with icicles in his veins. You're it. Now I'll give you the lowdown, as far as I can without reading those sealed orders. We're on a raiding cruise. We head north toward the China Sea, skirting Borneo and coming right up against the Jap supply lines to Singapore and Sumatra."

"All right," Frank answered. "But what do I do? Ride a torpedo or something?"

Paul chuckled. "No—the Japs can do that. There are

few submarines like this one. In the first place it's big. And we have an airplane aboard."

"A plane? Aw—quit kidding." Frank waved the idea aside. "How can you carry a plane in this tub? It isn't wide enough to put a trainer into."

Paul Kent arose and slid past the bunk. "You'll find out soon enough. By tomorrow night we'll be in position for some action. Until then, this cabin will be your quarters. If you like, I'll have somebody take you around to see what makes this tub tick."

"No thanks," Frank said. "I didn't ask for this assignment. I don't like it. This is a punishment detail, but you can depend on me. I'll see things through."

The hours aboard the sub were ghastly to Frank. He felt like trying to burst through the sides of the craft. He wanted to see the sun or the stars, to feel cold air whizzing around his neck, hear the roar of his engines. Instead, he was beneath the surface of the sea, cramped into a vessel hardly fit to live in. He knew now why they called them pig-boats.

Time was endless and without meaning. The monotonous humming of the battery-fed engines got on his nerves. Then, suddenly, they were checked. The floor of the sub slanted upward. Paul Kent climbed up the conning tower ladder. The hatch opened and Frank drew in fresh, soothing air. He climbed up on deck, too.

Paul Kent indicated that odd-looking superstructure on the deck and led the way to it. From inside, somebody operated mechanisms and a water-tight door opened. No lights were turned on and men were on constant watch.

This was decidedly the enemy's sea and no chances could be taken.

Frank edged into the water-tight compartment and saw his new ship. He closed both eyes and groaned. With her folded wings she was about the size of a kite compared to the planes he had been used to flying. She was pontoon-equipped, had a small engine and two machine-guns. There were no bombs, no depth charges, no torpedoes.

"What am I supposed to fight with?" Frank asked. "How do I roll that flivver off the deck and how do I get back on? Or don't I?"

"You'd better go below and get into your flying togs," Paul Kent said seriously. "We have information that an enemy squadron is coming this way. Convoying troopships. Your job, Pilot, is to fly this flivver, as you call it. You will spot the enemy formation from as great a height as possible and radio the location. We won't answer. Subs never use their radios on a job like this. After we attack, your map will indicate the rendezvous far away from the scene of action. We'll surface there and wait for you."

Frank, warmly dressed, squeezed into the narrow cockpit and wondered just what he would do if a Jap pursuit plane spotted him. A catapult was turned to port side. Paul Kent stood by, one hand raised. Frank Corrigan braced himself for the impact of the launching.

When it came it almost broke his neck. Then he was roaring away into the darkness and swearing in unison with the explosions of the motor. Next time, he vowed, he would handle his patrols differently.

Report the coming of enemy craft and then get out of

their way, eh? Courage and heroism didn't pay off in this war. Not so long as Colonel Drake had anything to do with it.

The top speed of this minute crate seemed to be about a hundred and seventy. Then Frank wondered what his rush was. He checked bearings and began to patrol. It was almost two hours later before he saw a faint light on the sea far below. Some sailor's carelessness had located the transport for him.

He didn't go down. That would give the whole game away. Instead he veered off and tuned in his radio. The sub, he knew, would be surfaced and listening. No confirmation came, as Paul Kent had said would be the case.

He cruised up and down at a lazy speed and cursed this kind of warfare. Then, suddenly, the sea below was lit up by an inferno. The explosion of the torpedo made Frank's light plane surge upward. He saw the guns of armored vessels go into action. There were grim rumbles of depth charges, and Frank gulped. What was he supposed to do if the sub was sunk? He didn't have fuel enough to reach land and even if he did, any shore would be hostile in these parts.

Then another torpedo slammed home and a second transport went down in flames. Frank's hopes arose somewhat until the guns and depth charges banged once more.

He veered off, his duty finished. He would have liked nothing better than to strafe the decks, but in the glow he could see that destroyers and a light cruiser were with the enemy convoy. They would be armed with anti-aircraft and this Lizzie he flew could be knocked down with a popgun.

He flew straight out to sea, checked his bearings again

and plotted the rendezvous. It wasn't far from the scene
of action, but he came down on the water, shut off his motor
and waited.

Hours went by. He realized the sub could not move without having the sound of her engines picked up, so he just
sat there swearing at wars in general, and at Colonel Drake
in particular.

It was not far from dawn when he gave a nervous jump.
The sea was parting and the giant hull of the sub started
to surface. Frank felt better then. He supervised the lifting
of the plane onto the deck, helped to fold its wings and
stayed at the conning tower until all was ship-shape.

Lieutenant Commander Kent slapped him on the
shoulder.

"Nice going, Pilot. We'd never have spotted that convoy,
but with your directions we waylaid those babies. Sunk
three of 'em. That's not such a bad night's work. Keeps the
Japs jittery. Now let's go below and open those sealed
orders. I have an idea they'll spell action in nice big letters."

Paul Kent opened the safe, took out a sealed envelope
and slit it open. He read the two pages of fine typing, then
thrust the whole business into a drawer.

"It's action, all right," he said. "Risky stuff, Pilot. Here's
the angle. We head for Tourane, on the east coast of French
Indo-China. Seems espionage reports indicate that the Japs
have assembled a huge ammunition and supply dump there.
No surface craft could get within a hundred miles of it, no
Allied aircraft are anywhere around so the Japs feel pretty
secure. They use the supplies to replenish their armies all
over the South Seas."

"And what do I do about it?" Frank asked.

"We'll reach Tourane in about four days. Right after dark you'll take off, spot the ammunition dump and drop a special flare right smack on top of it. We'll be surfaced and ready to let go with our guns. We've some pretty good ones, you know, and a few well-placed shells will destroy the dump. Your job is to furnish the target by a flare."

Frank Corrigan nodded. "I figured it would be something like that. I set the stage and you fellows do the business. Makes me quite a lad. How about letting me use bombs instead of flares?"

"No—that little plane wouldn't carry even a three-hundred-pounder, and she's not equipped with bomb racks. Sorry. I know just how you feel, but orders are orders. We'll keep traveling at full surface speed all night. Daytimes we have to lie low. That's why the trip will take so long. Anyway, you proved the worth of a scouting plane attached to a sub, Pilot. I'm grateful."

The next several days were agonizing ones for Frank Corrigan. By day, he flopped in a bunk or played pinochle with members of the crew. At night, he walked the tiny deck when the sub surfaced for air and to charge her batteries.

He thought of the patrols on which he had been, streaking through the sky. The whole world had been his kingdom then. Now he was packed into a tin can. Colonel Drake had no right to treat him that way.

When they reached a point well off Tourane, Frank felt a little better. At least he could fly again, smell the sweet air.

They were getting set to catapult the plane. Frank went below decks and summoned a junior officer.

"I'm to carry a submachine-gun, plenty of ammo and some time bombs. Can you furnish 'em?"

"Yes, sir. I'll see they're put aboard your plane."

"Good." Frank grinned. "You never can tell when things like that will come in handy."

The catapult hurtled him off the deck. He had fuel enough to reach the Jap base, fly around it for half an hour, then return to meet the sub well in toward land. It would be a risky business once the sub's guns started to fire, because land batteries were bound to open up on her and the Jap planes would take off with their bomb racks loaded.

Flying at a top ceiling for this plane, Frank had no trouble in spotting the ammunition dump. It was in a huge, sprawling wooden building. He could see horse-drawn carts pulling in and out of the gates around the place. No attempt had been made to black out the city. It was far away from Allied operations and apparently the Japs had not given a thought to a puny sub.

Frank seized a flare and cursed his luck. A flare! That was his part when a couple of thousand-pounders would reduce that dump to rubble. He held the flare overside, then hastily drew it back. Lights of a flying field were suddenly turned on and he saw medium bombers rolling across the runways. A whole squadron took off and headed out to sea.

The Japs were not trusting entirely to good luck. They were patrolling the coast. If the sub surfaced, they would blast it to the bottom.

Frank started to sweat. He realized now that he liked Lieutenant Commander Paul Kent and the whole doggone crew aboard that tin can. He even liked the sub. He gained more altitude and talked into his radio transmitter.

"Corrigan calling Operations Base," he said. "Nothing doing here. Better duck your head under the covers and get some sleep. Music a little too hot for comfort. Will return as scheduled. Stand by under cover."

He hoped that Paul would understand what he meant. There was a chance that his message would be picked up.

He had to act fast. Putting the plane into a slow dive, he streaked across the settled portions of the mainland and finally started hedge-hopping a lot of trees while he looked for a suitable landing place. It meant wrecking the plane, but that didn't matter so long as he could reach that ammunition dump.

About ten miles inland he saw a glimmering surface below. A lake. He howled his glee, circled it once, and came down to a smooth landing. He taxied close in toward shore, grabbed the submachine-gun, lashed the time bombs around his middle and waded to land.

A minute later he was headed back toward the town. Just what he could do wasn't clear, but if the sub couldn't shell that ammo dump, it was his job to destroy it somehow.

He saw a lighted farmhouse and wondered if the natives around these parts were for the Japs or the Allies. A lot of them would be French, but Vichy had turned the whole area over to the Japs. Perhaps the people were pro-Jap, too. Corrigan crept up to the farmhouse.

He stepped from behind a barn and a horse whinnied

nervously. At the same instant a voice called out a low-voiced command to halt. Frank froze, but his submachine-gun was ready for action.

He saw a man step out of the gloom, rifle in hand. He was not a Jap soldier. In a moment, Frank realized his captor was white and certainly French because he spoke that language only. Frank knew a little of it.

The two men stood about ten feet apart, weapons menacing each other. The Frenchman squinted through the darkness.

"Who are you?" he demanded.

Frank took a long chance. "American! Yank!"

Instantly, the Frenchman dropped his gun and rushed forward to plant a kiss on Frank's cheek. He pushed the man away, but grinned at him. It was nice to meet a friend in an alien land.

"I speak English," the man said. "Pretty good. *Oui!* I learned to speak it from American soldiers in Paris during the last war. *Eh bien,* it is well that I and not some yellow dog found you."

"That," Frank answered, "is no lie. You live way out here?"

"Since the yellow pigs came. Before that I had a big house in town. A friend of mine who got away left me his papers. I used them to prove I am but a poor peasant, and the yellow ogres only force me to carry supplies to town. They pay me with kicks and curses, but if they knew who I was, I would be shot on sight."

"So you have free run of the town?" Frank Corrigan

asked. "Don't any of the people there like Vichy well enough to expose you?"

"*Non!* I am their friend. They did not wish this to happen. They watch the yellow dogs pile up supplies. Their ships come to load and they go away with bullets and shells to reduce this part of the world to ashes, as that pig Hitler has done in Europe. I know, because I furnish hay with which they pack their cursed shells and bombs."

Frank whistled. "Say—maybe you and I could do some business. Those Japs have no idea I'm around. As I landed, a patrol was taking off and their motors drowned out mine. How'd you like to blast that ammo dump to smithereens, Frenchy?"

The Frenchman coupled both hands together and raised them toward the sky.

"*Mon Dieu,* nothing would do my heart more good. But how?"

"When do you take the next load of straw to town?"

"Any time that I have it. I could bring two loads now, if I wished. I often bring it at night because the dogs say I must work in the fields by day."

Frank asked him a score of further questions and an idea dawned on him. He talked to the Frenchman, whose name was Argal, and Argal was enthusiastic about the idea.

"It's an old American Indian trick," Frank explained, "but I'll bet the Japs never heard of it."

In short order a hay wagon was hitched up. The horse was sleek, well-fed and fast. Frank Corrigan stowed his submachine-gun and time bombs beneath a huge coat which Argal provided.

An hour after Frank had landed his ship, he was hidden under the load of straw. Argal, driving the wagon, kept singing at the top of his lungs.

Frank stuck his head out from beneath the straw.

"Hey—do you want to draw the Jap patrols on our necks?"

Argal waved both hands. "But, *oui,* if they hear my voice, they know I do not try to hide. It is difficult to reach town now. The patrols are spread out and cover all areas. More than one man has been shot by nervous sentries."

Frank ducked under the straw and made sure those time bombs were dry and intact. The wagon creaked to a halt and Argal hissed a signal. Frank slid off the wagon to the ground. Without wasting a moment, he hurried up to the horse and worked on the harness. When he had finished, he told Argal just what to do.

"It's pretty dark," he explained "When you get about a hundred yards from the barrier, get your horse going fast. Slam on the wagon brakes and the harness will give way. I'll be on the horse and if those Japs see me, it's Hollywood's fault for showing so many Western pictures in Tokyo."

Argal didn't quite know what it was all about, but he shrugged and followed orders. There was a barrier across the narrow road and Jap soldiers stood guard there. Argal swallowed with some difficulty, flicked his whip and the horse started running. Argal estimated the distance, jammed on the brake and watched Frank who was astride the horse. Horse and wagon parted company.

Frank slid off the side. By what seemed to be a miracle so far as Argal was concerned, Frank became invisible against the dark skin of the horse. He was guiding the animal too because Argal saw the horse veer to the left of the barrier, go around it and keep running.

Argal was running also, shrieking commands for the horse to stop. Sentries, with level rifles, saw nothing of Frank Corrigan who was on the off side of the horse. They guessed that the horse had merely broken loose and they began laughing at Argal's chagrin.

Frank let go of the horse as soon as he was fairly well blended with the darkness. He fell into a ditch, rolled over several times and crawled behind a bush.

He waited there until Argal came along, accompanied by two soldiers. The horse was grazing contentedly. Argal called it profane names, led the animal back to the barrier, and hooked him up to the wagon. Soldiers had already searched the straw and passed Argal through the barrier.

Frank leaped aboard as the wagon rolled slowly past his hiding place, buried himself under the straw and breathed normally for the first time in what seemed to be many hours. Being caught here, wearing a civilian coat over his uniform, meant a firing squad.

Argal bumped into town, proceeded down several narrow streets and finally turned into the gates of the munitions dump. Guards here made no attempt to search him. They knew that wagons were carefully gone over by sentries on the outskirts and that there wasn't an ounce of explosives in the possession of villagers or farmers.

Stopping his wagon alongside the great wooden structure, Argal selected a likely-looking spot. He hissed and Frank slid from the wagon, minus the time bombs which were now set. The submachine-gun was under his coat.

Argal knew what to do. He turned the horse loose, jabbed it with an elbow and the startled animal ran away for the second time. Argal started yelling imprecations and pursued his horse. Frank joined in the chase. As they came abreast of one another, Argal spoke out of the corner of his mouth.

"May the *bon Dieu* confine the soul of that horse to a pasture where there is nothing but cactus. He is slow—so slow as syrup. The time bombs are set. In a few minutes they will go off. Then, *mon ami,* we must work fast because all whites will be arrested immediately. It will not take the yellow dogs long to see through our trick."

"You head for the docks," Frank said. "I have the submachine-gun under my coat. Do you need it?"

"*Non.* It is better that you handle the gun. When we reach the docks, what then?"

"Not we—just you. Get into a speedboat. Use that knife on Jap guards if necessary. Head out to sea. I'm going back to the plane and take off. Show a light when you hear my motor and I'll convoy you to where a submarine will pick both of us up."

The Frenchman had a gleam in his eyes and he turned toward Frank quickly. Frank put up both hands and gestured him away.

"You can kiss me when we're inside that sub," he whispered. "The fuses were set for ten minutes."

"Then, *mon ami,* it is time to part. Good luck."

Frank veered to the left at the next street intersection and slowed down to a brisk walk. Argal was still chasing his horse and at the same time herding it toward the docks with skillfully thrown pebbles.

Frank was half through the town when those bombs let go. They were big and powerful. They exploded in five distinct blasts. There was a second or two of complete silence, then the earth rumbled under his feet as tons upon tons of explosives let go. Flames lit up the sky for miles.

Frank started running. Jap soldiers poured out of the buildings, but no one paid any attention to him. The upturned collar of the greatcoat shielded his features. He reached the outskirts and unlimbered that tommy gun. If he could skirt the barrier set up across the road, so much the better. If he couldn't, the gun would clear a path.

Someone shouted a challenge and Frank ducked. Three soldiers, with guns ready, came toward him. He let them get close enough so he couldn't miss and with one burst mowed the trio down. He quickly shifted the gun toward that shack. As the lieutenant and more men came out, Frank greeted them with steel.

The Japs didn't fire a shot, but he knew that racket would be heard back in town. He started running madly, but skidded to a halt, remembering that two motorcycles were parked behind the shack. Within a minute, Frank was bouncing over the winding road on one of them.

Pursuit came in a matter of seconds, but he reached the plane and was skimming across the lake when the first contingent of motorized soldiers appeared. Frank climbed to a thousand feet, circled and came back to strafe them with his machine-guns. They were light, but did splendid work.

He headed out to sea then, flying around the city. A beautiful fire was roaring and every few seconds another part of the building would blow up. Frank Corrigan swung back after he raced well out to sea. He worried about the Jap patrol which had taken off. Seconds were precious now, yet he was determined to save Argal at any cost.

He saw a light show briefly and dived toward it. Argal had a flash and turned it on his face for a second or two. Then he pointed. Frank saw a fast boat racing to overtake Argal. He swept down on it, guns pounding away. The boat began to weave a crazy course. Frank emptied his guns at the boat to make doubly certain of no further pursuit, then he flew above Argal and kept doubling back so the Frenchman could maintain the proper course.

A glance at his watch indicated the sub would be coming up to look for him.

He dropped a flare. Blinker lights answered. When Frank's pontoons skidded across the water, Argal was already being helped aboard the sub. Frank pulled up beside it, the small crane was hooked to the plane, and it was raised to deck. The moment the water-tight doors closed on it, gun crews sprang to the guns and began blasting away at the town.

Frank Corrigan watched the sky intently. The glow from the ammo dump brought the Jap patrols into view. At his signal, the gun crews rushed below. Frank dropped through the conning tower and as Paul Kent came down the ladder, the sub was crash diving.

Paul looked glum. "Look here, Pilot, he said, "that was

the McCoy about those patrols? You didn't just radio that to get a hand in on the job yourself?"

"You saw 'em," Frank protested. "Ask Argal if you don't believe me. It was a break—just what I needed for my own personal morale. Now I'll ride this tin can until doomsday if you wish. Believe me, I hope Colonel Drake hears about this. Imagine the guy—punishing me because I tackled a couple of dozen Japs, smashed plenty of their planes and lost mine."

"Punished you?" Paul exclaimed. "Pilot, you didn't read those sealed orders. Listen—they were pretty explicit. They said you were probably the nerviest pilot in the South Seas, that this job called for the very best man and you were it, that you'd proved it in that dog-fight over Java. Colonel Drake wasn't punishing you. He was handing you a chance to get a raise in rank and a medal—right on a silver platter. And, brother, I guess you rate it."

Argal made a dive for Frank Corrigan then. The pilot just stood there, grinning like an ape. Drake wasn't such a bad guy after all. Neither was Argal, even if he insisted on decorating him with cheek kisses. Lieutenant Commander Paul Kent was all right, too, and the submarine—why there wasn't anything like it in the world.

An undersea aviator! That was something!

# JIM CREAVY, HOODLUM

*By*

## DON TRACY

THE tall young man walked up to the desk and saluted. He had black hair, a lock of which swept down over his forehead, giving him a sullen appearance that was in keeping with his smoldering eyes and straight, thin mouth.

Behind the desk the older man, gray-haired, grave-eyed, looked up and nodded. The tall man's saluting hand swept down.

"Yes?" asked the older man.

"Jim Creavy, sir," said the black-haired youth. "Detailed to this squadron from training, sir."

He proffered a slip of paper which the gray-haired officer accepted without speaking. Silently, the officer read the lines inscribed on the slip. He looked up and nodded his head toward a chair beside the desk.

"Sit down," he invited. "Glad to know you, Jim. Glad to know all you American chaps who've come over here to help us with this go."

Gingerly, the black-haired Jim Creavy seated himself, his

cap held between large, spatulate hands, the fingers digging into the rough cloth. The officer looked down at the slip again.

"How is it," he asked, "that you didn't sign up for the Eagle Squadron or another of those American outfits? Should think you'd prefer being with your own countrymen."

"I'd rather be with a Canadian outfit, sir," Jim said. "I've —I've known a lot of Canucks—Canadians, and I've always got along all right with them."

The officer's eyes were keen as he looked across the desk. "Better than with Americans, eh?" he asked mildly.

Jim looked down at his cap for a moment, then up again. His voice was defiant.

"Well, yes," he said. "I might as well admit it. I—I don't particularly like Americans, even if I'm one myself. At least, I suppose I'm still one. I tried to sign on with the R.A.F., but it was no go. The Canadians were the next best thing. Not that the Canucks aren't swell fellows, but—"

His voice trailed off. The officer at the desk touched the underpart of his clipped mustache with a finger, then bent to open a drawer and pull forth a sheaf of papers.

"Curious case, yours," he said. "You seem to have interested Intelligence no end, Jim. They've been keeping an eye on you, ever since you tried to sign on with the R.A.F."

The black-haired man's face flushed dully, and his jaw set. The officer looked up and smiled.

"No offense, really," he explained. "Can't be too careful, and all that. But you'll admit it's a bit odd for an

American suddenly to show up in London, trying to join—of all things—the Polish Squadron."

"My mother was Polish," Jim explained, sullenly. "I—I'm still sore about what happened to the Poles. As soon as Hitler destroyed their country, I knew I had to sign up."

"Ah, yes," the officer said. "And was your father, perhaps, French? Was that why you tried the Free French after the Poles turned you down? And who in your family was Dutch? It says here you even tried the Free Dutch group, before you went to the Canadians."

A deadly serious expression changed the gray-haired man's face.

"Young man," he said, "you may not know it, but you came close to landing in an internment camp as a suspected enemy agent. If you hadn't been so free and aboveboard in all your maneuverings—so open that you couldn't possibly have been even the most amateur spy—you'd have been clapped behind barbed wire in no time. As it was, Intelligence spent quite a little time finding out who you really were."

Jim Creavy looked down at his cap and said nothing, as the officer flipped a page of the report and read:

"Jim Creavy. Born in San Francisco. Graduated in—hmm, we can skip that. Joined U. S. Army, 1933. Assigned to Kelly Field for flight training. Dismissed 1934, discharge without recommendation. Hmm. Stunt flier, crop-duster—what in the world is that? Refused employment by airlines as unfit for commercial pilot's license. According to C.A.A. Inspector Diggs, admittedly capable flier, but headstrong, uncooperative, reckless."

The keen eyes flashed across the desk again. Jim kept staring at his cap.

"Signed aboard tanker *J. V. Grant* at—hmm—Atlantic port. Jumped ship at Liverpool."

"I had to, sir," Jim burst out. "I had no money, and it was the only way I could get over here. I had to get into this war and have a whack at the Nazis, sir, and I just had to jump ship."

The officer laid the report on his desk and touched his mustache again in his distinctive gesture.

"I see," he said. "Well, perhaps we can afford to overlook things like that in times like these. Suffice it to say, you finally signed on with the Canadians. Your training report is excellent. You're ready to join your combat squadron—except for one thing."

Jim looked up questioningly. The officer's face was deadly serious now.

"The report Intelligence got from this man Diggs in the States says you were headstrong, uncooperative, reckless. The recklessness—well, maybe that has its place, but the other doesn't, Jim. In this war, we get orders and we follow them. There's no place in the fighting forces of this Empire, of any of the Allies, for anybody who won't take orders. You know that."

"Yes, sir," Jim said in a low voice.

"From the pilot of the biggest Flying Fortress to the newest man in the mechanic's crew, orders are to be followed," the officer went on. "One individualist, one headstrong, uncooperative individualist, might do untold damage."

"Yes, sir."

"I'm not going to ask you why you are down on your own country, Jim," the officer said. "That's your affair. But I'm going to give you fair warning. One misstep on your part, and you're going to land in trouble, my boy. Serious trouble. You're in this country without any kind of official papers. You could be held for deserting your ship. You could be shipped back home, where, I imagine, you don't want to go. So when the urge to do some of the things hinted at in this report proves too strong, Jim, remember the consequences, son, remember the consequences."

Jim folded the cap between his long, strong fingers, and didn't answer. The officer's voice took a new tone.

"I don't want you to get the wrong impression, Jim," he said. "I don't want you to think that Britain isn't grateful to you Yanks who come over here and fight side-by-side with us. Yes, and proud, too. I'm only giving you this warning for your own good, you see. That will be all. Major Mc-Naughton is your C.O. Report to him immediately."

Jim Creavy got out of his chair and stood at attention. He saluted, wheeled and strode out of the office. Behind him, the man with the decoration stripes on the left breast of his tunic pocket frowned faintly, tapping his fingers on the desk top.

"I wonder," he murmured. "I just wonder how that young hoodlum is going to make out."

Outside the administration building, Jim, his cheeks still hot in remembrance of the officer's lecture, stopped on the top step and adjusted the cap at a jaunty angle, scanning the scene that lay before him.

It was an inland base "somewhere in England," used principally by the small fighters whose duty it was to beat back invading bombers that, not long ago, had swarmed over the British Isles like deadly locusts but which now, in the summer months, had dwindled to a few isolated specks in the sky, coming at widely separated intervals.

Nobody, Jim knew, had been fooled by the drop-off in Hermann Goering's blitz. The long summer months had been disadvantageous to Nazi bombing tactics and, while the R.A.F. had been hammering at invasion points and industrial cities deep in the heart of the Reich, the *Luftwaffe*— or that part of it not engaged in the furious struggle on the eastern front—was lying low, waiting for the long nights of winter, before emerging from secret, underground hangars and roaring off in another attempt to break the back of the British lion.

This particular landing field was not a large one. It had three hangars, a sizeable repair shop, and the usual other buildings which housed the personnel. Being a secondary base, it was protected only by a scattering of anti-aircraft batteries, the idea being that if the Nazis were striking at air bases, they would find much more important game closer to home than this field.

The base was one step up from a training field, Jim knew. It was here that pilots who had just completed their fledgling course were put under the command of wise, seasoned veterans and led out on reconnaissance flights during which they might contact the enemy but never in force. It was a shaking-down process, during which the young newcomers were expected to learn how to act at the controls of the

Hurricanes, Spitfires and Tomahawks that supplanted their slower, more easily handled training ships.

This secondary base housed a Canadian unit, fresh from training fields in the Dominion. Jim knew that he was a replacement to the unit, taking the place that had been held by one boy who, on his first flight with a Hurricane, forgot that he was riding an actual whirlwind of speed and power and had paid for his lapse of memory by hurtling to his death.

The sun was hot on Jim Creavy's neck as he descended the steps of the administration building and walked across the field, arms swinging loosely at his sides. The officer's words still rankled. So they had dug up the dope about him, had they? Snooped around, as if he was a criminal wanted by Scotland Yard. Found out all about him from Diggs.

Here he'd come across the ocean to fight for them, and they were treating him like a burglar! He had left good money in the States—crop-dusting paid all right, even if you did have to ride flying coffins on the job—to come over here and work for next to nothing, to get shot at in a fight that really wasn't any of his affair. Maybe he had been all wrong when he had let the headlines get him all hot and bothered about the Nazis. Maybe he would have been better off to have stayed home and minded his own business. December 7th, 1941, was still a long time in the future.

He reached the building that housed the C.O. of the Canadian squadron and walked inside, the screen door flapping shut behind him. Major McNaughton lounged in a chair over in a corner, pulling at a pipe, laughing at something that had been said by one of the pilots who swung a leg over the corner of the C.O.'s desk. Jim Creavy saluted again.

"I saw the colonel, as you told me, sir," he reported. "It—it was all right. The colonel told me to report back to you."

"Fine," said McNaughton heartily. "Knew it was going to be all right. Just a matter of form, Jim. Some fool brass hat somewhere had a form he wanted to fill with statistics, and the war couldn't go on until he had it all filled out."

The major put Jim at his ease. He was a genius at it. The American had already discovered that, although he had met the laughing officer only a short time before. There was none of the rigid formality about this Canadian flier that there had been about some of the British big-wigs, yet Jim knew that McNaughton had made an R.A.F. record of which any British flier could be proud before he had taken over command of this Canadian group.

"Glad to have an American in this squadron," the major was saying. "Used to spend most of my vacations in the States. Funny, too, seeing that most Americans, those days, were heading for Canada to spend their vacations up our way. Maybe we've got mutual friends, Jim."

"I—I don't think so," Jim said.

"Never can tell," the major went on. "I rummaged all around the States in my old car—New York, Florida, Yellowstone, California. You come from California, don't you, Jim?"

"I was born there," Jim admitted. "But I've been all around. Can't call any special place home."

McNaughton pulled at his pipe thoughtfully.

"I see," he said, in a tone that clearly expressed the fact that he didn't.

He glanced at his wrist-watch and yawned.

"Better climb into your duds, Jim, and you, too, Perry," he said. "We go up for a tour in five minutes."

Perry sauntered out of the office and, as Jim turned to follow, McNaughton stopped him with a word.

"Jim," he said, "I always respect another man's privacy as much as I can, but I'm C.O. of this outfit, after all. You're pretty close-mouthed about yourself, but I've found out that Intelligence was pretty busy finding out things about you. Apparently, you're okay. Anyway, you're okay with me until you prove otherwise. But I've got one question to ask you."

"Yes, sir," said Jim.

"Are you running away from the law, Jim?"

Jim looked down at the floor, his face dull red.

"No, sir," he told McNaughton. "I'm—I'm not running away from anything."

There was a brief silence and then McNaughton's hand hit him a hearty slap on the shoulder.

"Forget it," he said, jovially. "It's just that some of these English up-noses think we colonials—colonials, they call us —are a bunch of gangsters. They expect us to pull tommy-guns out of our sleeves any minute. Not most of them, but there are a few. I'd hate to have my outfit get a black eye because one of us turned up wanted by the police, or anything like that."

Jim burned with resentment.

"The Intelligence report would have showed it up if I was on the lam," he burst out. "They seem to have gone to a lot of bother trying to pin something on me."

"Take it easy," said McNaughton mildly. "And get into your outfit. We hop off in three minutes."

It was three minutes later when Jim Creavy sat in the cockpit of his Hurricane, listening to the surging thrum of the motor. He checked his instruments automatically and found them all right. He looked out over the side to see the man of his ground crew, the one who had given him a hand into the ship, waving a thumbs-up at him. He raised his own thumb and grinned.

It was warming to have this Britisher who didn't know him from Adam give him the signal. The men assigned to each plane, he knew, made special objects of the pilots of those ships. When a plane failed to come back from its flight, the other pilots were custom-bound to make no mention of the loss. The ground crew, however, could and did show their emotions.

"My third man," Jim had heard a grease-grimed mechanic tell another. "Now 'e was a boy. Always laughin', 'e was, and 'e called me Disney; said I looked like Mickey Mouse. 'E got 'is over Plymouth, they told me, and the—" and here he went off into a string of unprintables directed at the Nazis.

Jim Creavy wondered if his mechanic would mourn him, the day he did not come back. Because, Jim knew, there would be a day when he would not come back.

The squadron leader gunned his motors and started out, racing across the field, lifting his plane into the teeth of the cross-wind and zooming sharply. The second plane followed, and then another. It was Jim's turn and he poured on coal, headed out across the field, conscious of the terrific power that lay under his hands at the controls.

As he lifted, he grinned, remembering what he would have been called for it, if he took off cross-wind at Kelly. Those days, like those old regulations, seemed very far away now. He wondered where Diggs was now. Probably wearing boots to society dances and swanking it all over the place, while Jim, the goat they all called a hoodlum, was flying in a war, with rounds of armor-piercing bullets in his wings.

The realization elated him as he found altitude and, at the appointed level, made his rendezvous and fell into his proper place. They circled the field until the formation was complete and then headed east, toward the coast.

The C.O., in the van, climbed steadily, until there were twenty-five thousand feet of air beneath the flight and the ground. A faint haze hung over the eastern coast. Below, Jim could see the neat pattern of fields and roads and towns of the English countryside. It was an idyllic scene. It made it difficult to realize that there was a war going on.

His earphones blatted suddenly, then cleared to let through McNaughton's voice.

"Number Six," the C.O. said. "In line, Six. In line."

The old man must have eyes in the back of his head, Jim decided. He looked at his watch and checked the time. He looked at the button on his stick, the button that would release streams of death at the first Nazi that came across the hairlines on the sighting pattern, affixed to the front glass. He looked about him, trying to find a flight of German ships that would provide a good target.

The flight droned on. East, then north, along the coast, then west and south, in a huge square that covered hundreds of miles. Below, Jim made out the wavering line of a convoy, nearing the end of its long, hazardous trip. A trio of Sunderland flying boats lumbered by, far beneath them, hovering over the convoy like mother hens over a brood of chicks.

Jim yawned. This wasn't much better than training flights, he decided. Jerry apparently had run to ground for fair.

Suddenly, to the north, he made out a V of fast-flying combat planes and tensed in his seat. This was it, then! He gripped his controls tightly, waiting for the C.O.'s command. None came.

The oncoming planes streaked closer and Jim swallowed his disappointment when he recognized their outlines. Tomahawks! They were British ships, on reconnaissance like the Canadians.

"There you are, Jim," came McNaughton's voice through the earphones. "Some pals of yours. Eagle Squadron."

Jim Creavy watched as the Tomahawks nosed up sharply and then leveled off, only a thousand feet or so beneath the Canadian squadron. They came so close that Jim could make out the insignia on their sides, the men at their controls. One of them, as he passed, raised a gloved hand in greeting.

Yes, pals of his. Pals of his who had worked together to get him booted out of Kelly, who had practically framed him, just to get rid of him. Maybe not these boys, but boys like these fellows, Americans who would never give him a fair shake.

Fellows like that Diggs, who had accused him of busting the law when he had flown that crazy photographer down close to the airliner wreck, so the guy could get a decent picture. Maybe it *had* been too close, but nobody had got hurt, had they? There had been no cause to ground him, had there? And later, when he had done a little crop-dusting with a phoney license—a fellow had to eat—that wasn't any big crime was it? And later—

"Heads up!" McNaughton said suddenly. "Northeast. Dorniers."

A thrill shot through Jim, wiping his mind clear of the memories that had wandered there. He squinted toward the northeast and saw the bombers, the first Nazi planes he had ever seen. There were six of them, long, pencil-thin ships with blunt noses. He waited for the C.O.'s command, thrilled again when he saw the major change course to intercept the bombers.

Then— What was going on? The Eagle Tomahawks were coming in from the opposite direction and they were much closer to the Dorniers than the Canucks. Unless the C.O. poured on more coal, those Eagles were going to get there first.

"Hold everything," McNaughton said. "It looks like it's their show. Shove 'em up to thirty thousand and look out for escort M.E.s."

The flight rose higher, while Jim Creavy gaped in amazement. Did the major mean that their squadron wasn't going in, with all those Dorniers presenting such tempting targets? He couldn't understand it.

At thirty thousand feet, the squadron leveled off and began circling in a wide sweep. Looking over the side, Jim saw the Tomahawks dive on the Dorniers, scattering the V of bombers like chickens scrambling under the swoop of a flock of hawks. As he watched, he saw one of the Nazi bombers sideslip curiously. Then, as smoke poured from the nose of the big ship, the bomber went into a lazy spin which increased in speed as the Dornier hurtled down.

The fight below them developed into a mad scramble, the Tomahawks buzzing in and out of the fight while the Dorniers twisted desperately to get out of line of the streams of bullets that were pouring from the wings of the attack planes.

Another bomber seemed to break in two, splintering into a thousand pieces before Jim's fascinated eyes. As he watched, he saw two parachutes blossom in the sky beneath the shattered plane and knew that the German crew—or part of it, at least—had managed to bail out.

The Canadians kept circling, even when one of the Eagle Squadron's planes turned over on its back and went plummeting to earth, out of control.

"This is my idea of nothing to do," Jim Creavy growled. "Letting those boys down there have all the fun while we cool our tails up here, looking on."

He looked at the gun-release button and scowled. What did the major think he was, anyway? He had come to England to fight, not to watch others do the fighting. What did he care about regulations; he was going to get into that scrap!

Deliberately, and disregarding the orders which came screaming through his earphones, Jim peeled off his Hurricane and roared down into the midst of the dog-fight beneath him. As he slanted downward, he caught a lumbering Dornier full in the sights, waited until it struck the cross line and pressed his trigger button.

He felt the pulse of the gun and saw his tracers streaking through the air. He was filled with elation and found himself shouting hoarsely, singing, yelling.

His tracers were too high and Jim Creavy dipped the nose of his plane to watch them disappear into the belly of the bigger ship. Then, because he was almost on the bomber, he hauled up sharply and zoomed, winging over to come back for another try. On his turn, he narrowly missed a Tomahawk that was coming in. The near accident got him off his aim and he swung again for another sight on the bomber.

Everything that had been taught him, all the instructions at the training field, had been forgotten. Instead, Jim was directed by a hot excitement that swept through him. This was better than the old stunting days or the dangerous crop-dusting jobs. This was the real thing, with the guns in his plane loaded with lead and an enemy who needed shooting down, cruising slowly ahead of him.

He set his sights on the Dornier again and streaked toward his target. He never reached it.

Instead, as he got his sights on the bomber, he felt the plane bounce as if it had hit a deep rut in landing. There was a noise like a million hammers pounding on sheet iron; a noise that stunned him with its impact.

The cabin was full of broken glass, his controls, when he hauled on them, were slack and useless. Looking over the side, Jim's amazed eyes saw one wing of the Hurricane fold up, like a piece of tissue paper, squeezed by a giant hand.

Thick smoke poured back into the cockpit as the plane lurched to one side and began to fall. Jim's hands were at his belt, his fingers struggling desperately with the catch. Free, he stood up, slammed from one side of the cabin to the other, and reached for the handle of the cockpit cover. He tugged and the cover slid back. He pulled himself out of the smoke.

Wind tore at him, snatching away his breath. A blast of heat seared him as flames streaked up at him. He made a last frantic lurch and toppled out of the cockpit, down into blessed smoke-free air.

The earth revolved around him before he yanked at his rip cord and felt the pull of the straps which suspended him from the silken mushroom that billowed out over him. His dizzy drop slowed abruptly to a gentle descent. He reached up, tore the smoke-stained goggles from his eyes and looked about him.

The dog-fight was still in progress, but more than a mile away and—Jim Creavy gaped—there were German M.E.s mixed up in the scramble now! He could make out the Canadians' Hurricanes dodging and diving among a swarm of Messerschmitts. The Dorniers and the attacking Tomahawks were bare specks in sky, far to the south.

Jim felt a chill of apprehension. He had done it again!

The squadron leader had told them to stay aloft, to keep an eye out for escorting M.E.s—and he had disobeyed orders. And now, because he had been bull-headed as usual, he had fallen prey to one of those unseen M.E.s—which probably got him with a cannon burst—and left the Canadians short-handed to take over their part of the job.

Fool! Would he never learn? He had lost his plane on his first flight without doing more than tickling the ribs of a Dornier. Probably, he had interfered with the work being done by the Eagles, by blundering in that way, where he had no business.

Misery swamped him. He wished that the M.E.s shots had polished him off. That would be better than being forced to return to his base, to face the major and admit that he had broken orders on his first flight, that he was not fit to fly in combat.

He looked below. The ground was coming up to meet him. He tugged at the shrouds of the chute, steering the thing toward a meadow bordered by clumps of trees. As he sank lower, he doubled his legs beneath him, hunched his shoulders and, when he hit, struck the ground with a fall similar to a football player throwing a block.

The landing jarred him, but he was on his feet in an instant, braking the chute and forcing it to collapse before it dragged him along the ground. When the parachute flattened, he unbuckled the straps, climbed out of the harness, and looked about him.

Two people were running toward him, a man and a woman. They came running over the uneven ground, the man brandishing a pitchfork. They arrived, panting, as Jim fumbled in his flying clothes for a cigarette. The prongs of the pitchfork were aimed at Jim's chest.

"Put it away," the flier said wearily. "I'm no Hun."

Reluctantly, the farmer lowered the makeshift weapon.

"You b'ant no Englishman either," he said, suspiciously. "You don't talk like an Englishman."

"Canadian," Jim Creavy explained briefly. "Where's a telephone?"

There followed a long walk to a phone and an interminable wait before Jim got through to his base.

"Jim Creavy," he said, into the mouthpiece. "I had to bail out, but I'm all right."

There was an instant's silence, and then the voice at the other end of the wire said:

"Righto, Creavy. The flight's just come in. We'll be waiting for you."

They were waiting for him, tightlipped, tense, when he reached the field, hours later. The pilots he met on his way to the major's office greeted him briefly, then looked away. They said nothing, but their eyes said: *"Hoodlum."* Jim attempted a swagger as he crossed the field, but it was not a success. He entered the C.O.'s office and saluted.

McNaughton looked at him silently for a full fifteen seconds, and then gestured wordlessly to a chair. The C.O. fumbled an empty pipe for a moment and then began to talk. His voice was quiet, penetrating, cold:

"Your first flight with the squadron, Jim, and you fluffed it. You had orders to keep with the squadron on the topside. We knew those M.E.s would be bound to be along, and it was our job to protect the Eagles while they polished off the

Dorniers. We knew that—or at least any man in the squadron who had any brains knew it.

"So you decided that you knew more than I did and you pitched into that bomber show that wasn't ours. You left your squadron disorganized, with a gap in its ranks, when those M.E.s hit. You were too interested in the Dornier you'd picked out to see anything else. You'd forgotten every particle of training they'd been drilling into you for weeks.

"You lost a ship, needlessly and carelessly. Britain needs all the ships she has, Jim. She can't be spending them to permit a pilot to satisfy his individual ambitions. You were duck soup for that M.E., Jim, because you weren't following orders."

He tapped the bowl of the empty pipe against the palm of his hand.

"You knew you were with this squadron on probation," he continued, "and still, at the first opportunity, you did everything you weren't supposed to do. I guess you know what that means."

"Yes, sir," Jim said. "And I'm sorry, sir."

McNaughton shrugged.

"Being sorry doesn't help now," he told Jim. "It never does. I guess you've done a lot of things in your life that you were sorry for later, haven't you, son?"

Jim thought back. Kelly Field—yes, he had done things there that seemed stupid in retrospect but, at the time, seemed plausible. Stunt flying, flying without a license, the arguments, the fist-fights he had had with Diggs—yes, he had been sorry about those, too. But when he had been sorry, it always had been too late.

He nodded, dumbly. He bowed his head so that Major McNaughton could not see the tears that trembled in his eyes. This was the last stop on a long road that, somehow, had never gone in the right direction. After this failure, there was nothing to look forward to.

"So," said McNaughton, "you see how foolish you've been—but there's no use going into that. I—I hate to do it, Jim, but G.H.Q. has told me to put you under arrest. In your barracks. Later, you'll go up before the colonel on insubordination charges."

Without speaking, Jim saluted and turned to go. He winced when, at the door, a soldier, his rifle slanted across his shoulder, fell into step with him. They didn't even trust him enough to let him go to his barracks unguarded.

They had nearly reached the barracks when the doors opened and men spilled out, running clumsily across the field, adjusting helmets, tugging at their belts. Behind him, as Jim turned, he saw the C.O. burst out of his office and head for the lead plane on the tarmac. It was, Jim knew, another show, and a big one.

"Straight ahead, sir," the soldier said, between tight lips. "I got me orders to see you to your barracks, sir."

"But it's a scramble," Jim protested. "You can't keep me on the ground when—"

"Straight ahead, sir," the soldier repeated.

Biting his lower lip, Jim stumbled on. As he reached the door of the barracks, the squadron was roaring away, whipping into the sky with the hungry whine of eager motors.

Inside, Jim ran to a window and looked out and up. He drew in his breath with a gasp as he looked at the sky.

There were hundreds of them, bombers, interceptors, pursuit and attack planes. It was a big blitz, the biggest of the year and he, Jim Creavy, was grounded.

Faintly, to his ears came the chatter of machine-guns as the British ships streamed up to battle. Formations of Nazi planes broke and engaged themselves in dog-fights while the bombers sailed stubbornly on, bound for London and the women and children who would perish there beneath the thundering bombs.

His face bleak, Jim watched plane after plane drop, smoking, earthward, whether Nazi or Britisher it was hard to tell. Formations were forgotten now. Up above, there was one huge mêlée with every man fighting for himself, taking on all comers.

Something within Jim burst in a flame of despair. His fist drew back and smashed at the window. His heavy flying clothes protected him from the jagged rim of glass as he scrambled, somehow, through the opening.

"Hi!" yelled the soldier who had been detailed to guard him. "You can't do that, sir!"

"The devil I can't," Jim yelled back. "Try and stop me!"

He was running across the field, toward two Hurricanes which still stood motionless on the apron. Mechanics he passed stared at him, open mouthed.

"Those planes serviced?" Jim asked, gasping, as he reached the apron. A mechanic swallowed and shook his head.

"Ripped up, sir, they are," he explained. "They've got a bit of patching to be done on them before they fly again."

"Which is the better one?" Jim Creavy asked. "The one damaged the least?"

The mechanic was gesturing with his thumb toward one of the two Hurricanes, when Jim felt the soldier's hand on his shoulder.

"Now then," panted the soldier, "come along. I've orders—"

Jim swung as he turned. His fist caught the soldier on the point of the jaw, and the private crumpled.

"Cor!" breathed a mechanic. "Wot a slosher!"

Jim already was lifting himself into the cockpit of the Hurricane the mechanic had pointed out. He ran his eyes quickly over the ship. Its right wing had been chewed up by machine-gun fire, but the controls still worked. His petrol was low. He supposed that the guns had not been rearmed. He was taking off in a damaged ship, without enough gas and insufficient ammunition—but he was taking off!

The plane had returned recently enough for the motor to catch immediately. Jim did not waste gas warming it up further. He jammed the gas lever back and sent the plane rolling across the field, lifting it into the air after only a hundred yards had been covered.

The ship was logey, but it flew. Like a tired, valiant horse, it buckled to its task and took Jim higher, up into the maelstrom that was whirling about in the heavens.

"This is the trip I won't come back from," Jim told himself, between set teeth. "Resisting arrest, stealing a plane, breaking orders—they'd probably shoot me for that. But I've got some things I've got to make up to myself."

He had to prove to himself, Jim Creavy, that there was some worth in him, that all the mistakes he had made in the past could be wiped out by one commendable act. They needed him up there now—they needed every plane they could get—and even an outcast American hoodlum, flying a battered plane, might be welcomed.

Outcast American? Who had cast him out? He had done that job himself. When things had gone wrong in the States, he had blamed Diggs, all Americans and the country, instead of blaming himself. America, he realized with a thrill that ascended his backbone, was his country. Maybe, now, he could strike a blow for America by hitting at the enemies of everything America stood for.

His laboring plane had reached the under fringes of the combat zone by now. As he roared higher, a flaming plane streaked down past him. He caught one glimpse of the pilot, trying desperately to shield his face from the flames, and then the horrid spectacle was gone.

A zooming M.E. came into his sights and he gave a short burst. Missed. He banked over, felt the plane slip as the damaged wing strained under the maneuver, and straightened up, seeking another target.

Directly overhead, a gigantic Condor was droning northward. Jim yanked back on his controls, pointed his nose at the belly of the big ship and pressed his releases. He watched his tracers bury themselves in the huge bomber.

He seemed to hang motionless on his tail for a minute before his plane fell off on a wing. As he turned, he saw smoke pouring from the entrails of the Condor. The big ship was beginning to wabble.

Jim turned, fought for altitude and came back at the Condor. He could see the bright splotches from the bomber's rear turret and he saw, from the corner of his eye, splinters flying from the damaged right wing. He gave the rear gunner a burst and saw the turret glass shatter, the gunner go limp. He was that close.

He kept his trigger button pressed down and poured lead into the body of the bomber. Suddenly, there was a blinding flash and the Condor disintegrated into a thousand pieces. One of Jim's slugs, apparently, had reached the bomb racks.

The explosion tossed Jim Creavy about like a toy boat in the surf. When he straightened out, he found an M.E. on his tail, chewing at his plane surfaces. He twisted, banked, and managed to shake off the German. Turning, he caught sight of the black crosses of another Nazi plane and fired. Another miss.

Swearing softly, Jim came about and spotted another bomber beneath him. He dived, every brace of the plane trembling under the strain and pressed his trigger button again. There was a brief burst, and then nothing.

His guns were empty!

Now, he should try and run for it, split-tailing as best he could back toward his home port. He had taken care of a Condor and that was enough. It was seldom that a single plane knocked down one of those big Condors.

But, somehow, he couldn't run for it. He had to stay, in a damaged plane with empty guns, because he was Jim Creavy, and he had a lot of things to make up for.

He nosed over and came around in a wide swing. What he saw ahead of him made him squint his eyes.

There, directly ahead, there was an Eagle Squadron plane in trouble. The Yank, whoever he was, was trying to get away from three M.E.s and he was having a hard time doing it.

From the actions of the Tomahawk, Jim guessed that the American flier was having motor trouble—either that or he had been wounded. His plane handled sloppily and, on every turn and twist, his Nazi pursuers came a little closer to the kill.

Rage swept through Jim. Three to one wasn't a fair fight, especially since the American was a cripple, an easy target for one first-class pilot.

And the man in the Tomahawk was an American—a brother American! A man like the boys he had known at Kelly Field, like the fellows in the group that may have high-hatted him, but still had been members of his squadron, before he got booted out. No three Nazis were going to do that to an American—not while Jim Creavy could help it!

Gritting his teeth, Creavy aimed the nose of his plane at the nearest Messerschmitt. He pulled the throttle all the way back and felt the ship leap forward in a burst of speed that belied its shattered condition.

Closer and closer to the unwary M.E. came the Hurricane. Closer, closer, until Jim could make out every mark, every scratch, on the tail fins of the German.

He saw the Nazi pilot turn in his seat and stare at him, his eyes wide with horror. For a second, time seemed hung in suspension. Everything stood still.

And then Jim Creavy's ship crashed into the Messer-schmitt.

It was later that night when the remnants of the Eagle Squadron gathered at their mess. It was a subdued meal, for the day's fighting had made an empty chair at the long table.

At the head of the linen-covered board, a tall, angular man arose and held up a glass.

"I don't want to go mushy about this, fellows," he said, "but I want to drink a toast to that Canadian who saved my life. There I was, with my motor conking and three Jerries on my tail. It was curtains for me, and I knew it. Then this Canadian came out of nowhere and slammed his ship right into one of those M.E.s. The crash flung the wreckage of his ship over on top of another one of the Heinies and—well, the third one quit. So, gents, I give you that Canadian, whoever he was."

The toast was drunk and Lucius Diggs, former inspector for the C.A.A., back in the United States, sat down.

# WINGS OF THE NORTH

*By*

## JOHNSTON CARROLL

"SURE, I know," said Perry Nolan. "Orders is orders. And here we are all cozy—and cold as blue blazes—on the hind side of Greenland. Greenland, he says! If I should see something really green up here, I'd drop dead."

Major Jordon, C.O. of the Thirty-first Bomber Command Squadron, U.S. Army Air Corps, chuckled in his throat and gently tamped tobacco into the bowl of his ancient pipe.

"Just the time of year, old son," he explained. "They say it's very beautiful up here in the summer. Wait a few months and the three feet of snow out there will be gone. There'll be lovely flowers, and birds in the trees, and—"

"And we'll not see them or smell them!" Perry said. "We'll all be six feet under—stiff from boredom. Joe Sucker, that's me! I should have joined the Marines. At least those lads see a Jap plane now and then. But us? Nothing but snow and ice!"

"Well, it can't last—I hope," Major Jordon sighed. "Maybe

one of these days the *Luftwaffe* will come sailing by, and we'll get in our cracks."

"No luck," Jerry complained. "That's been the tag line of my nightly prayers for weeks now. And nothing's happened. Nothing but that crash last week that took good old Johnnie Rucker and his crew."

Jordon nodded solemnly but said nothing. For six weeks, now, since five days before Pearl Harbor, the Thirty-one Bombers had been stationed on the southwest coast of Greenland at a point halfway between Julianehaab and Godthaab. Their job was to patrol the coast as far south as Cape Farewell, and to maintain a constant lookout for any signs of Axis infiltration by sea or air. And perhaps most important of all, to hunt out any secret Axis radio stations set up for meteorological or propaganda purposes, or both.

The idea had been good, but the execution had been enough to drive strong men stark, raving crazy. Which is to say that not one single thing of even a little interest had been sighted. Nothing but snow and ice, and more snow and ice. Then last week had come the only break in the freezing monotony, but a break that brought heart-ache, and not joy.

One of the planes with its pilot and crew of four had not returned from a routine patrol. Next day the plane had been found—what was left of it—a fire-blackened tangle of wreckage at the bottom of a two-thousand-foot canyon. A black smudge high up on the mountain side marked where the plane had struck, and jagged black marks, like black crayon on white paper, showed the path of the crashed plane as it went hurtling in flames down into the canyon.

That all were dead was certain. If not killed by the crash, then by the sub-zero cold that night. To attempt to reach the wreck before summer was out of the question. It would take an experienced rescue party at least three weeks to reach that point from even the nearest settlement. And then they probably would not find the wreck under fresh blankets of snow.

And so the Thirty-one gang had returned to their base, downed a toast to pals lost, and continued with the monotonous, nerve-fraying grind.

Major Jordon finally shrugged aside the unhappy thoughts, and reached for a match.

"I'll still stick to it that one of these days the *Luftwaffe* will be coming along," he said. "I've got a feeling. Meantime, I've got something special for you, son."

Perry Nolan sat up, bright-eyed.

"Yeah? Then let's have it quick!"

The C.O. stabbed his pipe stem at the clock hanging on the wall and grinned.

"You're due off in your sky chariot in twenty minutes," he said. "You can cut the patrol an hour short if you want to. How's that?"

The bomber pilot groaned and pushed his six feet-two up to a standing position.

"There's only two things that stop me from bobbing you right on the nose, for that crack!" he growled.

"Only two?" Jordon echoed with a chuckle. "What are they?"

"Well, one's because you've been my friend for close to fifteen years now," Perry grunted.

"And the other reason, son?" Jordon wanted to know.

Perry shrugged into his heavy service coat and scooped up his helmet, goggles, and radio-jack off the desk.

"Because there's an army rule against it," he growled and turned toward the door. "Of course I don't *hope* that fire goes out and you freeze stiff. However ... see you again, Sir Slave Driver!"

"Have a nice flight, Captain!" Jordon called after him.

The reply was not in words. It was just a long sound made with the lips and the tongue, and cut off as the door slammed shut. Jordon chuckled and reached for some papers on his desk. It was then he saw the frown of disapproval on the face of the young second lieutenant seated at the adjutant's desk in the far corner.

The lad's name was Ned Peters, and he was all of six months out of West Point. But everything was so different from what he had been taught behind those gray stone walls up the Hudson a ways. It obviously distressed him a lot.

"Something bothering you, Ned?" Jordon asked casually.

"Why, no, sir," the youth gulped. "That is—well, Captain Nolan certainly doesn't show much respect for your rank, sir."

"He doesn't, does he?" Jordon chuckled. "But he flies like a fool, and spends twice as many hours in the air as any other pilot in my command. Also, about five years ago he saved my life when a couple of ships we were flying tangled in the air. My 'chute fouled and I would have gone down with the wreck if it hadn't been for Nolan. He hauled me out, and hung onto me and took us both down in his 'chute. True, we each broke a leg, but we lived. Did you think he

got that D.S.C. he wears from cutting off box tops and sending them in? Respect for my *rank*? Be patient, Ned. You're
only six months away from the Point, you know."

"Yes, of course, sir," the youth mumbled and went beet-
red in confusion.

Jordon sighed heavily.

"Forget it," he grunted. "No offense, son. It's this blasted
frozen end of the world, and the continued inactivity. I'd
give my right eye if the enemy would only come this far
west just once. If they came in balloons it would be okay.
We'd promise only to heave hunks of ice at them. We'd—
oh, well, let it go. Where's that report I'm supposed to
sign? Or hasn't the ink melted yet?"

Outside, stamping across the hard-packed snow, Perry
Nolan was offering not one eye but two eyes for a touch of
honest warfare.

Perry kicked viciously at a clump of snow, but it was
actually ice and he got pains in his foot. He shoved open
the mess lounge door and stuck his head inside.

"Good news, bums!" he shouted. "We're going for an airplane ride. Shift it, boys!"

He pulled the door shut and walked over to the line of
Pratt & Whitney-powered Martin B-26 long-range bombers.
Number 8 was his plane, and the grease balls already had
the engines turning over and were checking the one hundred and one little things before take-off. The sergeant in
charge saw Perry and hurried over, a hopeful grin on his
face.

"You said yesterday, maybe today, Skipper," he said.
"Any chance? Honestly, I'm going bats just stamping my

feet on the ground. Lieutenant Bellows wouldn't mind if I took the tail gun for just one trip, would he, sir?"

"He'd love it," Perry grunted. "I only wish you would *fly* one of these things, Casey. Okay, climb aboard. I'll tell Bellows he can go back to his gin rummy."

Sergeant Bert Casey almost broke a leg scrambling up the belly door ladder. Perry grinned and waited for his crew of four to come trudging over from the mess. There was Gil Macey, his co-pilot and navigator; Corporal Larry Hicks, his bombardier; and Sergeant Arthur Yates and Lieutenant Sam Bellows, his gunners. They arrived looking as happy as kids heading for the dentist, but when Perry spoke to Bellows, the tail gunner let out a whoop of joy and tore back into the mess lounge before Perry could take a second breath.

The bomber's commander gave the mess door an envious glance himself and then climbed inside and went forward to the controls. A five-minute instrument and engine check, and then he trundled the big craft around and to the head of the snow runway that was packed as hard as brick and just as level as a billiard table top. Another couple of minutes and the B-26 was in the air, the hydraulic gear pulling the nose and wing wheels up into their sockets.

At seven thousand Perry Nolan leveled off and circled the field twice while he checked with radio operations on the ground. He got his "okay-check" and put the bomber on the first leg of its seven-hundred-mile "snow patrol." Presently, when he was sure that all was in tip-top shape, he swung the Dep wheel over to Gil Macey.

"Go ahead and earn some flying pay, my boy," he said.

"Same course as usual. But watch those fog banks. They like to sit right on these damn mountains. And to think that guys sell their very souls to explore this kind of country!"

Perry glanced down at the scenery below as he spoke the last, and shivered slightly. Actually, it was a beautiful sight, but in a heart-chilling, and breath-catching sort of way. As far as the eye could see there was range after range of snow-covered glacier mountains that stabbed their jagged peaks up toward the slate-gray sky.

Between the peaks were yawning green and black-streaked canyons and crevasses into which whole cities could be dumped and never seen again. Bleak, icy desolation in all directions, save where here and there a tiny cluster of buildings and shacks marked where civilization waged its unending struggle for existence on this left-over of the Ice Age.

"A fat chance," Perry said and slid out of his seat to go aft for some coffee. "The Nazis may be baby killers, but they *have* got some brains. They'll let us keep this ice-cube parking lot all to ourselves and welcome to it!"

A little over an hour and a half later Perry Nolan was taking his spell at the controls. Increased patches of fog had forced the big bomber up to ten thousand feet, and Perry was skirting the fringe of a bank that completely hid a mountain range which, when not shrouded by the misty stuff, seemed to rise right straight up out of Davis Strait like a wall that barred all possible approach from the sea.

It was in this tricky range Johnnie Rucker and the four members of his crew had lost their lives, and as Perry stared flint-eyed in that direction the familiar ache returned to his heart. Johnnie had been a swell guy. Tops. They'd got along fine. And the same went for every member of his crew, too. Each lad a real man, ready for a fight or a frolic. What a tough deal that they should have—

He never finished the rest. At that moment the surprise of surprises came blasting out of the gray air. It happened with such startling suddenness that for a couple of split-seconds Perry could only sit frozen in the seat and gape wide-eyed at two all black Nazi Messerschmitt 109-Fs that came rocketing up at the big Martin like two jet-black comets in high gear.

Two split-seconds to gape and stare, and then he snapped into action.

"Gun stations!" he roared into the inter-com mike. "Enemy aircraft approaching to port. Give them the works!"

Even as he roared out his commands he heeled the Martin over and around on wing-tip, as though it were a P-40, and got into position so that he and Sergeant Arthur Yates in the nose could let fly with the forward guns.

They both missed. The two Messerschmitts arced out of the line of fire like greased lightning, darted earthward a short two hundred feet, and then came tearing up again for a blast.

Perry felt the Martin shiver and shake as machine-gun bullets and air-cannon shells ripped into the metal covering. But he also heard his tail gunner blazing away. He grinned for an instant, then wiped it off with a groan as he remembered that Sam Bellows wasn't riding the tail this trip. It was Flight Sergeant Bert Casey back there on a joy ride. No chance Bert would be able to handle those guns.

Perry shouted loudly with joy and dumbfounded amazement as the miracle happened. Perhaps Bert Casey was shooting with both eyes closed, or perhaps one of the Messerschmitt pilots just didn't give a hang. At any rate, slugs from Bert's guns and the Messerschmitt met head-on. And the Nazi plane lost.

Out the corner of his eye Perry saw the enemy plane come apart in a shower of blazing pieces that slithered out in all directions and fell earthward like red rain. First blood for the Yank Air Corps in Greenland! And it had certainly been just that. The Nazi pilot was dead before he could even think of shoving open his greenhouse and bailing out.

The instant he saw the plane disappear in a shower of blazing embers Perry hauled the Martin around to the left and dropped the nose for a power dive on the second Nazi ship. But this cagey German had cut off his zoom and was now spinning around and racing for dear life toward the blanket of fog that shrouded the mountains.

As the Messerschmitt seemed to stagger a bit in mid-air and lose speed, Perry's heart leaped with joy. This made it possible for the Martin to overtake the faster ship. Another few moments and the Yank skipper would have a perfect nose-on shot. But before those few moments ticked by, common sense, and a wild hunch suddenly took charge of Perry Nolan's brain.

Just before Johnnie Rucker's radio had gone off the air forever a jumble of signals had been heard back at Thirty-one Operations. Static, or something, had garbled the message, and then suddenly there had been absolute silence. Had Johnnie and his boys been attacked in just this same manner? Had two mystery Messerschmitts caught him off guard and sent him crashing into those mountains under that fog before he realized what had happened? And was this lone Messerschmitt waiting to lure Bomber Number Eight into that fog, and smack a mountain?

Nolan hesitated, held the Martin in its wild dive for a brief moment longer, then shook his head. He mumbled through clenched teeth as he hauled the nose up toward the slate-gray sky and let the Messerschmitt go slip-sliding down out of sight into the fog. He heard an echo to his own growls and turned his head to see Gil Macey staring at him in wide-eyed disbelief.

"He was crippled!" the co-pilot shouted. "If you'd followed him in a minute longer we could have let him have it!"

Perry shook his head and leveled off the bomber on the top of the fog.

"Not in my book," he replied. "That lad was pulling something funny. I don't think his plane had even been hit. He was trying to make us come into the fog after him— and smack into a mountain side."

"What about *him* smacking one?" Gil demanded.

"He had it figured not to," Perry said with a shrug. Then in a harsh tone, "Do you think I'd have let him go if I'd thought there was half a chance of slugging him? Forget it, son. Check with the crew and find out if those rats did any damage worth worrying about. If not, then we'll do a little exploring in these parts. Two Messerschmitt planes up here! Maybe I've just been dreaming."

A check with the crew at their battle stations brought to light the information that the Messerschmitt pilots had shot a lot of holes in the Martin, but the bullets and air-cannon shells hadn't hit anything worth writing home about. Just to make sure, Perry turned the controls over to Gil, with orders just to circle, and went aft for a personal inspection.

The Martin was very much in tip-top flying condition, and there was only one "casualty." That casualty was Flight Sergeant Bert Casey in the tail. He was so amazed and over-joyed that he had lost all power of speech. He could only gulp and bob his head when Perry Nolan congratulated him and gave him an affectionate slap on the back.

Returning forward, Perry took over, and for two solid hours he "straffed" all sides of the fog bank, save the under-neath side. The stuff, however, was as thick as chilled pea soup and, in view of the fact the Martin wasn't the quickest of planes in the turns and zooms, he was forced to stick around the fringes and not try to grope his way down under on instruments.

At the end of two hours when the wall of fog continued to hold his curiosity in check, and there was no further sign of any Nazi planes, Perry banked southward and went roar-ing home to Base on full throttles. He landed smoothly on the packed-snow runway with its strips of metal grating to allow tire traction, and finally wheeled up to the hangar line.

Thirty minutes after that he and each member of the crew had made an individual report of the flight and fight to Major Jordon. The C.O. listened in silence, then asked a couple of questions. He finally signaled all but Perry to trot over to the mess and celebrate with Flight Sergeant Casey.

When they had left, the C.O. reached for his pipe, settled back more in his chair, and fixed quizzical eyes on his senior flight leader.

"Okay, Perry," he said. "You're just busting with words. Go ahead and spill them. You've got ideas. I can see them sticking out all over you. Go on, shoot."

Perry grunted and jerked his head at the detailed topographical map of the west and south areas of Greenland that covered the entire rear wall of the squadron office.

"Did some thinking on the way back," he said presently. "Among other things it suddenly occurred to me that during the six weeks we been up here I've only seen that particular mountain range without fog just once. That was the day we spotted Johnnie Rucker's crash. Maybe the gods decided to be kind to us that day. But, anyway, that was the only time I've ever seen those mountains without the fog. Strikes me that the pea-soup stuff is probably a permanent, year-around fog in that locality."

"So?" Major Jordon grunted, though a keen gleam had come into his eyes.

"Look at the map," Perry said and jerked his head again." From the air those mountains *look* like they rise straight up from the shoreline. But the map says different. You can see there's a small bay there and quite a stretch of flat ground before the mountains start. There's also jottings on that map that say the prevailing wind is north to south. Up and down the coast. Begin to catch on a little?"

Jordon swiveled around in his chair and squinted at the map in silence for a couple of minutes. Then he swiveled back to face Perry Nolan.

"A little, I guess," he said. "You think the Nazis have established a flying field right under our noses?"

"What else?" Perry murmured with an appropriate gesture. "Those two One-nines certainly didn't fly over from Occupied France just to have a crack at my ship. And, if you want my hunch, it was Nazi planes that caught Johnnie and his boys off balance. Johnnie was too good a pilot to barge right into fog on a routine patrol and end up against a mountain. And don't forget, we heard some garbled signals just before his radio went off the air. They've set up a field there, or I'm crazy!"

"Could be, the crazy part," Jordon said with a grin. Then knitting his shaggy brows in a scowl, "But what about the fog? A fog-bound field certainly isn't the best of places to take off and land ships. You'd have more crack-ups than completed flights, I'd say."

Perry shrugged. "If it *is* fog-bound," he said in grim significance. "There may be a certain ground wind that keeps part of it open at all times. I remember a field at which I spent a while during training days on the California Coast. Every morning the field was fog-bound save for half of the south side. When the take-off wind was right you could get off and on again without any trouble. Gave you the feeling of flying in and out of a circus tent. True, a few of the greenhorns did mess themselves up. But it was easy for a bird who knew his ailerons and tail flippers."

Major Jordon hunched forward in his chair and stared intently at Perry, the frown deepening on his face.

"Maybe you're right about that, Perry," he said softly. "Maybe they do have a field there that they can slip in and out of. We'd never spot it in a thousand years of patroling. But, answer me this. Why is there a field there? Also, why Messerschmitt One-nines? What do they hope it gets them?"

Perry didn't answer at once. He had already asked those three questions of himself a hundred times since he'd last seen that remaining Messerschmitt cutting down into the fringes of the mountain range's obscuring fog bank. He had guesses, but that's all they were. Just guesses.

"I wonder, too," he murmured more to himself. "If the fog opening is big enough, perhaps they've got bombers based there. And maybe their fighter escorts are fitted with extra tanks for long-range work against convoys close to the North American coast. Maybe, they've only just arrived, and are getting set to pile down on us and blast us right into the Davis Strait. Who knows? But, there's one thing certain. At least, it seems certain to me."

"Such as?" Jordon prompted when Perry paused and scowled at his folded hands.

"That Johnnie Rucker and I went just a little too close for their comfort," Perry said. "We usually give that particular range a fairly wide margin, but I was more than close to it today. I got surprise-jumped. I've a hunch that Johnnie was extra close to it the day he died."

"But what about the next day when we hunted Johnnie's ship from the air," Major Jordon said. "We were right down among the peaks then. But we didn't get jumped. We didn't see the sign of a Nazi plane, in fact."

"Too many of us," Perry said. "And with very little fog there was no chance for ambush. Then, too, it's possible they wondered if Johnnie had got anything back by radio, so they were lying doggo and waiting to see if we'd start hunting for something else besides Johnnie's ship. Come to think of it, maybe Johnnie's last signals were garbled because they had jammed the air on him. Anyway, there are some of the rats nesting up in that locality. That's definite."

Major Jordon smashed one clenched fist against the palm of the other hand and shot up out of his chair.

"So we load up everything," he announced, "and go up there and blow that whole mountain range into the sea. Maybe they've got some nice pea-soup fog to hide under, but fog never stopped bombs."

"And maybe they would laugh themselves sick at our bombing attempts!" Perry Nolan snapped. "And we'd get rid of them that way. Rot!"

His commander gave him an angry stare.

"What do you mean by that?" he demanded.

Perry jerked his head at the map again.

"That mountain range covers an area of about three hundred square miles," he said. "And maybe their secret field, counting camouflaged hangars, and everything, covers an area of about four or five hundred square *yards!* You could bomb from now until doomsday and still not come close enough to sprinkle powdered snow on their field."

Jordon started to speak, but didn't. He scowled down at the floor and heaved a long sigh.

"Okay, let's have it!" he finally said. "You're working up to something, aren't you?"

"It's a job that has to be done solo," Perry said. "Done solo in a small ship. We've got a Grumman Navy carrier job here that's just the thing for poking around low down in fog. It has speed and all the rest of it, *if* I should run into trouble. In short, my idea is for me to nose around up there and see what I can see. Then report to you *where* the target is, exactly. And *what* it is. Then we can all go up and give them the works, right on the old noggin. As soon as I find out what's what up there I'll come back here on the run. After all, that shipboard Grumman can't stay out more than three hours. I'll have to come home."

Jordon didn't say anything for a long time. He walked over to one of the windows and stared bleakly out at the Arctic wind-swept, snow-covered landscape. Eventually he turned and glowered at Perry.

"I always was a sucker about a request from you," he said. "Okay, go ahead and see what you can find out. But I'll give you three hours and no more. If you're not back then, the whole lot of us will come looking for you, fog or no fog.

"And here's something you can do to let us keep track of you. Keep blipping your radio cut-off switch. When we cease to hear the clicks we'll know you're in trouble, and we'll come up there as fast as we can. Of course, if you can get signals to us, so much the better. But if they are jamming the air we wouldn't catch them clear enough for translation. So keep blipping your switch."

The squadron C.O. paused and leveled a stiff forefinger.

"And don't try to be a one-man air corps!" he ordered. "Or, so help me, I'll burn your hide right clean off when I do catch up with you. Okay. And all the luck in the world, son!"

"Thanks, and don't worry about a thing," Perry said, reaching for his flying jacket and stuff. "I'll be back in practically nothing flat with all the dope we need to have fun in Greenland. See you later."

Perry waved his hand and dived out the door. Jordon stared at the closed barrier for a long time then turned and shuffled over to his desk.

"Well, Ned," he said to the ever-present, silent adjutant in the corner, "you should be able to easily spot a complete and utter fool the next time you meet one."

"Captain Nolan has courage to make that kind of a flight," the young adjutant said. "I certainly don't consider him a fool, sir."

"Huh? Who said anything about Captain Nolan?" Jordan said and dropped heavily into his chair. "I was referring to his superior officer."

Scarcely an hour later some thirty pairs of anxious eyes watched Perry Nolan lift the Grumman carrier fighter off the snow-grid runway and send its prop charging up around to the north. Every pilot and mechanic standing on that well-nigh sub-zero tarmac breathed a silent prayer of hope as the Grumman quickly became a black speck against the gray sky and finally disappeared altogther. Then without a look or a word to his mates each man turned away and continued with his own particular task of the moment.

There was no anxiety glowing in Perry Nolan's eyes, however. There was nothing there but grim purpose, plus a wild tingling that pricked his body like countless needles and pins. This was the real thing at last. This was a patrol against a lurking and hidden enemy. It was more than that, even.

In a way, it was a revenge patrol for Johnnie Rucker and his boys. That their death had been the result of a patrol accident was definitely out in Nolan's mind, now. He was as sure as he was of his own name that Nazi planes had jumped Johnnie and smashed him up against the icy mountain side before anybody aboard the bomber knew what had happened.

"As a matter of fact, son," Perry mused aloud and leveled off at an even eight thousand," but for some darn good shooting by Bert Casey, chances are you'd be a frozen mangled corpse in some canyon right now yourself."

With a nod for emphasis Perry pressed his free hand hard against the already wide-open throttle, as though in so doing he might get added revs out of the powerful Pratt and Whitney. Then as the Grumman tore through a patch of cloud scud and came out into clear air again he sighted the fog-shrouded mountain range ahead and to his left.

It looked just the same as it had a few hours ago. Wind had not seemingly moved a single wisp of the murky gray stuff. It looked like a mile-high pile of dirty laundry hanging motionless in the sky. Rather, it looked as though the section of Greenland below had been consumed by a great fire and this was the pall of smoke hung waiting for to-morrow's winds to drift it away.

Perry Nolan throttled a hair, and hunched forward to peer intently at the stuff. Not a mountain peak could he see. And the fog seemed to seep right down into the ground and go on through. As Perry stared at it little fears and doubts began to form in his brain. It seemed impossible that there could be a secret flying field somewhere down under that stuff. Yet, there must be.

He had seen a Messerschmitt 109-F dive right into the fog bank. It was certain the pilot had his altimeter set accurately and knew just how far down in he could go without strik-ing one of the hidden peaks. Yet, on the other hand, unless the Nazi had X-ray eyes, there was no way for him to tell if he was heading straight for a peak once he was below the danger altitude.

"So maybe he just went in a ways to lose himself," Perry said and veered the Grumman across the top of the stuff toward the west where Davis Strait blends with the southern end of Baffin Bay. "Maybe he just carried on through and went down on the other side. Yes, maybe a lot of things. Maybe I'm striking out on three pitched balls!"

As a sudden hunch came to him he zoomed a bit for altitude, then whipped the Grumman over and down in a roaring power dive that must have been heard all the way back to Thirty-one's field. He did that five times without results. On the sixth dive the hunch became a reality. Two Messerschmitt single-seater fighters came booming up out of the fog like comets gone haywire. Their machine-guns and air cannon were barking savagely as they came up through, but a fast turn to the left and a zoom took Nolan well into the clear. He grinned, tight-lipped, blipped his radio cut-off switch again to continue signal contact with Operations at Thirty-one, and then slid his thumb down onto his own gun button.

"Thought the racket might make you curious!" he shouted into the roar of his engine. "But only two of you, huh? The guy's just a greenhorn, so we start off with insults, huh? That it? Okay! Stick around while I become a veteran!"

As he barked out the last, Perry whirled on wing-tip, let the Grumman's nose drop like a rock, and went power-diving down and in at one of the Messerschmitts. He let fly with a one-second burst, but saw his tracers miss the mark by plenty. That didn't bother him, though. It was the way he planned it.

The Messerschmitt pilot started to rocket around toward him, but Perry didn't give him a chance to use his guns. Quick as a flash the Yank hauled out of his dive and cut straight across the sky at the second and completely unsuspecting Messerschmitt pilot.

Maybe that Nazi let out a startled cry. Maybe he jumped clean out of his safety harness, he was so startled. At any rate he did little or nothing to get out from in front of Perry Nolan's withering fire. He took the whole works broadside, and at the end of a couple of seconds the Messerschmitt was a ball of fire, and a dangling figure was dragging a half-opened parachute down into the fog.

"How's that for a greenhorn, tramp?" Perry shouted and cut his fire. "Thought I'd forgotten all about you? Yes, me and the elephants, chump! And that's another one for you, Johnnie, old pal!"

Perry whispered the last as though in prayer, rocketed upward in a power zoom that made the Grumman's wings virtually groan in protest, then half-rolled over and down for a go at the first Messerschmitt. But there wasn't any first Messerschmitt. That is to say, there wasn't one for Perry to blaze away at. The German pilot had seemingly decided that the odds of a one-to-one scrap were too many for him. He had wheeled away and down and was heading for the eastern side of the fog bank with every ounce of speed his Benz-Daimler engine could dig up.

Kicking rudder slightly to veer westward, Perry leaned hard against his safety-belt, and opened his mouth to relieve ear pressure caused by the power dive. He kept his thumb resting lightly against the electric gun-trigger button, but he did not press it, even though there was a slight chance that a lucky shot might catch the fleeing Messerschmitt and ground it for good.

To down it wouldn't help him any. It was his job, now, to spare the rat's life and tag him back to his hidden field. To find the opening in the fog so that he could return with Jordon and the others and lead them in to blow the hidden field clear out of Greenland.

"Yes, but I can think of easier jobs!" he said as the Messerschmitt nosed down into the fog. "That lug knows where he's going, but I don't. If I lose him I've got to zoom up into the clear. These Grummans are nice, but they're not built to go through mountains. So, I've got . . ."

He let the rest trail off, scooped air into his lungs and

held it there for a moment or so. He was down in the fog himself, now. And the Messerschmitt was just a moving faint blurr up ahead of him.

The Nazi had leveled off from his dive and was streaking westward. But he was zigzagging to throw off Perry's aim in case the Yank opened fire. But Perry Nolan continued to keep his guns silent and flew hand on throttle, eyes straining ahead.

In the next couple of minutes he thought he had lost the "ghost" Messerschmitt no less than a couple of hundred times. But on each occasion when the warning cried out within him to zoom up to safety he caught sight of the German ship again. It had not varied altitude an inch either way. But suddenly it went slanting down sharply by the nose. The warning cried out in Perry and for a split-second he dared not drop his own nose. Perhaps the Nazi was bent on hurling himself against a mountainside rather than to let the Yank continue to tag him all the way back and down to the secret field—if any.

That thought, and countless other disagreeable ones, whipped through Perry Nolan's brain as his hands froze briefly on the stick. Then he tossed all caution overboard and poked the Grumman's nose down, too. For three seconds, or three years, or perhaps an eternity, he went rocketing down through thick, murky fog.

A thousand heart-stopping shapes and shadows leaped out at him, but his wings cut through nothing save fog-filled air. And then suddenly the stuff grew thinner and he could clearly see the Messerschmitt ahead and below him. The

German was going down in a tight spiral that took him out into clear air on the western side.

Sight and action became one for Perry. He threw the Grumman into a spiral right above the other plane. And around and around he went. For one-half of each turn he was in the fog. For the other half of the turn he was in clear air and could see the ice-clogged waters of Davis Strait some four thousand feet below.

Each time he came out into clear air he snapped another quick glance below. But for all he could see there was no opening in the fog on the water side. The fog seemed to wall upward from the very surface of the ice-choked strait.

When he was at two thousand feet, and the Nazi not more than five hundred feet below, it happened!

The base of the fog bank seemed virtually to explode Nazi Messerschmitts. At least a score of them came ripping out from under the fog and prop-screamed up at him with all guns blazing. He could only gulp and stare for a split-second or so. Then he let out a bellow of anger and alarm and started hurling the Grumman all over the sky.

He tried to duck back into the fringe of the fog, lose himself, and zoom upward toward higher altitude and safety. But the swift Messerschmitts came up like polished slivers of greased lightning and hung a wall of hissing bullets and air-cannon shells between his plane and the fog.

To attempt to fly through that curtain of fire would be the same as asking for certain death. Perry's only chance of escape was to out-maneuver and out-climb the Messerschmitts in clear air and make his getaway to safety in that manner. But even as this knowledge came to him, hope died.

The Messerschmitts had caught him in a dive, and before he could begin to pull out they were all around him and over him like a tent. His mouth went bone-dry and there was a chunk of ice stuck in his throat. His heart! Cold sweat oozed out all over his face, and with each passing split-second, as he hurled the Grumman this way and that and fired blindly at every shadow of Nazi-marked wings that crossed his sights, he expected to feel the stinging bite of death in his flesh.

Death did not come, however. His plane was riddled from wing-tip to wing-tip, from prop to rudder post, but Lady Luck had seemingly thrown her cloak of protection about him. Then suddenly his spinning brain grasped the fact that he was little more than three hundred feet above the ice-choked waters of Davis Strait. An instant later the mystery was no longer a mystery.

He saw that there was a three-hundred-foot space of clear air under the towering clouds of fog. Unless you went down almost to the surface of the strait and risked plowing head-on into little hills of ice pushed up by the winds and the tides, you would never realize in a thousand years that there was a three-hundred-foot ceiling at that point.

No sooner did he realize that there was this ceiling than he stared inland and saw the stretch of level-packed snow that extended around all three sides of a small inlet. In that one sweeping glance allowed him he saw the cluster of snow-covered huts, painted white on the sides.

He saw, also, the double row of cleverly snow-camou-flaged Nazi bombers of the Focke-Wulf type. They were huge things, every bit as big as the Yank Air Corps Flying Fortresses, and in between them, even parked under their broad wings, were Messerschmitt 109s that looked like little black beetles by comparison.

One sweeping glance at the strangest, weirdest sight he had ever viewed in his life, and then the Pratt and Whitney in the nose received a direct burst from a charging Messerschmitt, and gave up the ghost for good. Instinctively Perry hauled back the throttle and then snapped off the ignition.

In practically the same instant he opened his mouth to shout what he could into his flap mike. But no sound passed his lips. He choked it back and swallowed hard instead, when his eyes fell on the radio panel. It was a mess of splintered glass and frayed wires. It looked as though it had been dropped from the top of a high building, and then stamped on by a couple of giants.

Perry suddenly realized that for the last ten minutes, at least, he had not blipped his radio cut-off switch once. Had the sudden silence started things moving back at Thirty-one? If so, what good would it do? Jordon and the boys would never be able to find this particular spot.

He himself was going to crash down under the fog. His controls were all shot, and the only thing he could do was to keep the nose up a little. It was impossible to change his direction, and the bullet-riddled plane was flip-flopping inshore beneath the fog bank.

"Nice work, fool!" he said aloud, and struggled to keep the nose from dropping down to the vertical. "You would try to do it all alone, wouldn't you! You got one Nazi and thought you were hot stuff. Yes! You let that other tramp lead you right down into this mess with a capital M. Never dreamed others might be waiting for you to get low enough, did you? No! Nice going, sap. A lot of good *you* are to your country, I don't think!"

In an abstract sort of way he realized that the mess of Nazi planes had stopped slapping away at him. They were riding herd on him like a black cloud of doom silhouetted against the gray sky. Any one of them could have slipped down a bit lower and chopped off his head with a single burst. He was clay-pigeon pickings, but the Nazis either didn't want to waste more bullets, or else they knew that the crash would finish him off.

Or, then again, perhaps they didn't want to chance his plane veering around and crashing on the choked ice of the strait where the wreckage would be seen from the air. Yes, perhaps a lot of things, but he didn't care a hoot about anything for the moment. His brain was too filled with rage at himself to bother concentrating on anything else.

"I deserve to get my darn neck broken in the crash!" he blamed himself. "Why didn't I do some low-level flying right off the bat? Why didn't I go down and look for the possible opening I was yapping to Jordon about? Oh, no! I had to be smart and raise a racket to get a couple of them to come up and *show* me the front door! Well, they did, and how!"

A series of snow- and ice-bunkers came sweeping up toward him. He stared at them glassy-eyed for a moment. Then abruptly the true fighter in him took charge. His rage at himself vanished, and in its place was a savage determination to cheat death in spite of hell and high water. He had made a mess of things, but he would not be the only one who had challenged failure in the very last moment and gone on fighting until there was no more strength left with which to fight.

"So long as I stay alive!" he mumbled through stiff lips, "so long I am not licked."

Further thoughts remained unspoken. The last few seconds had arrived. The white snow- and ice-covered inlet shoreline swept upward like so much frozen doom. He braced himself just long enough to pull the Grumman's nose toward the sky as much as he could. Then he let go of the controls, buried his face in his crossed arms, and let his whole body go limp.

He felt the tail wheel bump the ground and serve as a drag anchor to the rest of the craft mushing forward at a belly-up slant. Then the nose whipped down and all Greenland seemed to explode in a mad riot of sound and color inside his brain. Black hands reached into his head and crushed everything into utter silence.

A thousand or so years passed and then sound lapped at the edges of his brain again. It was harsh, unintelligible mumbo-jumbo sound that could mean anything, or nothing. It was like waves lapping against loose boards in a shore tunnel. It was like the rumble of cannon fire in the distance.

His aching brain suddenly stopped whirling around in a world of total darkness. The sound poured into his ears and made sense. Only in the nick of time did he check himself from opening his eyes. He sensed, rather than saw, the two figures who stood close to the bed. And he heard the two voices speaking German. Both harsh and rasping with anger, hatred hanging on every syllable.

"—may spoil all our plans, now!" one voice was saying. "Karl von Stultz was a fool to have attacked that American bomber a week ago. He should have let it go on by. The swine suspected nothing. We would be safe under this fog until March, at least. And today again. Twice! I am not sorry that he is somewhere in the mountains where he landed by parachute. Perhaps a few days in the snow will teach him that even a favorite of Goering cannot have everything."

"True, *Herr Kommandant,*" the second voice spoke. "But I would be careful if I were you. Karl von Stultz has friends here in our little *Staffle*. They might overhear your words and tell him when he returns—if he ever does."

"Let them, the swine dogs!" the other snarled. "I am *Kommandant* here. It was not my wish that von Stultz be included in this little expedition. I have had enough of his insolence, and his fool actions. I do not care if he is *Herr* Goering's son! I have *Der Fuehrer's* ear, myself. We shall see about Karl von Stultz. When and *if* he returns, he is not to so much as to get in a plane without my permission. He is no longer in charge of the escort planes. These are my orders. You will take command of the Messerschmitts, beginning now. You understand, Meuller?"

"Perfectly, *Herr Kommandant*. And Stebbins and Khole, who went aloft with von Stultz? I have your permission to ground them until Zero Hour?"

"You have!" the one addressed as *Herr Kommandant* snapped. "But, the Zero Hour. It was to be tomorrow at noon. *Gott!* Will we be lucky, I wonder? Von Stultz' foolishness today may change everything. The swine Americans must certainly know that something is amiss now. They fly bombers, yet this dog came nosing around in a fighter plane.

"It is obvious they suspect this fog hides something. Do they know what, and exactly where? And will we be able to remain hidden until we have left on our glorious flight tomorrow? Curse that fool von Stultz. I curse myself for not objecting to *Herr* Goering's demand that he be placed in command of the Messerschmitts. *Gott,* yes! I curse the fates that did not send him to the Russian Front. I—"

The man broke off short, cleared his throat with an angry sound, and then spoke again.

"Give this dog more brandy!" he snarled. "Either wake him up or drown him in it. I have things to ask him. And the swine will not live long if he does not tell me what I want to know. Give him stimulants, slap his face and hands —kick him, if you have to, but wake the dog up. He is not even injured. Just a bump on the head."

As the words died away to the echo, Perry Nolan struggled silently to slow up his spinning brain, to beat back the white-hot pain that stabbed at his head like a heated needle. Then he felt himself lifted up. A glass was forced between his half-clenched teeth, and liquid fire went pouring down his throat. He choked and groaned aloud, and raised a hand as though to push away the cup with the burning liquid.

The hand propping up his body was suddenly removed, and he received a stinging blow on the left cheek that popped his eyes open in spite of his efforts to keep them shut.

"That will be enough sleep for you, swine dog!" a giant of a man in German gray-green thundered at him. "Sit up and listen to me. There are questions you will answer!"

The stinging blow cleared most of the fog from Perry's brain. In fact, it seemed to act like a valve that released a reservoir of pent-up strength within him. His brain was suddenly crystal-clear, and warm, refreshing blood surged through his veins. His first impulse was to leap from the bed and smash both fists into the snarling face that seemed to hang in front of his own like a soured moon. But he checked the crazy impulse, shook his head and let his body sway from side to side.

"Hold everything, fellows," he muttered thickly and peered cautiously about through slitted eyes. "What happened, and where am I?"

A hairy hand grabbed his tunic front and jerked him up straight. The big moon face of *Herr Kommandant* was bent close to his.

"You were shot down, swine!" the man boomed in guttural English. "You are a prisoner. What were you doing in that American fighter plane? Where is your base? How much do your comrades know? Speak up, or you'll die this minute, like the dog you are!"

Perry gaped glassily at the German and continued to act as though his brain was too befuddled to grasp the meaning of anything. On the contrary, though, he was completely alert. And there was renewed strength flowing through his body, too. He didn't even feel the pains and aches caused

# WINGS OF THE NORTH

by the crash any more. He stared foolishly, but he didn't miss a thing.

Behind the big German was a wall, and hanging on that wall was a huge map of the Western Hemisphere. It was covered with navigation notes and symbols. Although Perry could not see all of them clearly, he saw enough to confirm what he had heard the Germans say, and to start his heart pounding like a trip-hammer against his ribs. The map on the wall was no more and no less than a preparation picture of a gigantic bombing raid to be made against the eastern seaboard of the United States.

The starting point was where he was right now—a fog-bound mountain range on Greenland's west coast just above Godthaab. The course of the raid flight, marked in red ink, was across Davis Strait, over Baffin Island, down Hudson Bay, and southward across the eastern neck of Canada, and into the United States through New England's back door for a perfect crack at Boston, New York, and Philadelphia. A four-thousand-mile, round-trip flight that would be duck soup for Focke-Wulf long-range bombers.

A sneak raid at the U.S. eastern seaboard, and then on out to sea to shake off pursuers on the way home. A daring venture, and one which would perhaps cost the Nazis dearly in planes that failed to return.

But surprise would all be in their favor. Yank home defenses would be watching for attack from the sea, not through the back door. It could well be turned into a second Pearl Harbor affair with no telling how much damage done before the defending planes and guns could swing into action.

A suicide raid, perhaps. So what? That wouldn't spare Boston, New York, and Philadelphia from the thunder and doom of bombs dropped by fiends who had already resigned themselves to their fate.

And it was certain that the escorting Messerschmitts would never return. They didn't carry the gas. But they would blast a path for the bombers, then each pilot would bail out to be taken prisoner for the duration of the war. It would cost the Nazis much, but since when had Adolph Hitler ever given a thought to the cost in German lives and blood?

"Speak up, swine!" went on the Nazi commander. "Where is your Fighter Squadron based? What is its strength? What do you know about this place?"

Perry's teeth clicked like castanets, and his eyes bulged as the Germans shook him as a dog would shake a rag doll.

"We know everything about you!" Perry suddenly blurted out. "You don't stand a hope of pulling your dirty raid on the east coast of the U.S. Not a chance! Every single plane that takes off from here will be shot down like a ton of brick. You. . . ."

Perry let his voice trail off as though he was too weak to go on. He let his body sag. The German let go of his tunic front and he slumped down on the bed. This was just what he wanted.

By a miracle the crash had not smashed his wrist-watch. A glance at it had shown that the hands pointed to a time that was two hours after he had left Thirty-one. That meant, that *if* Jordon and the boys were coming, they must be well on their way by now.

It meant also that his only hope was to show them in some way the exact location of the hidden field. And there *was* a way. There was a way—*if* he could only live long enough.

From his position, half-slumped down on the cot, he could see a half-dozen submachine-guns in their wall racks to his left. They were the heavy-duty, but light-weight type that had proved so effective with British Commandos parties raiding Norway.

These, of course, were the German type of gun with half-moon-shaped cartridge clips that stuck up from the top of the loading breech. The clip moved a notch downward, each time a bullet was fired, coming out the bottom in front of the trigger where it could be taken out and refilled when it was empty.

But it was more than just the sight of the guns that set his blood to racing. It was the fact that the clips contained more than the ordinary nickle-jacketed lead bullets. They were loaded as aerial machine-gun belts are loaded—with incendiary and explosive bullets as well. If he could get his hands on one of those guns, and dive through the window to his right, the target waited out there for him!

The big German's mouth opened wide to roar out again, and his big, hairy hands reached down to grab the supposedly weak prisoner. But that prisoner was not weak. That prisoner was doomed to death. He knew full well that he would never live to see tomorrow's dawn. But he didn't care. He had one last job to do—and Captain Perry Nolan was going to do it!

Even as Perry coiled his muscles to strike out with every ounce of strength in his body, he heard the drone of many engines high up in the sky above the fog. So did both of the Germans, and the big one with hairy hands froze motionless as anger and fear flared up in his eyes.

"*Gott!* Those are engines of American planes!" he choked out. "Meuller! Issue orders that not one plane is to take off. They cannot find us under this fog, and we must not be fools enough to—"

The German commander never finished the last. Perry Nolan's driving feet caught him smack in the stomach and darn near drove his belt buckle out through his back-bone. The surprise attack had been sudden, swift, and deadly. And momentum carried Perry right up on his feet as the big German went tumbling over backward like a felled ox.

The instant Perry's toes touched the floor he pivoted like a spinning streak of light and caught the second German flush on the chin even as the Nazi's eyes went wide in dumb-founded alarm. The man buckled at the knees and stumbled to the floor, weakly pawing at his holstered Luger pistol.

By then, though, the Yank had leaped over his prostrate body and wrenched one of the submachine-guns down off the rack. He slipped his finger over the trigger, clicked off the safety, and whirled.

"Stay just like that, or you get it in the belly, both of you!" he barked at them in their own tongue, and side-stepped quickly over to the window. "I'm leaving, and if I hear one peep I'll come back and blast you if it's the last thing I do. So hold it!"

The big German was too full of belly pains to hear, let alone pay attention. He lay huddled on the floor, hugging

his mid-section and groaning like a stuck pig. The other
German was still trying to get his dancing eyes to focus. He
had forsaken his holstered Luger entirely to clap both hands
to his swelling jaw.

Perry gave them both one last glance, then half-turned,
knocked out the window glass with the butt of his gun,
and dived headlong out into the snow. He was up on one
knee in a flash, and had the submachine-gun trained on a
canvas-covered pile of fuel and oil barrels not thirty yards
away.

He sighted for the middle of the pile and pressed the
gun's trigger. The gun pounded out flame and sound, and
the barrels in the middle of the pile seemed to melt away to
so much gray and brownish liquid that poured down over
the others. For a split-second, perhaps, and then it was as
though the Devil himself had reached up and put a torch
to that high-test gas and oil. A sheet of livid flame shot
high up into the fog with a thunder-clap of sound, and
clouds and clouds of swirling yellow and black smoke went
belching up after it. The terrific heat seemed virtually to
burn a path through the mountain of fog to the clear air
several thousands of feet above.

"That'll tell you, Jordon, old sock!" Perry Nolan cried
hoarsely and cut his gunfire. "There's your target to drop
the eggs on. And drop them, for our country's sake, Jordon!
Never mind if they hit me. I don't count any more. Get
these rats! *Get the whole works!*"

He choked up and sprang to his feet. The snow-blanketed,
fog-hidden flying field had become a wild bedlam of sound
and fear-crazed action. Pilots and mechanics seemed to pop

up out of the snow like rabbits, cast horrified eyes at the blazing inferno that had two minutes ago been the squadron's fuel dump, and then started dashing madly about in circles.

A scream of rage cut the air in back of Perry. He had just time to let his body drop, swing up his submachine-gun and pull the trigger as the hairy hand of the big German poked a Luger out at him. He saw it spit fire, and felt something white-hot kiss him on the side of the neck. Then *Herr Kommandant's* head and shoulders disappeared from view as Perry Nolan's bullets slammed the dead man back into the room.

Cutting his fire, Perry rolled over in the snow, scrambled onto his feet and floundered around the rear of the hut to the other side. He got just a flash glimpse of pilots and mechanics hauling white canvas covers off a row of Messerschmitts, and then the skies seemed to fall down on top of him and knock him flat. The roar of doomsday was in his ears as he saw one corner of the snow-packed strip of flying field belch flame and smoke high into the air.

The sight was terrifying, yet his heart sang with joy. The smoke from the blazing fuel dump had gone up through to the top of the fog and shown Jordon and the boys exactly where their target was. A "stick" had already come down to blast part of the place into nothing. There would be more sticks of bombs, and then some more.

"Drop them, gang! Slam them down! Blow the bums to Hades and back! Give them the old one, two, three!"

Perry was hardly conscious of the fact that he was yelling at the top of his voice, and even less conscious of the fact that he was racing headlong across the packed snow toward the line of Messerschmitts. Something had seemed to snap in his brain, and all the world about him was bathed in a red mist.

He became a wild man who didn't care where he was headed, how he got there, or when. He just went charging that line of Messerschmitts with his submachine-gun thrown up and pounding out the last of the bullets in the clip.

So sudden, so startling, and so utterly mad was his one-man charge that the Nazi pilots and mechanics broke in terror and fled off in all directions as though a thousand devils were after him. True, three or four did hold their ground, did grab for their Lugers and attempt to stop the madman practically running them down.

But they might just as well have tried to stop a tank with snowballs. Perry Nolan's shower of bullets cut their legs right out from under them almost before they could apply pressure to their trigger fingers. The third One-nine along the line took some incendiary bullets in the gas tank and the ship became a pillar of flame.

Then, as Perry flung his empty gun away and vaulted into the pit of the nearest One-nine, three more sticks of American-made bombs came sailing down. For one brief instant Nolan had the impression of being torn apart in small pieces by blast. Then he realized that he had fed gas to the idling prop and was booting the plane out to the near end of the runway.

Behind, the hut where he had been held prisoner, and a few more huts close by, were nothing but a great, smoking black crater in the snow. He had time only for one quick look at the sea of flame that seemed to splash out in all directions, and then the Messerschmitt was rocketing forward at full revs.

The instant he picked up enough speed he lifted the plane clear, and went into a vertical bank that took him out over the ice-choked Davis Strait, through the three-hundred-foot "tunnel" and into clear air. There he hauled back the stick and pointed the nose toward the sky. Toward the sky and a squadron of Thirty-one bombers that were circling the point where the black smoke came up through the fog.

"Okay, it's me, pals!" he shouted crazily and waved one hand wildly out the opened glass hatch. "I'm out from under, so really let 'em have it!"

One of the bombers broke out of the circle and came piling down. Perry recognized Major Jordon's personal markings, and just in case no mistakes would be made he let go of the Messerschmitt's controls and stood up so that from the hips up he was clearly visible to those aboard the bomber. Instantly the bomber's wings were waggled, and the big plane went curving up to rejoin the others. Perry gulped with relief and dropped back into the seat, and wiped beads of nervous sweat from his face.

"Praise to Allah they recognized me!" he breathed and leveled off from his climb. "The way I went tearing up they might have thought that I was—"

He shrugged the rest away unspoken, curved around and fixed hopeful eyes on the point where the fog met the ice-choked strait. But he didn't get his hope. Not a single German plane came rocketing out from under that mountain of fog. And the reason that none appeared was only too obvious.

There wasn't any mountain of fog any more. Rather, there was a mountain of glowing red flame. It was as though all of Greenland was on fire. With a chance at last to take a crack at war, Jordon and his boys were doing it up brown—or red. They sent ton after ton of earth-blasting doom hurtling down on the red flame and black smoke-marked target.

Perry didn't even try to picture in his mind the horrible sight that secret field under the fog must be. It was something one couldn't even imagine. It was doubtful if anything was left down there. Nothing but a huge fire-belching crater on the west coast of Greenland. And the way Jordon's bombs continued to rain down it was probable that even the mountain of fog would be blasted away so that tomorrow the entire Axis world could see the smoking results of their latest attempt to sneak one over on the winged warriors of Uncle Sam.

"But it was close!" Perry breathed and shivered slightly. "If that von Stultz hadn't taken a crack at poor Johnnie and at me, they might have pulled it off. But they *didn't*. And I guess that in this nasty business it's what *doesn't* happen that counts most. Happy landings, Johnnie, old kid. Today is only the beginning. We'll go right on paying up for you, kid, until there aren't any of the rats left—anyplace!"

Bowing his head in silent prayer to his lost pals, Perry Nolan then climbed his stolen Messerschmitt 109 up toward altitude where Major Jordon and the others were waiting to escort him back to Thirty-one's Field. There would be countless questions, of course, but a good old-fashioned Army Air Corps celebration would get underway, and last through the night, at least!

# DIRECT HIT

*By*

## JOE ARCHIBALD

I N THE ready room of the giant carrier, the crews of the Dauntless' were getting their final blackboard instruction pertaining to the early morning patrol. Flying sheets were being passed out and bombers, pilots and navigators bent over their portable chart boards to work out the grim business of the task at hand.

Data such as temperature, dewpoint, recognition signals and radio calls and codes. The latter were to be resorted to in dire emergency only, for obvious reasons. There is nothing wrong with Nippo flyers' ears.

A scout plane had come in and reported a Jap convoy headed west, possibly for a thrust at Dutch Harbor. It seemed incredible, but the Jappos had shown imagination ever since they had messed up Pearl Harbor. The tentacles of the horrible yellow octopus reached out everywhere, defying the combined forces of the United Nations to cut them off.

Data dispensed with, the men who were to man the Dauntless' pulled on canvas jackets, helmets and goggles.

They adjusted their yellow inflatable life jackets—yellow because that color is easy to spot on the surface of the sea. Compressed-air cartridges filled these jackets with air when the water came too close to the men who wore them.

Airpilot called out: "Are all men ready to man planes?"

All were ready. They spilled out of the ready room to the flight deck where the SBD's were clustered aft.

The great bow of the carrier rose and fell and below the deck the turbines pulsed. Up ahead and off to the right of the floating drome, destroyers knifed the sea.

A long, lanky ensign fell in step with his navigator and there was a lump in his cheek. It was not his tongue, for the gaunt Tennesseean took his war seriously.

Jimmy Hatford had come up the hard way, up from an isolated valley in the Smokies where a schoolbook had once been considered an instrument of the devil. A circuit rider and a congressman had helped lift him out of the valley and get him to Pensacola where he had been introduced to the flying boats.

He had become a polished flyer, but his carrier mates doubted that he would ever become a polished gentleman. But polished gentlemen have no advantage whatsoever in the war in the Pacific. Uncle Sam knows a fighting man when he sees one, and he had taken a good look at Hatford.

"Reckon we'll mess 'em up, if we just catch up with 'em," Jimmy drawled, as he plugged cotton in his ears and adjusted his helmet again. "Them torps pack a powerful load, Lieutenant, they shore do."

Lieutenant, junior grade, Tom Corbin muttered in return and tried to outstep Hatford. Tommy Corbin had come from Virginia and his grandfather had fought with Lee. Corbin had graduated from Annapolis and had been All-American tackle on the Navy team two years before.

He was proud and a bit intolerant of a raw-boned mountaineer who had slept a good part of his life on corn husks. He had made it plain to Jimmy that the war could not change a man's position or richen his blood.

Lieutenant Corbin looked upon tobacco-chewing as the filthiest habit in the world, forgetting that some of the greatest fighters of history had ridden over the enemy with a great cud in their cheeks.

"Can't understand how you can use that stuff," Corbin had said to Jimmy more than once. "You're an officer in the navy, Hatford. There are certain things a man must remember when he is part of the service, when he has a commission. His personal pride, trimness—oh, you wouldn't understand."

"Think I do," Jimmy had said. "You just can't make a silk wallet out of a razorback's eah, Lieutenant. But this ain't sure 'nough dress parade, this wah. It's a he-man's game."

Carrier ready for action! On the island, the great superstructure built along the starboard side, a light blinked. Behind the battened ports of the island, the air officer and his aides worked out the plan of the attack.

Along the catwalks on the flight deck, gun crews were at their posts. Up there on sky control, the bull-horn blared out its orders.

On the flight deck, men garbed in yellow, blue, red and green jerseys hustled about. Plane directors, firefighters, handlers and arresting gear crews. Halfway up the island, a light glowed red. A whistle blew and the carrier began to pick up speed into the wind.

The bull-horn kept booming. The light on the island turned green. Overhead the sky was brightening, losing its stars.

"Pilots, man your planes."

Hatford and Corbin were in No. 3 of the squadron commander's section. Walking to the closely arranged rank of planes aft, Jimmy Hatford tried to get under Corbin's reserve.

"Like to meet up with a rattlesnake, Lieutenant," the Tennesseean grinned. "Sometime I'll tell you how I got one down home. His eyes were looking right into mine, slanting beady eyes, an' I figgered any second—"

"You talk too much, Hatford," Tom Corbin said coldly.

There were rattlesnakes out there on the heaving sea. There were deadly foes waiting to strike from the sky. Lieutenant Corbin knew that there was a good chance that some of them would not get back. Diving at a Jap ship was not a healthy business, not when you had to come down to eighty feet to get that torpedo away. It was their business to get rid of it.

Jimmy Hatford climbed into the pilot's seat and went through the ritual of checking control tabs and mixture, prop controls and battery and generator switches.

The bull-horn on the island called for the mechs to stand by to start engines. Hatford, the taste of tobacco heavy in his cheek and the smell of it reaching the noses of the two men behind him, fooled with the wobble pump and built up fuel pressure.

Again the ghostly bull-horn spoke.

"Start engines!"

Jimmy tripped the starter and opened his throttle. He took a yellow sheet from under his gun sight and laboriously scratched his initials on it and handed it overside to the captain.

It told the officer that Jimmy was satisfied with the Dauntless and was ready to get it off the carrier. The great floating drome increased speed and the whistle on the bridge was blasting. The carrier pointed into the wind and everything was ready.

The squadron leader went first, the prop wash from the Dauntless shaking Hatford's plane. Jimmy watched the flight deck officer in his jersey of brilliant yellow. The man's arm came down and Jimmy opened up. The Dauntless flashed past the island, its tail up.

Once off the carrier, Jimmy held the ship level to gather speed and when it was sufficient, he pointed the left wing tip toward the lighting heavens and went up in a great climbing turn. A thousand feet a minute, the SBD's climb.

They went up to ten thousand—eleven. The air was getting a little cold and a little thin, but oxygen masks are not needed under twelve thousand. The flight went through a strata of clouds and Jimmy looked at the other ships and spoke into his hand set.

"High enough," he announced.

The leading section seemed a little too tight and the man

from Tennessee watched the leading edge of his left wing.
It seemed about to kiss No. 1's aileron.

"Ought to have spittoons in these crates," Jimmy said.
"Don't worry, Lieutenant, a good chewer never spits."

"You're a mug, Hatford," Tom Corbin said. "You'll never
be anything else. Don't forget that."

Jimmy read between the Lieutenant's words. He knew
the meaning he was supposed to take from them. They
might just as well have been "She's not for you, Hatford."

She had come to see Corbin at Guantanamo. She was just
about the prettiest thing Jimmy had ever seen. So delicate
he had jettisoned his cud of tobacco at the first sight of her.

Jimmy wondered why the movie fellows hadn't picked
her leading parts. Corbin's sister, Clarabelle. The name
smacked of Virginia and cotton fields and great white
houses with wisteria growing up their sides.

The girl had amazed Lieutenant Corbin. He had had a
man all picked out for her, but the girl seemed to have forgotten that she needed someone to tell her what to do. She
had asked especially to be introduced to Jimmy Hatford.

A couple of times she had walked with him along the
shore at Guantanamo. Not ten days ago, Jimmy had received a letter from Clarabelle and Corbin had opened up on
the ensign.

"You don't belong in her class," Corbin had told Jimmy
in front of a score of flying officers. "Keep away from her,
Hatford. You've got plenty of gall trying to reach for the
moon."

"I'm a flyer," Jimmy had told the man. "I can go as high
as the next man. Reckon yo'-all had better talk that over

with Clarabelle. You and Cupid both got wings, Lieutenant, but you ain't got the stuff Cupid has. This is a free country. There was Abe Lincoln who was born in a cabin and look where he got, Tommy."

"I don't want you corresponding with her, Hatford. Is that clear?"

"Nope. When she says not to, I figger I'll quit," Jimmy had said.

For almost a half hour, the formation held their course and below them the ceiling was thickening up and that was good for the Jap convoy would not spot them too soon.

Jimmy figured that they must be near their objective, if the charting had been right. He looked down through two cloud layers and caught occasional glimpses of the vast ocean.

There was a pressure at his temples and a tingling under his knees and he always got that when danger was imminent. In a few minutes, he saw the convoy. They were like toy boats floating in a bathtub and seemed to stand still.

From eleven thousand feet, they created that illusion, but the crews of the SBD's knew they were knifing through the water at great speed. Little streamers of white at their sterns betrayed their speed and the smoke from their funnels lay flat against their backs.

The crew of Number Three knew the method of attack. A bomber or two went down there for a frontal attack, the purpose of which was to distract the Nippo gunners. The crate that was to drive the first torpedo home came down in a zigzag course to avoid A.A. fire.

The torpedo was released eighty feet above the water so

that it would not be damaged when it hit. It generally hit the surface a thousand yards from the objective and then cut through the white caps at a forty-knot speed. It was risky business and it needed men specially trained for such work.

At a signal from the the squadron commander, the formation started downward. Not too steep. Another signal put the SBD's in echelon and Tom Corbin thought of the shift the coach had taught them for use against Army. The leader peeled off and so did Number Two.

"Now," Jimmy said. "Our turn."

He shoved the stick forward and there came that feeling of pressure in the stomach of the trio riding that torpedo plane. Down—down at terrific speed with the wind shrieking past the windows and trying to tear the wings off.

Ears clogged up until the whine of the engine was heard only abstractedly. Always going down with the sea coming up to slam you to pieces.

The Jap cruiser loomed up bigger and bigger. Down there, the squadron commander had dropped his steel fish and was turning away to climb if he was able. The Jap guns were barking from the monkey islands and a plane went off the catapult of the Shinto battle wagon.

A. A. fire began to thicken. Near the stern of the cruiser, the torpedo went off. Not close enough. Number Two was attacking now. Its torp knifed into a supply ship and seemed to lift it halfway out of the water when it exploded.

All the excitement of a sea and air battle was at the zenith now. Four Nippo planes were up and two of the convoy were going down.

It was the crew of Number Three that got that Jap cruiser, Jimmy Hatford at the controls. The torpedo struck full on, and a sheet of flame leaped from the cruiser's magazine.

Then Number Three was off the level of the approach and climbing. Great weights dropped away from the stomachs of the crew as the Dauntless turned away and climbed with A. A. exploding overhead.

The rat race was on. A Nakajima 92 was in for the kill and Number Three engaged it at a height of seven thousand. Jimmy got it with his guns just before a burst of Jap A. A. shattered the greenhouse behind Corbin.

That was where Ensign Andy Traynor sat. The Dauntless staggered and pitched and rolled and the Tennesseean fought it to even keel and kept climbing.

Down there on the gray wastes were great geysers of white water and fire and smoke. The convoy was scattered and the SBD's kept knifing down and unloading.

Jimmy Hatford yelled for Andy Traynor in his set, but he got no answer. He checked Tom Corbin in with a voice that was as dry as Tennessee corn stalks in September.

He got a Nakajima in his sights, let the forward guns squall, and saw the tracers go through the Nakajima as if the Jappo plane was made of butter. The yellow man in the cockpit jackknifed and his crate fell away with him, a thin pennon of smoke trailing out of it.

The fight was over in a few more minutes. The Jap catapult planes were wiped out and four Nippo ships were getting ready to settle beneath the broad Pacific. Another was limping far behind the decimated convoy, black smoke boil-

ing out of it. Life boats packed the sea. Little figures claw-
ing to keep above the surface. Wreckage.

Jimmy swept his eyes over the sky to quickly estimate the
damage to the attacking planes, but quickly swung his head
back to his instrument board again. The engine was dragging badly and he quickly checked.

He caught the strong odor of oil that resolved into a taste
of acrid smoke. There was no prop control and needles
spun crazily around the dials. The motor died and its dying
breath was fiery.

"We're out the window, Tommy, sho'nuff," Jimmy said:
"Tough luck."

It was a long way down. The sea was ugly and seemed
to be the only world there was. Jimmy thought of the
chances a man had down there, the chances to go right
down to Fiddler's Green—the sailor's deep-sea drome where
a hero could drowse throughout eternity, each with a bottomless tank of grog. Two men on the Pacific held up by a
pair of inflated life jackets.

Jimmy went overside a few seconds after Tommy Corbin.
He saw the man's parachute fan out and knew the proud
man was getting ready to inflate the yellow camisole. A
lifesaver for a while until the waves beat you around the
head and knocked the senses out of you and filled your
stomach with bitter brine. Or froze you like a fish on ice
with its terribly cold water.

Ships were few and far between on the great expanse of
water between Tokio and San Francisco. And there were
sharks.

Jimmy thought of a dreamy day in the valley of the Smokies. A day with a dog and a gun.

The chute opened and pulled at his arm sockets and jolted the muscles of his groin. He folded his arms, grinned a little, and fished into his pocket for a golden flat plug. He took a big bite of tobacco and felt better.

He guessed he had about three thousand feet more to go. He started working his chute, thankful that the wind was not too violent, and tried to follow Tom Corbin down. The man was not a powerful swimmer, and he did not have the toughness in him that you get from eating sidemeat and pone during your growing years.

Tom Corbin hit the water and began to cut himself loose from the collapsing chute. A wave tossed him high and for a moment the water engulfed him. Jimmy dropped in about a hundred yards away, and he had his knife out and slashing at the harness that held him. Once loose, he began the fight to live.

Sometimes the sea is deadly, shows no pity. At times it is a soft-hearted creature that lifts a man up and lets him breathe and gives him half a chance to survive.

There was wreckage all over the sea. The SBD's had strewn it there. Jimmy kept navigating and at the end of an hour he was close to Tom Corbin and he reached out a hand and held to him. The lieutenant's face was blue with cold and his grin was terribly forced when Jimmy yelled at him.

"We'll lick it," the Tennesseean cried out. "We'll make it to some wreckage and hang on. I see a landin' field over there—sho' nuff, Tommy."

"Save yourself, Hatford," Tom Corbin gasped out, after

a wall of brine nearly tore him loose from the gaunt flyer's grasp.

It was hard to keep hold of Tom Corbin. Jim's own hands were getting numb. The life-jackets bulged out and prevented close contact. Jimmy got a look at the floating thing. It looked like a lifeboat that had slid off the deck of a Jap ship. If it was, it would have air-tanks to keep it afloat.

Tom Corbin was losing his grip. He couldn't talk loud enough for Jimmy to hear him above the pound of the sea. Hatford was losing his grip too—with his hands.

He managed to get his knife out and while he opened the blade with his teeth, the bulge in his cheek got as big as an apple.

He plunged the blade into his life jacket and drove the air out of it. He went under a little and got a good hold of Tom Corbin and then he started swimming for that precious chunk of flotsam.

Ensign Hatford made it and kept talking to Tom Corbin, keeping the man from dropping off. Using all the strength left in him he got Corbin over the bow thwart before the Virginian passed out. Jimmy's weight nearly put the drifting lifeboat under when he fell across Tom Corbin and got strength back into him.

When Jimmy opened his eyes he felt that tingling under his knees that was his danger signal. The boat had another passenger, and he wore the uniform of an officer in the Japanese navy.

His face was square, with high cheekbones that seemed ready to burst through the skin. His teeth were perfect and as white as snow and he had them bared for Jimmy's benefit.

"Good morning," the Jap said in perfect English, and lifted the gun he held in his right hand. "There is not room for the three of us, I assure you. Unfortunate of course." He wormed his way a little closer to Jimmy and his grin broadened. "You are one of the American flyers who gave us such a warm reception, I believe. A lot of my companions were not as lucky as I."

"We have a right to live, Toto, or whatever your name is," Jimmy said, and he felt Tom Corbin stir under him. Corbin cursed thickly, resignedly. "Any man who comes out of a scrap like that should have half a chance. Throw your gun away, Toto, and we'll settle it like men."

"No, thank you. You might live to fight against the Mikado again," the Jap officer said, losing his smile. "Two less white devils to stand in the way of our conquering forces. Do I sound too melodramatic?"

Jimmy edged forward a little as if trying to relieve Corbin of his weight. The Jap was just seven feet away from him and the gun muzzle was coming up.

"I shall not waste time listening to you beg for your life," the enemy said scornfully.

Here was a rattlesnake, Jimmy thought. The most deadly of them all. Sometime he would tell Tom Corbin about a rattlesnake back in Tennessee—if he lived.

He had to live. There was Clarabelle and the promise she had made. He drove his teeth through the lump in his mouth.

"You dirty yellow rat," Tom Corbin gasped out. "Hurry up and shoot."

"I shall oblige," the Jap said, his slant eyes getting to be mere slits. "Unfortunate of course."

Jimmy thrust his head forward and Lieutenant Corbin, steeling himself for a bullet, heard his squadron mate make a sharp sound with his lips. Brown tobacco juice spattered the two deadly slant eyes under the close-cropped black hair of the enemy sailor, and his first bullet went wild and cut into the wood close to Corbin's head.

The Jap fired blindly again, one hand pawing at his eyes, but Jimmy had him before the third shot came out of his ugly automatic. He had him around the throat and his strong wiry fingers exerted pressure.

No pity for the yellow man. Jimmy pressed and pressed until the man's black eyes started to bulge out of their little sockets. Lieutenant Tom Corbin clung to the pitching life boat, unmindful of the numbness in his arm. His eyes were glued to Jimmy's powerful hands.

Jimmy threw the rattlesnake overside and lifted his head and looked at Tom Corbin.

"Just like I got that rattlesnake back home." The Tennesseean grinned like a gargoyle. "I was goin' to tell you about it, Lieutenant. You're hit."

"In the arm," Tom Corbin said as he watched Jimmy roll the cud of tobacco in his cheek. "His last shot did it. Thanks for the life, Jimmy."

The ensign shrugged. "Wa'n't nothin'," he said, getting a firm hold on the tossing lifeboat. "We shore ain't out of the woods yet, Tommy. If it rains, we can catch some fresh water in our undershirts. Wring 'em out an' drink 'em.

Let's get these belts off. Tomorrow—if we're here tomorrow —the sun's goin' to be powerful hot."

Corbin said: "I've been a fool, Jimmy."

"We all get to be fools sometimes," the ensign chuckled, and looked out over the gray wastes.

"You deserve anything if you get out of this," the lieutenant said. "You know what I mean."

"Reckon. You know I think I can give up this tobacco-chawing easy if I try. Clarabelle don't like it. I said I'd do the rest of my chawin' durin' the war an' sicken myself of it. Here, let's look at that arm, Tommy."

They drifted all night. Toward morning, Jimmy lashed Tommy to the boat and tied his own left hand to a thwart. That was about all the strength he had left. It looked like Fiddler's Green and the bottomless grog tankards for the flying sailors.

They had their yellow life jackets deflated and draped over their shoulders so that a scout plane might spot them.

Just after sunup, Jimmy saw the sharks. The devils were waiting to get what a rattlesnake missed. He cursed them and his voice sounded hollow on the surface of the sea.

The wind whipped up and angered the waters and the boat they were clinging to began to pitch and toss like a chip and the salt got into their dry mouths and nearly gagged them.

Tom Corbin was motionless. Jimmy tried to shake some life into him, but he knew he didn't have much more left in him than he did himself. He tried to stop from dropping off, but it was no use.

They were in a dive bomber again, up in the sky where

the air was very blue and clean. Tom Corbin was telling Jimmy that it would be a big wedding. Guess there would be quite a crowd and they would need about a hundred Virginia hams. Jimmy said a Tennessee ham could lick a Virginia pig any day. Jimmy could smell the ham.

And that was the smell that was in his nostrils when he opened his eyes on an old tramp steamer bound for Hawaii.

"They've sho' nuff got a galley in Fiddler's Green," the flyer said wearily. "The stuff a feller likes. Beans for ghosts from Boston, scrapple for ghosts from Philadelphia and ham for us critters from the Smokies."

"Kind of bleary yet," a man said to the grizzled skipper of the tramp. "He smells that ham and cabbage."

"The other one is still out of his head, Mr. Ordway," the skipper said. "Lucky for them we got a lookout with eyes like Dracula, Mr. Ordway. By Godfrey—five days floating on the sea—"

By nightfall Jimmy was willing to admit he was not a ghost sailing toward the Great White Anchorage. The ham was very inferior grade, but it would do all right.

Lieutenant Tom Corbin sat across the table in the galley, his arm bandaged and all he could take was some thin soup made out of a hambone and cabbage. Nothing ever tasted as good to the Virginian. He told the skipper and the first mate how Jimmy had got a rattlesnake.

"Knew the flyer ate tobacco," the skipper said. "Have a chew, sir?"

"Nope," Jimmy said. "I've swore off. I'm goin' to try and be a gentleman."

The carrier picked the two Dauntless pilots up in the

Hawaiian Islands, three weeks later, and Jimmy had a cablegram from Clarabelle Corbin in his pocket. He knew all the Japs in the world could not stop him from answering the message in person when the war was over.

The radio in a forward stateroom was going full blast when the two flyers came in to see the commander. An announcer was talking about a hero who had downed a Jap with a well aimed stream of tobacco juice.

"I wish I could have seen that shot," the commander was saying. "Hatford had to direct that shot at the Jap just right. He had to figure wind drift to get right to the mark. No wonder Number Three ship tagged that cruiser dead center."

Ensign Jimmy Hatford grinned and nudged Lieutenant Tom Corbin. They walked very close together when they stepped up to take the commander's hand.

"Getting that cruiser was mighty important, of course," the commander said after he had finished with his high praise of the flyers. "What is more important, I see you two chaps got something else out there. Especially Lieutenant Corbin. Let me congratulate you."

"I know what you mean, sir," Corbin said.

This time he nudged Ensign Jimmy Hatford. He knew the rawboned man from the Smokies would not be an ensign very long. He could tell by the way the commander measured the ensign and himself with his eyes. He would see to it that Hatford was put on an equal footing with a Corbin from Virginia, where he belonged.

# BOMB TRAP

### By

### WILLIAM O'SULLIVAN

I

T WAS a tough assignment. The Philippine bridgehead for the landing of Jap supplies from the southern tip of Formosa, two hundred miles into the north, was the target. Knowing its importance, the American command in the Far East had ordered it smashed at until made useless.

For their part, the Japs had moved in scores of archie pieces and crisscrossed archie trajectories at various altitudes, until it was all but impossible for any effective bombing at high altitude. And to bomb this position at low altitudes was sheer suicide.

But a tough crew in the U. S. Navy's air arm was now working on that very problem. Friction between pilot and bombardier, however, threatened to spoil the show.

"Hold 'er still, pal!" Sam Carhart, the bombardier, snapped into his phone. "How can I bomb if you let the ship jitter all over the sky?"

Pete Yancey's reply was dangerously smooth.

"Maybe you got somethin' there, brother! Maybe you can't! Looks like we've been flying over this beach long enough for the average bomber to score a direct hit once in ten!"

"Why, you—"

"Enemy aircraft coming!" "Sunny" Darville, the third man on the team, blared into his phone. "Better hold off the bombing, you two, until we clear these two Japs off our tails!"

The rearmost man in the three-place Devastator swiveled his turret guns and coolly got ready for the two Kamikaze monoplanes that were angling in for a blast. Sunny was grimly amused to find he was actually relieved that some diversion had interrupted the growing feud between Sam Carhart and Pete Yancey.

Pete lifted his eyes to the rear-view glass. For a moment the truculent stares of pilot and bombardier locked. Then Pete was whirling in a fast chandelle and coming out of it with his wing guns blazing.

*Rat-a-tat-tat-tat—*

One of the Japs veered off in a split-S, while the other Jap hurdled the Yank plane and reached for altitude with an Immelmann. Sunny Darville came into action with his turret guns. He yelped his glee when a Jap wing broke under the leaden stitching the U. S. Navy gunner gave it. The Kamikaze flew apart in mid-air.

Archie fire, which had left off to give the Japs a crack at the Navy plane, now opened up again with a murderous fire. The second Jap had veered off, was lurking a few miles away hopefully, looking for help before he tackled the hard-bitten Navy dive bomber again.

"Lay yo' eggs," Pete crisped to Sam over the phone. "The

wind has shifted. Ah've got to dig for our rendezvous with
the *Sussex* now! The gas is low."

"Huh?" Sam blared. "Listen, I got to get lined up again!"

"No time for that," Pete said flatly. "Ah'm boss, mister.
Lay yo' eggs. You fused them, didn't you? Well, we ain't
gonna land with 'em!"

"You're boss when I'm not bombing," Sam said heatedly.

"Which is now. Ah'm boss, because I'm pilotin'. Lay yo'
eggs, suh!"

Sam released his bombs aimlessly, his eyes bitter. As the
plane hit east for the rendezvous, picking up needed speed
for the run as the bombs fell free, Sunny Darville frowned
his worry.

"Trouble ahead," he thought, "and plenty of it. And not
all for the Japs. Unless I'm nuts, my fire-eating South Caro-
lina pilot and my frank-talking Indiana bombardier will
take up the Civil War where Grant and Lee left off!"

Captain Alfred Janes, commander of the aircraft carrier
*Sussex,* looked thoughtfully at the chart spread on the table
of the Operations room. He tugged at his chin, eyeing the
strip of land that was the Jap beachhead.

"Of course, it's out of the question for us to get down at
low altitude and wreck this supply depot of theirs. There's
no earthly way we could, without losing valuable planes,
and we haven't enough as it is. No, Mapley—we'll have to
stay high and try to do the job with our bomb-sights." He
smiled slightly. "You get the idea?"

Commander Harold Mapley nodded.

"Yes, sir. Peck away at that spot so as to keep their men
and guns busy. While the Army mines the forward posi-

tions the Japs will move across. Then—" He gestured, his gray eyes hard. "Blooey the Japs!"

"Right." Captain Janes liked a man who minced no words. "We must act as if our very lives depended on that beachhead. Actually, we want them to land every man and every pound of stuff they can. When those land mines blow up and our men go into action, we'll recapture the Philippines from the yellow little runts!"

Commander Mapley grinned.

"I've got a pretty tough bunch working over that objective. If they ever find out I'm really not expecting them to wreck that beachhead, those youngsters will raise cain."

Janes looked interested.

"Yancey and Carhart, eh? Those two look good to me. But—" He paused, frowning. "Funny, but I've got a sneaking notion those two are good individually, but not so hot as a team. How about it?"

"They'll spark," Mapley assured his superior. "Believe me, they're a trio of wildcats."

Ten minutes later, Commander Mapley was glowering severely at his crew.

"What is the Navy coming to?" he barked. "I told you I wanted that beach blown to smithereens!"

Sam Carhart stirred.

"Got any ideas on how a ship can be held still so a bombardier can do his work?" The man's hard eyes shifted to Pete Yancey.

"Maybe some practice, somewhere?"

Pete Yancey flushed angrily.

"Commander Mapley, suh!" he protested. "Ah would

like to know if you have any ideas on how long a man is expected to hold a plane still against murderous archie fire. Maybe if we jettisoned some bombs out of the cargo and put in a few more gas tanks, maybe Ah could stall long enough for my bombardier to make up his mind on the target!"

Mapley opened his mouth to say something. And shut it again. Mapley didn't like signs of friction among crew members. But if it helped to focus this particular crew's interest on the target, it was all right with him.

"You have my orders, Yancey. You are not to lose your Devastator. Not under any excuse you can think up! That equipment is too valuable to set up for the Japs to knock down! Understand? Good! But—I want you to pound that beachhead until a fox would break his leg trying to cross it!"

"Yes, suh!"

"Right, sir!" Southern drawl and Indiana twang merged and clashed. The trio saluted smartly and withdrew.

Outside Sam Carhart grimaced disgustedly.

"Heck, if only I could fly my own plane! I'd see those bombs were planted, believe you me."

"Ah reckon we'll have to believe you—since you don't seem able to prove anything otherwise," Pete Yancey snorted. "Now, if Ah could only handle the bombin', as well as all the flyin'—"

Sunny Darville broke it up.

"Hey! Look at what is coming in!" he exclaimed.

A Devastator, so badly shot up that it fairly staggered in to a landing, was wobbling astern the carrier, its pilot fighting the sluggish plane into position for the set-down.

One wing was shattered badly. The hatches had been

shot away. Of the lowered landing gear, only one wheel remained. The fuselage was riddled from stem to stern.

The three of them watched, breathless, as the game pilot made his try, judged it beautifully, slid down on his one good wheel and contacted the arrestor hooks. The plane canted slightly as it slid along the deck, but a throttle blast leveled it again. Then the hooks had it, were slowing it, had stopped it. The damaged plane's deck crew raced anxiously to take over.

The pilot was haggard from loss of blood. A bullet streak furrowed his neck redly. The gunner-radioman swayed weakly in his pit, then collapsed into the arms of the crewmen.

"Look! The bombardier's office!" Sam Carhart said grimly.

From under the fuselage dangled something that they made out to be a human arm. Or what was left of it. So savagely had archie fire torn the bombardier's working space, the crewmen were able to reach in and tenderly remove the lifeless body.

"Looks like that lad held real still," Pete said. "I'd say maybe two shells hit through to him." His eyes touched over his own bombardier. "You'd like somethin' like that?"

"I'd like to carry out my orders," Sam snapped.

A flush stained Pete's cheeks.

"Ah'd admire to help you, suh. But Ah've got orders, too. *If* Ah could hold the ship steady against the buckin' when the archies explode. But Ah still have orders to save my ship! If only Ah could figure out some way to bring her in real low, so you'd have an easier time with yo' sights."

"Why, drat your eyes!" Sam blared. "You mean I'm not good enough to work my bomb-sight? If I had a pilot with nerve enough to fly me where I want, when I want, despite shells, Japs or high winds, I'd show you some bombing!"

"Break it up," Sunny said nervously. "People are staring at us. Crewmen, pilots, deck officers. We're fighting Japs, you fellows, not one another!"

They broke it up. But there was a thoughtful look on Pete Yancey's face when he watched the hangar crew trundle the crippled ship to the power elevators, for the trip down to the repair quarters.

"Ah wouldn't say that plane was worth much, would you?" Pete drawled to Sunny. But his eyes were watching Sam out of the corners. "Ah would say a crate like that could maybe be spared for—well, for a trip it might not come back from! Stripped of its bomb-sight, and other valuable equipment. What do you think, Sunny?"

Sam Carhart was not waiting to hear what Sunny Darville thought.

"I think you haven't got the nerve," he said harshly. "How do you like that, pal?"

For once Pete didn't answer. Instead, he crossed to the senior deck officer.

"Suh?" he addressed Lieutenant-Commander Miller. "Ah wonder if Ah could speak with you about that plane. You see, suh, we have very important orders for a certain mission. And we have orders not to wreck our plane. Now, that plane strikes me as bein' already wrecked. If you get my meanin', suh."

Miller got it, with eyes that widened in surprise.

"Let's hear the rest of it, mister."

Sam ad Sunny heard it, too. Sunny was patently awed. But Sam was grimly amused, his eyes studying Pete ever and again, as if to find where the joker was. He was still trying to find the joker when Miller gave his answer.

"I'll see if Captain Janes wishes to survey the equipment out—to the Japs," he said dryly. "I'll let you know."

But as the deck officer left, his eyes were round with astonishment. It isn't every day that you hear a man pleasantly asking to be sent to his sure death.

Commander Harold Mapley glanced at his wrist-watch in irritation.

"What is that, Miller? Of course! Any plans Carhart and Yancey may have for accomplishing their mission are all right! What the devil sort of question is that, mister?"

But Lieutenant-Commander Miller wanted to be certain. There might be questions, later. He did not intend that anybody would forget.

"Very good, sir. Now, about Morrison's flight—that N-Twenty plane. It just came in, shot to pieces. It would need a major overhaul, sir, and I think it best to—"

Mapley was on his feet, his face flushed with annoyance.

"You are to do as you think best, and not to bother me with it. Don't worry about my opinion, mister. Must I be plagued with every small detail of what goes on aboard this ship?"

"No, sir," Miller said mildly. "Then I may take it that any disposition I make of N-Twenty is my responsibility? And that any help I give Carhart and Yancey in carrying out a mission is your responsibility?"

Mapley shook his head at thought of the dozen things he had yet to do. Being executive officer aboard a warship the size and the importance of the *Sussex* is not a sinecure. Especially with a skipper like Captain Janes. And yet you still had to take time out to listen to the plaintive murmurs of junior officers!

"I believe you understand me, mister," Mapley said, his mind and his eyes already busy with other things. "That will be all."

"Thank you, sir." Miller saluted, did a neat about-face and marched out of his senior's cabin.

*   *   *   *   *

He saluted again when Pete Yancey and Sam Carhart climbed up into the hastily patched-up wreck that had come in several hours earlier. He saluted because he liked them, respected what they were doing—and because he knew the chances were strong he'd never again salute them.

He eyed the carefully cleared deck of the aircraft carrier.

"Snap into it, fellows! I'm with you in not advertising this stunt to anybody. Not even to those on this ship. If you are to succeed in this—er—mission, there must be no fore-knowledge. But—I can't keep the landing deck cleared for long!"

"Yes, suh," Pete said, with a half smile.

"Don't say 'good-by' too quick, sir," Sam added grimly. "I still have a hunch we don't take off! This is too good to be true! Imagine coming back and not hearing somebody say: 'What? You didn't bomb that beachhead out of existence!'"

Miller coughed.

"Imagine coming back!" he said under his breath.

Sunny Darville had climbed up to his seat. Now he stared at his crewmates, puzzled.

"Hey! How am I to ride with all this junk you have in here? What is this stuff, anyway?"

"Forgot to tell you, fella—but you aren't booked for this trip," Pete Yancey drawled.

He glanced up from a scrutiny of the erstwhile instrument board. Everything of any value had been removed.

"Be seein' ya, friend," Pete grinned.

Sunny raged. "I'm part of this crew."

"Chop it short, Sunny!" Sam warned. "Look—we don't need a radioman-gunner-observer for a crate that doesn't plan to gun, nor observe, nor radio, do we? Besides, your seat is needed for more bombs." He stared at Pete. "What are those bags, anyway? I mean, they're tied up. How do we bomb with them?"

"I'll explain later, suh," Pete said, stiffly formal. "Ready?" he called to Lieutenant-commander Miller.

He whirred the starting gear alive, relaxed visibly at the roar of the powerful motor.

"Thank you, suh!" He saluted Miller carelessly. "Want to step down, Mistuh Carhart?" he added with a taunting grin.

"Get going!" Sam howled. "What is this, a Southern Coffee Club? Let's go!"

The ship left the deck with a blasting roar and headed instantly for the northwest stretches of the Pacific—and the tip end of Luzon.

At precisely the same moment the plane bucked from the

archie barrage at Luzon's eastern edge, Commander Harold
Mapley was making a routine inspection aboard the *Sussex*.

"Ah, Miller! Hope you settled all those little details you
saw me about? Good! Very good!"

The executive officer trod the decks of his ship a few paces
further, then stopped when his eyes discerned the disconso-
late figure of one Sunny Darville.

"I thought you were out on that mission, Darville!"

"The only thing I'm out on is luck, sir," Sunny muttered.
"I'm clean out of that." He shrugged unhappily. "They
were a good pair, sir. If only they had straightened out their
squabbles."

Mapley stared at Miller, then at Sunny again.

"Would I be inquisitive if I asked you to explain just
what it is you are saying? *Who* were a good pair? *What*
squabbles would they have straightened out? *Why* are you
out of luck, young man?"

"Sam and Pete, sir," Sunny said. "Their bickering. And
—I was left out of their 'suicide flight,' so they'd have more
room for explosives." He sighed. "They'll get their objective
this time, sir. And probably Navy crosses and Congressional
medals, to boot!"

Mapley's features had congealed in horror. Now they
broke and swam in a half-dozen directions at once.

"Miller!" he blared, forgetting his naval etiquette.
"Miller!" He gripped his junior's arm and shook it.
*"What's happened?"*

Miller blinked nervously.

"At your express orders, sir, I assisted Carhart and Yancey
in arrangements to carry out their mission. Also—at your

orders, sir—I made disposition of N-Twenty. Carhart and Yancey are in N-Twenty, sir—with a superload of explosives. I—I don't fancy we shall be hearing from them again, sir. Not directly, that is." Mapley, his face drawn, signaled Miller to follow him. For once the executive officer was shaken to the depths.

Captain Janes listened, his eyes wide with astonishment.

"Of course, I told you to let them think it was our single purpose to wipe out that beachhead! But—confound it, man —I thought you would use some discretion!"

Mapley's glare at the junior officer said, "Later, for you!" Then aloud: "Anything we can do now, sir?" he asked Janes.

Captain Janes considered, then wrote a message hurriedly.

"Code that, and radio it to the American attacking force on Luzon. Yes, yes—the Japs will decode it! But who cares what they do an hour from now? We've got to let our forces know!

"Give them the story, and the approximate time you think those—those fool youngsters will be over the beachhead. They won't die in vain!"

\* \* \* \* \*

Pete Yancey banked sharply, lost some altitude in a fast slip, and then slammed on for the northwest tip of the island of Luzon. He spoke into the mouthpiece strapped to his chest.

"If you want, Sam, shed a few eggs on anythin' you see. Er—Ah mean, Ah don't think you'll have much chance after the next ten minutes."

"Or ever again after that, eh?" Sam Carhart asked

calmly. "No, pal—I am satisfied to ride it down. Any way at all, so long as it gets there. But—what about this junk in Sunny's pit?"

"Oh, that!" Pete said. "Ah thought we'd like to strap some bags of grenades on, as we parachute down. They aren't fused until we fuse 'em, see? No fear of their goin' off, when the chutes open." He chuckled. "But it'll give us somethin' to pitch with, as we sail down on those danged Japs!"

Sam grinned, then chuckled back.

"Nice idea, pal. By gum, I didn't think of that myself!"

He went back carefully, got the bags of grenades, passed one of them up to Pete's seat. The other bag he adjusted himself, about his waist. He touched the ripcord ring of his chute, nodded his satisfaction that all was in readiness.

For the next five minutes, they rode hard for the beach-head. As they were raising it, a flight of fast planes showed in the distance, to the south.

"Looks like Wildcats," Pete said flatly. "Navy fighters. And Airacobras, of the Army, with 'em. But we haven't the time to inquire."

He lost altitude rapidly, the nose of the plane hard down and the throttle cracked. The Devastator whistled faster and faster. The archie puffs that now bloomed up around the plane didn't more than rock it gently in its speeding plunge toward the target.

"Hey, Pete!" Sam said. "While I still think of it, I—" He paused, his eyes embarrassed. "Well, what I mean is, I take back all I said. Anyway, I think the Southerners are pretty good fighters. Some of them. My grandpappy said they were, and I guess he ought to know!"

He laughed a little uncertainly.

"Oh, heck! I'm sorry I sounded off, Pete. But I was afraid that a good pilot like you wouldn't want to have anything to do with a bum bombardier!"

Pete grinned back as he nosed the ship faster.

"And Ah thought you figured like you said, that Ah was just naturally a rotten pilot." He was silent a moment. "Maybe we could of been a good team, Sam!"

Pete yelled his mirth.

"Boy, maybe yo' grandpappy is a-lookin' down and thinkin': 'What in thunder is that boy shootin' at Japs for, when he has him a Johnny Reb dead to rights in that front pit!'" He sobered. "Ah wonder if they met—our two grandpappies—at Gettysburg?"

Sam shouted his astonishment.

"Hey! You never told me your grandfather was at Gettysburg!"

Pete grinned with pardonable pride.

"Ah thought perhaps you might of read about it, friend. Or maybe yo' grandpappy told you. That's where Ah get my name, suh. Peter Pickett. Pickett's Charge. Ever hear about that?"

"That's where my grandpop lost his leg!" Sam exclaimed. "In Pickett's Charge! The craziest, bravest, wildest infantry charge in history! And they danged near made it, too. That charge would have won the Civil War!"

"The *what* war?" came back the cold inquiry.

Sam grinned.

"The 'War Between the States,'" he amended. And chuckled loudly.

Both ends of the phones rang with laughter.

The Japs around the ammunition dump stared with anxious eyes at the sky, as the dive bomber's roar came to them above the pound of their own anti-aircraft. The Yank artillery was picking up also, was for some reason concentrating a blasting attack on a column of tanks—the Jap column that was so cunningly disguised with palm fronds and other greenery.

"They cannot know," one Nipponese officer said worriedly. "But—that noise! That airplane! It comes this way!"

"No plane can live through our anti-aircraft fire," another replied with contemptuous disdain. "It will be shot down, surely. And the men in it will die!"

"Of what benefit," wailed the first, "if it falls on us!"

"It—it cannot." But there was doubt in the answer, now. "No, it cannot, I assure you. You see—*Ai-ee!*"

The wail of despair came when the U. S. Navy dive bomber broke the cover of the horizon ahead, pursued by a swarm of Japanese attack planes. And off to the right coursed an angry group of fast Navy fighters.

"*Ai-ee! Ai-ee!*"

Japs broke from the ammunition dump and ran madly, despite the intensified Yank artillery fire. It was a drum barrage that was eating its way slowly along the jungle paths, ever nearer the camouflaged tank column and the all-important dump.

"Boy, lookee there!" Pete Yancey howled, his eyes keen

on the running Japs. "A tank column, camouflaged. Boy, maybe Captain Janes didn't know what he was talkin' about when he sent us to clean out this nest!"

"Stop debating and let 'em have it!" Sam laughed. "But give me some room to get my feet clear when I pull the ripcord! You're so close to the ground, I'll stub my toe on a tank!"

"Had to get there," Pete apologized. "Hang on, pal! Ah'm zoomin' for altitude!"

The Devastator all but shed its wings when Pete leaned back on the stick and reached for the sky. The plane shuddered, then plunged upward. Pete, his eyes fixed on the earth, yelled with the excitement.

"Ah'm goin' to peel her off right near where all those Japs are—*were*—standin'! See? Maybe that's important, that spot! Ah'll peel her off, and before she starts down, Sam—jump for it. And remember yo' grenades! For gosh sake, don't land with any of 'em left!"

"Okay, Skipper!" Sam shouted back. "And—happy hunting, fellow!"

Pete moved, and the plane veered on a wing, canted there as if the laws of gravity had been suspended. From the rear pit a figure shot out, legs and arms pinwheeling until the chute-cloth snapped wide. Another such form shot from the front hatch.

Sam started throwing his grenades as fast as he could grab them from the bag strapped to his middle, fuse them and let them go. But Pete held back, staring with startled eyes at the swarm of Navy attack ships that were slanting in, tracer streaking from their wings. Then, with a grin of hope that he had denied himself a moment before, Pete Yancey settled down to his own individual bombing.

The Devastator, loaded with its terrific bomb cargo, shot by the parachuting airmen like an express train. It seemed to merge with the ground, at a spot where a short time before a horde of Jap soldiers had milled. Then all creation seemed to bucket upward in a belching, flaming wall.

The Navy airmen were slammed aside by the hot breath of the explosion, were lifted hundreds of feet, and then they were dropping again. But under them now, instead of the camouflaged tanks, was a line of flaming junk.

Pete shed his remaining grenades hurriedly, when he saw the column of tanks detonating fuel tanks and explosives under the impact of that first sundering blast. Little yellow men scattered frantically, to drop in smoking bundles of clothing.

The U. S. Navy fighting planes were streaking lower and lower now, were adding their own detonation bombs to the uproar of confusion that had taken hold of the erstwhile Jap advance. Artillery fire, suspended to let the parachuting figures of Pete Yancey and Sam Carhart slip safely earthward, waited a painful lull, then blasted ahead with savage rapidity.

From the cover of the palms, perhaps a mile away, lurched the hidden Yank tanks, gouging a way through the forest and down into the nightmare that had succeeded the orderly Jap alignment. Navy planes flew close over them, spearing down with flaming wing guns to prevent any ground troops from recovering for a defense, no matter how futile.

The beachhead was isolated behind the yawning chasm that the exploded ammunition dump had dug. Not for a long time would invading Jap troops beach their boats and supply ships on that particular corner of Luzon. And the time was coming when they would be driven back to their own miserable homeland.

\*    \*    \*    \*    \*

Peter Pickett Yancey, recovered from the shock of his fall after his chute had collapsed against a tall palm, got gingerly to his feet and reached out his automatic. Carefully, he ducked from tree to tree, and all the time his voice shouted: "Sam! Ah say, Sam, can you hear me! Sam!"

A flat, smacking explosion went off almost in Pete's ear. A Jap sharpshooter plunged from an adjacent palm tree. Sam's dry Indiana twang sang out. "Take it easy, pal! Sure I could hear you. So could that Jap! I was drawing a bead on him, so I couldn't answer!"

Sam showed his smoking automatic in his hand. He oriented himself with a glance at the spots of sky that broke between the tropic forest.

"Get going, Johnny Reb," he snapped. "Come on, Pick, maybe we'll make it away! Somehow, we seem to have landed right in the path of an Army attack!"

"Started it, maybe," Pete guessed, as he followed after Sam. "Maybe they were just waitin' for us to blast that ammunition dump, and then they attacked. Lucky, huh?"

"Looks like more'n luck to me," Sam grunted. "Hey!"

Sam dropped when a small, speedy tank raced close, spun on swift treads. Pete dropped with him, but came to his feet when the turret of the tank swung up. His gun was trained carefully on the head that emerged.

"Don't shoot, Navy! Hold your fire! And climb in here! This is friends, pal! And all of it in very good American! Hop to it!"

Pete and Sam gasped, then raced for the turret and scrambled aboard. The soldier in charge stared at them with wide eyes, and shook his head.

"Darned if I didn't think I was crazy, joinin' up with the tanks," he said. "But darned if the Navy Air's not crazier!"

"This is a crazy war," Sam grinned. "Don't get your wind up because nothing makes much sense."

The Yank continued to shake his head as the tank whipped along toward the rear, past the advancing American column.

"Our Headquarters got word you two fellows mistook a feinted maneuver for the real thing," he finally explained. "Anyway, you boys did a heap of damage!"

"Good grief!" Pete Yancey gasped, as the situation came home to him. "Sam, we've been bulldozed! Captain Janes bamboozled us!"

Sam's grin was something to see.

"You're telling me! A couple of saps, that's us. Listen, Johnny Reb. Just think what we'll do when we're not kidding!"

Pete shuddered, holding on tight as the tank plowed along.

"You think about it!" he shouted above the motor's roar. "That bomb trap we just got out of will last me a lifetime!"

# BLUE WATER PILOTS

*By*

## PHILIP SHERMAN

OMMANDER C. K. BUCKLEY, of the Forty-ninth Scout Bomber Group, U. S. Naval Aviation, Canal Zone Area, tossed the official-looking yellow slip of paper on the Ready-Office desk, and half nodded at the two score or more eagle-eyed pilots and gunner-observers gathered about him.

"Well, there it is, fellows," he said. "Defense Operation Sixteen from now on, and for keeps. You've all got your orders and instructions. No need to go over them again. However, there's one part I do want to repeat—and paste it in your helmets! If any of you go down—and I mean, shot down, a forced landing, or an act of God—don't let a sound about your tough luck go out over the radio."

The commander paused, fished for a cigarette, and lighted up.

"That's important!" he continued, after a moment. "We don't know what enemy ships are on the waters in this neck of the world, and less about craft that may be under it. An SOS, and your position, will be heard by anybody listening in. It might be one of our own merchant ships close by. Her skipper might go soft-hearted and change course to give you aid.

"A U-boat may be waiting right there—and the loss would be more than it should have been. So remember! Use your radio *only* when you sight enemy craft, and go in to attack. There aren't to be any exceptions, no matter what. Well, shove off. Good luck, and try not to get your feet wet."

A final smile and a nod dismissed the group. Like an eager bunch of school kids busting outside for recess they went stampeding through the Ready-Office door and across the sun-flooded field of the Chagres Naval Air Station to the double row of Wright-powered Douglas "Dauntless" scout-bombers on the far side.

Two of the group that charged over to the waiting planes could well have been twins; only they weren't. Both stood five-eleven from flying boot soles to helmet tassel. Both tipped the beam at a hundred and eighty-five in their birthday suits. And both had hard, rugged faces that would not be good for advertising Arrow collars, but which wouldn't scare little children, either.

In background and family, though, they were as opposite as the poles. Lieutenant Jake Barker's first toy had been a gold-plated miniature battleship given him by his grandfather, the late Vice Admiral Barker, one of Dewey's line officers. He had grown up with gold-dust, gun-powder, and salt spray in his nose, and managed not to let any of it spoil him.

He had taken his lumps at Annapolis the same as any of the other fellows, not letting the fact that his grandfather had been a vice admiral either hinder him or help him. He had graduated fourth in his class in 'Thirty-five, and had gone straight into Naval Aviation.

For the last year he had been assigned to scout-bombers. Both high rankers and low rankers alike agreed that he was tops in any kind of a sky crate, but particularly in scout-bombers.

Ensign Mike Cheviski's father had been born in Poland, and his mother in Ireland. Mike had first seen the light of day on the tough side of Milwaukee. At five he had been living with an aunt. Flu had taken his mother and father away. From then on a smart head on his shoulders, and a hammer-head fist at the end of each arm had thought out, and pounded a way through life for him.

His football really had put him through Wisconsin. And it had been in the Navy-Wisconsin game that these two opposites had met for the first time—head-on. For a full sixty minutes they had beat the tar out of each other. And when they finally staggered off the field, with a tie score for their aches and bruises, the Fates must have decided that here was a pair that matched up good for things to come in the future.

Perhaps not, though. Perhaps it just so happened that Mike Cheviski got a sudden ambition for flying in his last year at Wisconsin. Perhaps it just sort of happened that he made a forced landing at the Great Lakes Naval Air Station that day when a recruiting drive was swinging into high gear.

And perhaps, a couple of years later, some dumb Navy Bureau clerk spilled a mess of file cards and put them back in the wrong places so that Jake's and Mike's cards were together. At any rate they suddenly met again at the Chagres Naval Air Station, and one thing led to another so that by the time the Japs hit Pearl Harbor they were teamed up together. And what a team!

"Oke, Mike?" Jake called back when both were in their ship, and she was quivering to go. "Got all of that hide aboard, Mister?"

"All I'm going to take!" Mike shouted back, and reached up to pull his glass hatch closed. "Maybe we have fun, huh?"

"And maybe this is another false alarm!" Jake Barker said, and put his hand on the throttle. "But remember about that radio. No tuning in Colon dance bands this trip. Keep it quiet."

"Yes, I catch," the gunner-observer agreed. "But that Madri-what's-his-name sure plays a mean tune, don't he? Me, I go for good music. Maybe I should have taken up music. I'da been wonderful, I got a hunch."

"As a piano mover!" Jake answered. "Draw in your belly! Here we go!"

The flight officer had dropped the flag before Jake Barker's ship. He nodded and rammed open the gate at the same time. The Dauntless gave one final shake, then charged forward. A quarter run across the field and Jake pulled it up into the air.

He circled once, got his wheels up, made a radio check with the field, then swung out over the blue Caribbean on the patrol course marked on his charts. In the rear pit Mike loosened his helmet strap, shifted his big frame to a more comfortable position, glanced longingly at the radio, and sighed.

"How about five minutes of it, Admiral?" he said, after a long minute. "Tuning in on a station don't change anything, you know. It ain't like we were—"

"'Ain't,' is right!" Jake replied. "Good gosh, what they turn out at Wisconsin these days! Nope! You ain't tuning in, son. And you ain't going to sleep, either. You stay awake this trip, and find us a U-boat."

"A U-boat, he says!" Mike exclaimed. "The Nazis are dopes, but not dopes enough to fool around with their steel fish in these waters. Like you said, it's probably another false alarm. Or maybe in Washington they figured our jobs are too soft. So they send us a scare to keep our courage up. You know what I figure, huh?"

Mike Barker didn't answer for a moment. He had suddenly seen something far out across the shimmering blue of the Caribbean. He took a second look and shrugged unhappily. Curse the sun bouncing off the water! It could turn a roller into a steaming battlewagon right before your eyes. Then wash it away just as quickly.

"So what do you figure?" he said.

"This is all a Nazi trick," Mike Cheviski said. "These Panama Canal scares that have been popping up all around. They want to keep us and the fleet units chasing around down here while they do things some place else."

"Such as where?" Jake asked. "Come on, Master Mind! Tell me all about it."

"Aw, bah!" Mike exclaimed. "How should I know? I ain't heard from Hitler in weeks. But, if you want my opinion, they ain't going to take any chances at the canal. They know they'd never make it."

"Okay—skip it," Jake said. "Get busy and check our course. I always like to know where I'm headed."

"Me, too, when you're up front there!" Mike retorted and went to work.

An hour or so later the Dauntless was just a small dot circling about in the air between a cloudless blue sky and a glass-smooth empty blue sea that stretched to the four horizons and spilled over. Up in the Dauntless Jake Barker and Mike Cheviski let tired, bored eyes roam about in all directions.

Despite their attitude and posture in the pits they were still on the alert for the first sign of anything. But they were becoming more and more fed up with staring at empty blue sea and empty blue sky. And the bright hope that had burned fiercely within them when Commander Buckley had ordered this special emergency patrol for all station aircraft had fluttered down to winking spark size.

Another day, another false alarm! That's the way it had been for three weeks now. Navy Intelligence was all steamed up with suspicions of terrible things brewing. And, true enough, a few mysterious events of late did give rise to all kinds of thoughts and suspicions.

Tankers bound southward never reached the other end of the Caribbean. Three of them had just up and disappeared without leaving a trace. A fourth, and the only one to do so, managed to flash out a garbled SOS. But her position wasn't clear, and when she was finally located there were only bits of floating wreckage, and not one single live man in the water.

More important than that—at least to the Naval Air Station at Chagres, was the fact that four planes never returned from these solo scouting flights. What had happened to them was a mystery. They must have gone down, certainly, for they had not returned to base.

But no radio had been received of their going down, and that had certainly seemed to indicate they hadn't run into enemy trouble. It had probably been a forced landing made so quickly of necessity that there had been no time to flash back any word. If the engine had gone out while they had been wave-skipping for a closer look at some spot in the blue water, there naturally wouldn't have been time to get to work on the radio.

Even so, that still didn't explain anything. No trace of wreckage had been found. What's more, a Dauntless would float for six or seven hours at least, even if she did crack up. A series of feather-light dural air tanks in the wings and tail make that possible.

And finally, where was the crash buoy that would float for days marking the general area where the plane had gone in? There hadn't been a single one of those orange-painted buoys spotted. Not one. In fact, not anything to give a clue to the loss of four planes and eight highly-trained Naval aviators!

"It's no use, Admiral!" Mike's voice suddenly cut through Jake's thoughts. "We're just using up Government gas and oil. How much longer you figure to keep us out?"

Jake opened his mouth to make some kind of reply, but

he swallowed the words unspoken. At that exact moment
the Wright in the nose chose to start gasping and coughing.
Jake's eyes flew over the instruments, but they were all in
order. He jazzed the throttle and the compensator, and
even switched over to the emergency tank.

But nothing did any good. The Wright sputtered a few
seconds longer and then went as dead and as silent as a
frozen fish.

"If this is for a scare, you can skip it!" Mike called out in
a tight voice. "I don't feel like being kidded today."

"You're not being kidded!" Jake replied, and glared at
the instrument panel. "This is the real thing. Puff some air
in your life-jacket, Mike. It's us this time."

Jake Barker caught his breath as that last remark of his
faded away to the echo. He had meant it for just a wise-
crack, but the sound of it in his ears suddenly made his
throat go a little dry. A creepy, clammy sensation prickled
the back of his neck.

For no earthly reason he could figure the Wright had
pulled up cold, and the Dauntless was sliding down to sit
on the stretch of sun-flooded blue water below. Was this,
then, what had happened to four other planes of Forty-
nine? Had they also been just sailing along, and then *bingo*
—the works?

On impulse he turned around and looked at Mike. The
former Wisconsin football star was grinning, but there was
a tightness about the corners of his mouth and his eyes. And
there was just the tiniest of white spots in each sun-bronzed
cheek. The man met Jake Barker's gaze for a moment, then
shifted it longingly to the radio, and sighed heavily.

"The commander shouldn't have issued that order," he muttered unhappily. "Don't know as I can swim that far."

Jake made no comment. He simply shrugged and turned front to pay attention to his knitting. There was some eight thousand feet of air between the Dauntless' belly and the blue Caribbean, but for all the good that did them, as far as gliding to land was concerned, they might just as well be eight feet in the air.

Just the same, though, Jake flat-turned around toward the west and nosed in the shallowest dive possible. After all, every foot westward they traveled before they sat in the drink might prove to be a big help later on. Just how, he didn't know, but it was better than gliding away from one source of possible rescue.

And so, holding the ship steady, he took a moment to blow air into the tube of his rubber life-jacket. Then he relaxed as much as possible and began casting his eyes about the reaches of blue water below, and the endless expanse of blue sky overhead.

He saw nothing but the brilliance of the golden sun above him, and its shimmering reflection on the water below. There was not a single sign of anything else, and before he realized it he was thinking bitter thoughts about Commander Buckley, and his confounded Defense Operation Sixteen.

It was fine, an efficient and effective operation order so long as props kept ticking over. On a single three- or four-hour patrol the planes of Forty-nine could cover an area of thousands of square miles in size. And if enemy craft of any description were sighted, a word or two over the radio could bring a powerful attacking force to that point in a short time. Sure, an efficient and effective plan of defense operation *if* props kept turning over.

That was just the point. The area to be patrolled was so huge that at no time was any plane in sight of another plane. And so, when one went down it went down alone, and nobody knew about it until all planes had returned to base. The "no radio" order fixed that.

"Bad business!" Jake said. "The patrol courses should overlap at some point, just to check on ships in the air. A fellow could crack up and sink before the others even knew his ship was missing."

"Well, don't!" Mike suddenly boomed in his ear. "Just skip that part, will you? There's more than just water down there. Barracuda and things that don't like me at all. Funny about that engine, ain't it? Got any idea, Admiral?"

"It just got tired," Jake answered. Then clenching one fist, "But when I get back and get my hands on those mechanics . . . Well, sit tight, Mike. I'll try and make this a nice one."

"Never mind trying!" Mike instructed. "Just be sure and *do* it!"

A minute or so later the Dauntless was in the water and down slightly by the nose. It had been a beautiful landing, but that small success didn't help Jake Barker's spirits any. He wiggled out of his parachute harness, made sure the crash buoy would bob free if the plane should sink, then shoved open his glass hatch, and unsnapped his goggles.

"You bring a deck of cards, by any chance, Mike?" he asked. "We might be here for a spell."

Mike laughed and made a face.

"You cheer a guy up so! No. And I didn't bring along any rubber boat, either. Think there's a chance of them finding us? Or a ship, maybe? I get seasick awful easy."

"Don't fall apart," Jake said. "There's lots of time. A good two hours anyway before the others get back to base and don't find us there. Another hour for them to get out here. Say four hours to cover everything. Four hours sitting here isn't going to kill us. And a surface ship might come along."

"Who's falling apart?" Mike asked. "I was only asking a question. You don't have to go babying me. I'm just thinking the things you're thinking—only out loud. And I mean about the four other ships that sat down some place. That engine went awful suddenlike, Admiral, you know."

Jake nodded somberly and absently fingered the throttle. He was thinking of sabotage, himself, yet at the same time trying not to. How anybody could have possibly tampered with the ship was beyond him. His mechanics were as loyal to the Navy as he was himself.

Also, it was a hard and fast rule with both Mike and himself to give their plane a thorough check before taking to the air. They had done it again this time, and there hadn't been so much as a hint of anything going wacky. And yet, the power plant had passed out as though it had been hit with an axe—and with all the instruments indicating that everything was in order!

He combed his brain for an idea of what might go wrong with an engine, and not show up on the instruments. The only thing he could think of was something going haywire with the carburetor. But the engine passing out so quickly would prevent the direct cause from being known until an inspection was made.

True, the temperature and pressure needles had shifted position on their respective dials, but that was only natural because the engine had stopped. But the gas gauges had been okay, the oil, too, and the feed pressure where it should be. So, it must have been something tricky that—

Jake killed the thought cold as Mike's beefy fist came down on his shoulder, and the fog-horn voice boomed in his ears.

"Will you look, Admiral! Off to port, there! We're getting company, and I don't feel so good. Lookit the size of that thing!"

A lump of ice took the place of Jake Barker's heart as he snapped his head around to the left. Not sixty yards away was a stretch of frothy water, and in the middle of it a submarine was surfacing. It was a submarine right enough, but it looked almost as big as a cruiser as it pushed up out of the blue water until the conning tower, bridge, and fore and aft decks were awash. The conning tower hatch opened up and the head and shoulders of a man appeared.

"Hey!" came Mike Cheviski's hoarse whisper. "It wouldn't be one of ours, would it?"

"Not that big," Jake heard his own voice reply. "No. She's not one of our pig-boats. She's German, that's what she is!"

"This would happen to me!" Mike said. Then quickly, "Look! I can swivel my guns around. Do you think I should—"

"Don't be a plain fool!" Jake retorted, not taking his eyes off the U-boat that was mushing in closer to the downed plane. "You'd only get us a couple of shells that would settle everything. We've got to take this!"

"But that don't mean I have to like it!" Mike answered. "Ain't it fine? I see my first enemy, and that's all I can do about it!"

"And see that you don't do anything else!" Jake said, and stood up in the seat.

The U-boat was close alongside, now. Only a few yards of open water separated the wing-tip and the glistening sleek hull of the underwater rattlesnake. A couple of other figures popped up through the opening conning tower hatch, and went scrambling down the bridge ladder and along the deck.

They grabbed hold of the Dauntless and held her off. The flat-faced man who remained head and shoulders above the conning tower rim smiled at Jake and Mike and motioned with one hand.

"Climb out and come aboard!" he called in heavily-accented English. "Step lively, please."

"Don't bother about us!" Mike Cheviski boomed out. "We're doing all right. You just run along, and—"

Something made sound and flame in the German's hand, and something that sounded decidedly unpleasant whined, passed over the heads of the two Navy aviators.

"He means it!" Jake Barker said. "You keep that big hatch of yours battened down, will you?"

As Jake prepared to climb out onto the wing he reached down into the pit, slipped the specially-made weights over the radio code book, and quickly tossed the whole business over the side. It sank out of sight instantly, and there was a howl of rage from the U-boat.

"I should kill you for that, you swine!" the German roared. "I should leave you to sink and be food for the barracudas!"

Jake looked at him, cold and flint-eyed.

"Did you think I would make you a present of it?" he said.

"Close your mouth, and come aboard!" the Nazi instructed. "One more bit of foolishness, and you *will* be very sorry!"

Faces blank of expression, but with dull aches in their hearts the two Americans crawled out on the wing, caught hold of hands reached out to them, and stepped aboard the U-boat. No sooner had their feet touched the water-washed steel than a couple of German sailors stuck Lugers in their ribs, and frisked them for side arms. They found none, and said so to the commander, standing in the conning tower opening.

The senior officer looked unhappy, then rasped out words in his native tongue that were too fast for Jake Barker to follow, and were ten thousand feet over Mike Cheviski's head. The action that followed was a good enough translation, though.

One of the sailors herded them aft and up the conning tower bridge ladder. There they were halted while the commander, looking thoroughly un-Nazi in grease-smeared, torn uniform, and with unshaven face, inspected them both with close-set piggish eyes. Presently he grunted and popped down out of sight as though a trapdoor had been sprung under his feet.

The sailor jabbed Jake and Mike with his Luger and pointed up the short ladder to the lip of the conning tower hatch. Both got the idea at once and climbed up, then down the vertical ladder into the bowels of the U-boat.

The stench of burned fuel oil, and the acrid smell of spilled battery acid, hit them like a wet blanket to clog their throats, and make their eyes smart. In the brief period of time allowed, Jake glanced about the control room of the U-boat into which they had descended, and his reaction was instantly one of amazement and reluctant admiration.

Familiar with the close quarters aboard most American submarines, where the crew members practically have to turn sideward to pass, to step into the interior of this U-boat was like stepping into the engine room of a battleship. She was positively ballroom size inside her hull, and Jake shivered slightly in spite of himself when he thought of the terrific amount of death and destruction she could pack aboard.

He was allowed only a sweeping glance around, however. Fingers closed on his arm almost instantly and he was led through a steel compartment door, and along a grated companionway. Halfway along he was halted, swung right, and none too gently shoved into a cabin.

The U-boat's commander sat behind a bolted-to-the-deck desk that faced the door. He had taken off his battered cap, revealing that not a single hair was on his egg-shaped head. Not even any fringe over the ears or at the nape of the neck. In a movie he would look as funny as they come. In his

U-boat he didn't look funny at all. He looked cruel, sinister, and deadly.

He waved the two Americans to places on the steel drop-bench fastened to the wall, and grunted at the two escorting sailors. That obviously meant for them to leave, for they left in a hurry, swinging the steel door softly shut behind them.

The commander smiled at the two comrades, seemed about to speak, but bent over an inter-compartment phone instead. He rapped out something at top speed. Jake caught only two words of what was said, but those two set his brain to spinning over in wonder. They were, "dismantle" and "stow." Then the commander snapped off the connection and gave them his piggish-eyed attention again.

"Well, gentlemen," he said, "you may now start regretting the folly of your stupid Government for making war on *der Fuehrer!*"

A long moment of silence followed the German's words. He goggled at the Americans triumphantly, as though he half expected to see them both drop to their knees, pleading. They did nothing but return his look. Then Mike Cheviski unbattened his hatch a little as he shifted his big frame on the hard steel bench.

"*Der Fuehrer?*" he echoed. "You mean that bow-legged little slob who cracks the whip over you? Listen! When are you dopes ever going to get wise? That *Fuehrer* of yours is just a—"

Mike clapped his mouth shut quick, for the Luger had popped into the U-boat commander's hand again, and it was pointed straight at the third button down on Mike's flying jacket.

"You will be taught manners later," the German said in a harsh, blood-chilling voice. "For the present you will speak only when I tell you to. So, silence from you, swine!"

"Okay, okay," Mike mumbled. "Put the cannon away!"

The German left the "cannon" right where it was and focused his eyes on Jake.

"You could have made things easier, Lieutenant," he said softly, "had you not tossed what you did over the side. Small loss, however. I already have a copy of your radio code. I do not believe that it has been changed in so short a time."

Jake started slightly, and the German looked at him, bright-eyed, and smiled.

"You are surprised, Lieutenant?" he murmured. "You think this is a chance meeting, eh? But, no. Let me assure you that I have been waiting for you. And—"

"As you waited for the other four?" Jake blurted, hardly conscious that he had spoken. "Then our engine was—"

Jake didn't finish. He stumbled to a stop and stared incredulously at the German's smiling lips and his nodding head.

"You see?" the Nazi presently echoed, with a gesture. "You see what fools you Americans are to war upon the Reich? You are no match for us. No race in the world is the equal of Germans."

Jake felt something snap in his brain. He knew he was a fool, but thoughts of the *Reuben James,* and the *Kearny,* and a few other Navy ships crowded his head. He remembered a lifeboat he had sighted just two days before Pearl Harbor. The five men, two women, and the child, had all been dead. Eighteen days without food or water under a burning sun had been too much for them.

"How about the rodent race?" he bit off, tight-lipped.

The German blinked and pin-points of fire showed in his eyes. Then he chuckled softly, shrugged, got up from his chair and moved slowly around the desk.

"Your dog companion, Lieutenant," he murmured, "I would expect such words from his mouth. But from you, it is a different matter. So!"

The last was little more than a hiss, and the German's hand came out so fast that Barker didn't even have time to think about ducking. The barrel of the Luger caught him a stinging swipe on the left side of his face, and he went spilling head over heels off the iron bench.

"That is your first lesson!" the German snarled. "Before I have finished with you, you will have received many more!"

Flat on his back on the deck, and with bells ringing in his head, Jake Barker stared stony-eyed up at the man. Then he heard Mike Cheviski's booming voice, and saw the big fellow of Polish-born parents go into action.

"Hey! You can't do that to my pal! Not with me around, you can't!"

The big fellow's arm was like a bull-whip, or maybe a curved bit of lightning. The fist on the end of it smacked the German on the ear and almost tore his head off. The startled U-boat commander did a complete cartwheel clear of the deck, then crashed up against the compartment wall.

The Luger made a clanking sound as it hit the steel, and it went flying from his hand. It dropped four feet from Barker, and his spinning brain screamed for him to lunge for it. Perhaps he started to. He never knew for sure. For in the same split second the compartment door whanged open and the place was filled with armed German sailors.

Jake saw Mike swinging with both fists, knew in a hazy sort of way that he himself had regained his feet and was swinging at Nazi faces. Then the U-boat seemed to do an outside loop or something, and fall down on the top of his head. There was a loud noise in his brain, a great sheet of white light, and then there was neither sound nor light. There was just nothing. . . .

When Jake again opened his eyes his first thought was that he was in jail. He was sitting on a steel bench in a room that had a steel floor, ceiling, and walls. And a steel door. Also, there were steel bracelets about his wrists and ankles. They were fastened to chains which in turn were fastened to rings in the steel wall.

On the opposite side of the room, that was barely lighted by a small caged blue electric light bulb in the ceiling, was Mike Cheviski. The ex-football star was also handcuffed and chained. He had lumps and cuts all over his face, and one eye was closed and surrounded by a beautiful purple sunset. But as he saw Jake Barker look at him the good eye lighted up, and the bruised lips parted in a grin.

"Hi, Admiral!" he said. "We kind of lost the ball on downs, I guess. There was too many, and too tough. How do you feel?"

"I don't know, yet," Jake muttered, and strived to recall memory. "What happened, and where are we?"

Mike's good eye popped wide.

"You don't remember?" he echoed. "They must have slugged you hard, the bums! Don't you remember? We had a forced landing, and a U-boat surfaced and took us aboard. We made wise-cracks to the commander, and he didn't like it. He did something about it. The whole gol-darned German Navy fell on us.

"When they got worn out hitting us they threw us in here. Couple of hours ago, I guess. But, there's three, four of them lugs that ain't feeling so good either right now, I bet you. You darn near threw one man right through the hull. I bet he don't know his own name for a week. Can you hit 'em, Admiral!"

Memory was coming back to Jake Barker in a rush. He made no comment. He hurt all over, inside and out. He checked over everything up to the time the lights went out. Then he sighed.

"I guess we both talked too much, Mike," he said. "A prisoner should keep his mouth shut. You say, two hours? We been underway that long? We're moving now, and below surface, too."

"Two hours, maybe lots longer—I don't know," Mike said. "Things have been kind of hazy. When the brain began clicking we were underway, and below. What do you figure comes next? Kind of crazy, isn't it?"

"It's at least not funny," Jake answered. "But what do you mean by that?"

"You and me," Mike said with a faint puzzled frown. "I

always heard that the Nazis never went out of their way to save a life. And we gave them a little trouble to boot, too. What they keeping us locked up for? Why ain't we at the bottom wrapped up in an anchor chain? Like a cock-eyed dream, ain't it, huh?"

"Maybe you've got something there, Mike," Jake murmured, and frowned a little, too. "Perhaps his nibs thinks he can use us."

"How?" Jake wanted to know. "I don't know a thing about running one of these things. And no Kraut slob is going to teach me, either. But, hey! Maybe that's an idea."

"What's an idea?"

"We could make like we'd seen lots of sea duty on our pig-boats," Cheviski said eagerly. "And get them to put us to work. Then maybe we might get the chance to open a valve, or something, and send this thing to the bottom, and—"

"And us along with it!" Jake cut in.

Mike's lips shut tight and his face went unhappy.

"Yes, that's right," he sighed. "I guess that wouldn't be such a good idea, would it?"

"No, it wouldn't," Jake said flatly. "But look, Mike. No wise stuff, or funny stuff, from here on. Let's not be dopes again. We've got to play this one close. It's big, Mike. I've got a hunch it's plenty big. Did you hear him say he already had a copy of our radio code book? And he just about admitted that he knew all about the four other planes we lost. And that our engine was fixed, and he was waiting for us. We're the next on the list, Mike. We've got to play it close, and do something about it."

Mike gulped, swallowed hard, and looked uncomfortable.

"Yes, he did say those things, didn't he?" he finally got out. "And that engine certainly pooped out like no other engine I ever heard. So they got a spy back at the Chagres Station, huh? Would I love to get my lunch hooks on him! Wonder who he could be?"

"What's it to us, now?" Jake said gloomily. "I'm wondering more what he could do to an engine that we couldn't spot on our check? But he certainly knew Operation Sixteen inside and out. It's three strikes on us for not sighting this thing from the air. I'm glad Buckley isn't here. He'd have a word or two to say about that fumble."

"Who says it was a fumble?" Mike asked. "Ten to one this tub's commander knew the time our engine was going to poop. And he stayed deep until we were in the water, or just about in. And even Admiral King wouldn't spot anything deep down with the way that sun was doing things with the water.

"Don't go taking it hard, Admiral. It wasn't our fault for not seeing things. But I'd sure like to know what's coming next. I'm getting plenty tired sitting here on this steel. And don't try to get these things off. I did, and they don't come. Gosh! Handcuffed and chained inside a sub! Now ain't that a sweet set-up!"

Jake Barker just nodded and let it go at that. His aches and pains were beginning to step it up, and his brain was a swirling torment. It wasn't that fear was getting his nerves. It was more the mysterious situation in which he found himself.

True, Uncle Sam was in the war, and no man living can

name a single thing that can't happen in war. But, up to now, things had happened to other people at other places. That war had actually come this close to the Canal Zone, and had reached out to tap Mike and himself on the shoulder was still a little difficult to believe.

Perhaps it was because it had all happened so suddenly. But, suddenly or slowly, it *had* happened, and. . . . And as Mike had said, "What comes next?"

As though the gods listening in decided to answer that question at once there came the click of the door lock and the door swung open. Framed in the opening was the undersea craft's commander.

For a fleeting instant Jake Barker felt joy in his heart. The Nazi had quite a lump on the left side of his face, and the left eye was considerably more puffed than the right. But savage hatred glittered in both eyes, and the crooked smile on the lips held all the mirth of an exploding bomb.

"So you do not feel so smart, now, eh?" the Nazi jeered and came inside. "A little lesson and your tongue doesn't wish to wag so, no? You Americans are fools! You have no brains. You never realize you are defeated until it is too late. When you are dead. It is so stupid."

The man paused as though challenging either of them to speak. They said nothing. They just stared and waited. The Nazi beamed and nodded.

"Good!" he continued. "You learn quickly, at least. I come to tell you that we make port very soon. You will be taken ashore and put to work. Hard work. But it is what you deserve. I have things to do, or I would explain all this to you later. So I do it now. If you wish to live you will do as you are told. If you wish to die, your wish will be granted —but not in a pleasant way. Remember that I have made it clear to you. And you, Lieutenant—"

The man paused long enough to focus his small piggish eyes on Jake Barker.

"And you, Lieutenant," he repeated, "have it within your power to make things easy for this dog, here, and others you are to meet. You will be able to save them a lot. Even their lives, no doubt. Keep that in mind when I speak to you again. That is all."

With a curt nod the U-boat's commander wheeled around and went out the door, crashing it shut behind him. Jake stared blankly at the closed door, then at Mike.

"You heard that?" he asked and frowned.

"Yes, I heard it," Mike Cheviski said, with a shrug. "He says *we* got to remember things!"

For perhaps an hour or more the two Americans sat silently in their steel-walled prison, each busy with his own thoughts, and not getting any place at all. Thinking simply added to the torment in their heads, and thickened the shroud of baffling mystery that hung over the past, the present, and particularly the future.

A thousand times over Jake Barker took the Nazi's words apart and examined them closely. And each time he reached the same conclusion—one that seemed a downright impossibility. In short, that Mike and he were being taken to some place where the pilots and gunner-observers of the four other Forty-nine planes were held captives at hard labor.

That seemed to be it—but impossible. However, the crazy

twist was the U-boat commander's crack about him, Jake
Barker, having the power to make it easier. And to remember that when the time came.

"I give up!" he suddenly said aloud.

"I did that hours ago!" Mike Cheviski muttered. "I . . .
Hey! We're going up. I can feel her. We must be making
that port he was telling us about. But where in thunder
could this thing go in the time it's had?"

Jake didn't answer. He didn't have time to answer. The
door was opened again, and two armed sailors came
inside. There was a surly anger in their eyes, too, and a
strip or two of surgeons' tape stuck on their flat moon-
shaped faces instantly explained why they bore no affection
for the two Americans. Jake looked at them calm-eyed, but
Mike Cheviski grinned from ear to ear.

"You both been in a little trouble, huh?" he taunted.

They glowered, but said nothing. While one stood back
where he could use his Luger on either of them, the other
unfastened the chains from the wall rings, but made no
move to take off wrist and ankle bracelets. Mike scowled,
held out his wrists, and opened his mouth, but Jake beat
him to it.

"Pipe down!" he insisted. "Don't start anything here!"

"Yes, okay," Mike said, and lowered his hands.

The sailor with the gun stepped to one side and jerked
his head at the open door. The other guard, who held the
chain ends as though driving a pair of horses, shook the
chains savagely and delivered two swift kicks where they
would get instant results.

Choking back the red anger that surged up in him, Jake

flashed Mike a warning glance, moved forward to the door, and through it into the companionway.

As he walked back toward midships he felt the U-boat come to a quivering stop. Orders were shouted hoarsely, and a few seconds later a gust of fresh air came sweeping down the opened conning tower hatch to push back the stench of the U-boat's innards. A moment later more orders were shouted, and there was the harsh grind of gears, the whine of an electric-driven deck crane, and a hundred and one other metallic sounds.

The sailors halted Jake and Mike just short of the control-room ladder reaching up into the conning tower. They stood there while the U-boat's commander, shaved, shined, and spick and span in tropical whites, went monkey style up the ladder with a couple of his junior officers at his heels.

When the last pair of booted feet disappeared Jake and Mike got kicked again, and were started up the ladder.

No sooner had Jake Barker's head and shoulders lifted above the conning tower rim, than he took a sweeping look about him. And no sooner did he take the sweeping look than he almost lost his hold in dumbfounded amazement.

The huge U-boat was made fast to a pier that extended out into a small lake completely surrounded by tropical growth. Not only surrounded but reaching out overhead so that not more than pencil-thick beams of light were able to sift down through entwined green masses of foliage.

But his first surprise was no more than a mild shock compared to the jolt he got when he glanced forward. It was really two jolts. The first was the sight of a sister U-boat tied up at the same pier. And the second was from what he saw down through the slowly opening bow hatch covers of the U-boat on which he stood.

Down in the craft was the dismantled Dauntless that he had flown out from Chagres Station! Wings, tail section, fuselage, and engine, were all separate and neatly packed together down in the hold. And even as he stared, unbelieving, the block and tackle from the deck crane was slowly lowered down through the hatch opening.

"They salvaged the ship!" he said in a hoarse whisper. "Took her right up out of the water. I—I can't believe it!"

"Me neither!" came Mike's equally hoarse whisper in his ear. "Gosh! These Nazis know lots of tricks, don't they. They . . . Look! Ashore! The boys from Forty-nine! There's Denton Duffy, and Arnold Clinton, and Ed Allen. Hey, I got to hit somebody. I just got to!"

A red film was pouring into Jake's brain as he stared shoreward. But he still had sense enough left to jab an elbow warningly into Mike's belly.

Ashore were six figures in little or no clothing. Their faces were blackened by stubble beards, and their bare backs were crossed and recrossed by long red welts from a lash. Their arms were free, but there were irons about their ankles with a connecting chain just long enough to allow for a little short of an ordinary step.

Two giant Germans, each armed with a wicked bull-whip and a holstered Luger, were watching over them while they hoisted up long flat-hewn logs on their shoulders and went staggering up a path cut through the heavy tropical growth. Despite the stubble beards, and the pain and fatigue drawn faces, Jake instantly recognized six of the missing eight members of Forty-nine.

"Yes, they are your comrades, Lieutenant. They do not look very happy, do they?"

Jake dragged his eyes from the frightful sight to look down at the U-boat's commander on the bow deck.

"You rat!" he shouted, and gripped the bridge railing until his knuckles showed white. "Come up here and I'll kill you with my two hands!"

The German leered and shook his head sadly.

"So that little lesson did not help, eh?" he murmured. "Too bad. Well, after you have spent a night with your friends, you may change your mind. I will see you in the morning, Lieutenant, perhaps!"

Rage engulfed Jake and he started to lunge forward. But all he succeeded in doing was to crash flat on his face as the sailor jerked viciously on his chains.

Stunned and pretty much winded he was not able to follow just what happened in the next few minutes. He realized in a confused sort of way that Mike and he were herded off the U-boat, and marched up the pier and onto spongy ground. The sweet, stifling smell of the tropics filled his nostrils, and he knew that three or four times he stumbled to his knees, and was quickly booted up onto his feet again.

He heard Mike's voice at his elbow, but it was just a meaningless sound in his ears. Then finally he was shoved from behind and sent pitching forward on his face. He got a kick in the ribs that seemed to drive his heart right out past his back-bone. Then Mike was helping him up to a sitting position, and haggard, stubble-beard-covered faces were swimming around in front of his eyes.

"Easy does it, Admiral!" Mike was soothing in his ear. "You kind of forgot we were supposed to keep quiet. Here, have a cigarette, and . . . Why those crooks! They took both packs I had on me. Hey! Any you got a butt for him?"

"Never mind, Mike," Jake heard himself say. "I'm okay."

Then he was looking at the six missing members of Forty-nine. He clamped down hard on his aches and pains, and shook the fog from his brain.

"Hello fellows," he said, and forced a grin. "Where's Dickey and Stafford?"

Silence greeted the question for a moment, then a red-headed ensign named Ed Allen licked his cracked lips and spoke.

"They're dead!" he said harshly. "Refused to work, and tried to fight the guards. They got shot down like dogs. That was four days ago—or maybe it was four years. You lose track of time here."

"Did the same thing happen to all you fellows?" Jake Barker asked, as he swept them with his eyes. "I mean, the engine went, and you sat down, and a U-boat took you aboard, and the plane, too?"

"Just that," Ed said, with a weary nod. Then pointing over toward Jake's left. "There they are, all four of them. Yours will be there by morning."

Jake twisted around and stared in the direction of the pointing finger. Not a hundred yards away and lined up prop to rudder were four Douglas Dauntless scout-bombers.

The section and pilot markings had been removed, painted over with battle gray, but apart from that nothing else had been changed.

The planes were resting on a fifty-foot-wide runway made of flat hewn logs placed side by side and bolted together. From the lead plane the runway extended forward through a sort of cleared tropical tunnel for a distance of well over a quarter of a mile. By leaning forward and straining his eyes Jake could see that the opening at the far end now was turned a blood-red by the rays of a dying sun.

"We made that runway, all of it!" he heard Ed Allen's tired but bitter voice drone in his ears. "You work, or else. If I could only just get one crack at them before I fold up for keeps! Hoping for that chance is all that keeps us going. But each day the chance gets less and less."

Mike muttered something deep in his throat, but Jake didn't pay attention. He was still staring at the parked planes, and at his immediate surroundings.

A thatched roof covered the spot where he and the others sat hunched on the ground, and the chains of each man were fastened to iron ring-rods driven deep in the ground. In the distance he could hear voices speaking in German, but he could not see the speakers. Or anything else, for that matter, because all was blotted out by thick growth. It was like being under a gigantic tropical growth tent with the air so close and heavy you had to breathe it in chunks.

Suddenly he realized that he had ripped off his tunic and other bits of his clothing, and that they were wound about the chains connecting his ankles. He stared at what he had done, then started ripping the seams to get the clothing free of the chains. When he had finished he was wearing only shorts, shoes, and socks. And he still felt as though he was smothering in a dozen woollen blankets.

"Why?" he suddenly asked of nobody in particular. "Anybody know what their game is, and where this place is? And those two U-boats! That's a lake where they are!"

A thin, hawk-faced lieutenant named Arnold Clinton laughed mirthlessly.

"Sure, we know *all* the answers!" he said bitterly. "And so will you, before you've been here a day. That's the best part of their fun, curse them! Telling us all about it. They're not worrying. They know they have us cold. They know, as we know, that we're going to die here. Yes! While *they* blast the Colon end of the Canal higher than a kite, and block it so it'll take months, and maybe years to clear. Oh, they've got it all worked out sweet. And they can get away with it, too!"

"Block the Canal?" Mike echoed in amazement. "They must be kidding you. They couldn't get U-boats within twenty miles of the Canal. We'd blow 'em right out of the water."

"Think so?" Arnold Clinton said, turning on him. "Well, I don't, see? I know what they're going to pull. They've boasted about it enough to all of us. You fool! That rat, Ensign Max Miller, was here just yesterday. I thought I'd go mad when I saw him. And to think I once bunked at Pensacola with that dirty rodent!"

Jake had to try twice before he could get the words out.

"Max Miller?" he cried. "Of Section Two? But he just

got back from sick leave this morning. You say he was here? That he—"

"Is why we're all here!" Ed Allen cut in harshly. "Max Miller is a Nazi agent. He admitted it to us yesterday. What's more, he said that you'd be with us soon. Both of you. He's the one that fixed our engines—but good. He told us how. It was simple. I read about it once in a magazine somewhere.

"He makes a little bag out of cheese cloth soaked in paraffin, fills it with water, seals it, and drops it into the gas tank. In about two hours, the raw gas eats away the paraffin and the water gets into the gas. When the engine sucks it into the carburetor float chamber your engine is all done!"

Mike bunched his big fists.

"I remember, now, Admiral, seeing him walking away when we went to our ship this morning! Him, huh? Well, I never liked his looks much, or him either! The yellow Nazi!"

"He's the one!" Arnold Clinton said. "He was here yesterday. Came in on one of those U-boats. Been one of Hitler's boot-lickers for years, only he didn't put it that way. And know something else? They've had this set-up here for U-boats ever since the war started!

"There are no Nazi U-boat bases on this side of the Atlantic, huh? So! Lindbergh and Senator Wheeler should have a look, is all I've got to say!"

"But the Canal!" Jake Barker persisted. "How are they going to work it? And where is this place, anyway?"

"This is a cay about a hundred and fifty miles off Costa Rica, as near as I can figure out," Allen spoke up. "And about two hundred from the Canal. There's an underground entrance so that the U-boats can come up in that little lake. Whether it's natural, or whether they cut it, I don't know.

"Anyway, they've got everything here from machine-gun bullets to aerial torpedoes. A perfect hideout way off the beaten track. I haven't heard the engine of a single patrol plane since I've been here, and that's two weeks.

"See those planes? They're fitting torpedo racks to them. Two, mind you, for each plane! When their Zero Day arrives—and it must be soon—they're going to put markings on them of ships *still* in Forty-nine. Max Miller will give them that dope. Then they'll be taken off by *Luftwaffe* rats, who arrived only three days ago, and flown out to a rendezvous with the U-boats just off the entrance to the Canal. And—"

Jake could not believe it possible.

"But—" he cried, but went no farther as Ed Allen silenced him with an angry gesture.

"Sure, but you're wrong," the redhead said. "Shore spotters will see a formation of five ships *from Forty-nine with known markings!* They'll figure it a formation returning from patrol.

"Meanwhile far underneath the water the two big U-boats are sneaking past the mine barriers. Then when all is set the U-boats let fly at our naval ships at the entrance to the Canal, and the planes pop down and let loose on the Gatun Dam and Locks.

"With what they'll be dropping they'll fix it so's a rowboat couldn't get through. They'll have the jump, see?

They'll be taken for Forty-nine planes. And they'll be flying right over the submerged U-boats as a perfect cover protection for them. Once past the mine barriers those big U-boats will be able to tear all creation apart."

"But they'll get theirs!" Mike said viciously. "And the planes too. They won't live to tell Hitler about it!"

"So what?" Ed Allen said. "Our fleet units are stuck in two oceans, and will have to take the long way around. Don't worry! These Nazis know it's death for them. But that doesn't bother them a bit. They've been taught it's tops to die for their rotten *Fuehrer,* you know!"

Jake started to speak, but quickly stopped. The sound of an aircraft engine came clearly to them all from somewhere up off to the right.

Every man froze stiff, held his breath, and cocked an ear to the roar that grew louder and louder.

It was Ed Allen who finally broke the heavy silence that settled over the group. He expelled clamped air from his lungs in a rush of sound, and struggled up onto his feet. His face was dead-white under the stubble and dirt, and Jake Barker's heart tightened in bitter anger as he saw the bleeding sores made by Ed Allen's ankle shackles.

"That's a Wright engine!" Ed announced in a trembling voice. "And . . . listen! He's cut his gun! Sounds like he's going down for that inlet on the far side of this cay. If we could only get a look at him, and signal, or something. But why's he going down to land? Or is he?"

Nobody said a word. Every head was thrown back, and all eyes were staring hard up at the thatched roof in the hope of catching a glimpse of the plane as it slid by overhead. Three of them did catch a split-second glimpse of wings and fuselage. And it was Jake who spoke first. His voice was tight and strained.

"A Vought-Sikorsky utility job!" he said. "And I think I saw the three-stripe marking of Forty-nine. He's landing, though. Hasn't goosed his engine once. He must be on the inlet, now, so—"

Jake didn't finish. He looked at the others, and they nodded gravely.

"So it isn't a friend!" Arnold Clinton said. "That leaves just one guess. Ensign Miller! Something's popped, is my bet. He took a Vought-Sikorsky up for a joy-hop and buzzed out here to report to his two bosses. And I'm the guy who used to make fun of those pulp magazine thrillers! I wonder what's happened?"

"Maybe they've decided to pull the trigger," Ed said, and jerked his head toward the four Dauntless planes. "Those ships are set to go right now. All you have to do is jab the starter button, and take off the wheel brakes. The runway's about long enough. Good pilots could make it easy. It wouldn't take them half an hour to put the torpedoes in the racks. If—"

The redhead choked and clenched his fists in a helpless gesture.

"That stack of TNT mine cartridges down by the pier!" he said a moment later, in a husky voice. "If I could only get hold of one of them! Just one is all I'd want!"

The man broke a little, sank to the ground, and began slowly to pound his two fists on his knees. Arnold Clinton reached out as far as his chains would allow and patted the redhead on the shoulder.

"Just hang on hard, Ed," he said evenly. "They can't ride this high forever. Somebody's going to spill them for a fall, some day. It isn't in the cards for them to grab off the whole pot."

Ed shrugged and stopped beating his knees. Nobody said anything. Jake looked at Mike and was startled slightly by the look on the big fellow's face.

The gunner-observer's chin stuck out like a chunk of marble. His muscles were bunched as though he were about to pounce on somebody. And there was a wild, mad look in his eyes that were fixed steadfastly on Ed Allen. His lips were parted as though he were about to speak, but no sound came from between them.

A moment later the huge hulk of one of the guards loomed up in the fading light. He gave them all a sneer, slapped his coiled bull-whip against his leg, and suggestively fingered his holstered Luger. A second guard appeared in back of him, stepped past and bent over Jake's ankle shackles. With a key he unlocked one and freed the chain from the ring-rod in the ground, then snapped the shackle back on again.

"Get up!" he ordered, and hit Jake on the side of the head. "You are wanted."

Mike doubled his fists, but Jake shot him a warning look. He got up and suffered one of the guards to curl steel fingers about his arm and jerk him into motion.

They led him along a cut-out path that led toward the small lake where the U-boats were berthed. But a hundred yards this side of them they wheeled him right and into a small clearing that contained the only sign of civilization. It was a small hut that had a door and windows that were covered by fine netting to keep out the night insects.

The guard pulled the door netting aside and gave Jake a vicious shove in the back. He tried to keep his balance but didn't even come close. He tripped and went sprawling on his face on a hard wood floor.

For a moment he stayed right where he was. Then as a booted foot prodded him none too gently in the ribs he struggled up onto his feet, eyes blazing, brain whirling, and ready to lash out at the first thing he saw.

The first thing he saw, however, was a short-barreled Luger pointed straight at him. It was held in the paw of the bald-headed U-boat commander who sat at a table that was completely covered by a huge marine chart of the approach and entrance of the Colon end of the Canal.

Beside him sat another German. He looked like a bloated frog in his tropical whites. So puffy was his face that the eyes were just slits in the skin. He was obviously the commander of the other U-boat, but Jake didn't give him more than a passing glance. What caught and held his attention was the third figure in the room.

The man stood a few feet in back of the two Germans, and he was turned slightly sideward as though ready to dive out the rear window at an instant's notice. He was short, and not bad-looking, save for the eyes that were close-set and too small for the rest of his face. They were restless eyes, rather fearful and shifty. They dropped instantly before Barker's burning glare and became fixed on the marine chart on the desk.

Jake swallowed hard, and came up a bit on his toes.

"Take off that Navy uniform, Max Miller, you yellow Nazi!" he shouted. "Take it off, or I'll rip it off, you dirty traitor!"

"And die at once for your foolishness, Lieutenant!" the bald-headed U-boat commander snarled. "The advantage is all ours. Don't be a fool. Will you stupid American swine never learn that in war it is not the method but *the goal!* Sit down, Lieutenant!"

Jake ignored the command. He kept his eyes riveted on a man who had shared Air Station life with him. Who had eaten in the same mess, smoked and binged in the same lounge, flown in the same section patrol, and done all of the hundred and one other things in Naval Aviation life.

Raging hatred, scorn, and contempt surged through him as he glared at Ensign Miller. Yet with it all he wondered if maybe he was just dreaming. Whether this was not all cockeyed, and not even a little bit so.

"Sit down, Lieutenant!" the U-boat commander's thundering roar blasted into his thoughts. "None of us is interested in what you think of him. The situation has changed, and I have decided to talk to you now instead of tomorrow. You have talked with your comrades, eh? They have told you a little of what is to be?"

Jake Barker took his eyes off Ensign Miller's face and focused them on the U-boat commander, as he sank into a chair.

"They told me about your pipe-dreams!" he replied. "You

don't stand a chance. Not even a little one. You'll be smoked out like the dirty rats you are."

"Are such words part of your Navy training, Lieutenant?" the German murmured with a sneer. "So useless, and so unnecessary. No, they are not pipe-dreams. But I did not call you here to discuss our plans. I called you here to offer you the chance of saving the lives of your seven other comrades. I pay them the compliment of saying they are brave men, Lieutenant. If I were you I would certainly consider their lives well worth the saving."

The German paused as though giving Jake a chance to speak. The Navy pilot said nothing. He simply stared unwinking at the bald-headed one. The German shrugged, leaned forward and placed a stubby finger on the marine chart.

"We have one little problem," he said presently. "These mine fields guarding the breakwater entrance to Limon Bay. I have discovered that they are changed rather often. I have also found out that you had a part in working out the mine field systems. You helped direct the laying operations from the air, I believe."

"You're crazy!" Jake said. "That comes under Coast and Harbor defense, and—"

"You're a liar, Barker!" Ensign Miller suddenly snarled. "It was done with Naval Aviation cooperation, so that there'd be areas where Navy planes could sit down without touching off something. You and that fathead, Buckley, worked out the charts. You both rode herd on the job from the air not three weeks ago. You know where every barrier is stretched night and day."

The rat in U. S. Naval Aviation spoke the truth. Barker had been assigned the job along with Commander Buckley. He did know the intricate mine barrier system as he knew the palm of his hand, but he would take a bullet right between the eyes before he would even so much as hint where a single spiked ball of roaring doom was riding at the end of its anchor chain just under the surface of the placid blue water. He looked at the traitor and dragged down one corner of his mouth.

"Have you tried selling them the Brooklyn Bridge, too?" he asked contemptuously. "I hear they're suckers for any kind of information."

Max Miller made whistling sounds through his clenched teeth, and his small eyes fairly spat out flames of anger. However, he did not take a single step forward.

"The information is true, Lieutenant!" the U-boat commander said coldly. "So you waste words with your breath. Listen to me! Tomorrow we render your beautiful Panama Canal utterly useless for a long, long time to come. Whether you tell me something I wish to know, or not, will not save your precious canal. It—is finished. But, your refusal to answer my question *will* make a difference regarding you, and your comrades."

"You're wasting breath, now, so skip it!" Jake said, tight-lipped, as the German paused. "I wouldn't tell you the time!"

The U-boat commander smiled coldly and fondled the Luger he had drawn from his pocket.

"I believe I can change your mind," he said. "My question is this. What will be the arrangement of the mine barriers tomorrow morning? There is the chart, and here is a pencil. You can plot it for me. And bear in mind, Lieutenant! I have a way to first find out if you lie, or not. False information will be the same as no information at all."

"I said you're wasting your breath, didn't I?" Jake said. Then glancing at Max Miller, "Too bad you don't know, bum! It would get you an extra bonus, I guess."

"By noon tomorrow," the baldheaded U-boat commander said, "this place will be completely evacuated. It has served our purpose, and we are abandoning it. Let me assure you, Lieutenant, that it was well selected. No ship comes within twenty miles of here. And no plane comes within signaling distance. Anybody left on this cay would be doomed to a most unpleasant death.

"Tell us what we want to know, and I promise that two collapsible rubber boats, and provisions, will be left for you and your friends to use to get out where you'll be picked up and saved. Refuse, or give us false information, and you will be left here with nothing. Not a bit of food, not one drop of drinking water.

"*Nothing,* Lieutenant. And your comrades will be told why. Not because you made the task *impossible* for us. The canal is doomed, whether you speak, or not. They will die because you refused to make it a little easier for us to accomplish our task.

"And so, Lieutenant—are their lives worth the satisfaction of delaying our triumph a mere hour, or possibly two at the most?"

As he gave his ultimatum the German crashed his fist down on the table. He fixed his piggish eyes on the Navy pilot's face. Jake returned the look, and said nothing. But his brain was whirling over at lightning speed.

Left deserted with neither food nor water, Ed Allen, and Arnold Clinton, and the others probably would last two days, if that long. Brave lives thrown away, and for what? Just as the German had put it! For the satisfaction of delaying their triumph an hour, or maybe two.

He knew what the German meant by that. It would take that much longer for the two giant U-boats to feel their way past the mine barriers. But supposing the U-boats didn't get past, struck a mine and were destroyed? So what? It didn't change much. If five Douglas Dauntless planes fitted with two torpedoes apiece reached Gatun Dam and the Gatun Locks, the canal could still be blocked off for nobody could tell how long.

Yet there was a chance that something might go wrong if the U-boats were destroyed. If he, Jake Barker, said nothing, perhaps some kind of a miracle would rise up to smite down these rats of the Reich. Yet—yet, was it worth Ed Allen, and Arnold Clinton, and Mike Cheviski, and the others? Did he have the right to snuff out their lives—for nothing?

The thoughts poured through his brain like liquid fire. He hardly realized it as he swayed forward slightly, his eyes fixed on the Luger in the U-boat commander's hand. The Luger being jerked back out of his reach, and the harsh laugh stopped him.

"Don't be a fool!" the German warned. "I'll not shoot to kill you, and end your torment. No! Just to maim you a little, and—"

The man stopped short with his mouth hanging open. Anger blazed up in his eyes, then dumbfounded amazement, and then a look of wild terror spread over his face.

"*Gott!*" he whispered hoarsely. "*Gott!* No! Don't!"

"Drop your cannons and reach!" the voice of Mike Cheviski boomed out behind Jake Barker. "Reach, I'm telling you!"

For one long second Jake froze motionless, hardly daring to believe his ears. Then he half twisted around and looked at Mike who was standing just inside the hut door. He stood spraddle-legged, with both hands stretched above his head. But in his two hands he held a black metal cylinder about ten inches long and eight inches across.

Jake took one look at that cylinder and felt his face go pale, and his knees turn to rubber. He had seen such "cans" often, and instantly recognized this one for one of the TNT cartridges used to load mines as well as torpedoes.

In short, Mike Cheviski was holding aloft enough explosives to blow the hut and its occupants clear across the Caribbean. And the big ex-football star was having the time of his life.

"Timed it just right, hey, Admiral?" he boomed. "Been outside listening to their song and dance. Get around in back of them, Admiral, and lift their side arms. This thing's getting heavy. I might drop it any minute, and—"

"*Gott,* don't!" the slit-eyed U-boat commander gasped in a strangled voice. "You would kill us all!"

"Yes, I thought of that," Mike chuckled. Then fixing agate eyes on Max Miller, "You, huh? Fix our engine, hey? Why you crawling worm, for two cents I'd—"

"Mike, don't!" the traitor screamed. "You've got us— cold."

Jake had slipped around behind the two U-boat com- manders, and Miller, and had frisked them of their guns. He backed over to Mike's side.

"Rest your arms, Mike," he said. "Put the thing down. There's some rope over there. Tie them up good. But how in the name of—"

"Ed Allen gave me the idea, saying where this stuff was down by the piers," Mike said out the corner of his mouth. "I eased down after they took you away. I knocked out a Kraut that I bumped into and took one of these. I came over here and let those two outside have a look.

"Did they drop their guns when they got that look! I made them lie down, then kicked their teeth in. I couldn't use my hands, you see. Anyway, they won't be bothering nobody. Tie 'em? I got it planned better than that, Ad- miral.

"The big slob of a guard on the right outside. He's got the key that unlocks those ankle bracelets you're wearing. Go get yourself free. Then we go over and let the boys loose. Then we take those crates and fly away. I'll drop this from the air. I can see the fireworks better from up there."

"You fools, you'll never leave here alive!" the bald-headed U-boat commander rasped hoarsely. "There are two hun- dred men on this cay. They'll shoot you down like dogs. You'll never escape!"

Mike didn't say anything. Still holding the can of TNT he stepped over closer to the U-boat commander then shot up one foot and kicked the German right in the belly.

"That ain't fair fighting, I know, Admiral," he said over his shoulder to Jake. "But I've been wanting to do that to some fat Kraut ever since Hitler marched into Poland. Okay, on your feet, slob! You three walk ahead of us. And if any of your pals come running tell 'em it's okay to shoot. When I drop, *you* go up, and I don't mean, perhaps.

"Go ahead, Admiral, go on. We took enough from them, didn't we? Huh! Don't be particular. These Nazis know only one way to fight. Well, we know that way, too. Let's go!"

Jake grinned in spite of himself. Here was a Mike Cheviski he had never seen before. Here was Mike Cheviski going into action his way when the chips were down. Navy or Army technique? Boy! The big ex-football star of Polish parentage was fighting the Nazi way—without rules.

Jake was tempted to take Mike's tip and slug Miller and the slit-eyed U-boat commander just on general principles, but something wouldn't let him do it. Perhaps it was because he had more Navy training in back of him than Mike Cheviski had. Or perhaps it was because his parents hadn't come from Nazi-devastated Poland. Anyway, he grinned but shook his head, then motioned with one of his Lugers for the two Germans and the Navy traitor to walk out the door ahead of him.

Once out in the open air his blood ran a little cold, and his heart skipped a few beats. It was still quite a long way from dark, and the other Germans might see them herding their prisoners over to where Ed Allen, Arnold Clinton, and the others were. A German with a rifle could pick them off like clay pigeons, and not realize what Mike now had tucked under his arm like a football.

A second later, though, he shrugged aside his fears and steeled himself. This was Mike's party, and he would play it the ex-football star's way. But, how in heaven's name had he got loose from his chains? It—

"That's the one there, Admiral," Mike broke into his thoughts and pointed. "See? There's a bunch of keys hanging to his belt. Get 'em, and let's go. The boys will be getting impatient."

Jake bent down to relieve the guard of the keys.

"How did you get free?" he asked Mike.

"Simple," Mike said. "Tried to tell you but there wasn't the chance. Besides, you were kind of out cold. When they tossed us in with the boys they took off one shackle to pass it through the ring. I sort of dragged it from the lug's hand by stumbling. Then sort of ground it into the dirt. He hit me, but it worked. Got the hollow end jammed with dirt.

"It didn't lock tight like he thought. I was able to yank it open a couple of notches. Enough to slip it off my foot. Somebody once showed me how. He'd done time in a Georgia chain gang. Boy! Do I thank him plenty if I ever see him again! I . . . Steady, you!"

Mike leaped forward and kicked Miller hard in the pants. The traitor sobbed in pain and terror.

"I wasn't trying to break, Mike!" he choked. "I just tripped!"

"Well, stop tripping, and walk!" Mike said. "Believe me, I'll get you first. Come on, the three of you. Move!"

It was perhaps a quarter of a mile to the prisoner compound but it seemed like ten miles to Jake. With every step he took he expected to hear a hoarse cry in German followed by the crack of a Luger or a rifle. But the Fates were kind or perhaps the gods stood in the way and made the light bad for the other Germans on the cay.

At any rate the strange party reached the other Yank prisoners without a single thing happening. Ed Allen saw them first, and leaped to his feet, eyes blazing. He seemed to see only Miller and the two Germans. He started to hurl himself at them, completely forgetting that he was chained to the ground. Had not Arnold lunged out and grabbed him in time, the redhead would have snapped every bone in his ankle.

"Steady, Ed!" Arnold panted and dragged him back. "Mike, I'll love you for life. You made it, big boy, you made it. Here! For crying out loud, give me the key! And you, Max! When I'm loose I'm going to—"

"*You* make it steady!" Jake Barker ordered, and stepped close. "We haven't got time to start slapping rats around. Mike's miracle won't last forever. I've got the key. As I release each man, leg for the planes. Mike and I will come last. When you hear me yell, start your engines and get going. And *keep going!*"

Jake's crisp voice of authority had instant effect. Blind rage caused by the appearance of the two Germans and Miller died down instantly. Each man realized there was more at stake than beating these three chunks of human vermin to pulp. And Mike Cheviski was the most relieved of them all.

"That's the stuff, Admiral!" he gulped. "Me, I'm no good at giving orders. You take over. I'll just make these fellows stand between us and whoever might come looking."

Mike Cheviski was still talking as Jake bent down and released Arnold Clinton. The man instantly whirled and started for the line of planes. Denton Duffy was next and went chasing after Arnold. Then Wilson, then an observer named Harris, and a pilot named Baxter. Without a word they all streaked over toward the planes.

Jake bent down and released Ed Allen's ankles and heard Mike slap a hand to his face. Then almost instantly there was a bellow of rage from the big fellow's lips. Jake jerked around just in time to see the two Germans, and Miller, go racing off down the cut path. At the same time he saw the can of TNT at Mike's feet where the big fellow had placed it while he slapped at a mess of tick-flies on his face.

At almost the same instant a low mad cry spilled from Ed's cracked lips, and the redhead became a streak of crazed greased lightning. Before Jake could cry out a warning, Ed Allen had leaped free of his chains, scooped up the can of TNT and gone racing along the path after the Germans.

Jake shouted at the top of his voice. But he didn't dare shoot because Ed's speeding figure was directly between his gun and the others.

"Get to the last plane, Mike!" he finally said and gave the big fellow a shove. "I've got to catch Ed. He's off, and doesn't know what he's doing. You get to the plane. I'll get Ed!"

Mike shouted something but Jake heard it just as a muffled roar. He was already pounding down the path after Ed

Allen. But with every stride he took his heart became a colder lump of lead in his throat.

The redhead was far out in front of him and gaining on the two Germans and Max Miller with every step. Then suddenly, when Jake lost them to view for an instant, and dashed suddenly around a bend in the path, he put on the brakes hard and flung himself flat on the ground.

He had reached the clearing along the edge of the little lake. The U-boat piers were no more than a hundred yards away. Miller had seemingly vanished into thin air, but the two Germans were leaping on the deck of the nearest submarine and racing toward the conning tower.

Screamed orders poured from their lips as they ran, but every sailor on deck froze motionless as though permanently paralyzed. And well they might freeze solid, for they saw a human torpedo come sailing through the air.

Ed Allen, clutching the can of TNT against his chest, hurled his body straight off the edge of the pier to crash down on the deck of the U-boat.

His body landed and then there was a great sheet of livid red flame that belched high up into the air, and seemed to spread out over the whole world. A split second later there came a sound as though mighty, invisible giants had split the earth in two. The ground heaved and shook under Jake, and his head felt as though it were going to fly apart in small pieces.

Through a whirlwind of red flame and black smoke he saw the U-boat break in two and rise right up out of the water. The stern half let go, and actually sailed through the air to crash down on the bow of the second boat. Instantly the place was rocked by a second and perhaps even more terrific explosion, and the little lake became a boiling, seething cauldron of doom.

Jake knew that he must be flying apart in all directions. Yet at the same time he realized that he had his legs under him and had spun around and was racing madly back up the path. Figures came racing toward him but he swerved by them, and probably wasn't even seen by the fear-stricken Germans running blindly toward the scene of disaster.

Then suddenly he was within sight of the planes. He saw his pals in the pits, all turned and staring back at him. Mike was in the rear plane, standing up and waving his arms like a madman. Putting every ounce of strength into his legs Jake cupped a hand to his mouth.

"Start engines, and go!" he bellowed. "Start—"

He never finished. At that moment a figure in German uniform popped into sight from the right. He was one of the guards, and carried a rifle in his hand. Oblivious to Jake, the man dropped to his knee and took a bead on Mike's big figure towering up out of the rear pit of the end Dauntless.

But sight and action were one for Jake. While in midstride he flung up his hand that still clutched the Luger and squeezed the trigger. The German fired his rifle but he wasn't pointing it at Mike by then. Jake's slugs had hit him and bowled him over. His bullet went ripping harmlessly up through the tentlike tropical foliage above him.

Four seconds later Jake reached the end Dauntless and scrambled up into the pit. Arnold, in the first ship, was already banging down the man-made runway. He was off and away in a flash. Then Denton Duffy in the second plane went off. Then the third ship that had only one figure in the pit, Harris. Ed Allen's flying partner was taking off without his pal. But he didn't leave until he looked back at Jake and received the meaningful shake of a head signal.

Finally, Jake Barker gunned his engine and went roaring along the take-off run. But, as though his parting was some kind of a signal to the gods, or somebody, the little uncharted cay became a thundering, blazing inferno in the Caribbean. Stored fuel, oil, and everything else let go. And as Jake cleared his wheels and went prop-screaming upward he turned in the seat to stare back down at a Nature-made death-trap.

The U-boat commander had said that there were two hundred on that cay. Well, if true, there would be nothing but two hundred fried corpses when that blaze died down. He shuddered and turned front.

"Poor old Ed!" he muttered hoarsely. "But, he wanted just one more crack at them, and . . . And I guess you're kind of happy, now, aren't you, fellow? You saved—"

He cut short the rest as Mike's fist banged down on his shoulder, and the big fellow's voice sounded in his ears.

"Hey, Admiral, look! We still got unfinished business. There's that Vought-Sikorski getting altitude. And Max Miller must be in the pit. Swing us over while I pepper him like he should get!"

Jake turned and stared out across the air space at the utility plane prop-clawing upward and to the south. He also saw the three Douglas Dauntless planes ahead of him swerve sharply and go banging off in that direction. Then he glanced back at Mike and shook his head.

"No, Mike!" he called and waved a hand at the other three planes. "They took more of a beating than we did. That yellow Nazi is their dish."

"Yes, I guess you're right, Admiral," Mike agreed, just a little sadly. "But say! I ain't thanked you for saving my life. Thanks! Boy, did you knock over that Nazi. Some shooting. Am I glad you were along!"

"You got that last twisted around, and how, Mike!" Jake cried. "And how, *and how!*"

"Huh?" the big fellow gulped with a scowl. "What do you mean, and how?"

"You'll find out when they pin the Navy Cross on you!" Jake said. "Right now, get going on that radio. Get a bearing on a couple of stations and give me a course."

"And I know just the two stations!" Mike cried happily. "Both hot bands this time of day, and ... But, hey! Buckley said—"

"An emergency, Mike!" Jake stopped him. "We're lost, aren't we? Or we can say we were, can't we?"

Mike Cheviski didn't reply. A blast of hot licks from Madri What's-his-name's boys did that for him.

# FLIGHT TO DANGER

*By*

## FRANK JOHNSON

SIRACUSA in Sicily had been turned into a raging inferno. Her docks and several submarine bases were throwing off pillars of smoke and bright tongues of flame.

Protecting the bomber formation, a squadron of Gladiators from the aircraft carrier H.M.S. *Vigilant* dived and zoomed, discouraging the Italians from taking to the air.

Huge bombers of the Fleet Air Arm were relentlessly demolishing the whole port. Squadron Leader Don Jackson inspected the damage, then spoke into his radio transmitter.

"Objective reached. Bomber formation, attention! Maintain altitude of five thousand. Gladiators—Squadron A at one thousand feet above bombers. Squadron B, a thousand below."

The entire flight wheeled and streaked out to sea, the fighters swarming like protecting hawks above the slower bombers. As the Island of Sicily vanished behind them dawn broke. Squadron Leader Don Jackson reported to the aircraft carrier by radio. He obtained his position, and the fighters escorted the bombers until they wheeled south and headed for their base seven hundred miles away.

Five minutes later one of the bombers called Jackson.

"Trouble below, sir. Looks like one of our fellows sitting on the ocean. We're getting ready to go down."

Don called orders for the others to keep on their trail home while he peeled off and roared toward the position which the bombers had given. He saw what they meant in a few moments. A small fighter plane, miraculously still afloat in a calm sea, formed a minute speck on the vast stretches of water.

One of the big bomber flying boats was trying to land. Her pontoons cut the water and she slowed down to a crawl, maneuvering slowly toward the wrecked plane. Don dived, flew just above the rescue operations and saw one man, in a British uniform, standing on the wings of the fighter, his legs awash to the knees.

The bomber maneuvered closer until her giant wing practically touched the wrecked plane, then the stranded pilot gave a herculean leap aboard. The bomber pushed off, set her nose in the wind and cut contact with the sea. Jackson, high above now, was staring into space. What seemed to be the tiniest dot on the horizon was rapidly fading into nothing. Another plane? He shrugged. An enemy fighter would have pounced on those bombers like a hungry hawk.

A radio message came from the bomber which had accomplished the rescue.

"Have aboard with us Flight Lieutenant Whiters, shot down by enemy pursuit squadron an hour ago. We are taking him to your aircraft carrier."

"Good work," Don Jackson said. "Tell Whiters I'll be glad to have him as my guest."

Don accompanied the bomber to the *Vigilant,* watched her settle down to transfer Whiters, then banked himself for the tricky landing on the wide deck of the carrier. Signals came and he slowly lost altitude. Then his landing gear hit the secret checking device and brought the plane to a smooth halt.

Don climbed out and reached the port side just as Whiters, in a watersoaked uniform, came overside. Don Jackson greeted him with outstretched hand.

"Rather off your course, aren't you?" he grinned.

Whiters smiled, too. "Quite a bit, sir. I was flying a replacement ship to Malta when those Jerries spotted me. Must have been a dozen. They put me down without much trouble, though I think I winged a couple of 'em. Thanks very much for taking the trouble to pick me up."

Don grabbed Whiters' arm and led him to the officers' mess. They ate a huge breakfast. Afterwards, Don left Whiters to entertain himself while he made out his report.

Don Jackson walked back to the mess, yawning and flexing his tired arm muscles. He was lean and firm-jawed. Canadian wheat fields had put those brawny shoulders on him and tanned his skin a nut brown. Whiters wasn't like that at all. Perhaps two or three years older and just as lean, he had prominent cheek bones and pale blue eyes, but there was a perpetual grin on his face.

"We could do with some sleep," Don said. "My cabin has bunks for two. Let's turn in."

They slept until late afternoon. Whiters was shaving

when Don awoke. He finished, shoved a metal shaving kit onto the dresser and sat on the bed while Don cleaned up and told him about his experiences aboard the aircraft carrier.

"We've been sunk half a dozen times according to Nazi reports," he chuckled. "Well, I've got an appointment with Wing. Why don't you go on deck for a bit of air?"

It was dinner when Don Jackson finished, but there was nothing to do the rest of the night. They were steaming about four hundred kilometers off the tip of the Italian boot.

Destroyers flanked the carrier, their sleek grey shapes hardly visible in the early darkness now. Don walked slowly to his quarters. Whiters was apparently at dinner because the cabin was empty. He glanced in the medicine cabinet mirror and wondered why his whiskers grew so fast, but decided against shaving anyway. Then he saw Whiters' shaving kit.

It was different from any he had ever seen.

Snapping open the cover, he whistled at the sight of a gleaming chromium-plated razor. He removed it from the kit to examine it more closely. His eyes narrowed. Beneath the slot into which the razor fitted he found a scratched-out portion, as if there had been a manufacturer's stamp there, but someone had obliterated it.

With an idle motion, he began to twist the long stem of the razor to the left. Suddenly the blade end of the razor flipped open, and the shiny single-edge blade fell out. But strangely enough the stem continued to turn until the top screw came off in Don's hand, exposing a hollow tube in which was wedged a tightly wound cylinder of paper.

Don removed the wad of paper, opened it and found it covered with an odd jumble of words.

Warning prickled the back of his neck as he heard a scuffle of movement behind him. He started to turn, then halted as the barrel of a gun was poked into his back.

"Walk over to your bunk and sit down or I'll put a bullet through you!" came the harsh command. Don stiffened, recognizing Whiters' voice. Now Whiters was sneering at him. "So you were snooping and found that sheet of German code in my razor!"

With arms raised shoulder high, Don Jackson walked over to the bunk and sat down.

"I was admiring the razor and found that paper by accident," Don murmured tersely. "You came in before I could make out what it was. You gave yourself away just now." Don's eyes blazed with temper. "So you're a Nazi! A pretty slick trick."

"You are right, my friend," gloated the other man with a wicked smile. "I am Captain Carl Lommel, commander of the squadron of planes which shot down Whiters."

Don forced his voice to remain spare and even. "What's it going to get you? You're one man aboard a floating fortress."

"It will get me everything I wish," Lommel declared tartly. "Whiters was killed, but his ship did not sink. I was flying a plane equipped with pontoons so I sat down. Then the idea occurred to me. We knew you were bombing Sicily and that your squadron was too big for us to attack. Therefore, I put on Whiters' uniform, transferred his corpse to my plane and had my crew stand by until your bomber formation was sighted on its way back. Then my ship took off."

Don's lips made a tight crease across his clean-cut features. "I know. I had a glimpse of it. Of course, I didn't recognize its identity. You must realize that you'll face a firing squad because you're an enemy in one of our uniforms."

Captain Lommel snorted in derision. "Do you think I am to be caught now? We Nazis lay our plans well. For months we hoped to get a man aboard one of your carriers. I have not been idle. I have learned many secrets. My report will help engineers to build craft like this. Soon we shall have a Navy strong enough to cope with yours."

"Before I allow you to get away with this, I'll make you shoot me," Don warned the Nazi grimly. "That will create an alarm. You forgot to include that in your plans."

Carl Lommel showed his gleaming white teeth in a nasty snarl.

"Everything is planned," he said. "I know there is a plane on deck capable of reaching Italy. One of your pilots is leaving in a few moments to fly dispatches. I shall take his plane. Already the aircraft carrier is turning into the wind and maintaining the proper speed for a take-off. Arrangements have been made by members of my own command to notify the Italians to expect me. Now I must be going. Of course, I am compelled to kill you."

The gun came up and centered. Don Jackson stifled the rage that seethed in his heart. What Carl Lommel could do with the information he'd picked up would be disastrous. In addition, Don was almost certain an attack would be made on the carrier. Lommel could broadcast her position the moment he was in the air.

Lommel backed up a step or two. His eyes glinted. He rested his left hand on a small flat desk top and leaned heavily on it.

"The shot will not be heard," he said. "There are no men near this cabin."

As he talked, the Nazi raised his pistol so he could squint through its sights. With all attention riveted on aiming the gun, he didn't see Don's foot sneak out and rest firmly against the leg of that small desk. Suddenly Don gave it a hard shove. Lommel lost his balance for a moment, and Don leaped from the edge of the bunk to attack.

The muzzle of the gun raked his cheek. Another blow exploded against his skull. He started to slump, but reached out and managed to dislodge the telephone.

Lommel cursed fluently and decided against shooting.

Don opened his mouth to yell a warning which the operator would pick up, but Lommel moved too fast. His clubbed pistol hit Don squarely on top of the head. The cabin spun madly for a fraction of a second, then blacked out.

Don hit the floor with a thud.

Lommel backed to the door, opened it and listened. There was a buzz in the phone. He quietly hung up the instrument, then hurried into the corridor. It required only a moment to reach the deck. He observed with smiling satisfaction that only a small watch was on duty.

A plane was poised on deck, too, a chunky little Fairey Swordfish. Lommel squared his shoulders, hid the gun in his pocket and drew a knife. He approached a man on duty near the plane. The launching officer, the officer on watch and the officer of the day were well forward.

The sailor saw only a man in the uniform of a British pilot and he wasn't at all suspicious.

The Nazi struck fast. The knife came up and slit through the sailor's throat, preventing any outcry and killing him almost instantly. Lommel eased the body to the deck and walked briskly toward the plane.

Another sailor was approaching, attracted by the faint scuffle. He saluted Lommel and the German spy snapped orders.

"Bring Squadron Leader Jackson here at once," he said.

"Yes, sir."

The sailor wheeled and took two steps before Lommel's knife repeated its bloody task. Then the German clambered into the plane, pressed the starter button and heard the motor roar into life. In a moment he was streaking across the deck. He took off with the precision that came from a complete knowledge of aircraft. The three officers and other men on deck were helpless to stop him.

In his quarters Don recovered his wits in time to detect the roar of Lommel's stolen plane. He staggered to the deck, saw the sailors sprawled out dead. Don cursed slowly and shouted an alarm.

He bawled orders. A Gladiator was quickly brought on deck and wheeled into position. Rear Admiral Thomas came topside in a hurry. Don saluted.

"The man we thought to be Whiters was a Nazi flier, sir. He came aboard to learn the secrets of this ship and our location. I'm going after him."

"After him? But, man, you don't know where he's going. How do you expect to overtake him?"

"I know where he's headed, sir. The nearest airport is Taranto on the Gulf of the same name. He stole one of our planes. But it happened to be a Fairey Swordfish—slow compared to the Gladiator I'll use. I hope to overtake him, sir, and shoot him down if I can. If that fails, I'll assume his tactics and try to meet him on Italian soil. There's a chance, sir. May I have your permission?"

"Yes, by all means, and good luck. This wasn't your fault, but get him if you can."

"Yes, sir." Don ran to the plane. He shouted back, "Better get all hands to battle stations, sir. The spy may radio our exact position so his forces can attack."

The motor throbbed. Don gave her the gun and roared off the deck of the *Vigilant*. He flew into the night and set his course carefully. Lommel had no more than a five-minute start. If luck held out, Don should overtake him before he reached land. The only hitch would come in trying to spot the man.

There was no telling at what altitude he would fly.

Don's eyes ached from trying to penetrate the gloom. A growing sense of defeat and despair began to plague him. Lommel would get away with this unless he could think up some counter measure quickly.

Lommel had notified the Italians to expect him. Taranto was the only place he could go. Don was sure that the German was far behind him now because the coast of Italy was already assuming definite shape, and Don had flown at full gun. The Italians would be expecting a British plane and a pilot in a British uniform! Don Jackson uttered a howl of glee and tried to urge a little more speed out of his ship.

Flying low, he reached shore and aimed for the airport at Taranto. If his hunch was right, they'd hear him coming and light the field. It happened just that way. The beam of a searchlight cut the darkness, passed by him and then came back to center its ray. Don dived and looped. Then he wiggled his wings and carried on in a manner which no enemy pilot would ever have done.

Suddenly the airfield was flooded with light. Don banked, streaked across the field, then returned to make a perfect landing.

Italian troops rushed up to the plane as Don climbed out.

An officer saluted smartly and jabbered something in Italian. Don glared at him.

"Speak German," he rasped. "Or English."

Another officer approached. "I speak English, Herr Captain. German I cannot talk. We have been prepared for you. A neat job, si?"

"Yes, but I am followed," Don Jackson said. "Order your men to man their guns. A British ship was on my tail. Shoot the dog down. Out with the field lights!"

The officer yelled orders and the lights winked out. Men raced to gun positions. Two minutes later the hum of a distant plane motor became evident. Searchlights went into action, pinned the Fairey Swordfish with Lommel at the controls, in its beams.

Expecting a friendly reception, Lommel was flying low and became an easy target. Shrapnel burst all around him. His plane rocked badly. Part of one wing broke off. He cut the motor, wisely estimated where the landing field would be between the guns and searchlights and strove to land. The guns followed him. More of the plane was knocked away. It started to plummit earthward.

Lommel was apparently making a desperate attempt to land, thinking his orders had been misunderstood and certain he could straighten things out once he was on the ground. The plane hit the field, bounced out of control, then did a perfect nose dive.

Before this occurred Don was running wildly across the field with a swarm of Italian officers at his heels. The German staggered out of the wrecked ship, his face bloody.

Then he saw Don and went completely rigid.

Don grabbed him by the leg and hauled him down. He pinned the man against the side of the plane.

"Remember me, friend? I owe you this."

He jabbed a short right to the German's jaw, battered his head back with a left. Lommel slumped to the ground.

Italian soldiers grabbed him. Don turned to the officer who could speak English.

"That is the way those stupid English *schweine* should be treated," he stated tersely. "He is not a spy, but perhaps we could arrange that he escape, eh? Just far enough."

The Italian gulped. "But, Herr Captain, they have many of our men prisoners, too. They would shoot them in retaliation. I do not like to disobey a man like you, but—"

Don Jackson scowled, and he pretended a terrible rage, though the Italians never recognized the nervousness behind his shout.

"Silence! You Italians always wait for us Germans to take

the initiative. Where is the man to whom I can safely entrust those things I learned aboard that aircraft carrier? I'll need an office or a hotel suite where I can be alone."

"Si, signor."

The officer saluted, wheeled and gave some orders. A military car rolled up. Don started to get in. Then he looked back. A squad of soldiers were clustered around Lommel's still unconscious form.

"The prisoner is for me to handle, do you understand? Bring him here at once."

Lommel was carried over and dumped into the car. It started off and Don suddenly remembered that there might be other Nazi officers in this port who would know Lommel. He whacked the driver on the shoulder and gestured for him to back up. The Italian officer came running toward the car.

Don Jackson opened the door and said in a curt voice. "Get in! I need you!"

The Italian shrugged and obeyed. He sat down beside Don and the car started away again.

"You are sure you do not understand German?" he asked the Italian.

"But no, signor, only English."

"Good," Don said, "because this pig tried to pass himself off as a German spy when I told him who I was. Are many of my friends at the hotel?"

"They have all gone with the exception of the Major General in command of all German forces in this area. He and his staff remain."

"By the way, what is your name?" Don inquired.

"Lieutenant Operti. We are almost at the hotel. You wish to see the Major General at once, of course?"

Don licked his lips. A Major General! It would be a nice bit of work if he could bring one of those monkeys back as a souvenir. But it was highly dangerous.

"Why, certainly."

The car stopped in front of an inn that resembled a great chateau. Two Italian soldiers sprang to attention. Operti got out and saluted while Don swaggered into the lobby. Several of the men gathered there gasped in astonishment as they glanced at Don's British uniform, but Operti quickly informed everyone what had happened.

Don suddenly thought of something.

"Lieutenant Operti, you will return to the flying field to order my stolen plane tuned and gassed up. I may wish to fly to Germany with this information. I await only the General's orders. Ah—you did not mention his name. Does he know me?"

"Of course," Operti smiled. "You served under him in the Greek campaign. What shall we do with the prisoner?"

"Watch him closely. If he awakens, put him back to sleep."

Operti saluted and hurried away. Don glared at the ogling villagers and Italian soldiers, then marched to the stairway and went to the second floor.

There he leaned weakly against a wall and wondered what the next step should be.

If Operti refueled the Gladiator, there was a slim chance he might get clear. The ship was slower than anything else on the field, especially the several Messerschmitts he'd noticed. However, if he could keep up this deception, they'd suspect nothing and allow him to depart. Don decided to wait about ten minutes, then walk downstairs again. He would indicate that he had talked to the Nazi General and was under orders to proceed at once to Germany.

A loud, jubilant shout reverberated outside the hotel. Don's heart skipped a beat. It sounded as if Lommel had regained his wits and his tongue, and had made somebody understand the real truth of the situation. Don Jackson rushed to a window, raised it and listened. He knew enough Italian to translate what the excited men and women were talking about.

The *Vigilant,* his airplane carrier, had been sunk in a sudden attack by submarines and torpedo-carrying planes. Radios were blaring out the news.

Rushing feet pounded along the corridor. Don looked around in time to see a German sub-lieutenant staring at his British uniform and reaching for his gun. The German got his gun free of its holster, but had no chance to fire. Don knocked him down with a beautiful tackle around the knees. He swarmed over the man and beat him into insensibility. What Operti meant by the General being along was now clear. He still had his usual staff in the hotel. This man must have been sent down to get the news, and had attacked Don because he had taken him for an enemy in his British uniform.

Don suddenly thought of Lommel again, remembering the German officer was still a great menace to his own safety. Sunk or afloat, many of the secrets of the *Vigilant* were tucked away in his mind. The devices he had seen were also used on other aircraft carriers. Don looked out the window. Enough light came from the lobby so that he could see Lommel was still curled up on the floor of the auto. Operti had disappeared somewhere. Don Jackson raised the gun and drew a bead on the unconscious spy.

Lommel was a murderer. He had stalked two sailors and knifed them. He deserved no better treatment. Yet Don couldn't bring himself to squeeze the trigger. Shooting a man down in a fight was one thing, but plugging an unconscious man, even one like Lommel, ran against the grain.

A door slammed somewhere on the third floor. Heavy feet pounded down the steps. Just as this new distraction sent chills up and down Don's spine, he noticed that Lommel was trying to get up.

Two Nazi officers stamped down the hallway. Don faded out of sight around the corner. Unfortunately he had no time to drag the unconscious Nazi lieutenant with him.

The newly arrived pair saw the Nazi lying in the corridor. They shouted an alarm and raised the man to his feet. He mumbled something in German, and Don caught the word Englander more than once.

The lieutenant was describing his assailant.

Nazi troops poured out of various rooms, and hurried to the lobby. Don sidled up to one room which had just been vacated, slipped inside and went to the window again.

Lommel was standing up in the car and telling the world what he thought of Italians in general. Two of the soldiers tried to pacify him. But with a great oath, Lommel looped a punch to one Italian's chin. The blow sent the soldier reeling backwards. Then Lommel jumped out of the car and started running. The Italians menaced him and he knew he had to get away from them.

Don quickly raised his gun, rested it on the window sill and took careful aim. His finger began to tighten on the trigger, then relaxed. Nazi soldiers streamed out of the hotel. All they saw was a man dressed in a British uniform, trying to get out of the vicinity. They called no challenge or warning, but just raised their rifles and blasted away.

Lommel leaped into the air, kept going another step or two, then fell forward, his arms reaching out ahead of him. Don Jackson smiled grimly. The Nazi had been killed by his own men, a punishment worse than being lined up against a wall and shot down as a spy.

But that didn't solve Don's problem. He was marooned among thousands of enemy troops. In a few moments Lommel would be identified. The Nazis would quickly guess the truth and a ruthless man-hunt for Don would begin. To save their faces the Italians would be compelled to exert every effort in the chase. As for the Germans, they were bound to track down this Englander who had flouted them, causing the death of one of their best pilots by the guns of his own men.

Glancing around the room, Don saw several dress uniforms carefully draped over the backs of two chairs. He hastily peeled off his British uniform, donned the German field grey and shoved his own clothing into the corner of a closet. If he were caught now, he'd be shot as a spy. He shrugged the thought out of his mind.

All the Nazi officers and men were gathered around Lommel's body. It was now or never. Don hurried downstairs, walked briskly through the lobby and straight to the car. Two Italians stood near it. The driver lolled idly in the seat, evidently not caring much what went on.

Don Jackson opened the car door and climbed in. He barked an unintelligible order at the driver and pointed down the road in the direction of the airfield. The car started with a jerk.

Don settled back until they had left the town limits.

He leaned forward then, and tapped the driver on the shoulder. In fair Italian he demanded to know where Lieutenant Operti had gone. The chauffeur answered rapidly. Jackson gathered that the lieutenant had hurried to the airfield to see that the Gladiator was refueled and ready for a long trip. Don groaned. That slow, under-armed little plane wasn't going to stand much of a chance!

The airport was blacked out when they reached it. The car slid to a halt a hundred yards away from the Gladiator.

A few flashlights were gleaming and Operti had one of them. Don got out and started running. It would be only a matter of seconds now before the Nazis in town realized what had happened.

A phone call to the airport would spell his doom.

He reached Operti's side and seized his arm.

"Lieutenant! I had to get out of that English uniform. It made my flesh crawl. This was the only German uniform I could find. Is the ship ready?"

"Of course," Operti said. "There are a few tools inside the plane. I shall get them. Follow me!"

Don tried to stop him, but it was too late. Then Don gaped because Operti ran to a sleek Messerschmitt—one of the new 115-E's. The fastest, best-gunned Nazi plane. Its prop was turning over smoothly. Don heard excited voices from the region of the hangars.

He knew the game was up.

There was no time to get rid of Operti who had disappeared inside the plane. Don climbed into the ship and pushed the cowling into place. Then, without paying any attention to Operti's yowls, he revved up the motor, swung around and shot straight toward the hangars.

Four planes were being rolled out on the field. Don's fingers touched the gun buttons and sent a hail of death at the planes. Two blew up when incendiaries hit their fuel tanks. Another fell over on one wing, and the fourth was jammed between the wreckage of the other three.

Don swung about again. There was plenty of shooting now, and the Me-115 shivered under the impact of slugs. He sent her racing down the cement apron and raised her smoothly off the ground. Operti was yelling and gesturing with his arms. Don nosed up for altitude, then leveled off. It wasn't going to be any picnic getting clear. Nazi patrols would be looking for him.

He twisted his head and Operti was amazed to see a gun pointed at him.

"What is wrong?" the Italian shouted. "Why did they shoot at you—a German?"

"I'm not a Nazi," Don yelled back. "I'm British. The man I took prisoner was the real German captain. His own men shot him back there, mistaking him for myself. Sorry, Lieutenant, but you're a prisoner of war."

Operti's lips parted in a broad grin, but there wasn't time

to talk any more. Winging down out of the night came a quartet of Messerschmitts. They had spotted Don's stolen plane in the light of a moon that had just broken through the clouds.

Don dived swiftly, then looped. As he came up, one of the Nazi planes flashed by, guns spitting. The machine guns on Don's ship broke into life, and the enemy ran straight into the V-shaped hail of steel.

There was another on Don's tail now. He had Operti to worry about, too. But the Italian was hunched down as far as possible. His eyes showed no fear.

The German opened up. Jackson felt his ship stagger. He nosed up, and the Messerschmitt followed. Two more waiting for him upstairs.

Don banked sharply, zoomed out of the Nazi's bullet stream and streaked for the moon. The three Nazi planes followed relentlessly. Don kept gaining more and more altitude, and the Messerschmitts climbed right along with him.

Then Don Jackson dived again, the steepest, craziest dive he had ever taken. Wind howled against the stolen plane's wings and threatened to rip them off. About four hundred feet above the sea, Don leveled off. Now he was flying above the Germans.

He dipped his nose and began shooting. One Messerschmitt started fluttering toward the water. The other two tried to bank and tackle Don from tow sides. He selected one of these planes, and darted over to meet it before the pilot could get into position for accurate shooting.

The Messerschmitt was just a dusky blur in the sights of his guns. It grew larger and larger. Then, at precisely the right second, Don pressed the buttons. The Messerschmitt began to weave and squirm like a wounded animal, but Don's guns were deadly and fast. He saw debris pop off the tail assembly. The Nazi pilot suddenly rolled over and away in a desperate attempt to reach land.

Don Jackson roared upstairs then, looking for the fourth Messerschmitt. A tap on the shoulder reminded him that he wasn't entirely out of danger. Operti could do a lot of damage if he wished.

"The fourth one fled like a coward!" Operti shouted. "Did you hear me? A coward! That is what they called us! They said we were afraid to fight. That is a lie. We are not afraid, but some of us cannot see what we have been fighting for. To let the Germans take over Italy? They have almost done that already. I am more English than Italian. I lived in England for years. I do not want to kill people I like. I was aboard a neutral ship when Italy entered the war. Italian destroyers took me off. Although I hadn't been in Italy for years, I was still subject to their conscription laws and in to the army I went. For months I have longed for a chance to escape. None came until now."

Don yelled back, "I thought you were a decent sort. I'll try to make things easy for you."

"But this is a land plane," Operti wailed. "It cannot reach any of your bases."

"We're heading toward my ship, the carrier *Vigilant*."

"The *Vigilant!*" Operti howled. "But it was sunk tonight. The radio said so."

Don Jackson grinned and edged over in his seat so that Operti could cram himself just a little closer.

"The *Vigilant* has a thousand lives when it comes to being sunk by Nazi planes or U-boats. She was sunk off Crete twice, off Gibraltar once and a day later near the coast of France. The sinking was done on German and Italian radios, Lieutenant. You have to get out of those countries to realize that the news bulletins are slightly exaggerated."

Don tuned in on his radio. Back came a reply from the *Vigilant*. He gave details of his adventure, got bearings and finally saw the deck lights of the great ship. Operti saw them, too.

"Such lies!" he marveled. "The Nazi pilots swore they watched her sink. Such exaggeration. It is like them."

"Sure," Don Jackson answered, "but you've got a few windbags spouting Italian, too. Wait, you'll hear them."

"Hear them," Operti groaned. "My friend, I have listened to them for what seems to have been ages. Once when I was lying in a shell hole at Tobruk, I heard a broadcast from Naples. It told how gloriously we Italians had charged and taken the garrison at Tobruk. I looked around me at the dead who lay in heaps. The Germans led us into that kind of propaganda. They are clever. You, too, my friend are clever. But I am the smartest of all!"

Don circled to get the wind right. He had to pancake on the water. But rescue ships were already being lowered from the aircraft carrier. The plane would stay aloft long enough to be reached. He glanced at Operti.

"I don't quite understand what you meant about being the smartest."

The Italian bared his teeth in a wide grin.

"You left me with Captain Lommel in the car. Remember? He was waking up before I left and he started to mutter in German. I understand the language better than I let you know. I was sure who he was and I guessed your identity, too. That is why I made certain a faster plane than yours was ready with her tanks and gun-belts full, and why I was also inside the plane when you took off. Now, perhaps, the British will let me help them fight this war against the mad Nazis."

Don Jackson just shook his head slowly from side to side.

"I shouldn't be surprised if they did. You certainly saved my neck as well as your own. Hang on. I'm going to see if this nice new Messerschmitt can swim."

# COWBOY IN THE SKY

*By*

## SAM MINES

LIEUTENANT TEX CONWAY U.S. Airacobra Squadron 33 stationed in England, blew his nose violently and hurled his handkerchief to the floor.

"They can't go up without me!" he protested desperately.

Major Amos Hartway, squadron leader, eyed him without warmth. "No flying with a cold," he said firmly. "Want to injure your ears permanently? Besides, this is routine patrol. McSweeney and Lincoln will be okay without you. If you're so worried about them, come over to Communications and listen to their radio report."

Lieutenants McSweeney and Lincoln waved mocking farewells to Conway as they raced to their idling planes.

"So long, cowboy!" McSweeney yelled. "Take care of your precious little nosey-wosey!"

"Don't blow too hard!" Lincoln shouted. "Might injure little man's eardrums!"

Lieutenant Conway swore ferociously and sneezed. Then he went back to his bunk for a fresh supply of handkerchiefs and ephedrine.

By the time he reached the radio room, reports were coming in. Major Hartway was standing near the radio operator, listening to a brisk babble of voices in the loudspeaker. Conway stepped up and sneezed. Major Hartway motioned him brusquely to silence.

Lincoln's voice came, thin with distance.

"Bandits at 10 o'clock, Mac. Two of 'em."

"I see 'em, baby. Let's go."

There was a chatter which might have been static, or machine-guns. Then an alarmed shout.

"Look out, Linc! Five Messups at four o'clock!"

"Hey, look—it's the Executioner!"

"I saw him first!"

In the radio room, Tex Conway drew in his tortured breath with a groan. The Executioner was a Nazi ace who was fast becoming the nemesis of Squadron 33. More than one of their planes had gone down under his slashing attack. His ME 109G was easy to recognize because of its insignia—a dripping headsman's axe.

The Nazi, whose name was Heinz Bulow, actually had been a state executioner in Germany before the war. Either because he was proud of his profession or because he realized its psychological effect, he carried on the name and painted his symbol, a bloody axe, on his plane.

The babble of voices in the radio broke out again. Then there was a fierce hammering which was definitely machine-guns. Abruptly the radio went *bloop* and there was only the thin howl of static.

Major Hartway made an involuntary movement toward

the dials, then checked himself. The Texan's big fists knotted.

"You wouldn't let me fly with them," he breathed.

The major's eyes were desolate, but still unyielding.

"Sorry, cowboy," he said, his voice little more than a whisper. "You wouldn't be much good to us deaf."

Tex Conway turned his back and strode out.

Blackness settled upon him, deeper than any he had ever known. He'd always had friends, back on the ranch at home: good friends, with the common bond of background, school, childhood and long years together on the range. But even that had been nothing like his friendship with McSweeney and Lincoln.

The three had been welded together in a common front against death. Their swooping wings and hammering machine-guns had fought off that grim old reaper time and again—brushed him aside as he was about to pounce on one of them. Nothing ties men together like sharing their lives and fates.

Hours later, Tex Conway was tramping the field where the woods crept close, still fighting his grief and despair. Suddenly the raid alarm went off.

As the sirens screamed he looked up to see Yanks pouring out onto the field and dashing for waiting Airacobras. But before anyone could even get to his ship, the invading plane appeared. It was a twin-engined ME 110, flying high and fast.

A hail of ack-ack stormed up to meet it. Miraculously the sky blossomed with puffs of smoke like black snowballs. The ship dipped, seemed to nose down, then rolled over.

A black speck dropped and then the white canopy of a parachute bloomed. The plane righted itself and zoomed away.

Tex Conway spotted the parachute's drift and saw that it would come down in the woods. He yanked his .45 from its holster and plunged into the underbrush to cut off the descending Nazi. Behind him he heard the pound of feet as his buddies followed.

The chute was spread over the brush in a little clearing and the crumpled body of the parachutist lay nearby. Conway slowed. Another flyer pounded up beside him.

"Looks like he's hurt."

"Take it easy, bud, might be a trick."

Several men converged on the still shape. As they got closer, a sudden familiarity struck Conway. He dropped caution and sprang in to turn the body over. It was Mc-Sweeney.

He'd been shot, several times. On his bloody tunic was pinned a card in good English. It read:

This one had the bad taste to get himself killed. I have the other, John Lincoln, alive and well. I shall have the pleasure of executing him tomorrow morning, myself. Perhaps next time you stupid Americans will not meddle in things too big for you. Heil Hitler!

The card was signed with the familiar drawing of the dripping headsman's axe and under it the neat signature, Heinz Bulow, Colonel.

A red mist obscured Conway's eyes for a moment. He remained on his knees beside the body until his vision cleared. Then he stood up.

"Pack him in for me, will you, boys?" he asked quietly, and, without another word, strode toward the field.

At the barracks he hunted up Michalsky, the daredevil Polish ace who'd been shot down in Poland, taken to Germany as a prisoner and escaped, to wind up eventually in the U.S. Army Air Force. Michalsky was said to have known Bulow in Germany.

"Yes," the Pole said quietly. "I know Bulow—the Executioner. He is mad, like Himmler. And like Himmler he kills because he loves it. But he is clever and dangerous in his madness."

"Tell me everything you know about him," Conway said, his lips tight. "Everything you ever heard or read or saw."

One bit of information came from this catechism—one clue to the madness of Heinz Bulow. He gloried in executions—and he lived in deadly fear of being some day executed himself.

Perhaps that was the key to his madness. He executed others in a frenzy to remove enemies who might some day wreak vengeance. Just as Hitler purged and purged in fear of assassination. This was Bulow's madness and weakness.

It was late afternoon when Conway left the Polish flyer. He went to the hangars, found his mechanic.

"The ban's been lifted," he lied cheerfully. "Gas her up, I'm going out."

"Yes, sir, Lieutenant," the mechanic asserted, unsuspecting. "Cold all better?"

"Sure," Conway replied. In truth, the consuming rage which was racing through his veins seemed to have scared off his cold. He went back to his bunk, dosed himself again with ephedrine and dressed for flight. Then, keeping a weather eye out for Major Hartway, he scampered for his plane and took off.

He was circling for altitude when Hartway's voice crackled in his ear-phones.

"Conway! Where the blue blazes do you think you're going? Return to the field! That's an order! Come back here!"

Conway turned the set off.

As he gained altitude his ears began to hurt. He opened his mouth wide, gulped air, trying to equalize the pressure. It helped somewhat.

At five thousand feet the Airacobra skimmed along with less effort than a bird. It was a beautifully sensitive ship to fly, easy on the pilot.

Conway knew where he was going. They had bombed Bulow's airdrome often enough to know its location. He came over the airfield at dusk, and Nazi interceptors snarled up after him at once. He circled the field and headed back toward England.

Locking the controls so the ship would fly herself, he slid back the canopy and climbed out.

Dusk shielded him as he dropped off the wing. He let himself fall as far as he dared before pulling the ripcord. And overhead Nazi planes snarled in pursuit of a pilotless Airacobra, headed back towards England. They'd catch it and shoot it down, perhaps—never know it was empty.

Conway came down in woods. His chute caught on tree branches and left him dangling in the air. He cut himself loose, gathered up the silk and climbed to the ground. He hid the chute under a rock and in the growing darkness headed for the field.

He counted on surprise, on the fact that the Nazis would never expect a one-man invasion of their territory. His outdoor training, years of hunting in the Texas hills, enabled him to move like an Indian in these open French woods. He evaded the sentries with ease and began a careful inspection of the field.

The Nazi fliers, celebrating a victory over the Americans, never knew that a Yank was making himself thoroughly at home in their base, looking them over, studying planes and hangars and making mental maps. Conway even looked in on the celebration dinner where Heinz Bulow was the principal speaker and honored guest.

Tex Conway was watching through a window when Bulow spoke. He recognized the swarthy, thick-necked man with the light of madness in his eyes from Michalsky's description. And he burned that likeness into his memory.

It was near dawn before he found John Lincoln. The field had a guardhouse—a stone building with barred windows. A sentry stood before the door, which was closed with a heavy iron bolt. It was the logical place for a prisoner.

Conway had never enjoyed killing. But for the first time in his life there was a grim satisfaction in his heart as he squatted in the shadows and drew a heavy, sharp hunting knife from his clothes.

A moment later a silent shadow leaped from the dark upon the sentry. An arm went around his neck, shutting off the cry that sprang to his lips. A knee crashed into his back, doubling him backward. And then the knife slid in with cold finality.

Conway drew his automatic, carefully slid back the bolt, and levered the door open. This was the riskiest part of the job. Suppose an erring German flier were in there instead of Lincoln?

"Johnny?" he whispered.

There was a stir in the darkness and a gasp of astonishment.

"Tex! How in the—?"

"Shut up. Come out of there."

Lincoln stumbled out. Conway closed and bolted the door. He caught the sentry under the arms, hoisted the prone body upright. The soldier's belt hooked over the bolt and held him there, although his head lolled forward on his chest. Still, in the darkness, it might fool anyone who did not come too close.

Shutting off Lincoln's eager questions, they ran for the tarmac. Planes were coming in and going out, others were being serviced by Nazi mechanics.

"We've got to swipe one of those 110's," Conway said. "They're two-seaters. Can you fly one?"

"I'll fly it if you steal it," Lincoln replied.

"I'd like to get one crack at Bulow first," Conway growled, "but it isn't sensible. We'll come back in our own ships to get him."

They crept up to the edge of the landing strip and picked out a plane. Mechanics were working on it, apparently readying it for flight. Another ship, a 109, was standing nearby.

"That's a single-seater. We've got to get the two-motored job."

Dawn was beginning to show over the trees to the east. The traffic at the field slowed down. From the hidden mess-hall in the trees came the continued sound of revelry.

Then came the alarm. From the direction of the guard-house they heard shouts in German. A rifle blasted into the night.

The men on the field looked up from their work. One mechanic started to run towards the scene of the disturbance. The other two stood irresolute. But the Yanks heard the racket from the barracks as the fliers barged out.

"Let's go!" Conway urged.

They darted from concealment and raced for the plane. The mechanics stared, at first mistaking the pair for Nazi fliers. Then they saw their error, and acted.

One was armed. He snatched for his pistol and Lincoln cut him down. The other turned and fled. In a moment the two Americans had scrambled into the plane.

Lincoln took the pilot's seat, up front. Conway slid into the back, on top of a parachute seat pack which had been left there, and grabbed the machine-guns. As Lincoln hurriedly fumbled for the starter and swore at the unfamiliar German controls, Conway swung the guns to cover the approaching Nazi mob.

"Hurry up, sonny," he said. "The welcoming committee is comin' fast."

"Where the heck is the—?"

A burst of machine-gun fire cut off his profanity. Some of the running fliers dived for cover, others fell and did not move. Rifles and pistols spat slugs across the field. Then the ME's motors roared into life.

They trundled forward, raced down the flight strip and lifted into the air. Peering down, Conway saw the Nazis racing over the field again, and poured lead at them. Then Lincoln banked the ME and dived.

Two 20-mm. cannon and four machine-guns thumped and stuttered. Pieces flew from the grounded Nazi planes. Men ran, staggered and fell. Gasoline blazed up with a sodden thump.

Linc pulled out and zoomed. He dived and raked the field again. Death and destruction blazed merrily behind them as they soared once more and pointed west for England.

The dark countryside slid under them and Lincoln chanted a war song. Conway tampered with the radio, trying to find out if he could adjust it to their own wave length so as to signal the field that they were coming in with an enemy ship. Suddenly his earphones crackled, and a harsh voice spoke.

"Wait for me, Americans! We have unfinished business for this morning!"

Startled, Conway looked back. Against the lighter eastern sky, an ME 109 was coming in fast, a scant mile back.

"Hey, Linc, Bulow's here!" Conway shouted. "What luck!"

He swiveled his machine guns, tried a warming burst. The fast 109 darted in. At long range Conway tried to connect. His tracers fell short. Bulow jockeyed for the 110's blind underspot but Linc was on his toes and got away.

The maneuver brought the two ships close and the machine-guns really opened up.

Conway saw the orange flames from the 109 twinkle like evil stars. Their plane leaped and thrummed to the hail of lead. Plastic flew in a shower as the storm swept briefly across the birdcage.

Conway felt the scorch of hot metal and the warm trickle of blood on his face. No bad hits. His own guns were hot with the barrage he had poured into Bulow's ship.

Bulow darted in again, clung to their tail. Conway braced himself for the hail of lead, but nothing happened. He stared through the shattered birdcage. Bulow's face was working, and he seemed to be struggling with something.

Had he hit the Nazi? No, the ship flew just as steadily as before, but no gunfire came from it. Realization struck him. His own bullets had smashed the electric firing control— Bulow's guns were out of action!

He cheered hoarsely.

"We got him, Linc—he can't shoot!"

"Is he down?"

"No, he's comin' up under us. Get away from him."

"I can't! He's made hamburger out of our controls—I can't fling this ship around like I did before!"

Conway leaned over to look. The Executioner was sliding in close under them. They could see his swarthy, gleaming face, teeth bared in hate. They could see the insignia—the dripping axe on the plane's cowling. What was he doing?

Memory stirred in Conway.

"Hey, Linc—he's trying to ram us!"

"He can't do that!" Linc shouted. "That's copyright by the Russians!"

"He's doing it. I guess they learned something from the Russians!"

Bulow was, in fact, trying to bring the shining arc of his propeller up under the tail surfaces of the 110 in the Russian ramming tactic. Properly done, the propeller would slice off the bigger ship's tail and send it plunging down out of control.

The maneuver was new to Bulow. He had now reached the 110's blind spot and was safe from the machine-guns above him, but he was having trouble. Craning his neck, Conway saw him reach up and slide back his canopy so that he could raise himself and see better. Now he was bringing his ship up again, his face lit with fierce triumph.

"Hey, cowboy, can't you do anything?" Lincoln shouted.

"Do anything? He's on our blind spot. I can't reach him with the guns and you can't kick this crate over— Hey!"

The word "cowboy" had suddenly rung bells in his mind.

He snatched his sheath knife and in a moment was ripping at the seat pack under him. He cut through the canvas cover, shredded the silk mercilessly and yanked out the shroud lines. Deftly he cut off several lengths, rapidly braided and knotted them into a sturdy rope. Even as he finished, he felt the first vibration of Bulow's propeller.

Metal screamed and their ship trembled in every part. Then it stopped as the Executioner's nervous handling dropped him away again. He began to creep up once more.

Conway got on his knees and leaned over the side. The rope in his hands had been swiftly fashioned into a loop.

Holding it in the deft fingers of a cowboy, he watched Bulow's plane rise under them.

The rope sailed out. Like something alive, the loop dropped through the Bulow's opened hatch and settled around the Executioner's neck.

Conway saw the man's surprise give way to terror. Bulow's hands flashed up, too late. The loop tightened. Conway took a turn around his machine-gun post. A moment later, Bulow's plane dropped and the Executioner was hauled, kicking and strangling, from his cockpit, to dangle in midair.

Lincoln gave a startled yell as the plane swung to the sudden new weight.

"Hey! What happened now?"

"The Executioner," Conway yelled, "is being executed."

Michalsky had said Bulow's one fear was of being executed. Staring now at the Nazi's popping eyes, his purpling face and flailing hands, Conway knew that all Bulow's fears and hates had indeed come home to roost.

It was with relief that he cut the shroud lines and let Bulow go to a quicker death. The plane righted itself.

"Home, James," Conway said. "And take it easy, whilst I contact our Major Hartway. He's liable to be mad enough to shoot us. Forgot to tell you, Linc, I'm A.W.O.L."

# BURMA BOY

*By*

## DON KEENE

TERRY DOUGLAS kicked his ship into a tight bank
and turned inside the Zero that was trying to dodge
him. The frantic Jap pilot, seeing that he had been
outmaneuvered, attempted a barrel-roll, but the guns on
Terry's Curtiss were speaking.

Streams of laden death poured into the Nipponese plane.
The Jap ship lurched like a wounded bird, zoomed wildly,
and fell off on one wing in an uncontrollable spin.

As it fell, the Rising Sun plane left behind a plume of
thick black smoke. Terry watched that smoke trail go down
until it hit the tangled jungles beneath him. There was a
brief flare of light, marking the explosion of the Jap ship, as
it struck. Then the jungle closed over the scene as Terry's
plane streaked onward over the wilds of Burma.

"That, my fine slant-eyed friend," muttered Terry, "was
for Scarsdale Jack Newkirk, and for Tom Cole, the chap
you machine-gunned after he bailed out. And for the
women at Manila and Hongkong and Singapore and Nan-
king."

Terry wrenched his thoughts back to reality and found the outlook far from good. True, he had got his man, but, as a matter of fact, he knew he was going to catch particular blazes when he got back to base.

He had been sent out on reconnaissance, with strict orders from the colonel not to engage in any fights he could avoid. But the sight of that lone Zero, apparently a stray from a squadron, had proved too much of a temptation. Terry had chased the Jap for nearly half an hour before he had got within striking distance.

And as for the reconnaissance report he was supposed to give the colonel—he hadn't the slightest idea of how many gunboats the Nips had brought up the Salween River during the past twenty-four hours.

"So," he told himself dismally, "it's Terry Douglas on the carpet again. The Patsy of the A.V.G., that's me."

He turned his ship, glanced at the compass, and set off for the Salween. His tank meter showed he had just about enough to make the flight he had been sent out on and get back to base, with luck. The dog-fight in which the Jap had engaged at the last moment had used up gallons of precious fuel and, Terry suspected, the belts of the wing guns must be close to their ends by now, after the repeated bursts he had fired at the fleeing Nipponese pursuit ship.

He could, of course, hightail back to the base and turn in a report to Colonel Fleming, saying that four or six or ten boats had moved up the Salween. The Flying Tigers of Burma had little if any photographic equipment and the Colonel would take Terry's word for it.

But that was just the trouble. The tight little band of

adventurous fliers had their own code and one which, while it irked Terry at times, demanded respect.

For instance, no man claimed a downed plane unless he saw it crash.

It might go, twisting and turning and burning, down into a cloud bank and be lost from sight, an almost certain casualty, and yet it had to be listed as a "probable."

"Let the Nips put out communiques claiming a hundred planes a day," the colonel had said. "We'll underestimate our claims, rather than have one word go out of this base that the Japs could prove was wrong."

Terry poured coal on his P-40 and came down to a hedge-hopping level as he came closer to the Salween. The sky was clear but he knew that there were emergency flying fields hidden in the locality—fields that the Japs had hacked out of the jungle, using coolie labor at the point of a bayonet.

It was better, he figured, to keep as low as possible so that the Nip spotters would have more trouble marking him, if the spotters were on their job. And they usually were.

"Not a very nice detail, Terry," the colonel had said, "but His Nibs (that was the British top-shot up the line) says he's got to have the information. Pete and Willie got shot up pretty badly in the go yesterday so I guess you're elected. But, for the love of tripe, don't go off tilting at windmills like the last time. Just do the job and split-tail back home."

Terry's ears burned in recollection of the colonel's words. That "tilting at windmills" stuff, he told himself, savagely, wasn't exactly fair. How was he to know that the one bomber he had sighted that afternoon, when his flight was resting after a go had been a Jap decoy? And, although he knew that he should have reported the bomber and awaited orders, he had taken off without notifying headquarters, hot on the tail of the Jap.

And he had nearly rubbed himself out on that jaunt. The skies over the bomber had rained Zero pursuits and he had had to scurry for base with his tail between his legs. Well, not exactly that, but the Nips had chased him home. And then, when he had come in, they had strafed the half-hidden Tiger base with some pretty hot stuff.

His squadron mates had blamed him bitterly as they had been hauled out of their rest period to take shelter and, as soon as possible, go upstairs and take care of the Japs. The colonel had been pretty angry about it, too, because it had meant a quick change of base before the bombers came. And they came, too, in plentiful quantities.

"I ought to kick you out of the A.V.G.," the colonel had said. "I ought to bust you higher than a kite. Here we spend a couple of weeks getting this base into shape and now you play sucker for the oldest trick in the world. The greenest cadet at Kelly or Randolph would know that the Jappos don't send out their bombers single-O. Did you ever buy a gold brick, by any chance, or snap up the option on Brooklyn Bridge?"

Terry had taken it, without reply. Nobody ever attempted a reply to the colonel when the colonel was angry. The man on the carpet stood there, with his fingers crossed, hoping that the colonel wasn't angry enough to throw the pilot out of the American Volunteer Group—the fightingest outfit in the world, bar none.

"I'm giving you warning, Douglas," the colonel had told

him, after that fiasco. "One more such incident and it's good-by for you. You're a capable flier and you love to fight, but in this outfit, sometimes we have to do a bit of thinking along with the fighting."

"Yes, sir," Terry had said, and that had been that.

The motor of his grotesquely painted P-40 roared evenly as he streaked up on the Salween, winding its sluggish way through the jungles. Suddenly, the river appeared beneath him and he shot up at an almost vertical climb to get a better view.

The gunboats were there, all right. One, two—five of them, and every one spitting lead at him. He winged over and dived down at the nearest Jap warship, his guns hammering. He saw the men on the decks of the gunboat scramble for shelter; saw a half dozen or so of them sprawl and lay still as his slugs reached them. Then he was over the ship and away, zig-zagging back toward base as the Japanese fire reached vainly for his plane.

If the Nipponese sent planes out after him, Terry did not see them. The P-40s could always lose the fastest Nipponese combat ship, even though the Zeros were more maneuverable in the hands of a good pilot.

Terry gave the plane full throttle and headed for home, his eyes going every now and then to the gas gauge. And his worried frown grew deeper with every glance at that inexorable marker.

He almost made it, but not quite. He was within sight of the secret direction beacon when the P-40 began to cough.

Terry moaned. "Won't the boss love this!"

He fought for altitude, then gave up the one-sided struggle. As the engine cut out, he reached up, yanked back the cockpit covering and turned the plane on its side. He went out easily, expertly, his hand reaching for the parachute cord.

The Curtiss hurtled past him, bound for its destruction, as he fell. Then there was the tug of the opening 'chute and Terry looked down, picking a landing place. What looked like an abandoned rice paddy offered the best place for him to set himself down. He manipulated the shrouds of the parachute so that he drifted toward that cleared space, spilling air from the 'chute now and then to avoid being carried beyond the paddy, into the jungle.

He struck, rolled over like a tumbler and came quickly up on his feet, struggling with the parachute. As it collapsed he unsnapped his harness, climbed out of the straps and reached for a cigarette. Then, as he inhaled his first lungful of smoke, he muttered:

"You fool, Douglas," he told himself. "You get sent out on a reconnaissance mission that one of those girl students you used to teach could carry out. You disobey orders to have a whack at a Nip and then you lose your plane! It's back to Cornfed Corners for you, and it serves you right!"

He whirled, his hand reaching for the gun in his shoulder holster, as he heard a voice behind him.

"Pardon, sir," said the liquid voice. "Hopefully you are not hurt probably, or yes?"

## II

It was a native, complete with turban who spoke, a tawny-skinned youngster with deep, black eyes and a mouthful of white teeth. Terry estimated his age at about twelve. The boy wore the inevitable cotton undershirt and *parong,* knotted about his middle.

"Hi, Squirt," Terry said. "Livvee here-around? American talk-talk?"

The boy's grin widened.

"Indeed, sir," he replied, "hope am fluent spokesman English. You, sir, am Tiger Flier I comprehend. It will be foolish matter guide and instruct you to home plate."

Terry tried to hide the grin that came despite the misery in his heart.

"Wonderful fine talk-talk you make," he complimented. "Mission boy, maybe?"

"Indeed, sir," the boy said, bobbing his head. "Top honor special student and baptized boy at mission school before"—here his talk went into adjectives that he certainly never had learned at a mission school—"Japanese annihilates and subjugate we."

His eyes were faintly troubled as he looked searchingly into Terry's face.

"Apology excuse," he said, hesitantly, "but you talk enormously and I cannot unhear. You get kicked the Tiger Fliers you say?"

"Afraid so," Terry said bitterly.

Suddenly, he found himself talking to this native boy, a youngster who could not possibly understand more than a tenth of Terry's richly colored words, about the fool he had made of himself and what the colonel was going to do about it when he presented himself. The boy watched him, as though fascinated, nodding his head as though he were an ancient sage, pondering on the facts of the case.

When Terry finished, he tossed his cigarette to the ground and stepped on the butt.

"C'mon, Gunga Dhin," he said. "Know way to Flying Tiger base?"

The boy nodded.

"Indeed, sir," he said. "If unmentionable Japanese assault you with the guns and harm your flying machinery, then, sir, the boss could not raise the roof, as you say, properly or yes?"

"No," Terry said. "If I was shot down, I was shot down, but if I ran out of gas, there's the question of why I ran out of gas and—" He stopped and gave a short laugh. "So what, Small Fry?" he asked.

"Was pondering," said the boy. "Was pondering over sight of you in flying machine, beating a hundred unmentionable Japanese and eliminating but one whom assaulted you to shoot down your flying machine. Or maybe two hundred. Then boss angry not be maybe?"

Terry laughed again and laid a hand on the boy's shoulder.

"Not two hundred," he said, as lightly as he could. "Let's be modest and make it twenty-five. And I only shot down a dozen of 'em. Come on, Wee Willie, show me the way to go home."

"Not Willie or Smawfry or Squirt," said the boy. "I Raga

Das, second son Abul Das who now brigadier soldier eliminating Japanese with British gentlemen. I showing you."

The boy was silent as he led Terry over a faint path in the jungle. As Terry walked along behind the youngster, he noticed how the lad's eyes shifted instinctively from side to side of the trail, marking every motion, every detail of the lurking jungle on each side.

The youngster, Terry told himself, had reason to be wary. For there never was real peace in Burma. Before the Japs had come, there had been tigers and, more dangerous, the wild water buffalo—a ton of tough muscle capable of rushing at express-train speed and able to take the slug of an elephant gun on its thick-skulled forehead without hesitating.

Since Time began, Man had waged war in Burma; against the jungle and the beasts of the jungle. And now they waged it against the beasts who wore the faces of men and called themselves subjects of the Son of Heaven.

Quietly the boy pattered along, guiding Terry through a tangled maze of steaming vegetation. Once, he stopped short and held up a warning hand. As Terry's hand went to his holster, the boy grinned and nodded, pointing upward. Terry looked in the fingered direction and shivered. There, looped over a low-lying limb of some tropical tree was draped the thick length of a huge python, waiting to drop with crushing force on anything that might pass beneath it.

The snake's lidless eyes stared at Terry as the flier sighted the heavy Colt and squeezed the trigger. The bang of the gun was astonishingly loud in the silence of the jungle. The python came crashing down, twisted itself into a convulsive series of death agony contortions and went pinwheeling off into the brush.

"Excellently good," said Raga Das calmly. "The little pigs the unmentionable snakes steal on occasionally."

"Tell me," said Terry, placing the gun back into its holster, "did they teach you those words in the mission school? I mean what you call the Japanese and snakes."

"Ah, impossibly no," said Raga Das. "Those words I learned myself from utterly no book. By staying near the camp of the Tiger Fliers I have instructed myself. I know the words—"

"Okay, okay," Terry interrupted hastily. "Never mind!"

"Gladly I would say them," said the boy. "You could tell me were it right pronunciation."

"I'll take it for granted," the pilot said. "Let's get going."

In less than an hour, and just as Terry was becoming convinced that Raga Das was lost, the boy led him into a clearing on the outskirts of the Flying Tiger base. In all the time that Terry had been at that position, he never had known of the path over which the boy had led him. And, when he got out into the open, under the strips of camouflage netting, he looked back at the solid wall of jungle and could not find the place from which they had emerged.

"Indeed, sir," Raga Das was saying, "I would inquire a favor of you."

"What is it?" said Terry. "I don't think I'm going to be around here long, but if it's cigarettes or chocolates you want, I'll be glad to oblige."

The youngster shook his head.

"It is not those," he told the flier. "It is I appreciately would honor being batman for you here at the camp of the Tiger Fliers."

"Listen, kid," said Terry. "We don't have batmen. You're thinking of the British. We brush our own teeth. Besides, I don't think I'm going to be here long enough to need anybody like that."

"If you stay," asked Raga Das, "could considerably me as Number One boy, probably?"

"Well—"

Terry hesitated. The boy had done him a big favor by leading him through the jungle on a path that, he suspected, not many humans ever traveled. This Raga Das reminded Terry of Kipling's Mowgli and there was something about the youngster that appealed to the flier. He could not give the boy a blunt turn-down. He stalled for time.

"Tell you what," he said. "You drop around some time soon and we'll talk it over. In the meantime—"

Terry reached into his tunic pocket and brought out the remains of a pack of cigarettes. When he proferred them to the boy, knowing that every Burmese native begins smoking at the age of six or so—and, miraculously, seem to suffer no ill effects—the youngster shook his head. From the pocket of the undershirt he wore, Raga Das plucked a villainously black cheroot.

"Unlike cigarettes," he said, apologetically. "Seegar is my preferable. But I will ask honor of seeing you again."

He bobbed his head and trotted off, not toward the jungle but toward the quarters where the native mechanics and laborers lived. Terry looked after him and smiled. Then he shrugged and turned toward the pilots' barracks—if those huts could be called barracks.

It was hot and the fliers were stretched out in deck chairs, each one shrouded in mosquito netting. They stirred somnolently as he stomped up onto the porch. One man, Pete Raleigh, opened an eye and closed it again.

"You back?" he asked plaintively. "I didn't hear you come in. I thought maybe my luck had turned and some Nip finally had drawn you as a booby prize."

"Quiet," Terry said. "Uh—how's the boss feeling?"

Somebody spoke from down the line of deck chairs.

"What you done now?"

Terry tried to keep his grin intact.

"Nothing," he said. "Nothing at all. Just lost my ship, that's all."

Heads jerked upright at that and all eyes swung toward him. He hunched his shoulders and spread his hands.

"Well," he said, defensively, "there I was—"

The voices of all the pilots came in the chanting chorus made famous by the R.A.F.

"Upside down at twenty-five thousand feet and out of petrol!"

Terry made his way to an empty deck chair and pulled the fly netting over him.

"I think, dear people," he said, fighting to keep his voice light, "that you're going to have to fight this puny little war without Terry Douglas. There'll be glad hearts in Hirohito's palace tonight."

"No kidding, Terry, what did you do?"

"Nothing, really. Nothing at all. I only—"

He stopped as there came an excited babble from the direction of the native quarter. One by one the heads of the A.V.G. pilots turned in that direction. From the porch of the rest house, the fliers could see the Burmese and Chinese workers cavorting about in wild excitement.

"What's up?" murmured one. "Maybe Tokio's been bombed. These natives get news a lot faster than by radio. Somebody get up some ambition and go see what's cookin'."

Terry, his eyes fixed on the jubilant crowd, suddenly gaped. He caught a glimpse of his erstwhile guide, Raga Das, slipping from one group of mechanics to another and, he noticed, when the boy left that group, the workers to whom he had just talked joined in the mysterious celebration. Then he saw one of the Chinese mechanics, a product of M.I.T., head for the colonel's headquarters.

"Oh—oh," Terry said silently. "Little Gunga Dhin has not been idle."

### III

Sitting quietly, Terry watched while one of the fliers disentangled himself from the mosquito netting and wandered down off the porch of the rest house. Terry watched him warily as he engaged a worker in pidgin English and winced when he saw the pilot's jaw drop. Raga Das, he thought, apparently had made up one lulu of a story in his determination to keep Terry at the A.V.G. base, so he could be Terry's Number One boy.

The pilot broke off his conversation and returned to the rest house, his keen eyes searching for an expression on

Terry's face. Terry stared back, blankly, feigning innocence.
The pilot climbed back into his chair with a grunt.

"What's all the shooting for?" asked Pete Raleigh.

"We," sighed the pilot who had interviewed the native,
"have a hero in our midst, believe it or not."

"A hero?"

"Yes. According to the story brought in by some native
kid who saw the whole thing, our Terrence Douglas shot
down, personally, five hundred—that's what that native said
—planes before Tojo's combined army and naval air force
knocked him out of the sky."

Eyes swung in Terry's direction and he managed a feeble
grin.

"You know how natives always exaggerate everything,"
he said weakly.

There were footsteps pounding on the steps of the rest
house and a bearded orderly, majestic in his cunningly
twisted turban, saluted.

"Pardon, sirs," he said sonorously. "The colonel is asking
for Pilot Douglas."

Terry got out of his deck chair and walked to the top of
the steps. He turned for a parting word at his mates.

"They sure give our D.S.C.'s quick these days, don't they?"
he asked mildly.

Somebody blew him a friendly Bronx cheer as he went
down the steps, the turbaned orderly following.

The colonel was behind his desk, the shadows about his
eyes the only sign of the intense strain under which he had
been for months. It was a legend of the A.V.G. that the
colonel had been visited by a fairy godmother who had im-

parted to him the secret of how to live indefinitely without sleep.

That would be the same fairy godmother who had given the colonel the gift of scenting Jap planes a hundred miles away, and the second sight which enabled him, apparently, to peer over the shoulder of Nipponese air chiefs when they plotted any campaign that concerned the Burma sector. For months, long before Pearl Harbor, the colonel had been outguessing the Japs so successfully that an official communique, issued in Tokio, had complained peevishly that the A.V.G. squadrons, the dreaded Flying Tigers, were "not conducting their warfare on orthodox lines."

Tall, as straight as a ramrod and burned deeply by the fierce Burmese sun, the colonel was a hard taskmaster, when the occasion demanded—and the occasion had been making increasingly heavy demands on the Tigers during recent weeks. He was the hard-bitten leader of a hard-bitten crew and he knew how to handle his men. When the men of the A.V.G. spoke of General MacArthur as "the Colonel Fleming of the Philippines," it was the highest praise they could give.

As Terry entered the headquarters shack and saluted, the colonel looked up from the papers he was scanning. He nodded in the direction of a chair and Terry seated himself gingerly.

"What's the report on the Salween situation?" Colonel Fleming asked. "I've been waiting for it. His Nibs has been on the radio four times since you took off, asking for that report."

"Sorry, sir," said Terry. "I just got in. There are five

gunboats, little shallow-draught jobs, lying in that cove just below the place we call Big Bend. I saw no troop concentrations. They're probably supply ships. Light ack-ack and three-inchers in the bows. I didn't see any mine-laying equipment, but I didn't tarry long."

The colonel scribbled something on a sheet of paper and called the turbaned orderly.

"Radio to L-Six," he said. "Tell Harmon to get an acknowledgment."

The orderly saluted and left. The colonel picked up the pencil he had used and began turning it, end over end, in his big hands.

"All right, Douglas," he said quietly. "What's the story?"

"Story, sir?"

The colonel leaned back in his chair, pushing his sun helmet back on his head. His eyes, as they bored into Terry's, were intensely searching.

"That's right," he said. "The story. Jimmy Soong just came bursting in here with the yarn that a native kid saw you shoot down a couple of squadrons of Japs before you had to bail out. How about it?"

Terry hesitated, started to talk, then bit his words back. Little Raga Das had told a story that the whole camp, even Colonel Fleming, might believe—with generous modifications—and there was a chance he could get away with it. But—

"Well," he told himself, "a guy like Newkirk wouldn't do it, or Pete Raleigh, either."

He straightened himself in his chair and spoke in a level, dispassionate voice.

"There's nothing to it, sir," he said. "I started out for the Salween and I met a single Zero. I chased the Jap, against orders, and knocked him down. Then I went on the reconnaissance flight, as ordered, and turned back to base. I'd used up too much gas chasing that Jap and I couldn't make it. I bailed out. The ship crashed."

There was a moment's silence, broken only by the tap of the pencil against the edge of the desk. Then the colonel said:

"How about this native boy? Why is he spinning this yarn for you?"

"I—I met him after I chuted down, sir. He led me through the thick jungle, to base. He's a mission kid with an old man in the British service. He's got the idea that he's going to be my Number One boy. He—he made up that story because he thinks I'm due to get kicked out of the squadron unless you believe I was shot down, sir." He stood up and looked around the headquarters shack. "I—I guess that's about all, sir," he managed.

"Sit down!"

Terry plumped himself back into the chair while the colonel studied the pencil in his hands intently.

"This Jap you knocked down, Douglas," the colonel asked. "Did he engage you?"

Douglas told himself, "It would be so easy to say yes. But Newkirk—"

"No sir," he said. "I chased him."

"Against orders."

"Yes sir."

"So you lost your ship, a P-Forty that don't come a dime

a dozen. A P-Forty that a lot of men in the States worked hard on, thinking that, if it went down, it would go down fighting. And you lost it because you ran out of gas. And you ran out of gas because you went against orders."

Terry remained silent. There was nothing to say in the face of that accusation. It was true—all true.

The colonel waited a moment and then sighed, heavily.

"Douglas," he said, "I'm afraid you've got to leave us."

Terry winced, although he had known, inwardly, that this was coming. He remembered, suddenly, being thrown out of school, expelled, when he had been a boy and the feeling he had experienced then, when the principal had given his final word, was exactly the same as the feeling he had now. But then, he had cried and now he kept his chin up, his gaze unwavering.

The colonel watched him in silence for a moment, and then permitted a faint smile to touch his lips.

"It's not as bad as you think," he said finally, and Terry's heart leaped. "You're going to fly with the R.A.F. for a while."

"The R.A.F.?" Terry asked in astonishment.

"That's right. His Nibs sent me a message just a short time ago. Seems that he's been a little luckier than we have been and he got a shipment of new planes from the States. They're the latest thing and strange to the British. He wants somebody to come up to his base from our bunch and do a little schoolteaching."

"But I—"

"You," said Colonel Fleming, fixing Terry with a direct stare, "know planes and how to fly them and fight them, even if you're a little—shall we say, impetuous?—as far as orders are concerned. I think you're the ideal man for the job."

His voice took on a more kindly tone as he continued.

"Don't think you're being thrown out of the Tigers, Douglas," he said. "This is an important job, a blamed important job. With those new ships, the British ought to be able to take the pressure off the northern flank and, in time, take the air offensive. We've got to get back Rangoon, you know, before we can start going places in this sector.

"So far, we've been limited to interceptor action against the Nip bombers. Now, with the British reinforced and with ships due to reach us soon, we can start out on some little jaunts of our own."

He paused and reached for the pipe lying on his desk. As he talked, he began jamming fragrant tobacco into the bowl.

"But all those new planes," he said, "aren't going to be worth a whit to the British unless they are taught how to use them properly. That's your job, Douglas, and I expect you to do a good piece of business."

"Yes, sir," was all Terry could say.

"You'll be picked up tomorrow morning. They're sending a ship down for you."

He got up and stretched his hand across the desk to Douglas.

"Good luck, Terry," he said earnestly. "If you could learn to obey orders, you'd be one of the top men in this outfit. Maybe the British can teach you what your squadron leaders couldn't—that there are times when it is more valiant not to fight."

IV

Terry saluted and left the headquarters shack. His heart was a lump of lead in his chest as he slowly made his way back to the rest house.

With reluctant feet, he pulled himself up on the porch and went to his deck chair. He knew that the eyes of every man there were focused on him, and he also knew that it was the code of the Flying Tigers that nobody would ask him what had taken place in the headquarters shack. If he did not choose to volunteer the information, not a man-jack would make an inquiry.

He settled himself in his chair and adjusted the fly netting.

"I," he announced slowly, "am now a member of the Royal Air Force. Tea for breakfast—good gosh!"

The other pilots waited expectantly.

"As a reward for having swept the skies clear of Nips," Terry continued, "I've been detailed to go up to the Limey base and teach Cecil and Geoffrey how to handle P-Forties —or at least I guess they're P-Forties. Anyway, they're new stuff."

Pete Raleigh spoke without opening his eyes.

"They'll probably be teaching you after an hour's instruction," he said. "Those babies can really fly."

"Yes," Terry said, moodily. "They can fly Hurricanes and stuff like that, but they'll probably have to start from scratch when they get a real ship under them."

"Listen to him," somebody scoffed. "I don't think the

British are goin' to like our Terry very much if they get that kind of talk."

"That would about break my heart," Terry said, bitterly. "Imagine, after flying with the Tigers to go up as an instructor to a bunch of haw-haw chappies."

"Skip that!" Pete said, sharply. "You've been reading too many cartoons and listening to too many radio programs. Those boys—"

He broke off as the sirens began to wail. As a man, the pilots broke from under their mosquito netting, hurled themselves to their feet and raced for the field. The mechanics were in place, propellers began to whirl as the fliers jabbed at the starter buttons. Within three minutes of the time the warning signal had sounded, every plane in the squadron was ready to take off, awaiting action.

Terry's squadron leader, a lanky Texan, came running from the colonel's shack with his mates in hot pursuit. The Texan raced from plane to plane, shouting his instructions into the ears of the nodding pilots. He reached Terry's ship and shook his head, waving his hands, palms out, in a wig-wag motion.

Terry groaned and cut his motors. He had been told, silently, that he could not fly with his squadron.

He waited in the cockpit of his plane as the Tigers took off, one after the other, roaring down the abbreviated runway and slanting up almost vertically into the sky. He squinted aloft as he watched the squadron make rendezvous at ten thousand, then streak off toward the east. Then, laboriously, he climbed out of his plane.

"Indeed, sir," came Raga Das's voice. "It is a sorry occurrence that you are not flying with them."

"Yes," Terry said, dispiritedly. "It's a sorry occurrence, all right." He glared at the diminutive native. "What's the idea of spreading that story about me shooting down a thousand Japanese planes?" he demanded. "Want to get the pants kidded off me?"

"But I—"

"But you, nothing!" Terry said, brutally. "Now you've got me transferred to the British base. Well, it's not exactly all your fault, but I'm not a Flying Tiger any more."

"Indeed, sir," the boy began. His mouth quivered and he seemed very close to tears. "I—I thinking—". He gulped and turned away.

Terry, relenting, made half a move to go comfort the boy. Then the distant drone of plane motors brought him up short and he gazed aloft.

The fight in the skies was just visible to the naked eye. A Jap bomber squadron, protected by Zeros, was trying to break through to some objective and the Flying Tigers were making sure that they did not get through.

As Terry watched, he saw one trail of black smoke start plummeting toward the ground and he groaned, not knowing whether it was Jap or A.V.G. A passing mechanic wore field glasses over one shoulder and Terry commandeered them. They were ancient binoculars, with the lenses scratched and fogged, but they brought Terry a bit closer to the fight in the sky.

The Tigers, he saw, were using their regular tactics—getting above the bombers to engage the Nipponese interceptors and, occasionally, getting a chance to power dive a bomber. For some reason known only to Tojo and the Mikado, the Nips had built their bombers to fly faster than their pursuits and to score a hit on a bomber meant to dive at them, with full throttle, from a thousand feet or so above.

And the Tigers were diving. As Terry watched, he saw one bomber halt in mid-air as though it had struck a stone wall, then drop its tail and go whirling down toward the earth. Another lurched crazily and staggered off, out of sight, leaving a trail of smoke.

Suddenly, Terry's eyes narrowed. One squadron of light bombers had left the dog-fight and was heading in the direction of the field. Terry passed the glasses back to the native and began racing for the hidden emplacements where the Bofors waited.

A Bofors gun, according to the legend of the A.V.G., is the offspring of a .22-caliber rifle that married a water pistol. Those that protected the Flying Tigers' field were some which, also according to legend, the Chinese had politely but firmly refused when they had been offered by the British. Still, when nothing else had been available, they'd had to be used.

Terry reached the nearest gunpit and practically shouldered the native gunner out of the way. He sighted the ancient Bofors and, as the Jap bombers roared in, caught one between the cross-threads. The gun yammered and the Jap sailed on, unharmed, laying a trail of light bombs in the jungles beyond the field.

"Good thing the Nipponese are the world's worst bombers," Terry said silently. "If a Yank had a chance like that, there'd be no field left. Hi!"

His gun stuttered again as he swung it on a Jap slanting in from his right. Bombs thundered and there was the acrid stench of cordite, the gritty taste of dust, the aching pound of the concussion. The Jap zoomed and winged over to come about again.

It was when the man from Tokio was practically ready to level off again that Terry did the impossible. He reached the light bomber with a burst from the Bofors. He saw the plane flinch as the shells miraculously poured into the ship and he shouted, his teeth bared, as he held his sights on the Rising Sun plane.

"Service!" he hollered. "Gimme more ammunition! I'm running out!"

Somebody handed him a fresh drum and he put it into place, watching the stricken Jap sag off to the right, obviously out of control. He heard the crash of the downed Nipponese plane, and he grinned.

The bombs were coming thick and fast now, as the Japs came in, unloaded and circled for a second try. Terry saw from the corner of one eye an explosion which marked the end of the rest house. His gun hollered again as he got a fleeting glimpse of a Jap plane. Miss.

Then he was thrown to the ground by the impact of a bomb that burst less than twenty-five feet away. The sandbags that protected the gun emplacement split like over-ripe tomatoes, spraying Terry with stinging sand that bit like needles into his flesh. The Bofors lurched over on one side, out of commission.

Terry clambered to his feet, spat out a mouthful of sand and looked around him, trying to pierce the blinding smoke. A vague figure was picking himself up at the other side of the gunpit.

"Come on!" Terry shouted. "Make for that gun emplacement over to the right. Savvy?"

"Indeed, sir," howled Raga Das. "I'm understand."

"What're you doing here?" Terry demanded. "Get under cover!"

"Indeed, sir—"

*Wham!*

More dust and sand. Terry picked himself up a second time and looked anxiously at the place where Raga Das had been. The boy again was struggling up through a sand-pile that had been built around him by the bomb explosion. His smile was visible through the cordite fumes and dust clouds.

"Dokey-okey," he said calmly. "Those unmentionable Japanese never shall kill Raga Das, son of Abul Das!"

"Get under cover!" Terry cried.

Then, because the Nipponese were coming in again, he scrambled over the edge of the gunpit and raced, zigzagging, to the adjoining emplacement.

Some Japanese pilot had trained his machine-guns correctly on that pit. The bodies lay motionless, riddled with slugs. As gently as possible, Terry moved the men away from the breech of the Bofors, on its makeshift pedestal, and squinted through the sights again.

A Zero, apparently some fugitive from the dog-fight that had moved to the west, came in low and Terry squeezed the trigger of his gun. He missed and the Jap banked sharply, having spotted the emplacement. He did a neat turn, leveled and came in again, head-on.

Tiny fountains of sand began jumping up from the parapet as the Jap's guns sought out Terry. Douglas stayed at the gun, screaming words he never could recall.

The Bofors bellowed. The Jap ship, entirely framed in the sights, came on—seemingly invincible, impregnable. It roared over, so close that Terry, swinging the gun, could make out the rivet-heads on the plane. He sighted the Jap as it banked, and squeezed the trigger. There were two bursts and then empty clicks.

"Here, sir," said Raga Das.

Terry gave the boy a hopeless look and took the fresh drum from him, slamming it into place.

"Apology excuse," yelled the boy. "You infinitesimally low on last shooting. Observation the bullets."

Automatically, and without questioning the fact that this sharp-eyed boy of the jungle could see bullets in flight, Terry raised his sights the next time the Jap came in and was ready waiting for him.

The Zero's guns hammered at the sandbags and the tired old Bofors gave its answer. As the red-spotted plane swept over, Terry shouted again. From the bottom of the ship spurted a plume of flame. The Zero was mortally wounded.

The Nipponese pilot banked again and started to come around for another try. He had started to level off when the fire burst about him. A sheet of flame came flaring out of the engine cowling and Terry had the distinct picture, as clear as an expertly made snapshot, of the pilot standing up, trying to shield his face with his arms and hands.

"Duck!" Terry cried.

"Indeed, sir," Raga Das asked, "and what is the duck?"

In lieu of an explanation, Terry picked up the Burmese boy and threw him under the protective shelf of the sandbags. Then, with a dive that would have done credit to a swimming meet, Terry hurled himself down beside the boy.

The plane hit the ground ten feet behind the gun emplacement. There was a horrid crash and then the spine-chilling crackle of flames gone berserk. Terry groped for Raga Das, tossed the Burma boy over his shoulder and climbed quickly out of the gun pit.

He staggered on with his burden for fifty yards before the plane blew up. It was as though somebody had struck him across the shoulders with a club, and he went down.

And out.

## V

When Terry Douglas fought his way back to consciousness, he found himself on a cot in the base's field hospital. The lanky Texan who was his squadron leader turned from the doorway, where he was blowing cigarette smoke out into the still, night air, and came over.

"How you feelin'?" the squadron leader asked.

"Fine," Terry said. He looked at the Texan's cigarette and the squadron leader put the cigarette between his lips. "How about the kid?"

"He's disappeared," said the Texan.

"You mean—"

The tall man hunched his shoulders.

"Hard to say," he told Terry. "That exploding plane half

buried you. It was like an H.E. shell. The natives dug you
out. They insist they saw the kid who was helpin' you at
the gun run away, but you know how those natives are.
Anyway, nobody's been able to find any trace of him."

He looked down at Terry with his calm, depthless eyes.

"You did a right good job, Douglas," he said.

"How did the squadron make out?"

"We got six positives, three bombers and three pursuits.
Four probables. We didn't lose anybody. Pete—Pete Raleigh—"

"Yes," said Terry, to save his squadron leader the agony
of saying it.

The Texan's face did not change but an edge came to his
easy voice as he continued:

"They did the same to him that they did to Tom Cole.
Pete caught fire and he went over the side. Two of them
gunned him on the way down."

"The—"

"Those two," continued the Texan, "were two of the
three positive pursuits we got. That's why those light bombers got over here to the field. Everybody was so mad they
went after those two ships. I guess everybody in the flight
had a crack at them. They came apart at the seams."

He reached down, took the cigarette from Terry's mouth
and puffed at it. Carefully, he replaced it.

"You know how many Nips you got with those old Bofors?" he asked.

"I know I got one," Terry said. "That was the one that
crashed right behind that gunpit."

"You got three," said the tall Texan. "And there's a probable, too. You did more on the ground than the whole squadron did, almost. You sure must be medal hungry."

"That kid was a big help," Terry said. "I hope he's okay." He looked up at his squadron leader. "Maybe—maybe, on account of what happened today, the boss won't ship me up to the Limey base," he offered.

The Texan's eyes gave Terry his answer. "Afraid not, son. You're booked for that job and in this man's war, you do the job you're booked for."

"Okay. Only—"

"Only what?"

"I—uh—nothing."

It seemed strange to Terry the next morning, not to see Pete Raleigh sprawled in his deck chair, his eyes closed, murmuring friendly insults at the others. The men were restless, itching to get into the sky. They talked jerkily and smoked too many cigarettes and looked up, every now and then, as though hoping they could see some Japanese plane on which they could take their revenge for easy-going, lazy Pete Raleigh.

The colonel, apparently, felt the same way. It was at about ten o'clock in the morning when the men under the trees—the temporary rest house to be used until the natives threw up a new building—stiffened. For, from the screened field to the south came the throaty voices of big planes— Blenheim bombers; used on rare occasions.

Then came the colonel's turbaned orderly to call for the bomber pilots, bombardiers, observers and pursuit squadron leaders. The group trouped off to the headquarters building.

"If what I think is true," somebody murmured, "Pete's going to get in his licks this morning."

Terry was muttering silently, a few minutes later, as he stood watching the bomber flight lift into the air, with its protective screen of P-Forties. The flight circled, then headed eastward, steadily reaching for altitude, bound for a raid on some base in Thailand or Malaya. He broke off muttering as the bearded giant who was the colonel's orderly approached and saluted.

"The colonel wants Pilot Douglas to know that the British plane will be here in about half an hour," the orderly announced. "The colonel suspected that you would want to pack."

The bombing flight was not back when Terry saw the big British ship come in. He tossed his sea-bag to a native and went down to the field, his innards gripped by a poignant ache.

The colonel was at the field, talking with a group of R.A.F. officers, when Terry arrived. Terry gave his salute and acknowledged the introductions as the Colonel made them.

"Captain Douglas, this is Captain Smythe-Arbitson, Lieutenant Kriss, Lieutenant Samuels."

Each of the men shook hands in a more or less tentative fashion. The Britishers eyed Terry, and Terry eyed the Britishers warily. The two services might work together—and the A.V.G. and the R.A.F. had worked hand-in-glove since Pearl Harbor—but there still existed that strange half-antagonism between the British pilots and the Yankee flyers. The antagonism, of course, was carefully fostered by the enemy. The old Axis slogan of, "The British will fight to the last American, or Chinese, or Australian," had been planted among the natives of Burma, months before. Also, the Americans had been told about the non-existent incident in which some British pilots asked when the Yanks were going to put another stripe in their flag—the yellow one!

During the early days Terry, along with the others, had half believed those stories. As they had been repeated, the Flying Tigers had greeted them with lip-blowing responses which proved their disdain of such tripe. Although Terry did not know it, the British pilots' eventual reaction was identical with that of the A.V.G. men.

"You're all set to go?" the colonel asked. He put out a hand and gripped Terry's firmly. "I want to say you did a mighty fine job yesterday. I'm putting it in my report."

The British pilots looked interested.

"Thank you, sir," said Terry. "And if that little native boy, Raga Das, should turn up, I'd appreciate it if you'd let me know. The boy—"

"I know all about the boy," the colonel interrupted. "We're trying to find him. He'll be rewarded, if we locate the youngster."

Terry stepped back and saluted, then turned to climb into the plane. The Britishers got in behind him. The propellers began ticking, then roared as the British pilot fed gas. Terry adjusted his earphones, checked the board and turned to see the second British flier—Lieutenant Samuels—getting into place at the midship gun position. The other lieutenant had made his crouching way back to the aft gun turret.

"Want to handle her out, old boy?" asked Captain

Smythe-Arbitson, his voice loud and crackling in the earphones.

Terry spoke into his throat mike.

"It's your party," he said. "Ground's a bit soft at the lower end. I've been flying lighter stuff. You know your lift better."

"Righto," said the British captain. "Samuels?"

"Okay, sir."

"Kriss."

"Okay, sir."

"Captain Douglas."

"Right."

The motors roared as the big plane trundled the length of the field and turned. A native waved a white flag and the bomber began to rush over the ground. Terry eyed the dark patch that marked the soft end of the field. He saw it speed toward him and, at the moment he was going to shout, the bomber went up.

He kept his eyes straight ahead but his mind was busy revising some of his estimates of British fliers. The undercarriage of that huge bomber, he knew, had not been a foot away from the soft section of the field before they had lifted from the ground. To judge that closely, giving the big ship every inch of take-off ground possible and still avoiding a nose-over, was flying!

The British captain threw his ship into a tight bank and then leveled, making altitude. At fifteen thousand feet, the bomber leveled and droned steadily northward toward the R.A.F. base.

"Glad you're goin' to be with us, Captain," said Smythe-

Arbitson, through the intercommunication system. "Those new American ships look top-hole to me."

"Ever flown a P-Forty?" Terry asked.

"No," the British pilot admitted. "I've never handled one. Of course, I'm Bomber Command, but I'd done a bit of interceptor work, before I came out here. We thought the Spitfire was about tops, then."

"They must have been all right," Terry said.

"They did very nicely, for a while. Dunkirk, London and all that, while *Herr* Hermann was giving us all he had."

"You were at Dunkirk?"

"Minor sort of way, old man. Our Flight had been knocked about a bit and I was attached to another squadron. Trying to keep 'em off the beaches and that sort of thing. Bad mess. One to twenty or thirty, I'd say. Very lucky to come through. But, I say, you chaps in the A.V.G. have really been doing things, eh?"

Terry bit his lip. He remembered having called British fliers "haw-haws" and had derided them for their His Nibs who asked for reconnaisance flights over the Salween. Yet, beside him, sat a man who had gone through Dunkirk and the Battle of London and still thought that the Flying Tigers, with the victories on their record, were tops.

"We did a couple of jobs," he said, "that were okay. But you boys really—"

"Captain!" came the voice of Lieutenant Kriss.

"Go ahead."

"There's a native boy back here, sir. Just found him, curled up under a gun-belt."

"Native boy!" exploded the pilot. "In heaven's name, what's a native boy doing back there?"

"He says he's Captain Douglas' batman," said Lieutenant Kriss.

As Terry groaned, the Britisher at the controls swung an inquiring glance at him.

"I—he—he's attached himself to me," Terry managed. "I bailed out yesterday and he led me through the jungle. Then, yesterday afternoon, he serviced a Bofors for me. I— well, if you could carry him to your base, I'll make sure he gets back where he belongs. He must have sneaked aboard while we were talking to the colonel just before we took off."

Captain Smythe-Arbitson chuckled.

"Kriss," he said.

"Sir?"

"Make the little beggar as comfortable as you can and keep him quiet. Tell him a million Japs will get him if he doesn't sit still. And give him a cigarette, once you get him out of that gun-belt."

"Yes, sir."

Terry turned and peered back into the tunnel that was the bomber's body. He just barely could make out the flash of Raga Das's grin before he turned back.

"Sorry, Captain," he said.

"No reason to be," said Smythe-Arbitson, laughingly. "I know how these native youngsters are. Had an Arab kid attach himself to me in Libya. Stole me blind, but I loved that nipper."

"What—" Terry began.

"We were based near the Mekili line," the Britisher interrupted, "and some Stukas came over and . . . I say!"

Terry switched his eyes in the direction of the British captain's stare. At the same time, the earphones sounded with the simultaneous warning from the center and rear gun bays.

"Nips to the right, sir!"

## VI

Terry squinted into the brassy sky, marking the dots that were Nipponese pursuit planes. There were—let's see—at least a dozen of them and they were bearing down fast. The dots grew larger as the Jap squadron rushed toward them. Captain Smythe-Arbitson's face tightened as he hauled on the wheel to bring the nose of the bomber up, trying for altitude.

"Sort of bad go, this," he observed quietly.

"It isn't good," Terry agreed. "What should I do?"

"Sit tight. Might need you. Here they come!"

The tail and center guns began slamming as the first Jap dived at the bomber. Terry heard the familiar sound that always reminded him of some kind of gigantic hailstones, hitting a tin roof. The guns of the ship sounded again and Terry saw a Nipponese plane slant off to one side.

"I've got to do something!" Terry protested. "How about helping with the midships guns?"

"Sit tight," said Captain Smythe-Arbitson.

"Captain," Terry heard in his earphones.

"Yes?"

"Got one. Could the American captain look over the side for verification?"

Terry wrenched himself in his seat and peered over the side. He saw a Jap plane twisting and turning as it fell.

"Saw it," he said briefly. "Okay."

"Thank you, sir."

Then the Japs came in fast. The wing guns of the bomber were blasting and the cannon in the nose was smashing out its message of death. Nipponese planes disintegrated in mid-air, or fell off, crippled, and still they came.

"Sit tight, Captain," said Smythe-Arbitson. "You may have to take over in a—"

The forward cockpit was rained upon with a hail of lead. The glass flew in a shattering hurricane and the bomber faltered. Terry looked at the British pilot and saw the man hunched over the wheel, his mouth twisted into a grotesque grin.

"Could you take over, please?" asked Captain Smythe-Arbitson. "I'm afraid I—I—"

Terry grasped the controls and brought the heavy ship out of its near-spin. The British captain slumped back in his seat, the tunic of his uniform crimsoning at the shoulder as the blood spilled out of his wounds.

The British bomber was hard to handle; balky and obviously hard-hit. Terry tried to zigzag the big ship as he would have a P-Forty and found the bomber reluctant to answer the controls, sluggish and tired. He gave up the idea of trying to dodge the attacks of the Jap pursuits and hauled back on the throttle in an effort to outrun them.

Again the Japs struck, while the guns of the bomber cried

their reply. Another Jap went twisting down into the jungle below. But, at the same time, there came a grunt in the earphones clamped on Terry's head.

"Kriss!" Douglas yelled.

There was no response.

"Samuels!"

"Righto. I—Here they come!"

There was the sound of riveters playing along the British bomber and the staccato reply of Samuels' guns. Terry gave a desperate wrench to the wheel of the big ship and sent it off in a sharp bank as the shadow of an attacking Jap flashed over.

The plane bucked like a bronc and Terry wrestled with the wheel.

"—know Kriss is gone, sir!" Samuels said, after the din had died down. "They're after the tail, Captain."

"Get back there," Terry ordered. "Give 'em hallelujah!"

"I—Oh, I say!"

Terry heard guns speaking from the tail of his plane. There was a long burst and then another. He twisted his head to see a Jap plane climbing in an unnatural zoom. The Nip went off at an angle and began performing a weird series of convultions that showed plainly that the man at the controls was dead.

"Kriss!" Terry cried. "Lieutenant Kriss! Can you hear me?"

After a moment, Terry said:

"Samuels."

"Righto."

"Give a look at the back gun-bay. Kriss must be on his guns but I can't raise him."

A Zero flashed across the sight fixed on the splintered glass of the fore cockpit and Terry pressed the gun button. A miss. Another came into range and Terry kicked the cannon release, feeling the bomber buck as the center gun bellowed. The Nipponese was struck squarely and clay-pigeoned into nothingness.

"Captain," came Samuel's voice.

"Go ahead."

"Kriss—Kriss is down, sir."

"I heard that tail gun talking."

"Yes, sir. That little native, your batman, is on the gun, Captain. He—believe me, sir, he's doing fine work. He really got the last Jap that came at him. They—I say, sir, they're pulling off. Had enough, they have."

Terry cast a glance at Captain Smythe-Arbitson. The British officer was slumped far down in his seat, with his light khaki tunic a carmine mass. Still, as Terry looked, the British officer's chest was rising and falling steadily. He had been hit and hit badly, Terry knew, but he was far from being mortally wounded.

"Samuels," he said, through his throat mike, "can you fly this job?"

"Oh, yes, sir."

"Come up here then and take over," Terry ordered. "I want to handle that tail gun and get that little Gunga Dhin of mine out of there."

"No need, Captain. They're bloody well getting out of these parts. I say, Captain, how is Smythe-Arbitson?"

"He'll do, if I can read this chart into your base. He needs some attention, but he hasn't cracked up. How about Kriss?"

"I'll go look and see. Carry on."

While Terry scanned the chart that hung in the forepeak of the cabin, with one half-inch hole through its middle, Samuels went to the tail of the lumbering plane to investigate. It was a few seconds later that a liquid voice came through the earphones.

"Indeed, sir," said Raga Das, "I hope you are unangry of my presumption. I had to batman you, sir, and there was talking in the compound about you dispersing to the British gentlemen in a flying machine to summon you. I anticipated the chancing and arrived in secret in this place when the British gentlemen's plane alighted."

"You little idiot," fumed Terry. "You might have been killed!"

"Ah, surely, indeed, sir," said Raga Das. "But the Japanese might be killed, in addition, which accomplished."

About that time, Terry saw the planes coming. They were in eschelon and a glance told Terry Douglas that they were Hurricanes. They roared over, as Terry waggled his wings, then turned and came back to escort the bomber into base.

Terry set the big plane down on the runway in a landing of which his instructor at Kelly Field would have been proud. Then, before the propellers had stopped turning over, he crowded his way back toward the tail of the plane, to the rear gun-bay.

There, he found Raga Das and Lieutenant Samuels, huddled in the cramped quarters of the gun blister.

"Now," Terry demanded, "just what is going on?"

Samuels smiled at him and put a hand on the Burmese boy's shoulder.

"*Pukka sahib,*" he said. "When he saw Kriss"—he jerked his head at the still form that lay in one corner of the gunbay—"go down, he got out here and handled the gun. Did all right, I'd say. I strapped the microphone on him, so he could talk to you. Captain Douglas, you've got a Number One batman, here."

Terry looked at the boy as Raga Das turned his brown eyes up to meet his.

"Where'd you learn how to handle a gun?" he asked.

"Surrounding the Tiger Fliers," said Raga Das, "I learned considerably things."

"Come on," said Terry, taking the boy by the shoulder. "I'm getting you on a truck going back to where you live. You did fine, Gunga Dhin, but this work is liable to prove a little too heavy for you."

He dropped Raga Das to the ground from the tiny door of the bomber, then turned to help Samuels with the unconscious Captain Smythe-Arbitson. After the captain had been taken away on a stretcher, the two men carried Lieutenant Kriss's body out of the riddled bomber. Then, and only then, did Terry lower himself to the ground.

His Nibs himself was waiting to greet him. Terry gave his report, as briefly as possible, and looked about him.

"The little native kid," he said. "Where did he go, sir?"

His Nibs scanned the ground around him and then shrugged.

"He's about somewhere, no doubt," he said negligently. "I say, Captain, just who is he, and where did he come from?"

"He," said Terry, swallowing hard, "is my batman, my Number One boy." He looked at His Nibs steadily as he added: "The best Number One boy in Burma, sir."

The British general smiled, understandingly.

"Well," he said, "don't worry about him. He'll turn up."

"Sure," Terry said. "He always does, when I need him."

# WINGS OVER CRETE

*By*

## LIEUT. JAY D. BLAUFOX

"ROCKY" HOWE angrily paced the board floor of the eight-foot shack that served as his guardhouse. He left nothing to be said of the past, present and future of the court-martial officers who stripped him of his flight-sergeant rank.

"Desertion!" he imitated the officer. "Where could a bird desert to on this blasted island in the middle of the Mediterranean—the mountain peaks? Whoever said Crete was a picnic ground *was nuts! Hang the court-martial and* everybody connected with it!"

As the sweat of anger trickled down his temples, he heard a pebble clatter to the floor and roll under the wooden bunk in the corner of the room. He looked up, startled, went to the small, barred opening in the wall that was called a window.

Steve Copely was standing on a rock, straining his neck to look in.

"Hey, Rocky!" Steve called out. "I hate to tell you this, but I thought I'd tell you before the C.O. does. The court-martial is transferring you out of the R.A.F. into the infantry."

"They can put me in the infantry, if they want to," Rocky said, "but they'll have one sweet time keeping me in it!"

"I didn't mean to get you sore, Rocky," apologized Steve. "I merely thought that if I tipped you off early enough, you might be able to do something about it."

"Do something about it?" sneered the irate little flier. "Ever hear of King's Rules and Regulations? It's a big, fat book with red covers and a lot of penalties for 'thou shalt nots.' Try to do something about it!"

One hour later the court-martial reconvened in front of the shack. The C.O. himself grinningly read the sentence.

The pale pilot had all he could do to keep from diving at the throat that read him out of the R.A.F. into the infantry.

He wouldn't have cared if he had merited the transfer, but he knew he hadn't deserted. The Merlin had played a dirty trick on him. It had knocked him into a forced landing and sat his Hurricane right down on one of Suda Bay's best night spots. It took three days to start the engine, yet the mechanics swore under oath that the engine started without their even having to wipe the grease off its nose.

The third day in Suda Bay, Rocky woke up with a Cretan goddess on his lap—and she wasn't marble. She had no tag on her. If he hadn't become involved with the lady, he might have been charged with being just A.W.O.L.

But he had spent three days away from the airdrome, right after the Heinies had driven the R.A.F. out of the Maleme Airport. The British were making for the beaches, preparatory to executing another Dunkirk, and the major's prize bit of Cretan statuary had virtually been confiscated.

He was lucky the C.O. hadn't called him a spy.

So Rocky was planted in a battalion of tough New Zealanders on the island and began freighting guns and grenades.

He wasn't in the infantry regiment long when another little fellow taunted him at mess one day about his being kicked out of the Air Force. Rocky plastered a bowl of hot porridge over the infantryman's cranium and the fight started. Naturally the Air Force won.

Rocky still didn't like the infantry, though. He decided to be a wolf, since he was being hung for one. He watched for his opportunity to do his bit for King and Country in the way he chose, not the way the court-martial had ordered.

The British were being pushed all over the island. The Nazis kept dropping their pot-bellied dogs with Madsen sauerkraut from motorless gliders, and Crete was getting too hot to live in.

Orders came through for the regiment to head for Sphakia and its beach on the southern part of the island, where they were to prepare for evacuation. Warships waited just off the shore to pick them up.

It was only a ten-mile trek through mountain passes and rolling terrain. Hagios Theodorra, where the regiment was billeted and camped, could be seen from Sphakia, in the valley beneath it. The regiment formed fours and started off for the beach after a hasty preparation.

The smallest men always draw up in the rear in a British column, since they form according to size. The tall men march in front, where they can get knocked off first, and the small men bring up at the tail. So Rocky and his porridge-receiving playmate marched together at the absolute end of the regiment, with the second in command bringing up behind them.

Rocky, still burning under his monkey suit, told the shrimp beside him that he wasn't going to run. He intended to stay and fight.

"You're such a big feller," said the New Zealander, "you ought to be able to do the job without the rest of us."

"That's what I was thinkin'," retorted Rocky. "I don't like your rotten infantry and I ain't stayin' with it."

"You'll write us, won't you?" continued the infantryman. "We'd love to know how you're gettin' on."

"Silence in the ranks!" the second in command ordered. "March to attention!"

Rocky stiffened, so did his companion. When he thought the officer wasn't listening, Rocky snarled out of the corner of his mouth:

"I'll send you a piece of red ribbon off my V.C."

The regiment plodded on. A small, flat plain between two of the White Mountains, which served the R.A.F. as a temporary drome, came into sight. It was Rocky's Hurricane squadron!

As he looked at it, he felt a stab of homesickness jolt through him. His anger rose again at the injustice of the transfer. Then the roar of Rolls-Royce Merlins reached his ears as he heard them warming up on the line.

"They're running out, too," he thought sadly.

There was a sudden rise in exhaust volume that was almost deafening as the regiment slogged by the field and headed for a narrow pass in the mountains. Six of the Hurricanes tore off the small field and catapulted into the air, heading between the low peaks in the direction of Maleme.

Rocky's nerves began to twitch as he witnessed the take-off. Automatically he worked the controls himself. He eyed the remaining planes, readying for the take-off.

There was a sudden commotion up ahead, but Rocky paid no attention to it. He was gazing at a lone Hurricane that was warming up on the line. It was so close to him, he could almost reach out and stroke it. He saw the grease-monkey stop the engine and climb out of the cockpit. The man stepped into the hangar and shouted:

"Ready, sir!"

The commotion in the column ahead grew still more violent. The second in command suddenly spurred his horse and raced past Rocky to see what was wrong. Rocky instantly realized that this was the chance he'd been waiting for. Dropping his rifle and equipment in the grass, he dashed for the open cockpit of the Hurricane.

"To blazes with the infantry!" he thought. "I'll fight the war my own way."

The infantry runt who hated the little pilot saw his opportunity to get even for the shower of porridge. He began screaming frantically at the top of his lungs:

"Deserter! Deserter!"

The Merlin thundered defiantly as the tail suddenly swung around, smacked the midget amidships and sent him sprawling in the grass. Shouts rose from the hangar, but they were drowned in the roar of the engine. The Hurricane headed down the field and rose into the air with the grace of a gull.

Rocky, now back in his element, began singing "Lorelei," which he had learned when he was a student at Heidelberg before the war. He was as happy as a lark. The roar of the Rolls Royce was music to his troubled soul.

He was free again!

Barely clearing the peaks of several mountains ahead, he saw the formation of six Hurricanes which had taken off before him. He glanced inside the cockpit and shouted for joy at what he saw on the instrument board. It was the face of the doll for whom the C.O. had transferred him to the infantry. This was the C.O.'s ship!

He howled with glee. Wouldn't that doublecrossing scamp be sore!

He reached under him. The C.O.'s parachute was there. He buckled himself into the harness, reached over and kiddingly kissed the picture of the Cretan doll. Then he pushed the Hurricane in the direction of the Maleme Airport.

Off in the distance he could see Junkers 52s, shedding their cargoes of parachutists. The blossoming silk looked like puffs of white smoke as they blew open and sank gently with their human freight. They disappeared among the mountains.

The six Hurricanes ahead suddenly broke formation and began smashing at the Junkers and landing 'chutists. Messerschmitts tore into the Hurricanes and the furious battle was on.

Rocky poured everything into the Merlin and it was only

a matter of seconds until his eight Brownings were chattering and tracing a perforated line along the fuselage of a 52. Parachutes opened over corpses. The spray of gunfire cut into the pilot's cubicle and shot the goggles off the eyes of the Nazi at the controls.

As Rocky thundered over it, the nose of the Junkers dipped, starting on its dive for earth. A screaming moment later the ship crumpled and burst into flames.

Rocky looked about him for another Junkers to knock out of the sky. He saw something that horrified him. The German parachutists were wearing the uniforms of New Zealand Infantry!

"Well, of all the dirty, rotten—"

Quickly two Messerschmitts started fighting for first place on his tail. He awoke with a start as the perspex cowling above his head was blasted with Madsen slugs. The pretty face on the instrument board suddenly disappeared, leaving a hole as big as a man's fist.

He stuck the nose of the Hurricane down in a hasty dive to get away, but he was too late. Black smoke rose up at him from the ports through which the exhaust manifold protruded. Nazi slugs had penetrated his oil tank, and the tracers had set it afire.

"What a shame!" he muttered, grinning weakly. "First they shoot the C.O.'s girl friend right off the instrument board. Now they've put the C.O.'s ship permanently out of the fighting. Poor, poor Major!"

Rocky forced the shattered cowling back. With a great deal of difficulty he succeeded in dragging himself out of the cockpit, after getting the smoky nose into level flight position.

Choking, he dived overboard and fell to earth like a rock, turning and twisting until his parachute blossomed open.

He descended slowly toward a gulley between two low hills, landed gently in a shrubberied area. He lay quietly for a moment, looking up at the sky, which was still dropping Huns. Bitterly he thought of the typically low trick they were using in the invasion of Crete, wearing the uniforms of New Zealand troopers—until he suddenly remembered that he was wearing the same uniform!

Rocky suddenly shot to his feet. An idea had smacked him in the bicuspids. He bit into it with grim determination.

Unfastening the parachute and harness, he hid it in some shrubbery. Then he crawled out of the gulley to a rise nearby and carefully looked about him. Not fifteen feet away lay the body of a German, riddled with Browning bullets, though the parachute was intact. The wind had blown the corpse toward the gulley and landed it on the rise. It was alone.

Rocky made sure he was not observed before stripping the body of its parachute and placing the harness about himself. He took the identification papers, Maxim machine-gun and started for the others who had landed successfully. Then he realized the papers might get him into trouble. Somebody would surely know the man. He stuck them back into the Nazi's pocket.

Throwing the machine-gun over his shoulder, he staggered on up the rise to the place where he had remembered seeing more of the invading troops. As he neared a group, a man in British officer's uniform shouted at him in German.

Two years at Heidelberg, during which time he had spoken no language but German, gave him an excellent command of the language.

"Yes, sir, here I am, sir," he answered in German, staggering under the weight of the gun. The officer looked at him peculiarly. "Where shall I put this, sir?"

"Over there. Take your position alongside that gunner." He indicated a Heinie, twice Rocky's size, manning a Maxim of his own. Rocky staggered so badly under the weight of the heavy Maxim that the officer shouted to him: "Put that gun down and come over here!"

Rocky did as he was told and came running. Stopping suddenly in front of the German in British officer's uniform, he cracked his heels together. As he saluted in good old Hun fashion, he thought how ridiculous it must look even to the Heinie.

"What is your name?" snapped the officer.

"Ziegfried Schultz," replied Rocky, standing as straight as if someone had rammed a poker down his neck. "Twenty-third Parachute Squadron."

The name he invented. The squadron designation he had seen on the papers of the dead parachutist.

"How did you get into this corps? You're not even big enough to carry a rifle, much less a Maxim." He did not wait for Rocky to answer. "Follow me!"

Rocky followed the man, with his heart pounding against his ribs and his knees wobbling slightly beneath him, wondering if he had been unmasked. He couldn't be shot for a spy even if they were wise to him, for he was in his right uniform. They were the ones who were on the wrong side of the firing wall.

The man hustled him to a small truck. He swung about to Rocky and demanded:

"Can you drive a truck?"

"I can drive a car," said the little pilot eagerly.

"Then you can drive this." A dark shadow loomed over their heads. "Look out!"

The warning was so explosive that Rocky dived under the truck. A great white dome suddenly covered them like a shroud as a huge, heavy object struck the earth. It had wheels, so Rocky knew it couldn't be a bomb.

After swallowing his stomach and forcing it back to its normal place, he succeeded in scrambling out from under the huge parachute. It had just landed another of the supply trucks from the air.

"So that's how they got this stuff onto the island," he muttered grimly.

He hopped into the driver's seat of the supply wagon. It was a small affair, with dozens of cubicles into which supplies necessary for the Maxims, small arms and cannon could be placed. As he dropped into the driver's seat, another man drove past in a truck.

"Follow him and bring back some ammunition belts for the Maxims!" the officer shouted. "Hurry!"

Rocky kicked his heels together as he sat in the seat, saluted stiffly and drove off in the wake of the other supply truck. He wondered where he was being led to and whether the men at the supply depot would ask any questions.

Overhead, men were still pouring from the Junkers transports, which seemed as though they would never stop coming. Hurricanes battled escorting Messerschmitts, while Bristol Blenheims laid tons of high explosive right in the laps of the invading Nazis.

As the two small trucks crossed an open plain nestling in the mountains, a Blenheim bomber rode high overhead. The air above the two supply wagons throbbed to the sound of a high wind that changed to a whistling noise and became a terrifying scream.

Rocky looked up for a split-second, shoved on his brakes and came to a dead stop. Instinctively he put his hands over his head and covered his face. He had seen one of England's best 400-pounders heading for the plain and the two supply wagons!

There was a terrific roar that almost shattered his eardrums. The concussion drove him back against the rear board, almost knocking the wind out of him. When he opened his eyes again, he saw the other truck lying on its side. The driver lay pinned under it, shouting bloody murder.

Rocky rushed over to the stricken man to see what he could do to help him. As he ran, he thought that the bombardier above should be sent back to bombing school for more training. His aim was terrible.

"My leg!" moaned the Hun. "It's caught under the sideboard."

"You're lucky the truck wasn't loaded," Rocky gasped as

he tried to lift the truck off the man's leg. "So—am—I!" He strained until the veins stood out on his forehead, but the truck would not move. "Just be patient a minute. I have an idea."

He rushed back to his own truck, drove it to the side of the fallen truck. He tied a rope to the rear of his own wagon, then to the top side of the other supply wagon. With the aid of his own gas-buggy, he raised the stricken man's vehicle into an upright position and dumped it on its four wheels again.

"There you are," he said as he bent over the man. "You are free now."

"I'm in such terrible pain!" bawled the injured man. "What can I do? Help me!"

"Let me see what has happened to you," said Rocky.

Carefully removing the man's shoe, he raised the trouser leg. Rocky had been preparing for a medical career at Heidelberg, consequently his knowledge of physiology and anatomy was greater than he usually admitted.

"You certainly are a very lucky fellow," he told the frightened driver. "You've nothing more than a few minor lacerations and bruises. Here, let me help you up. I'll get you to the nearest first aid station, if you'll direct me to it."

"You're saving my life," moaned the German. "I'll never forget you."

"You probably won't," agreed Rocky.

He helped the fellow to his truck and drove off with him in the direction of Maleme and the airdrome, where the wounded man directed him. A mile this side of Maleme lay a huge ammunition dump, fed by Junkers which landed there with deadly supplies. These were transferred to the dump by small motor lorries similar to the one Rocky was in command of.

The first aid station was just a hundred yards from the dump. Rocky left the injured man in charge of a doctor, to whom the German still insisted that Rocky had saved his life.

At the dump, Rocky loaded up with ammunition and supplies, then headed back for the Nazi lines. It was a miserable thing to do, he thought, supplying the Huns with the means to destroy his own friends. But he had a job to do and he was preparing to do it. Just how or what he would actually do, he didn't know yet, but he knew the opportunity would come.

He reported to the officer who had ordered him to the truck, explained what happened to the other driver. The officer turned him over to a Heinie sergeant, who took the ammunition in charge, and ten minutes later Rocky was on his way back to the ammunition dump.

As he reached the heavily guarded gates, several men were standing outside. One man in German officer's uniform, obviously a high-ranking official, was looking his way. Near him stood the driver Rocky had brought to the dressing station. The driver recognized Rocky and shouted:

"That's the man!"

Rocky's heart sank. They knew he was no German, but an Australian on a mission of destruction. His brakes squealed as he stopped the truck short. The officer had stepped directly in his path.

The diminutive pilot wanted to shove the truck in reverse

and get away while the getting was good, but he knew the getting away was worse than ever. The officer was coming around the car toward him and the patched-up driver of the other wagon was shouting again:

"That is the man, Heinrich! He is the one who saved my life!"

"I'm Heinrich von Heiswasser," the officer said, saluting. Rocky stood up on the truck at attention and saluted stiffly. The man continued, now craning his neck to look up at Rocky: "I am this private's brother. He tells me you have saved his life. For this I shall recommend you for a decoration and promotion to sergeant."

Rocky wanted to tell him that he already was a sergeant. Couldn't he do better? But the man's neck was beginning to ache.

"Please step down to my level," he asked.

"Sorry, sir," replied Rocky.

He climbed down and stood at mechanical attention.

"That is all," said the officer. "You will hear about this in the near future."

"Thank you, sir," said Rocky.

The officer saluted. Turning on his heel, he strode away. As he passed his effusive brother, he said:

"*Auf wiedersehen,* Gustave."

The moment the officer had gone, Gustave joined Rocky and clung to him like a leech. He presented the little ex-pilot as his friend to the others in the dump, who accepted him as what he appeared to be. Now he knew he could go and come in any part of the place.

Gustave showed him around when he said he had never

been on this detail before. Here were the Maxim ammunition belts. There were the 30 millimeter shells for the Messerschmitt aerial cannon. In another corner of the dump, Gustave showed him the 110-pound bombs used by dive-bombers. Nearby on the ground lay the 1,100 pounders and not far from them were thousands of two pound incendiaries. Close to the incendiaries were stacked several hundred time-bombs.

The time-bombs were located near the rear gate, where Gustave introduced his "friend" to the sentries and told them the story all over again.

Rocky loaded his supply wagon once more. He drove Gustave back to the plain, on his way to the front lines, and saw him start back to the dump with his retrieved truck.

As Rocky was emptying his truck of its load at the front, the sergeant became talkative.

"The *Englische Schweine* are beaten. We've driven most of them off the island of Crete and taken fifteen thousand prisoners."

A chill ran through Rocky. He wanted to kick the Heinie sergeant in the teeth, but at that stage of the game it wouldn't have been wise. He had a job to do, and now he knew what that job was.

"Not only that," the sergeant continued, "but we have fifteen thousand more of them—Australians, I understand they are—trapped on the beach and they can't get off."

"I should think they would have ships to help them get off," ventured Rocky, hoping for more information. "I know we Germans, if we were caught like those rats, would have our ships take us off."

"They have ships waiting off Gavdos, but they can't get near enough to shore because of our batteries." The Nazi grinned at Rocky and added: "That's why your job is so important, my friend. Keep the guns supplied with ammunition from the main dump, and we'll wipe out every one of those Australian dogs."

"What can I do alone?" asked Rocky, apparently unhappy.

"Who told you you were bringing up ammunition by yourself?" encouraged the sergeant. "There are dozens of you."

Rocky knew that, for he had passed them on their way to the batteries and other stations. But he could have kissed Gustave for what he had done. He had virtually given Rocky a pass to every part of the main ammunition dump, and the little ex-pilot was going to need it badly.

On his return trip to the dump, he noticed that new objects were being rolled into the dump. They were barrels of gasoline that had been brought in by Junkers transports and were being piled up not far from the time-bombs.

Eager to show his gratitude, Gustave helped Rocky reload his truck. The German limped a bit from his accident, though otherwise he had been unhurt. The alley between the munitions was just wide enough to permit a hand-truck to be loaded and taken out. Gas trucks naturally were not allowed inside the dump. Gustave and Rocky were handling shells for the light cannon, which were piled opposite the section where the time-bombs were racked.

There was another hand-truck nearby. Rocky strode over and drew it into place near the time-bombs. As his glance fell upon the cigar-shaped missiles of death, his heart pumped with excitement.

Fifteen thousand of his own men were trapped on the beach at Sphakia, unable to get off. Just a few hours more and they would be completely annihilated. He had to work fast!

"Gustave," he said, turning to the Heinie, "do me a favor. If you'll take that hand-truck out to the wagon and unload it, I can be loading this one. In that way we can get the stuff to the men faster. What do you say?"

"Of course!" Gustave replied enthusiastically. "Did you hear how many Australian *Schweine* we have trapped on the beach at Sphakia? Fifteen thousand!"

"That's what I was thinking of," replied Rocky, his jaws tightening in grim determination. "Good, my friend. Let's get busy."

He turned away and began loading the second truck. Gustave started off toward the gate with the first load. The Australian watched him go out, then carefully looked around to see that no one could observe him from any part of the dump.

He quickly reached across to the time-bombs, pulled the safety pin from one, right in the middle of the stack nearest the barrels of gasoline. He set the mechanism to explode in an hour and went back to his loading, just as another of the ammunition carriers stepped through the gate.

It was all over in a second, yet executed none too soon. Rocky could still feel his heart pounding against his sparsely covered ribs. He was almost sure the man in the dump with him could hear it, too.

Gustave returned with the empty hand-truck as Rocky put on the last shell that it would hold.

"All finished, Gustave," he panted. "Let's get out of here."

"Sure," answered the German, grabbing one side of the truck's handle.

When the loading was finished, Rocky suggested that Gustave take a ride with him. He hadn't the heart to see the simple Gustave blown into Kingdom Come with the Nazi horde. After all, he had made the realization of the dump's annihilation possible, so it was the least Rocky could do for him.

"I'd be glad to," agreed Gustave. "I'm on sick leave for the day, anyway."

He hopped on beside Rocky. The truck coughed past the dump, headed out for the plains and the front lines near Hagios Theodorra, a few miles away.

Rocky started to worry about halfway from the dump. Suppose the time-bomb didn't go off. The men on the beach would be wiped out completely and he wouldn't know how safe it would be to try again. Suppose it went off too soon. He wouldn't be able to tell his friends that it was safe for them to make their getaway. There was another danger if it went off too soon.

He might be caught and shot, thereby not being able to tell them anything at all.

The perspiration gathered on his forehead. Even Gustave noticed his quivering hand when he lit the cigarette the German gave him.

"You cold?" he asked.

"No." The little ex-pilot laughed nervously. "This truck is making butter out of the milk I drank for lunch."

They reached the auxiliary dump just back of the German front lines. Rocky could even make out the fire of the small arms on the British side, well ahead. The flashes of fire seemed to be falling back as the German line in front of him advanced. The clatter of Maxims mingled with the shouts of the officers in command, the cries and moans of the wounded and dying.

Rocky couldn't tell which were German wounded and which were the Anzacs, for both were wearing the same uniforms. It made him mad all over again. Why didn't that bloody bomb go off? Although he was about five miles from the main dump, he knew that when it blew up he would know it. This explosion, if it ever came off, was going to be felt clear to Berlin.

Gustave had dismounted and was beginning to unload the shells. The German line was steadily advancing. It had driven the British out of Hagios Theodorra and was pushing them farther and farther toward the sea. When Rocky had gone back for the last load, the German line had rested a quarter of a mile behind Theodorra. Now it settled almost two miles beyond there.

The sky was still pouring down hundreds of parachute troops. Rocky looked up at them and cursed under his breath. He looked at his watch. It was exactly 55 minutes since he had set the time-bomb. He looked back at Gustave.

The German was gingerly setting a shell down on the ground.

"Here I come, Gustave!" Rocky yelled.

He started to get down. He had not stopped the engine and it was still idling. Gustave approached the truck, reached in for a shell. Rocky let out a shout that almost startled the Heinie out of his boots.

"Look out, Gustave! Look out!"

The truck gave a sudden lurch forward as the clutch engaged the transmission with a grinding jerk.

"Stop it, Ziegfried!" Gustave bawled frantically. "Stop it! You'll be killed."

"I can't stop it!" cried the seemingly frightened Rocky as the truck raced for the German lines. "I can't stop it! Something happened, Gustave!"

Gustave tried to run after the truck, but his sore leg impeded him.

"He can't stop it!" he kept shouting. "Help my friend, somebody. He can't stop it!"

He was soon left far behind as the runaway truck dashed across the rolling country, drove through olive woods and trampled shrubbery in its mad path.

Rocky continued yelling and waving his arms wildly, until he raced into a battery of machine-guns and sent the gunners toppling.

"Stop that truck!" a German officer shouted. "Stop it instantly!"

"I can't!" Rocky shrieked back frantically, all the time carefully steering it through the German infantrymen lined ahead of him.

The men scattered in all directions to avoid being run down. A shell fell off the truck and landed with a thud among several prone Huns. One man jumped to his feet, tried to hop on the truck, but a heavier shell rolled into him. They both fell to the grass and lay there.

The officer ran after the runaway ammunition truck, still shouting. A British sniper nipped him and he stopped making so much noise.

Four other Heinies almost reached the flying ammunition truck just as another shell rolled off into their path. A stray Anzac bullet struck pointblank on its explosive nose and the shell blew up in their faces.

The truck was getting nearer the British lines when suddenly it seemed that the whole world was ripped apart. The island shook and shivered, as though a thousand volcanoes had given up the ghost with a last great explosion.

Enormous avalanches rolled down the sides of the mountains and crushed everything in their paths. Mountain goats were hurled from the heights and left dead in the wake of the avalanches that still tumbled down. Men shrieked with pain and fright, and ran to get out of the way of the thundering devastation, only to slip into vast, jagged seams that appeared abruptly in the tortured earth.

Rocky tried to stop the truck, but he was too late to save himself from being hurled out. The front wheel had dropped into a chasm that had opened before him.

As he lay on the grass, stunned for a moment, he laughed in shaky triumph. The time-bomb had done its work well. He had known there was a lot of high explosive at the main dump, but he hadn't thought there was enough to do all this damage.

He rose to his feet, saw the Anzac line just ahead, saw the blue Mediterranean not far beyond. He started to run for it. Three shots rang out on the shocking stillness after the explosion. He fell to earth again with three Anzac bullets inside him.

The world started to swim about. He heard someone yell:

"Hold your fire! He's one of our own men!" He saw the little fellow rush forward and drop down beside him. "S'help me, it's the blinkin' deserter!"

Rocky looked up and grinned sickly. He recognized the diminutive New Zealander he didn't like.

"Hello, midget, is that you?" He had difficulty rising, and the little fellow helped him up. "Better get me in—I've got good news—for you little—Georgie Porgies. . . ."

Two other men ran out. Together they carried Rocky in and placed him well behind the lines, under some shady olive trees.

"Sorry, I done you in, pal," one of the men apologized. "I thought you was a bloomin' Nazi parachutist."

Rocky grinned his forgiveness. An officer joined them, dropped to his knees beside the wounded man.

"The German batteries have stopped firing. Do you know why?"

"I think—so, sir," gasped Rocky. "You can signal the—ships to come in—and get the men off the—island. It's safe now. I—just blew up their main—ammunition—dump."

Rocky heard a low whistle of amazement rise from the men about him. That was all he heard before he passed out.

When he awoke, he was resting very comfortably in a nice, clean bed in a ship's hospital. One of the prettiest girls he had ever seen in his life was holding his hand. No, she was taking his pulse. No, she was holding his hand!

He grinned at her through his pain.

"Did they all get off?" he whispered.

She smiled back at him and it seemed that her lovely face was a radiant sun.

She squeezed his hand very affectionately.

"The whole fifteen thousand of them," she replied happily.

He fell asleep again and dreamed that she had kissed him. Who cared about the C.O.'s doll? The major could have her. Here was a doll that *was* a doll!